REBELLION . BOOK ONE

MAN OF WAR

M.R.FORBES

Published by Quirky Algorithms
Seattle, Washington

Cover illustration by Tom Edwards
http://tomedwardsdmuga.blogspot.com

1

"Slipstream return path is set and locked. Reactor online. Realspace engines online. QPG primed and ready."

Captain Gabriel St. Martin leaned back in the seat of his starfighter, closing his eyes and putting his hand around the crucifix his father had given him when he was three years old. He remembered his mother at that moment, the same way he did every time he prepared for a recon mission to Earth.

A mission that would take him sideways into the jaws of the enemy, with the odds of making it through somewhere around fifty-fifty.

Gabriel had never met his biological mother. She had been dead for nearly fifty years. She was dead twenty years before he had even been born. A casualty of the invasion of Earth, when the aliens they called the Dread had arrived in their terrible black ships, overpowering all of humankind's defenses, slaughtering billions, and swiftly seizing absolute control.

He remembered her now in pictures and videos, a limited history of a woman both young and beautiful, happy and carefree with the love of her life, then Captain Theodore St. Martin, a pilot in the United States Space Force. Things had been so simple then. So easy. The United States was only one of the countries reaching for the stars with the help of new technological breakthroughs and shared initiatives.

At the time, it had seemed unfortunate that the only way to get funding for that reach was to funnel it through the military. To build machines of war in a limitless expanse where there was enough territory for anyone who wanted it. According to his father, there had been numerous arguments across the House and Congress about how and where to fund the new space race; the race that would determine the future of every nation involved.

Nobody had known how all of those arguments would be wasted.

Nobody had expected there was something else out there.

Nobody had guessed they wouldn't be friendly.

Once, it had been fun to create stories about hostile aliens. They were exciting and adventurous, and made for heroes that children could look up to. Besides, most philosophers, scientists, and think-tankers had tended to believe that any race that managed to reach the level of technological achievement needed to make a starship and access the slipstream would have evolved beyond such uncivilized, wanton destruction.

Gabriel wished the smartest men in the room had been right. If they had, he wouldn't be about to take a ride through Hell.

"Everything checks out," he said through the ship's comm. "Wish me luck, 'Randa." He lifted the crucifix to his lips, kissed it, and then dropped it back under his flight suit.

Senior Spaceman Miranda Locke laughed, the soft tone of it crackling in his ears. She was nowhere near as pretty as her voice suggested. It didn't matter. She was a good person and an even better friend. "Like you've ever needed luck. Firing launcher in five, four, three..."

Gabriel reached out and took hold of the main control stick of the small starfighter. The station's rail launcher would accelerate him out into space at over 5,000 meters per second, hurling the ship into the calculated inception point of the slipstream without any manual intervention.

There was usually no need for a starfighter pilot to get themselves into slipspace.

The pilot was for after the vehicle came out.

"Two, one... Go!"

Gabriel was pressed back in his seat, the station's artificial gravity extending its reach into the launch tube. His teeth clenched as the inertial dampeners fought against the sudden and intense g-forces. He could feel the crucifix pressing into his chest, reminding him of his mother and her lost dreams even as he hurtled toward space. He could see the metal walls and lights passing him as an increasing blur, along with the rapidly approaching darkness of the universe beyond.

He always asked for luck when he made a run. As the most successful recon pilot in the New Earth Alliance Space Force, he always wondered if the next time out would be his last.

He had seen so many pilots come and go. More than a few had never returned from their first mission. This would be number sixty-seven for him. He had earned the right to retire and spend the rest of his days on Alpha Settlement seventeen missions ago. He could meet someone, start a family, and be given all of the comforts the closest thing humankind had to a war hero could want.

The thought had never crossed his mind. Retirement wasn't in his family's lexicon. Neither was the concept of quitting. Like his father, General Theodore St. Martin, the Old Gator, was fond of saying: "Your mother gave her last breath to save the lives of thousands, including you and me. We ain't never going to let that be for nothing. We'll find a way to beat those couillons off our planet. They think we ain't good for nothing? Heh. I'll tell you what, son, I ain't never gonna die until they're gone, and you can't either."

Of course, that had been before the accident. Before his father had lost the use of his legs. Before he had become addicted to medicine that sucked away both his pain and his mind.

General St. Martin's days as a productive member of society were done, and the Dread continued to hold the Earth. His old man was still alive, though. Still as good as his word.

It was up to Gabriel to do his part, and that meant making run after run until his luck ran out.

2

Gabriel's starfighter shuddered as the onboard computer triggered the quantum phase generator. Gabriel looked to the left when it did, watching as the pock-marked, triangular wings of his craft began to blur.

The QFG was the most advanced piece of tech on the ship. It was also something he barely understood. Even after ten years as a recon pilot, it still seemed more like black magic than actual science.

From what he understood, the QPG worked by creating a shift in the quantum properties of the spacecraft's specially engineered and painted surface, a process called phasing. This process enabled the vehicle access to the strange and barely understood currents of time and space that ran both above and below what was now called realspace. These currents, known as slipstreams, weren't controllable, but they were measurable. The measurements allowed calculations, which in turn allowed humankind to take advantage of them. By phasing into a slipstream, a starship could be carried from one part of the universe to another at faster than light speeds without any of the unwanted time dilation side effects, without having to worry about crashing into some other celestial body, and without the possibility of being attacked.

In other words, the slipstream was a free ride from one part of the universe to another, at speeds that averaged out to between forty and sixty thousand times the speed of light. For Gabriel, it meant that the trip from the New Earth Alliance orbital station in the Calawan system back to Earth would take somewhere in the range of five to ten hours.

That was one of the biggest downsides to slipstreams. The currents were just that, rippling waves of time and space distortions whose relative strength or weakness had a very real effect on travel. At the distance between Calawan and Earth, this variance wasn't a problem. It was; however, a remaining limit on humankind's ability to explore more of the universe. There was always talk within the Alliance of abandoning the planet and finding a new, more suitable home further out amidst the stars. In fact, it was what the colony ship they had escaped on had been designed to do. One problem with that idea was that trying to ride a slipstream in distances greater than a few hundred light years made logistics a challenge.

The other problem was the simple fact that not everyone on Earth was dead, and not everyone who had escaped was of a mind to leave them behind. Theodore St. Martin had been one of the most vocal supporters of remaining in Calawan, and his position as the man who had piloted the only ship to escape during the evacuation gave everyone cause to listen to him.

A tone from the cockpit dashboard signaled to Gabriel that the phase was complete, and the slipstream had been successfully joined. Not that he needed the computer to tell him that. The entire universe changed once a craft entered slipspace, the myriad stars fading away and leaving the view as a gigantic, blank, black canvas just waiting for God to come along and start painting again.

Gabriel tapped a few commands out on the touchscreen beneath his right hand. Then he reached up and lowered the secondary visor on his flight helmet, covering his view with an already running virtual reality simulation, lest he risk succumbing to what doctors had termed 'the slips,' caused by staring out into the void for an extended period of time. It was one of his favorite sims. A lifestream recording he had made seven years ago of himself and his fiancee, Jessica, having dinner. She had been a pilot, too. Everyone had told him not to get involved with another soldier like him. Everyone had warned him about the dangers of getting attached.

He had been young and stubborn. He had already survived twelve missions by then, and at the time he had believed that only the fools died young.

He knew better now. Jessica was anything but a fool, and it hadn't saved her in the end. She had gone on a run the day after the recording was made.

She had never come back.

He didn't watch the lifestream to depress himself, or to ruminate, or to fill himself with regret. He watched it when he was feeling weak. When he was losing hope. When he had the sinking notion that he wasn't coming back this time. He watched it to remember the sacrifices that had been made and to reinforce his belief in the value of what he was doing.

After all, if he went on the mission and survived, it meant that someone else wasn't taking his place. It meant that someone else wasn't dying.

Of course, the part where they danced against the backdrop of an Ursae Majoris solar flare always brought him to tears. She had been so beautiful, so talented, so filled with joy and life and hope for the future. They had been a perfect match. Maybe too perfect in a time as dangerous as theirs.

Hope for the future. That was what being a recon pilot was all about. It was the reason Gabriel risked his life to go back there again and again, making daring runs across the atmosphere for the smallest possibility of picking up any little bit of intel the planet-side resistance could provide, even when most of the time they didn't transmit at all.

And how could he ever give up that hope when there were still people alive on Earth doing their damnedest to fight back?

3

"Move it, move it. Let's go people. We don't want to be the last squad on Earth to be gunned down by those alien bastards."

Major Donovan Peters waved his arm in a furious windmill, motivating the rest of the men and women behind him, twenty in all, to surge forward across a dangerous chasm of twisted steel, cracked concrete, and shattered glass.

It was a warm evening. Too warm, as far as Donovan was concerned. And too dry. The ash and dust were hanging heavy in the evening air, picked up and left there by heavy winds earlier in the morning.

It was lousy weather for a transmission mission, or t-vault, as it was more commonly known. Green cadets liked to have fun saying "transmission mission" as many times as they could as fast as they could before they tripped up.

They stopped right after going on their first one.

Donovan wasn't really sure why they even bothered anymore. There had been nothing new to transmit in months.

Major Donovan Peters. He had been promoted two months earlier, rising to Major not because he was especially suited to the position but because he had managed to survive. Rank these days didn't mean anything close to what it had when the countries that sprinkled the Earth maintained standing militaries. It was chain-of-command, sure, based on the United States structure since it originated with General Alan Parker, the man who had first organized the survivors into a unified resistance. Back then, they had tried to follow the military guidelines, and for a while they had even managed to make something they liked to call progress in their guerrilla war against the alien invaders.

Back then. This was now, and now the promotions came as people died. There was no other system left to it.

And people had died. Nearly half of their forces in the last year alone. Donovan had no idea why, but the Dread had come to the decision that they were finished playing games with the remaining free humans, and they were going to end the resistance once and for all. He had heard the reports from the other militias around the globe, and they were all the same. The Dread were intent on wiping them out and ending the war once and for all.

"Sweep left," Donovan said, keeping his voice low and tight and guiding the squad with his hands.

They ran together out amidst the shattered buildings of what had once been Mexico City, Mexico, turning left and heading through a break in the debris. They were clothed in simple uniforms, dark green and roughly woven by hand, damp after a quick dump of water. Their faces were coated with a light orange clay, as were the back of their hands and bare feet, whose hardened soles beat down on the broken remains without being pierced. Boots were hard to come by and hard to maintain, and runners needed to be nimble without the distraction of a shoelace coming untied, or an old sole coming loose.

Donovan scanned the field ahead of them, his eyes picking over the charred city. He was only twenty-three years old. He had been born to this life, as had his mother. His grandfather had been in Los Angeles when they had come, only a child himself at the time. He had told the story in more personal detail than any video could show.

Not that he hadn't seen the videos of the first attack as well. All of them had. It was an important part of their upbringing, a remembrance of why they lived the way they did, and why they fought.

As he searched for a break that would lead them north to the building he had picked out for the needle, he could picture the massive plasma flume pouring from the sky, superheating the air around it, vaporizing millions and turning Mexico City into this. He shuddered slightly before regaining himself and motioning the team ahead.

He was the oldest of the group of twenty charging through the wreckage. Other than worn rifles, they were carrying only the equipment that would enable the needle to make the transmission. He didn't know what the message they carried was. He never did. General Rodriguez never briefed the t-vault team on the contents.

Donovan waved the team to the right, around an old barricade of burned out cars that had probably been constructed thirty years earlier. He had once thought it strange that the surrounding jungle had never encroached on the abandoned urban center and that everything stayed so well preserved despite the passage of years. Their Chief Science Officer, Carlson, had told him it was because of the nature of the Dread's plasma weapons. They had rendered the earth infertile, unable to sustain plant life wherever the flumes had scorched.

They were getting closer to the old skyscraper, once fifty or sixty stories tall but reduced in the attacks to fifteen or so. They needed to get the needle up over the terrain to ensure it would transmit with a good spread, making it easier for the passing starfighter to capture the message.

His Lieutenant, Renata Diaz, suddenly raised a closed fist. Within a heartbeat, Donovan and the rest of the squad were down behind whatever cover they could find.

Donovan crouched behind the barricade, pressing his body close against it and forcing his breathing to slow. The ability to control fear and panic was one of the most important for a t-vaulter, as the alien's scanners were able to not only sense heat, but to pick up the rhythm of a rapid heartbeat. It took a lot of practice to become adept at staying calm in such dire circumstances.

His eyes stayed forward, focused on Diaz. She had been the first to put eyes on the enemy scout, so it was her job to track it. It was a dangerous role, as the scout would notice all but the smallest of motions. It was hard to watch something without moving. Her head turned slowly, deliberately, her eyes locked onto the craft.

Donovan didn't need to see it. He had seen too many of them already. The scouts were relatively small and oblong, their undersides bristling with sensor needles. They were one of the few things the aliens used that wasn't covered in the black, ridged armor that protected them so well.

He counted the seconds in his head. By the time he reached sixty, the scout had passed over them and continued, sweeping through the empty city. The Dread knew that they were out here somewhere. They had been searching for the fifth iteration of the Mexico rebel home base for nearly fifteen years without success.

Diaz reached the second sixty at the same time he did. She lowered her raised fist, and the team got back on their feet and into formation.

"Damn close," Donovan said. "Let's try to open our eyes next time."

"Screw you, Major," Diaz said, glancing back at him with a smile.

"Is that an invitation?"

"In your dreams."

He put his finger to his lips. She gave him a different finger.

"In my dreams, or yours?" he asked, smiling. He knew where he stood with Diaz. She was pretty, but she was also his best friend's sister. The banter was a tension release. Nothing more.

Donovan scanned the sky, double-checking for any more of the scouts. When he didn't spot any, he waved his team forward again.

"Let's keep it going, soldiers. Who wants to live forever, anyway?"

4

The squad reached the top of the building, picking their way up an emergency stairwell and then over a pile of rubble to get there. As soon as they had moved into position, each member of the t-vault team unloaded their cargo and hooked it up with practiced precision. Their only light came from the nearly vanished sun and the rising stars, giving them the barest illumination. They quickly snapped together battery packs, signal amplifiers, trackers, and finally the twenty-foot tall transmission needle that would send the message out.

Donovan crouched next to the needle, pulling a dark green homespun bag from his back and untying the top. A small box sat inside, and he lifted it out and placed it next to the needle. Then he went back into the bag to remove a wire, which he connected to both the box and the whip.

"How long until the flyby?" Corporal George Cameron asked. He was the youngest of the group, fourteen years old. This was only his second time out.

Donovan put his hand on his wrist, feeling the time on a braille watch. They didn't dare risk using anything that emitted light out here. Once the needle was up, the only things they had to protect themselves were darkness, dampness, and stillness.

"Not too long now if the slipstream calculations were right," Donovan said.

He didn't know exactly how the ground force managed to coordinate with the space force. He knew there was something to slipstream patterns that made certain days and times more likely than others. That wasn't to say they hadn't crossed signals in the years since they started the information dumps, and he knew there were plenty of times that the space forces had passed by the Earth and his team had nothing to send. In fact, this was the first message he had delivered in nearly six months.

"Everything is online," Diaz said, running her fingers along a flat board on the ground in front of her.

"Ears are open?" Donovan asked, looking over to Private Gabriella Sanchez.

She was wearing a pair of headphones, and would be listening for the signal from the passing ship that it was receiving. It came in as a minor blip, a tiny anomaly in the normal static of celestial noise that took keen attention and hearing to catch.

She put her thumbs up to signal she was monitoring.

Donovan tapped the ground with his hand, signaling the rest of the team to spread out and watch for the enemy. It was the other reason t-vaulters went barefoot. Once the light was completely gone they would use vibration to communicate.

Donovan took a seat next to Sanchez, putting his back against the remains of a wall and tucking in his legs. There wasn't much to do once the needle was up and active, at least not until the package had been picked up and it was time to go home, or until they were spotted and they had to run.

Except they wouldn't be running this time. The squad didn't know it, but he had been ordered to hold position and get the transmission off no matter what. According to the Colonel, this was the most important message they had sent in nearly a dozen years. It was a message that was deemed worth the lives of the twenty men and women gathered in the burned out husk of a skyscraper, sitting in darkness and listening to the sky.

Donovan wasn't afraid of those orders. He was honored to be the one to take on the mission, and he knew his squad would be honored, too. Why hadn't he told them? Honor or not, knowing they had no options would get into their heads and change their approach. He needed them in top shape, as precise as always.

He was sitting in the same spot for close to an hour when Diaz slid down next to him, careful not to make any sounds that would distract Sanchez. She pushed her shoulder against him, smiling when he looked at her.

"Nice night," she mouthed.

"It's too hot," he replied.

Mexico had always been too hot for him, even though he had spent his entire adult life with the resistance here. He still had nightmares about the days spent on the run, when the Dread had discovered the Los Angeles base. He remembered holding his mother's hand, the look of fear in her eyes, along with the anger that burned there. He remembered the heat of the explosions behind them and the screams of the dying. He remembered his fear of the monsters that hunted them, large and black and spitting fury. That fear had transformed into anger as he had aged and learned that they weren't monsters at all. They breathed, they bled. They lived and died.

He wanted nothing more than to kill them. All of them.

"Are you okay?" Diaz asked.

Donovan hadn't realized he'd sank into those memories again. He blinked a few times to clear his head before nodding.

"Memories," he said.

Everyone had them. There wasn't a free human alive that couldn't relate to loss or death or destruction. It didn't matter that the invasion had happened three generations earlier. The stories lived on; the videos and images lived on, the resistance lived on. In a lot of ways, humankind had grown strong in their failure and their weakness. That they were still fighting was a testament to that.

"Matteo's birthday is next week," Diaz said. "Did you get him anything?"

Donovan shook his head. "I tried to carve a baseball bat from an old tree branch. I spent three weeks on it. Maybe I'll tell him it's a wizard's staff instead."

Diaz shook, laughing silently. "He hates that fantasy stuff."

"I know."

"Hey, do you think Gibbons likes me?"

Donovan glanced over at her, and then looked out across the darkness for the Corporal. He was crouched at the edge of the wall, peering out into the night and watching for the enemy. He was one of the biggest men in the squad, over six feet tall and heavy with muscle even though he was only eighteen. The same age as Diaz.

"You like Gibbons?" he said.

She shrugged. "He's kind of cute, in a brutish way."

"It's not like there's a lot to choose from, is there?" Donovan asked.

She stuck her tongue out at him. "He's not that bad."

"He's a good soldier. And yes, I think he likes you."

Sanchez reached out and tapped Donovan on the arm, giving him a thumbs up.

The messenger had arrived.

He tapped a code into the ground to alert the others. They tapped their feet back in return, acknowledging the message. Diaz worked the control board, sending more power from the fuel cell to the needle to increase the signal output.

Donovan felt his watch. The pilot was later than expected but within the calculated time. He had no idea how the scientists were able to track the slipstreams so well, but he was glad they were. The less time they had to sit out here-

The thought was interrupted as a flash lit the sky and Gibbons fell backward, a smoking hole in his chest that cast an eerie light on the rest of the squad.

They had been spotted.

5

A soft vibration against Gabriel's arm woke him from his sleep. He evacuated into the tube connected to his flight suit, and then opened his mouth and found the smaller tube that would allow him to drink. His throat was always parched after sleeping in the cockpit, his limbs always stiff. He tapped his control pad a few times, and the vibrations spread to the rest of his appendages, getting the blood flowing again.

He checked his mission clock. The currents were slow today. Eleven hours.

He was almost there.

He tapped the control pad again while clearing his throat.

"Captain Gabriel St. Martin mission recording sixty-eight. Successful join with the slipstream. Time to arrival, eleven hours fourteen minutes. Preparing for departure. Engines online. Weapons system-" He paused to turn it on. Not that it mattered. Everyone knew they had nothing that could pierce the armor of the Dread defenses. "Weapons system active. All systems nominal."

The recording was standard operating procedure. From now until he re-entered the slipstream, everything he did would be saved for review upon his return to Calawan.

He leaned forward and flipped a few switches on the dashboard. A small screen lit up in front of him, giving him a map of the solar system. The stream would drop him near Earth's moon. It was dangerously close, but they were under orders to conserve fuel whenever possible. While the stations had hydrogen converters, the growing population and expansion of the colony required that more and more of it be diverted to keeping people alive. Gabriel could only imagine if Theodore were still lucid. He could picture his father storming into a council meeting and cursing up a storm about chopping the dicks off the resistance so that Joe and Mary Scientist could make another mouth to feed.

Not that they didn't want mouths to feed. The remains of free human civilization was in a constant, delicate balance. Too few heads and their life support systems wouldn't have enough hands to maintain them, the excavation equipment that fueled their expansion would have no one to drive it, and the military wouldn't have enough soldiers to prepare to fight a war that might never come. Too many heads and they would starve.

Children had been and still were a priority, though there was less desperation now than there was thirty years ago. Not all of the eggs that had been carried off Earth with the fleeing colony ship had ever been fertilized and implanted into a surrogate. Gabriel had been lucky because of who his father was, and even then he had been left to wait his turn. Theodore St. Martin hadn't wanted a son until he was older so that he could stretch his family's involvement in the resistance for as long as it took.

Gabriel drew in a breath. Held. Released. He took in another. He was nearing the end of his slipstream route, and in less than a minute the QPG would deactivate and the ion thrusters would kick on. He would have eight minutes to blast across the upper Earth atmosphere and listen for a transmission from the freedom fighters on the ground before rejoining the slipstream on the other side.

All he had to do was avoid the Dread defenses.

As long as it took. Gabriel often wondered how long that would be.

Fifty years had passed. They had been sending ships back to Earth for the last twenty-seven of those. At first, they had done little more than take pictures and record video which was used to monitor the enemy's build-up on the planet. It hadn't been as dangerous then because the Dread didn't care that much about the initial sorties. They weren't worried about the one that got away, not when they had defeated everything the governments of the world had to throw at them without losing a single ship.

Then the first transmission had come. Until then, the resistance in space had no idea there was a resistance on the ground. Somehow, small pockets of people around the world had managed to stay hidden from the aliens and to find shelter and food. The initial communications had been simple and straightforward messages about who they were and what they were doing. Later transmissions had described the situation on Earth.

It wasn't good, and time hadn't made it any better. The ground-based resistance was shrinking. The messages were fewer and further between, as the forces either had nothing new to report or were unable to find a safe place to set up a transmit needle.

As long as it took. Gabriel wanted to believe he would live that long. He wanted to believe his father would live that long, and fulfill the promise he had made all of those years ago.

The truth was, they had lost everything in the initial attack. It was only stubborn determination that kept them going despite every bit of evidence and logic pointing to their eventual demise.

Gabriel held onto hope because hope was the only thing he had.

It was the only thing any of them had.

6

"Departing slipstream," Gabriel said for the sake of the recording. "Firing ion thrusters."

The starfighter shook like it was entering the atmosphere as the QPG brought him back in phase with realspace and his main control thrusters began to fire. Gabriel held the stick steady, lifting the secondary visor from his helmet and putting his attention forward.

The craft shuddered one last time and he was back out into space, the moon a large mass ahead of him and the Earth barely visible beyond.

"Here we go," he said, shifting his free hand from the control pad to a smaller stick that would handle the vectoring thrusters. One eye landed on the fuel monitor. Every move he made would have to be measured against his power supply.

He increased the thrust, angling the fighter to swing around the moon, using its limited gravity to help boost his acceleration.

It had taken him almost a dozen sorties before he had grown accustomed to what humankind's home planet looked like now, compared to what he had been shown in videos and pictures salvaged in the colony ship's datacenter. While the general size and shape and color remained the same blue marble as it had always been, it was the change in the surface features that was the most striking.

There was a time before the Dread had come when the dark side of the planet would be lit with the glow of cities, lines of illumination that spread through small areas and left the rest of the land in darkness. The light side would reveal itself in spreads of green or brown or gray, where sister cities rose into the atmosphere, the tallest being almost six kilometers in height.

The wasted remains of those cities were still visible. On the light side, their majestic silver forms had been reduced to dark black splotches that on closer inspection revealed heaps of slag and broken concrete and glass. The surrounding countryside was also obliterated, transformed from forest or grassland to barren stone and dust.

On the dark side, there was nothing. No light, and no indication that a civilization had ever existed there at all. There was so much emptiness. So much death and destruction hidden yet hinted at in that space. Even now, it caused Gabriel to feel a chill.

The alien construction was more centralized, though there were smaller outposts positioned in strategic locations around the globe. An endless array of networked tunnels, towers, and spires occupied the bulk of the land within the planet's tropical zone, between the Tropic of Cancer and the Tropic of Capricorn. The structures were dark, no more than black spots in the day that made it seem as if a colony of giant ants had settled itself across most of Africa and the northern part of South America. At night, they too were lit with a glow, though it took on a more blueish hue and was dimmer than anything humans had created.

The aliens' orbital defenses were a blockade that hung between Gabriel and the ruined Earth. They hadn't always been there. They had started to appear only after the resistance had made their first successful broadcast, and the NEA's flyby had been rewarded with a choppy recording of a man known only as David revealing the first of the aliens' secrets.

The reason why they had come.

Those defenses materialized as small satellites that surrounded the planet, numbering in the hundreds of thousands. They were round and ridged, coated in the same dark carapace as everything the aliens made, the damned armor that none of humankind's weapons were able to pierce. Not even nuclear warheads had broken through the material, detonating directly against it and leaving nothing but a minor wound. It was the one and only reason they had lost the planet. How do you defeat something that you can't hurt?

It would never stop them from trying.

Those satellites came to life as Gabriel drew closer, their sensor arrays picking up the arrival of his starfighter. Small thrusters hidden beneath the carapace began to fire, turning the satellites toward him, while their plasma cannons extended from cover like a turtle poking its head out of its shell.

"I have been targeted by the enemy," Gabriel said calmly. Every mission started with the satellites firing at him. His skill and experience would get him past this first line of defense. "Taking evasive maneuvers."

His hands worked the two sticks with practiced ease. Gabriel kept an eye on his power reserves while adjusting to take a more chaotic path. The satellites changed their position to line up the plasma cannons and opened fire on him.

Gabriel switched up his vectors, bouncing and dancing as he drew ever closer to the defenses. The fighter was armed with a heavy ion pulse cannon, but there was no point in trying to use it. The beam weapon would strike the armor without a hint of damage made, and it would use up too much of his precious fuel.

Instead, Gabriel scanned the field of satellites for an opening. He found it a moment later, a gap in the defenses that would allow him through. He spun the fighter in a tight rotation while creating a bit of wobble in the flight path with the vectoring thrusters. It was enough to keep the enemy's targeting computers from getting a solid lock, and their shots scattered around him.

He was centimeters from death with every blast yet he remained completely calm. He had done this so many times. He had survived so many times. Luck was important, sure, but so was skill.

The starfighter slipped silently into the open lane, racing past the satellites within seconds. Gabriel eased up on the throttle then, changing course and heading further down toward the thermosphere. The satellites ceased operation behind him, their instructions limited to monitoring space outside of the ring.

He dove quickly, keeping his eyes open and scanning the field ahead of him. The satellites were dangerous, but they were the least of his concerns.

"Entering the thermosphere," he said, using the two sticks to maneuver the fighter. He flattened out some, running a horizontal arc along the upper atmosphere. All of the debris from the initial attack had long ago burned up or had drifted unencumbered out into deeper space, yet somehow a few non-functional human satellites had managed to remain in their orbit, unaware of what had become of the people who had put them there.

He took his hand off the thruster control and moved it to the touchpad. He tapped in a rapid sequence, opening up the onboard receivers. He wouldn't know if he had gotten anything until he returned to Delta Station, but it was better that way. To pause or hesitate for even a moment would be the difference between life and death.

"Activating receivers. Let's hope we get something this time."

He kept his head moving side to side, while at the same time watching the HUD for any hint of motion from his sensors. He knew this was the calm before the storm, even if he wouldn't see the storm coming until it was almost too late.

He swept along the atmosphere, racing over the northern hemisphere, not too far from the Tropic of Cancer. It had been so long since they had captured anything, Gabriel wondered if there was anyone left down there to transmit, and if not, how they would ever know it.

It was a wayward thought that almost cost him his life.

7

Donovan didn't hesitate as he tapped out orders with his foot, getting the team moving. Three to try to draw the enemy away, five to keep a tight defense on the needle, and the rest to hold the perimeter. He didn't need to be quiet, but some directions were more efficient to issue by feel.

"Diaz, go," Donovan said, choosing her as one of the decoys. Not because they were usually able to escape alive. She was their fastest runner.

Diaz looked like she was about to argue, but then she hopped to her feet and ran, sliding down a fallen girder with acrobatic ease. Plasma rifle fire blasted into the space behind her as the enemy soldiers tried to get a bead.

"Fox, cover her," Donovan shouted.

Private Fox aimed his rifle, opening fire with conventional bullets. The weapons were vastly inferior to the alien plasma rifles, but they were all the resistance owned, taken years earlier from gun shops and homes from as far south as Acapulco and north into the southwestern United States. It didn't matter that much, anyway. There was nothing the humans had that could pierce a Dread soldier's carapace armor.

The slightly better news was that the Dread rarely sent their real soldiers after t-vaulters.

Donovan felt his watch again. The flyby would take about eight minutes, but only twenty seconds or so would put the pilot in range of the transmission. There was a small switch on the computer that would pop out when a connection had been made, and the signal sent. Sanchez had her hand on the box, waiting to feel it happen.

Thirty seconds passed. Mexico City was a nightmare, lit by the flashes of plasma as the bolts poured into the surrounding concrete and steel, burning into it where it hit. Donovan heard a thud, turned and saw Amallo was down. He unslung his rifle and rushed to the Corporal's position, looking down toward the street.

A half-dozen enemy combatants had gathered behind the charred wreckage of a car. They were the typical Dread response to a transmission, what the resistance called HSCs or human simulacrum combatants. Clones. They were all identical in appearance: six and a half feet tall, bald, muscular, and wearing simple cotton shirts and pants.

From what Donovan had heard, the clones were easier for the Dread to make than the impenetrable armor they used to build pretty much everything else, and so they would grow them out, program them, and send them to find the resistance. Once in awhile, after an HSC put eyes on a t-vault, a real Dread soldier piloting one of their mechanized armor would show up. It would then blow the hell out of everyone and everything nearby, ending the transmission and the t-vault team in a hurry.

At least, that was the rumor. Donovan was still alive, which meant he had never seen it happen.

The clones stared back at him, finding him with alarming ease, genetically modified to see in the dark. Donovan barely slipped behind the wall before a gout of plasma fire spewed up at him.

"What have you got, soldiers?" he shouted.

"Counting twenty-four, Major," Rollins replied. "They aren't going easy on us today."

Twenty-four? Not going easy was an understatement. That was twice the normal number of clones scouting for a t-vault squad.

"Sanchez?"

He looked back at the Private. She shook her head. The transmission hadn't been sent yet. Damn.

He peeked around the corner of the building, taking a quick shot at the clones below. His bullets hit the car in front of them, and they returned fire, sending him back to cover again.

A shout and Rollins was down.

"Come on," Donovan whispered, glancing up at the sky.

He could see the dark splotch of the Dread's orbital defenses blotting out a pattern ahead of the stars. He knew it wasn't easy for the pilots to get through that mess.

It wasn't exactly a cakewalk on the ground, either.

A groan and Mendoza fell off the side of the building, her head torn in half by plasma. Davids went to cover her position, firing a steady stream down at the clones. His gun clicked empty, and he ducked to the ground, grabbing a magazine from his pocket and slapping it in. They had been traveling light and fast, and only had two reloads.

"Sanchez?" Donovan asked again. Only a dozen seconds had passed, and he was getting a bad feeling about this one.

She shook her head again.

He glanced down at the HSCs. They were gone.

What?

They wouldn't have retreated. It meant they were either making their way up through the building or the decoys had managed to pull them away. Except the decoys rarely worked anymore.

"Stay on it," he said to Sanchez, putting a hand on her shoulder. "I'm going to intercept."

Sanchez's eyes opened wide. He might as well have told her he was going to kill himself.

Donovan reached the steps and started down, leading with his rifle. He could hear the plasma sizzling against the walls above him and the echo of the return fire from his squad outside. It was nearly pitch black in the stairwell, good for the clones and bad for him. He dug a small wrist light from his pocket, slapping it on. It gave him just enough illumination to see the stairs before he tripped down them.

A plasma bolt lit the area, and Donovan threw himself to the ground, barely avoiding being hit. He rolled down the steps, feeling the edges of the concrete digging into him, leaving cuts and bruises as he fell. He hit a landing and rolled to his feet, directing his rifle down while he tried to get his bearings. That had been too close.

He kept his back to the wall while he listened for the footsteps of the clones climbing the stairs. When he picked them up, he started to descend again, his bare feet silent as he went down. In the glow of the wrist light, he noticed he had lost a lot of the clay that would hide his heat signature. It didn't matter much in here, but if he survived long enough to run?

He would worry about surviving that long first. He hadn't made it to Major by being stupid.

He stood still again. The clones were getting closer. He pulled the wrist light off and turned it over. There was a small switch on the bottom, and in one motion he flicked it over and threw it down the steps.

The light flared from it, a bright flash that revealed the enemy position and blinded their sensitive eyes. Donovan charged at them, weapon firing, cutting them down in a hail of bullets. He didn't stop shooting until his magazine was empty, reaching them as the last one hit the floor and stopped moving.

He knelt down and grabbed one of the plasma rifles. It was rounded and slender, designed to rest on the forearm of one arm and stabilized with the opposite hand. It deactivated as it left the clone's grip, and he tossed it aside. It was a foolish hope to think they might forget to pair the weapon.

He slapped a new magazine into his gun and continued the descent, feeling his watch as he did. Four minutes had passed, and the fire from both sides had calmed somewhat. The transmission had to have been sent by now.

He reached a pile of rubble, stepping carefully out onto it and surveying the area. Gomez's body lay at a crude angle across the lower portion of the debris, his arm blown off by a plasma bolt. A dead clone lay nearby.

"Sanchez," he shouted, his voice echoing. He looked back and up. Her face appeared over the edge a moment later, illuminated by her wrist light, and she gave him a thumbs up. The transmission was sent. "Where are the clones?"

She put her arms out to the side and shook her head. She didn't know.

"Grab whoever's still alive up there and let's get the hell out of here. The stairwell is clear."

A heavy vibration shook the ruins, sending small bits of debris rolling down and a cloud of dust into the air. A second rumble followed. Then a third. He heard the soft whine of moving parts. What was that? He crouched low, scanning the buildings around them. The vibrations were steady, and getting stronger. He caught a bit of motion in the corner of his eye and turned to aim his rifle.

"Donovan," Diaz said. Sweat had washed the clay away from half her face and left her hair a damp mess. "Run."

8

The enemy starfighters came out of nowhere, darting through the cover of lower clouds and taking a direct vector toward him. His sensors beeped in a panic as they picked up the burn from the thermosphere, and he cursed himself for letting his focus slip for even an instant. He put his hands on the controls and added thrust, shooting ahead of the enemy ships and forcing them to tail behind.

He kept an eye on them on his HUD. They appeared as red triangles there, but he knew what they looked like. Wide and slender, the wings rounded and sharp at the fore and aft, with a cockpit that swept up from an inverted center. They were made of the same ridged black carapace as the satellites and the alien buildings. Some pilots called them Bats. Others called them Rays. To Gabriel, they were nothing but trouble.

There was still some debate about whether the alien craft were piloted manually, remotely, or autonomously. Since no one had ever shot one down, it remained a point of contention. Unlike a human starfighter, the cockpit had no obvious viewport, but that didn't mean the aliens weren't using some advanced tech, or even something as simple as camera feeds, to see out of the ship. They certainly didn't fly like they couldn't see, and they hugged Gabriel's aft as he juked and jived across the sky, doing everything he could to prevent them from getting a lock.

His heart was racing while his head remained calm. If he panicked, if he lost concentration now, he would die. No matter how the enemy ships were flown, they were extraordinarily skilled and impossible to defeat. The only option was to keep going, to keep trying to avoid their efforts to bring him down.

Gabriel threw the stick hard to the right, and the starfighter tipped over and turned. He threw it to the left, and it rolled back the other way. His computer complained as it registered the enemy fire, and Gabriel felt his first pang of true fear as a shot from a plasma cannon nearly tore a wing from the fuselage. As it was, it left a long, trailing scorch mark on the back of the fighter.

"Come on, come on, come on," Gabriel said, forgetting about the recording. "Is that all you've got?"

His hands worked the sticks, keeping the fighter from ever flying a straight vector that the enemy ships could target. He checked his mission clock. Two minutes to egress. The run was almost complete.

The sensors cried out again as a second pair of enemy ships were detected, coming at him from the front.

"Damn," Gabriel said, throwing both sticks forward. The fighter dipped and headed down toward the surface as the four enemy ships blew past one another before circling back to follow.

Gabriel's eyes jumped from the mission clock to his power reserves. He had gotten closer to the surface, and deeper into Earth's gravity than he had wanted. It was going to cost him. He couldn't shake the enemy fighters and make it back to the slipstream in time.

A million calculations darted through his head. A million options for how to make his next move and try to get back to Delta Station. He had outmaneuvered four enemy ships before, and he could do it again. The one place the aliens didn't have human starfighters beat was in overall thrust.

He slowed down, easing off on the throttle once more. The enemy fighters were wedges on his display, sliding into position behind him and gaining.

Good. He wanted them close.

He was more cautious with his maneuvers now, making short, tight jumps and turns that were just enough to keep the alien fire from scoring a direct hit. Plasma cannons sent bolts scattering around him, close enough to scorch the frame and raise more warnings from the computer. He ignored it, keeping his focus on the result.

He slowed even more. The alien ships continued to close in, their shots drawing dangerously near as he dangled the bait. What he was doing was insane, and he hoped he would never have to do it again.

The four alien fighters were only a few hundred meters behind him. At their current velocity, if he had cut his thrust they would slam into him and tear him apart without taking a hint of damage themselves. In fact, one of the ships began to accelerate harder, inverting the idea.

That was Gabriel's cue. He pulled back hard on the left stick while pushing the right stick forward. The fighter changed direction as the thrusters went to full burn, and he shot up and away from the enemy. They were too close to change direction easily and too slow to catch up.

They were smart enough not to try.

Gabriel kept going, watching his power levels sinking further and further. He could see the orbital defense ring up ahead, and he narrowed his eyes and gritted his teeth. He couldn't risk slowing down or he might not have the power or the velocity to get back into the slipstream.

His eyes scanned the ring, picking a path through the round devices. He wasn't worried about their fire on the way back out, especially not at this velocity. He would blow past and be gone before they could touch him.

He was only seconds away from the ring when he saw the wedge enter his display, coming on from his left faster than anything he had ever seen before. He turned his head to watch one of the alien starfighters bearing down, using constant heavy thrust to gain a velocity that would be unmanageable for maneuvering.

Except it didn't need to maneuver. It was headed right for him.

Gabriel couldn't believe it. After sixty-seven missions, had his luck had finally run out?

Not yet.

"Pic kee toi, asshole," he said, using one of his father's favorite cajun cusses. He flipped a switch next to the thrust stick, engaging the emergency overdrive. It would nearly drain his fuel cell but it was either that or die.

The fighter's velocity jumped, throwing him into the midst of the satellites at high speed. He deftly shifted the vectoring thrusters, whipping the craft this way and that, somehow managing to avoid the satellites, in some cases by a meter or less.

The incoming enemy fighter tried to follow. Gabriel looked back over his shoulder, watching as its plasma cannon loosed a stream of bolts into the satellites to clear a path, his eyes opening in wonder as the satellites blew apart beneath it. There had been rumors forever that the aliens' weapons could overcome their shields, but there had never been any definitive proof.

Until now.

Gabriel put his eyes back forward. The enemy fighter was still behind him, but the obstacles had forced it to slow, its design not able to maneuver quite as well as he could. He angled the fighter to the inception point, checking his velocity. Then he hit the touchpad to activate the quantum phase generator.

The wings began to blur, the ship shaking heavily as the unharmed phased surfaces compensated for the damaged ones. The computer continued to beep warnings; a new one added as his fuel cell reached critical levels. There would be just enough juice to keep the QPG powered and to run life support.

Gabriel found the enemy ship still racing toward him. He had never seen one so intent on stopping a sortie before, and he wondered if he had picked anything up from the resistance on the ground, and if so what it was. The intel he had just gathered on his own was more than enough to have made the trip worthwhile.

Watching the enemy's plasma beam pass harmlessly through the fighter as he joined the slipstream was even more rewarding.

"This is Captain Gabriel St. Martin," he said, a little less calmly than before. "Mission complete."

He switched off the recorder and leaned back in the seat.

It was going to be a nice, quiet ride home.

9

Donovan didn't question why Diaz had come back. He spun around again, looking for his team. The vibrations were getting stronger and closer, the whine louder with each passing breath.

"Damn," he said, returning to the mouth of the stairwell. He found the remainder of the t-vault squad almost down. Sanchez and Cameron. Were they the only ones left?

They had abandoned the needle and the equipment, carrying only their rifles. Donovan waited until they caught up to him, putting his hand on their shoulders to guide them out the door. He heard Sanchez gasp as she exited.

"Dios Mío," she said, her face pale and afraid.

Donovan followed her eyes out to the corner of a distant building. A dark shape had emerged from behind it.

It was easily twenty meters tall, a wide, squat body resting on massive mechanical legs that ended in three claw-like toes that dug deep into the broken pavement. A massive plasma cannon rested on either side of the torso, serving as arms, while smaller weapons jutted out on either side of a rounded bulge in the center that had to be a cockpit or remote control unit of some kind. The whole thing was a rippled black, covered in the protective carapace.

Donovan had been a child the last time he had seen the Dread's mechanized armor, when they had been laying waste to the ruins of Los Angeles in an effort to root out the resistance. In his nightmares, he remembered them only as black monsters.

The real thing wasn't much different.

Its presence only confirmed what he had already guessed. The aliens were done being patient with the resistance and had every intention of ending it now.

"Come on," he said, running ahead of them, letting himself slide down the pile of rubble to where Diaz was still waiting.

She had her rifle against her shoulder, facing the armor. There was nothing their guns could do to hurt that thing, but maybe it made her feel better to act like there was.

"What are you doing here?" he asked as he reached her.

The armor was closing in fast, and before she could answer a massive flume of plasma launched from the left cannon. He could feel the static and heat of it as it passed overhead and struck the top floor of the building where they had set up the needle. The entire thing vanished in pulverized rock and superheated slag that rained down on them as ash. It burned where it touched the skin.

"No time," she replied. "Follow me."

The remaining members of the t-vault team followed Diaz as she sprinted away. They had only gone a few meters when a spray of pulsed plasma tore into the rubble behind them, lighting up the sky in a red hue and leaving a burning heat at their backs.

"This way," Diaz said, reaching a building and turning left down a tight alley.

Donovan could feel the vibrations on his bare feet. The Dread armor was following them.

"It knows we're out here," he said. "It can see us."

"You lost all of your clay," Sanchez said.

Donovan looked at the others. Sanchez and Cameron were still coated.

"Diaz, wait," he said, bringing his Lieutenant to a sudden stop. "Sanchez, Cameron, go that way and find a place to hide."

"We're not splitting up, sir," Cameron said.

"Yes, we are. They won't be able to track you, and we can't afford to lose any more soldiers. Do it. Now."

They hesitated for a heartbeat before bolting. The Dread machine was catching up with them.

"You just wanted to get me alone, didn't you, D?" Diaz said, smiling.

"I want them to survive this," he replied, not in the mood for jokes.

"Come on," Diaz said. She started running again.

Donovan followed. It was a challenge to keep up with her as she made tight angles through the wasteland of a city, vaulting wreckage and squeezing through small gaps. Donovan could feel his lungs burning from the dust, smoke, and effort. He could hear the armor behind them, gaining ground with every passing second.

A whine, and projectiles chewed through the buildings behind them, sending shards of concrete into the area. One hit Donovan in the shoulder, burying itself in his back. He stopped himself from crying out, desperate to keep moving.

Diaz looked back, seeing he was hit. A concerned look flashed across her face, but she didn't slow. They reached another alley, and she pointed to an open door. They ducked inside, finding themselves in what had once been the lobby of a hotel. There was debris everywhere, along with a few old corpses and some rats that scurried away at their approach.

"Where are we going?" Donovan asked. He held his left arm across his chest to ease some of the pain.

"Here," Diaz said, leading him to the back of the space and ducking under a partially collapsed ceiling.

He followed her through to a bank of elevators. One of the doors was open, and Diaz brought him up to it. He looked into the shaft. There was nothing but darkness below. The vibrations of the armor were growing stronger behind them, so close that Donovan was surprised it hadn't turned them to ash already. The rats had to be confusing its thermal sensors.

"Now what?" Donovan asked.

Diaz kicked some of the debris into the shaft. A few seconds passed until he heard the distinct sound of it hitting water. He didn't need a verbal answer to his question.

He grabbed her hand and jumped.

10

Gabriel leaned forward and hit the switch to deactivate the QPG. The fighter shook slightly as it disengaged from the slipstream and reentered realspace. Warning tones immediately began ringing out in the cockpit, and the power indicator flashed red.

His main battery was dry. He had two hours of reserve power to keep his life support going.

It was more than enough.

Delta Station floated ahead of him, a few thousand kilometers distant. It was brightly lit from here, its large, saucer-like head spinning slowly while the narrow docks and launch cannons remained stationary below, trailing downward into a near spike where the sensor array and communications antennas poked out from the bottom. It was a simple design and looked a lot more impressive from the outside than it was on the inside. Every part of it was function over form. Every ounce of material that had gone into its making was calculated and planned. Their printers could only manage so much per day, and everything that was constructed was essential to someone.

"This is Captain Gabriel St. Martin. Miranda, are you back on duty?"

"Gabriel. Welcome home."

Miranda's voice made him smile. He hadn't been worried about making it back once he'd joined the slipstream. It still wasn't the same as actually being home.

"I could use a lift back," Gabriel said. "My cell is empty."

There was a pause at the other end. She knew what that meant. How close he had come to not making it back at all.

"I guess you needed my luck after all," she said.

"For sure," Gabriel replied.

"I'm sending Captain Sturges out to bring you home. ETA, ten minutes."

"Sounds wonderful. Did I miss anything while I was gone?"

"Around here? In one day? Not much. One of the compressors broke on Alpha. All of the build jobs had to be reorganized to emergency print a replacement. Oh, and Shawna had her baby."

Gabriel tried to remember who Shawna was. With a total population of around twenty-thousand, there were some people who were able to keep track of nearly everyone else. Gabriel wasn't one of them. He wasn't interested in entertainment through gossip.

"Boy or girl?" he asked.

"Boy. Bradley Williams. Twelve pounds, four ounces."

"Big boy."

"Yup."

"Did they assign him yet?"

"Not yet. Space Force is arguing with Engineering over him."

"He sounds like he might get too big for Space Force."

"He's the right size for infantry. They're projecting him at over two meters."

"Just what we need. Another mouth to feed and body to train for a ground war that will never happen."

"You sound like your father."

"Good."

His father was right on that account. Twenty-thousand people and a quarter of them were infantry. Ground soldiers with guns that couldn't pierce Dread armor and no protection of their own. They weren't going to get the aliens off of Earth like that. Their only chance at victory would come from space. They needed to blast the Dread like the Dread had blasted them.

The existence of the infantry division was an asinine waste. It was also proof that despite his father's stature in the government of the New Earth Alliance, it hadn't been enough to guide every military decision. The council thought the infantry was good for morale, and General Cave loved having the resources and the control.

Just because humankind had nearly been wiped out of the universe, it didn't mean the survivors would give up on their politics.

Sometimes he wondered if things would be different if one of the colony ships launched from India or Japan had survived the exodus.

"Do you know if the resistance sent a message?" Miranda asked.

"You know I don't," he replied. "But that was a good nonsequitur."

"I don't want to bring any more of your father out of you. I'll be listening to you rant for the next thirty minutes."

"He ranted because he was passionate."

"I know. And so are you. That's not always a bad thing."

"Not always?"

"Sturges is approaching. I'm going to leave you in his capable hands now. Locke out."

Gabriel laughed at the abruptness of her disengagement. She really was afraid to get him going. He turned his attention to the ship that was vectoring toward him. It was a simple supply transport, also known as a BIS, or box in space. As the name suggested, it was nearly square, with a large front viewport and a couple of small thrusters breaking the shape on either side. He could see Captain Sturges through the transparency, his wrinkled face wrinkling even more when he smiled.

"Captain St. Martin," Sturges said, his voice gruff and aged. "I heard you needed a ride home."

"Yes, sir," Gabriel said. They may have been the same rank, but Sturges was forty years his senior and a survivor from Earth. The last part alone meant he deserved respect.

"Close call?"

"Too close."

"I can see the burn marks on the frame. You're lucky you didn't lose integrity or shake apart when you joined the slipstream."

"How lucky?" Gabriel asked.

The BIS was getting closer, slowing and turning so that Sturges could collect the fighter in the rear cargo hold.

"Son, you don't want to know. You might not go back out there."

"As long as I'm not dead I'll go back out there. How lucky?"

"I'd say a few extra prayers tonight if I were you. You'll have to divert some of your backup power to thrusters to get in line."

"Yes, sir," Gabriel said. He worked his touchpad to shift power, ignoring the warnings from the computer.

He took hold of the secondary stick and gently fired the vectoring thrusters until the fighter was lined up with the back of the BIS. The transport's cargo hold was easily big enough to swallow him, and Captain Sturges directed the ship expertly, taking the fighter inside and then closing the bay door. A light on the front of the bay turned green once the space had been filled with air and the suppressor was reactivated. At that point, Gabriel opened the cockpit and got to his feet, feeling the blood rushing back to his legs.

He shook them out for a few seconds before climbing onto the wing. He took a moment to survey the damage, surprised to see how much of the frame had been burned away, leaving the inner skeleton and wiring of the craft exposed. He clutched the crucifix in his hand again, quickly thanking his mother for her intervention.

Then he jumped down to the floor and made his way to the front of the BIS, opening the cockpit door and entering.

"Captain Sturges," Gabriel said.

The older man glanced back at him. "Gabriel. Have a seat."

Gabriel sat down in the open co-pilot's seat. The BIS had been designed before the Dread had come, back when they had the manpower to use two people to fly a transport.

"I'm going to haul you back to Alpha," Sturges said. "That fighter of yours is going to need some reconditioning."

"I'm supposed to deliver the recorder to Colonel Graham on Delta," Gabriel said.

He laughed. "I know the procedure. I already spoke to Graham. He's on Alpha, too. You can drop it with him there."

"Why is he on Alpha?" Gabriel asked. He knew Graham. The man didn't like leaving Delta. He didn't trust that his subordinates could run the station without his constant oversight.

"General Cave ordered him there. Before you ask me why, I don't know. I get more intel because I'm old and people think I'm special for riding the Old Gator's ship away from the Dread, but they don't tell me everything."

Gabriel was silent. General Cave wouldn't have called in his officers if he weren't thinking big thoughts.

"Anyway," Sturges said, breaking the silence. "I'm sure your father wouldn't mind seeing you."

"He doesn't even know who I am anymore."

"Maybe not outwardly. Deep down, I think he knows. When was the last time you visited him?"

Gabriel thought about it. "I don't know. Six months?"

"He's getting up there, Gabe. You don't want to regret not spending more time with him when he's gone."

Gabriel stared out through the viewport. They had taken a wide angle around Delta Station, and now he could see Alpha Settlement up ahead. It was a long, low network of domed buildings that spread from a large central hub, all of which was resting at the bottom of a deep crater in the largest of Taphao Kaew's three moons. The original settlers had named the moon Manhattan after the famous Earth city.

Behind Alpha Settlement, sitting at the far edge of the crater was a starship. The U.S.S.S Magellan, a nearly three-kilometer long dagger of scarred and dirty metal that had transported the escaping humans from Earth to Calawan over fifty years ago. She was sitting abandoned and empty, a half-century restoration project still underway, working to convert humankind's only large space-faring vessel from a passenger ship to a military one. Over the years, she had been bolstered with extra layers of armor and newer damage control systems, while the inner configuration had been re-imagined to add fighter launch tubes and landing bays and provide for the needs of both the flying and ground units of the NEASF. It was an incredible amount of work for a population as small as theirs and a testament to what they could all achieve when they worked together.

It was also a constant and sad reminder of the cold hard truth of their existence. The restoration was unfinished, and who knew how long it would remain that way? The Magellan had no weapons systems or offensive punch of any kind. She was sitting dormant, waiting for the day when a means to defeat the enemy's defenses would be discovered.

A day that might never come.

To Gabriel, the sight of the ship was a strong reminder of his father. It had been a while since he had paid the man a visit. It was hard for him to bring himself to do it. He preferred to remember his old man as the spitfire he had been, not the invalid he was today. Still, he knew Sturges was right. He didn't want any more regrets.

"I know. Okay, I'll stop by."

"Good man."

11

Gabriel waited for the loop transport to come to a stop and the entry hatch to swing open. He stepped into the small cylindrical vehicle, taking the first of two seats at the front. The loop system would carry him quickly from the hangar at the western edge of the settlement to the central hub where the Star Force Headquarters were located. He had changed from his flight suit to a standard issue pair of dress blues, grabbing a pair from the general commissary after showering off his hours inside the cockpit. A satchel was slung over his shoulder containing his fighter's data recorder.

Captain Paul Sturges sat down beside him. The older man had also showered and changed though he was wearing more casual utilities. A few other NEASF members filed in behind them, filling the small pod in no time. The hatch closed and the pod rushed ahead through the connecting tubes, a trip to that would take less than thirty seconds to complete.

"I know that you don't know why Colonel Graham is on Alpha," Gabriel said. "Do you know anything else that isn't common knowledge that I might be interested in?"

Sturges glanced over at him, flashing a wry smile. "I should have known you would ask me that when I sat here."

"You have about fifteen seconds to answer."

Sturges shrugged. "Nothing more than rumors and hearsay."

Gabriel watched the man's face. He didn't like Sturges' expression. "Anything credible? And please don't lie to me, Captain. We've known each other a long time."

"Heh. I've known you since you were still crapping your diapers. I know something, but you aren't going to like it, and I don't want that news to come from me."

Gabriel hadn't been expecting that answer. He felt his heart start to thump. "Paul-"

The loop slowed.

"Nothing definite, Gabe," Sturges said. "Just some things the military leadership and the Council have been talking about."

The pod came to a stop, and the hatch opened. The passengers disembarking in the central hub stood to depart. Sturges wasn't one of them.

"What kind of things?" Gabriel said, leaning over the man as he crossed the pod.

"I shouldn't say."

"Come on. Spill it."

Sturges looked back to check on the other soldiers. Then he leaned up and forward to whisper.

"Some members of the Council think we should start preparing the Magellan to take everyone into deep space. The science team believes they've discovered an Earth-type planet a year out."

Gabriel felt the heat rush to his face, his anger rising. "They want to abandon Earth?"

It wasn't the first time the subject had come up. Every time the scientists claimed they had found an E-type, someone on the Council decided to start pushing to take the colony there, even if it meant leaving the resistance behind.

"You know Siddhu is on the council," Sturges said. "She said the team presented a very compelling case. They believe they've really found one this time."

Gabriel barely heard him. He stood straight and stepped out of the pod, turning his head back over his shoulder. "Thanks for the tip."

He stormed away from the station, his mind a sudden blur of anger and frustration. Captain Sturges' wife was a strong woman, and she was usually on the side of the military. The rest of the Council wasn't nearly as accommodating. If the case were strong enough, they would vote to leave Calawan and their home world behind.

And there was nothing he could do about it except be angry and follow orders.

Sturges didn't want to tell him about it. He shouldn't have pushed. They said ignorance was bliss, but it was a lesson he still hadn't managed to master.

Gabriel made his way into the central dome. It was a massive structure, hundreds of meters high and wide and the home to all of the New Earth Alliance's government facilities, twenty-five floors worth in all. It was the place where every decision concerning the remains of free humankind was made, and a place where Gabriel always preferred to avoid. As soon as he stepped foot on it, he couldn't wait to catch a transport back to Delta Station.

He headed directly to the middle of the structure, where a centralized administrative station sat ahead of the elevator tube that carried people up to the offices. It was early morning, and the area was relatively quiet. He was thankful for that. In the middle of the day, there would be hundreds of people crowding the floor, either waiting for a scheduled appointment, transferring from one loop to another to cross the settlement, or enjoying a work break by socializing.

"Captain St. Martin," the receptionist said when he reached the station. She was dark-skinned and chubby, with a big, welcoming smile and bright eyes. "Welcome back. How was the mission?"

Gabriel tried to remember her name. "Good morning." He paused. "I'm sorry. It must be the slipspace fatigue. I can't remember your name."

"Danai," she said.

Gabriel shook his head. "Danai. I can't believe I forgot a pretty name like that. I came back; that's about as good as I ever hope for. I heard Colonel Graham is here on Alpha?"

"Yes, sir," she replied. "He's in one of the visitor offices upstairs."

Gabriel smiled. He had been worried the Colonel would still be asleep. He slipped the satchel from his shoulder and handed it out toward Danai. "Can you do me a favor and make sure that he gets this."

"You can deliver it to him yourself," someone behind him said.

Gabriel turned slowly. He knew that voice.

"Captain," Major Vivian Choi said.

Gabriel stood at attention. "Major," he said, saluting.

"Relax, Captain," Choi said with a warm smile. She was a handsome woman in her fifties, her graying hair suited to her matronly face. She was wearing similar dress blues to his, though her jacket had a lot more decorations on it. "We've been waiting for you to get back."

"You have?" Gabriel asked, releasing his stance.

"You sound surprised. Why wouldn't we be relieved to get our best pilot back from his sixty-fifth mission?"

"Sixty-eighth," Gabriel said. He was sure she was happy that he had returned. He wasn't convinced the reason was purely personal. "I almost didn't make it back at all."

"Thank heavens you did. Is the data recorder in that satchel?"

"Yes, ma'am. Like I said, I was going to send it up to Colonel Graham."

"I think he'd prefer if you delivered it yourself. Come with me, Captain."

"Yes, ma'am," Gabriel said, following her as she headed for the elevator.

He waved to Danai on the way past, who gave him a quick wave back. He would have rather left the recorder with her and made his way over to see his father. The less time he had to spend on Alpha, the better.

They stepped into the elevator, the doors closing behind them. Major Choi turned to face him, her mouth open to speak. Gabriel decided to beat her to the punch.

"Forgive me for being blunt, Major, but does your impatience over my return, and Colonel Graham's presence on Alpha have anything to do with the rumors that we're going to be leaving this system and abandoning the resistance on Earth?"

12

"Where did you hear that?" Choi said, her face turning to stone.

"I'm not going to rat out my sources," Gabriel replied. "Is there any truth to the rumor?"

"There is always some truth in rumor," Choi said.

"Playing coy, Major? Whatever is going on, you can fill me in. I don't have the power to change any of it anyway."

"Not directly, no. But you have the respect of your superiors, and that still counts for something."

"Did you just compliment me?" Gabriel asked.

"I did. I'm not only interested in that data recorder, Captain. Your presence here is important to me on a personal and a professional level."

"Why?"

"Personally? You should know why. Beyond that, because your father saved my life when I was only a little girl, along with the lives of my brother and my parents. Professionally? Because I need all of the support, I can get."

Gabriel didn't like the sound of that. "What do you mean?"

Her eyes fell on the data recorder. "If you got the information from Captain Sturges, then yes, what he said is true. I'm trying to stop it."

Gabriel was silent. He couldn't believe that this argument was going to come up again. "Does it have legs?"

"Strong ones, unfortunately. A lot of the population is tired of living this way."

"A lot of the population has only lived this way."

Choi smiled. "Funny, isn't it? Most of the New Earth Alliance has never set foot on Earth. Hell, most of the NEA has never even seen Earth. They're in love with the fairytales their parents tell them about how wonderful it was. I'm not saying it wasn't wonderful, especially compared to this, but isn't that the reason we keep fighting for it instead of packing up and heading out? The grass isn't greener in another system. Life is going to be harder than we want wherever we go."

"You're preaching to the choir, Major. I don't keep risking my life because I was drafted. I care about what happens to the people on Earth."

"I know you do. That's why I need your support."

The elevator stopped at the top floor, the doors sliding open.

"What about Colonel Graham?" Gabriel asked. "Is he on our side?"

Choi didn't have to speak to answer. Her face wrinkled, and she shook her head lightly. Gabriel felt a slight chill at the response. Graham was one of the last people he could ever imagine giving up the fight.

"Mind your words, Captain," Choi said as they crossed from the elevator to the outer corridor at the edge of the dome. Small viewports in the side gave him an impressive view of the Magellan, sitting vacant and lonely at the edge of the chasm. "Graham is going to be on the offensive. I know you have your father's temper sometimes. Don't let him bait you."

"I'll try."

They rounded the dome, reaching a pair of wide doors guarded by an infantryman in dark fatigues and carrying a rifle. His presence was purely symbolic. There had never been a violent incident in the NEA settlement.

"Major. Captain." The soldier saluted as they approached.

"Spaceman," Choi said, returning the salute. "Is Colonel Graham still in the visitor's office?"

"Yes, ma'am."

"Thank you."

Like everything else in the settlement, the offices of the New Earth Alliance Space Force were spartan, designed with a bare minimalism where every piece of equipment existed because it had a specific value and purpose. The main reception area was nothing more than a flat table affixed to a central support pillar, with a small hinged panel to allow the receptionist to get into a lightweight chair behind it. A small tablet sat on the table in front of him, while a second chair occupied the corner for people to sit in while they waited.

"Spaceman Owens," Major Choi said, approaching the desk. A smaller man with a bald head and glasses sat behind it.

He stood and saluted. "Major Choi." He saw Gabriel behind her and saluted him as well. "Captain St. Martin. Congratulations on your mission."

"Thank you, Gene," Gabriel said. He had known Owens since childhood. "How are you feeling?"

"I have good days and bad days," Owens replied, in reference to his heart condition. It was the reason he had been relegated to desk work. "Today is pretty good so far."

"We'll take what we can get, eh Gene?"

Owens smiled. "Absolutely."

"Spaceman, we're here to see Colonel Graham," Major Choi said.

"Of course, Major. He's been expecting you. Are you bringing Captain St. Martin in with you?"

"Yes."

"I should go and inform him, ma'am. He doesn't like surprises."

Choi chuckled. "There's no need to warn him that I'm coming. I'll take full responsibility for his bluster."

Owens didn't look happy about the idea. He motioned towards the hallway behind him. "Second office on the right, ma'am."

"Thank you."

Gabriel followed Choi past the desk. They didn't have to go far to reach the visitor's office. The door was closed, but he could hear Graham tapping furiously on his tablet behind it.

"Mind my words?" Gabriel whispered. "You're going to get him riled up before I say anything."

"That's the idea," Choi replied. "That way he won't blame you."

She knocked on the door. The tapping stopped.

"Come in," Colonel Graham said. His voice was rough and hoarse, as though he had been born screaming at people and had never stopped for a breath of air. Gabriel knew the Colonel well enough to know that probably wasn't far from the truth.

Major Choi opened the door. She entered first, with Gabriel right behind her. Graham's eyes narrowed at the sight of him.

"Colonel," Choi said, as both she and Gabriel saluted him.

Graham got to his feet. He was a large man. Over two meters tall, with broad shoulders and a thick frame. He had a long forehead with a wisp of black hair laid flat on his scalp, brown eyes, a flat nose that had been broken a few times, and a crooked smile. He was an imposing figure who had driven cadets to tears on more than one occasion.

"Major Choi, you're early. And Gabriel, I heard you got into a bit of a scrape on your run. I'm glad to see you here in one piece."

"Thank you, Colonel," Gabriel said. He stepped forward, opening his satchel and pulling out the data recorder. "Mission complete."

Graham smiled. Gabriel knew those were the Colonel's two favorite words. He didn't reach for the recorder, instead putting up his hand. "Normally I would take this from you and arrange to have it transported back to Alpha. Seeing as we're already on Alpha, you might as well bring it down to the lab yourself."

"Yes, sir," Gabriel said, tucking it back into the satchel.

"Thank you. Dismissed, Captain. Major, please, have a seat."

Gabriel didn't move right away. Major Choi had obviously come early to time her arrival with his. She wanted him to be there.

"Do you need something, Captain?" Graham asked.

"Colonel," Choi said. "I'd prefer if Captain St. Martin participates in our discussion."

Any sense of lightness that the Colonel had managed to project vanished from him in an instant. He clenched his jaw, his eyes burning a hole into Choi.

"I see," he said, pausing.

"Permission to speak freely, Colonel?" Choi said, not backing down.

"Sure, why not, Vivian? I don't want to be accused of running away from a fight."

"I didn't come here to fight, James," Choi said. "But I think Teddy's son has a right to be a part of this in his father's place."

Gabriel took that as his cue. "If you don't mind, Colonel?"

Graham looked at him, and then back at Choi. Then he sat down. "Fine. Speak your mind, Gabriel. We've known each other too long, and I respect you and your father too much not to let you."

"The Major told me about the Council and the Earth-type planet. She said you support the option to leave Calawan."

"I do. It may come as a surprise to you, Gabe, but not all of us want to spend our entire lives committed to a war we can't win. Let me rephrase that. A war we can't even fight."

"I thought you believed in the cause."

"I believe in the future of humankind. I believe that our civilization deserves to carry on beyond this." He waved his hand at the sparse office. "We've been living on borrowed time since we came to Ursae Majoris. We were never supposed to live this way. The Magellan was intended to carry us thousands of light-years away, not a handful. Yes, we have the printers and the compositors, and they've kept us up and running, but every year we spend more and more man-hours maintaining what we've got and fewer and fewer able to construct anything new. We can't let the technical debt keep piling up forever. Eventually, something is going to give, and we're all going to wind up dead."

It was a good speech. A good argument. Gabriel could feel his opinion losing strength as he absorbed it.

"There was a reason we decided to stop here instead," Choi said. "A reason we didn't keep going into deeper space."

"Because we weren't ready," Graham said. "The astronomers hadn't come up with a viable system they were confident contained an Earth."

"That isn't the only reason," Gabriel said. "And you know it."

"You mean your father? Yes, he convinced the others to stop here so we could send back one of the scout ships. The goal was to see if there was any way to get anyone else out, not to start plotting some magical rebellion that was going to liberate Earth. I've supported your father in that for years. You know I have, Gabriel. I've been in charge of Delta Station since it was built, and I've dedicated all of my adult life to the mission."

"Then how can you just turn your back on it?"

It was the wrong thing to say, and Gabriel knew it as soon as the words left his mouth. Every remaining member of the Magellan's original population had some degree of survivor's guilt.

"Turn my back on it?" Graham said, rising to his feet again. "Don't make the mistake of thinking this is an easy decision, Captain. Or that I haven't spent sleepless nights wondering if I'm doing the right thing. There is no good decision here. Whatever we do, we lose something important. I've been trying to ignore the facts for years. I sided with your father the last time the Council was considering moving on. We can't win this fight. We never have, not once, managed to so much as scratch an enemy ship. It's been fifty years, and we still have nothing that can hurt them. How do we fight that, Gabe? How do we sit here and ask all of these people who have never breathed real air, who have never walked around without a dome over their head, who have never seen daylight just to hang in there while we figure something out? We've had fifty years to figure something out. The scientists have found us a new home, and it's time to go and claim it."

Gabriel stood in stiff silence, working to control his anger. He could feel his fingers digging hard into his leg, trying to relieve some of the sudden tension he felt. It wouldn't do him any good to yell back at the Colonel, even if he did have permission. No. He had to push back with facts.

"We have a home, Colonel," he said, at last, his voice somehow managing to come out flat and calm. "We still have people there. We know that the enemy used the healthiest and most intelligent as templates to update their genetics because centuries of cloning and modification drained away their diversity. It's the same reason the Magellan carried the frozen eggs and sperm of over a million people. It's the same reason I'm standing in front of you right now.

"We also know they took others as slaves to do menial work that they believe is too demeaning or too dangerous to waste their kind or risk damaging their machines on. Finally, we know that the war on Earth isn't over. We've received this information from the remaining free humans that have continued to fight back against the Dread since they arrived, in spite of the fact that as you say, they never have so much as scratched the enemy.

"You think our people are tired of their life? Imagine spending every day in hiding, afraid that you won't survive to see the sunset one more time. Imagine having to claw and scrape for everything you have, knowing it might be taken away at any moment. Imagine the effort it takes to reach out to the only people in the universe who might be able to help you. To the military that abandoned you. That gathered up their personnel, loaded them in a starship and escaped to the stars, lucky as hell they had a hero at the helm.

"Daylight? Fresh air? What do those things mean in the absence of security? Those are our people down there, Colonel. People we swore to protect, and a war we promised to fight. Not win. Fight. Humankind may survive by fleeing further out into the universe. But what kind of legacy will we leave? And do we deserve to carry on with a history like that?"

Gabriel drew in a deep, calming breath, unclenching his fists. His father's passion was more volatile and animated. He tended to stay more introverted.

Both Major Choi and Colonel Graham stared at him. Choi had a big smile on her face. Graham was stoic though it appeared to Gabriel that his words had at least been heard.

"Thank you, Captain," Graham said in a flat monotone. "I'll take your comments into consideration. Dismissed."

Gabriel came to attention, saluting and then spinning to head out the door. Major Choi's hand ran gently over his own in support as he passed.

He paused as the door slid open, turning back to Colonel Graham. "By the way, Colonel, I watched a Dread fighter blast one of their own orbital defense satellites to dust. The technology to defeat their armor exists. They have it. We need to discover it."

He exited the room then, satisfied with the surprised looks on both Graham and Choi's faces.

"He reminds me so damn much of his father," he heard Graham say as he headed away. "You knew he'd be able to push me."

"I didn't know for sure," Choi said. "I had a feeling he could bring you to your senses."

"I'm not quite there yet. Anyway, even if you can change my mind, it won't be enough to convince the Council."

"That's the trouble with history and legacy. Time forgives all sins."

13

Gabriel stood at the edge of the platform, waiting for the pod that would carry him along the western loop, beneath the chasm to residential. He still had the satchel with the data recorder slung over his shoulder, having decided he would deliver it after he talked to his father.

Well, tried to talk to his father, anyway. The last time he had stopped by to see him, his old man had remembered who he was but thought Gabriel was four years old and kept asking him for his mother. Gabriel had walked out when Theodore had started to cry.

He couldn't stand to see a man like his father bawl like a baby.

The pod arrived, and Gabriel climbed in, taking a seat next to a younger man he didn't recognize. The man smiled politely before turning his attention to his tablet, where a page full of gray numbers swam against a black background. The hatch closed, and the pod raced off, reaching the western loop before the man could finish looking over his page.

Gabriel climbed out, joining the handful of passengers on their way into residential. The younger man was one of them, and he stared at the tablet as he walked, nearly knocking into a woman with a child. His face turned red, and he apologized as he shuffled past them.

An engineer or an astronomer, Gabriel guessed. They were the ones who tended to have their faces pointed down instead of out, more interested in calculations than other people. He moved with the line, through the archway, and onto a long, wide concourse.

Residential was carved into the rock beneath the chasm, and so it was more open and natural than the central hub and one of the few places to trade gray, metallic walls for multi-colored stone. The bottom level of the concourse was designed for socializing and shopping, with some storefronts, restaurants, and pubs in simple stalls along the floor. In the early days, the NEA had tried to bypass the token economy for more of a communist-style arrangement. It had failed miserably. The Magellan was a United States colony ship, and despite the fact that most of its passengers had been part of the military, they had adjusted more easily to a new life that was as close to their old as possible.

Gabriel crossed the lower level, taking in the smell of cooking meats and the colors of fresh vegetables laid enticingly out along the thoroughfare. It was all transported in fresh from Beta Settlement on Taphao Thong daily. The meats were grown in vats of nutrients, the vegetables on hydroponic farms. All of it was made possible by the water and chemical rich atmosphere of the planet. He had to admit that as much as he hated the more chaotic and busy nature of life in Alpha Settlement, he did miss the food.

He paused at a stall and picked up an apple. "How much?" he asked, holding out his thumb to transfer the money from his account.

"For you, Captain? It's free," the merchant responded, giving him her best smile. She was young and pretty, and might have elicited more interest from him if he were in a better mood.

As it was, he barely noticed her flirtation. "Thanks. Enjoy your day."

He savored the taste as he walked. The NEA didn't have the resources to waste on printing kitchen equipment for Delta Station, leaving his regular diet as ninety-percent nutrient packs: a dark, foul-tasting liquid that contained everything a healthy soldier needed. They would also get occasional shipments of things like cocoa and coffee, but it never lasted long.

He climbed the steps near the center of the concourse up to the second level. Residential was composed of cutouts in the rock, with most of the spaces consisting of three or four small rooms and assigned based on need. As the population had grown they had continued building up to the five levels they had today, though the signs of further excavation were obvious in the corner of the area. The population was still growing, which meant residential had to grow with it.

Gabriel made his way to the back, eating the entire apple, core and all, as he did. Gabriel had spent his childhood in the same, simple two-room space near the front of the concourse where Theodore had been living since it had first been excavated. Gabriel approached it with a growing sense of anxious trepidation. He never knew who he was going to get when he came to see his old man.

He was surprised when the door to the home slid open before his reached it. He was even more surprised when General Alan Cave ducked through it.

"General," Gabriel said, coming to attention and saluting.

"Relax, Gabriel," Cave said. "I'm not here in any official capacity. I just stopped by to pay an old friend a visit."

Gabriel relaxed his posture. Alan Cave hadn't even been a member of the military when he had boarded the Magellan back on Earth. He was a government contractor at the time, who happened to be in the right place when the order to launch was given. It was Gabriel's mother who had gotten him allowed past the barricades, eager to save every person she could. The act of sacrifice had made General Cave and Theodore fast friends, and over time the man had joined the military and used his intelligence and charisma to rise through the ranks and eventually become their CO.

He was a tall, lanky, gentle man, with a tight crop of curly gray hair, dark skin, blue eyes, and a soft but powerful voice. He wasn't a soldier, not in the traditional sense, but he was an exceptional motivator and leader of men. He was well into his eighties and still as fit and hearty as ever.

"How is he?" Gabriel asked.

"Pretty good, today," Cave replied. "He remembered my name. It's been a few weeks since that happened."

"Do you come to see him often?"

"At least twice a week. It's tough to see him like this. I imagine it's a lot tougher for you. Even so, I owe him a debt I can never repay. This is the least I can do."

Gabriel wasn't sure how to take the second part of the General's answer. It was Theodore's influence that had gotten him pulled from the freezer and inserted into a surrogate in the first place. He owed his father for his life, even more so than a child of a traditional pairing.

He suddenly felt guilty for making such infrequent visits that he had never run into the General before now.

"I was over in the hub earlier," Gabriel said, shifting the topic away from his father. "I joined a meeting with Major Choi and Colonel Graham."

"Oh?" Cave said. "So you know about the plans to remodel the Magellan again?"

General Cave's choice of words didn't go unnoticed.

"I do," Gabriel replied. "I assume you're opposed to the idea?"

General Cave hesitated before answering. "The Council is concerned with the level of resources being dedicated toward militaristic ends while the population continues to expand. You know that we can only grow so far before we reach a maintenance level. We're getting close to it now. We're exploring every option."

"That isn't a no," Gabriel said.

"It isn't," Cave agreed. He put up a hand before Gabriel could speak. "Look, I know how you feel. And I certainly know how your father feels, even if he can't say so himself. The fact is we have to consider everyone in the settlements. We can't barter the future of the human race on the promises made by dead men."

"Not all of the men are dead. You're one of them."

Cave laughed. "So is the Old Gator. Who else is left? Sturges. Siddhu. Patel. Maybe a dozen others who were adults when we arrived in this system. The past is dying. The future still has hope if we're brave enough to see it. Even if that means breaking those promises. We can refit the Magellan, take the civilians to a new planet, and then come back and continue our fight. It won't take more than ten, twenty years."

"Twenty years? There may not be a resistance in twenty years."

"I know. Believe me, I do. The messages have been fewer and farther between with each passing year. It was getting harder to ignore the truth before the reports on the E-type. Even I can't ignore it anymore. I don't want to betray the trust your father had in me, but there's more at stake here."

Gabriel couldn't believe what he was hearing. First Colonel Graham, and now General Cave? It was as if all of their leaders were losing their faith and courage at once. After fifty years they were ready to let the aliens have their home, and everyone left on it.

"I can see you're disappointed by my answer," Cave said. "I understand why, Captain, and I wouldn't expect anything less from you. You're your father's son, and you should be damn proud of that." He reached out, putting his hand on Gabriel's shoulder. "I'm sorry it has to be this way."

Gabriel looked up at the General and nodded, fighting to keep the disappointment from showing. Cave released Gabriel's shoulder, straightened his jacket, and started walking away.

"I'm sorry, too," Gabriel whispered, too low for Cave to hear. If only he had spared a few seconds worth of power for thrust, he could have brought his fighter back to Delta and stayed oblivious to everything that was happening down on Manhattan.

He would rather be ignorant than feel disappointed and betrayed by the people he had spent his entire life looking up to.

He took a moment to gather himself before approaching the door to his father's home. If only he could tell his father about any of this. If only his mother had made it to the starship on time, or Jessica hadn't died.

The door slid open, and the smell of fresh urine wafted out.

Gabriel had never felt more alone.

14

Gabriel entered the small home, every step he took tempting him to turn his heel and walk back out. He could hear motion in the back of the living quarters, where the heavy smell of sick piss was making the air in the space hard to breathe.

"Come on now, General," he heard his father's nurse, Sabine, saying. "We need to change your pants. You've wet yourself again. It's a good thing General Cave left before you did."

Gabriel remained in the front of the quarters to wait. There were two bedrooms at the back of the excavation. His father's door was on the left and open, though he couldn't see his father or Sabine through it. His eyes shifted to the one on the right. That had been his room once, long ago. He was sure it was in the same condition as he had left it when he had headed off to NEASF Officer Training fifteen years earlier. He doubted his father had ever even opened the door after Gabriel had closed it on the way out. Theodore St. Martin believed in a person's right to privacy, almost to a detrimental degree.

If he hadn't, he would have known of his wife's plan to stay behind and guide the others to the Magellan when the Dread came. As it was, he had only learned of her betrayal once they were well underway. A betrayal that had only led him to love her more.

Gabriel blinked a few times, trying to wipe the stories of the past from his thoughts. He was almost successful, until his traveling gaze fell on the far wall. It was smooth, solid stone, painted white. A projector affixed to the ceiling directly above the wall was beaming a near life-size photo of his mother against it.

He had seen the image a million times before. He had grown up with the vision of her timelessly placed against the wall whenever they weren't using the system to watch a video, or communicate with someone else in the settlements. For some reason, maybe because of what he knew was happening with the Council, the sight of her face nearly brought tears to her eyes.

She was standing in a field of marigolds, wearing a simple blue dress that hung loosely from her athletic frame. Her red-gold hair lay in a braid over her right shoulder, and her blue eyes squinted involuntarily in conjunction with a wide, white smile. Her face was heart-shaped and filled with life, and just looking at it made her selfless compassion obvious. His father had always called her an angel, and Gabriel had never had reason to doubt it.

He clutched at her crucifix without thinking, gripping it beneath his shirt. The necklace had been delivered by one of the families she had saved, dropped into his father's hand with a simple, painful message.

"I love you. I'm sorry. Get these people to safety."

Theodore St. Martin always did what his angel asked.

Gabriel clenched his fists. As far as he was concerned, his mother had meant all of the people on Earth. And now they were considering abandoning them. It was bullshit. Plain and simple.

"Oh, Captain St. Martin. I didn't know you were here."

Sabine's voice pulled Gabriel out of his anger. He looked at the nurse, forcing a smile. She was only fifteen years old, still in training to become a full member of the medical staff. She was rail thin, her face innocent. Gabriel could barely remember being innocent anymore.

"How is he?" he asked, his voice a whisper that made Sabine shrink away from him.

"He voided in his pants again," she said. "It's been happening more often the last few days. I was going to get Doctor Hall to come and look at him."

"Is he lucid?"

"I just gave him his medicine. It always steals some of his strength, but he screams in pain without it. If you want to talk to him, your timing is pretty good."

Gabriel nodded, looking back at the bedroom. He wasn't sure he wanted to go in there. Especially not with the way he was feeling.

"Are you okay, Captain?" Sabine asked.

"Yeah, I'm okay. Thanks for asking. I just got back from a mission, and I think I'm still a little shaken."

"Do you want to take anything? I have a benzodiazepine that might help."

"No. Thank you. You're going to get Doctor Hall?"

"Yes, sir."

"Can you give me ten minutes?"

"Of course, sir."

"Thank you, Sabine." Gabriel took a couple of steps toward the bedroom before pausing. "Sabine?"

"Yes, Captain?" the girl asked, stopping at the front door.

"Did you give my father the benzo?"

"Yes, sir. A pretty high dose, in addition to the painkillers. General Cave's visit made him pretty upset. I think that's why he wet himself."

Gabriel turned the rest of the way around. "What do you mean?" he asked. "What did he say to him?"

"Oh, I don't know, Captain. He made me stay up front, and he spoke softly so I couldn't hear."

Gabriel wondered what Cave might have said. Had he told Theodore of their plans to convert the Magellan back into a transport and give up the fight for Earth? Why would he do that?

"Thank you, Sabine," he said again, spinning around and moving more purposefully into his father's bedroom. He had a sudden need to speak to his father before the meds took full effect.

15

"There isn't anything going to bust that armor of theirs, sir," Theodore St. Martin said in his signature Cajun drawl, his eyes flicking back and forth as he sat at the edge of his bed. "That nuke was a direct hit. I swear it hit that coullion dead on."

He was silent for a moment while the other person in his waking dream spoke.

"No, sir," Theodore replied. "I ain't saying we should give up, but we need to get these people out of here. If Command is going to call an evac, now's the time to do it." Another pause. "Already called? Yes, sir. I'm on my way."

"Dad," Gabriel said, entering the room and approaching his father.

Theodore was clothed in his dress blues, his wrinkled shirt tucked neatly into a crisp pair of pants, his suit jacket slightly askew. His chair sat at a right angle to him, within easy reach should he decide he wanted to move.

He wasn't moving right now. He was reliving a moment Gabriel had seen him relive before.

"Dad," Gabriel said again. He wanted to pull him out of it before it got painful for both of them.

"Reactor is online," Theodore said. "Thrusters are warming up, QPG nacelles set and locked. What's our load look like?"

Theodore paused again, waiting for the answer.

"General," Gabriel said, still trying to get his father's attention.

"I can see them all coming in. You sure that many are going to fit? Look at the heifer down there. I don't recognize her. She got clearance to board?" A pause. "My wife? Where is she? Not on board? You kidding me, Sergeant? Well damn, boy. Don't just sit there, go and get her. This litter ain't leaving without its Queen."

Gabriel felt his heart begin pounding harder. He didn't want to hear this. Not again. He knew what came after. The bawling. The tears. Why did he have to show up now? It would have been better to come once his old man was already sleeping. Sit with the corpse for a few minutes and take his leave. His conscience would be salved, but he wouldn't have to deal with the memories.

"Damn it all," Theodore said. "We need to get these people loaded double-time. Sergeant, why are you still standing here? Orders? I don't give a damn about your orders. You find my wife, you hear me boy, or we're all going to die."

He rocked side to side, as though he were feeling an explosion.

"Took some flak to the armor. This ain't looking good. Who the hell is letting all these people through? Those are civvies out there, and this boat is for VIPs only. Two by two onto the damn Ark. All the right kinds to keep civilization going, just like we drilled. Can't you people get anything right?" A pause and his face reddened. "Where in the name of all things holy is my wife?"

"General St. Martin, atten-shun," Gabriel shouted.

His father froze. Gabriel knew it wasn't because of him. He stepped forward, throwing out his palm to slap his old man.

Theodore caught his wrist, squeezing the nerve and making his whole hand go limp and numb.

"Who the hell you think you're striking, boy?" Theodore said, his eyes suddenly alive and looking up at him. "Don't even think of telling me it's me."

Gabriel shook his hand, trying to rid it of the sudden pins and needles. "Dad," he said, feeling a sense of relief. "It's Gabriel. Do you know me?"

"Why in the world wouldn't I know my own son?" Theodore asked. "Of course, I know you."

"How are you feeling?" Gabriel asked.

"My legs are itching like crazy," Theodore said, reaching out to scratch limbs that weren't there. "Feel like I'm buried up to my balls in bullet ants. Hurts like a son of a bitch."

"You need your stimulators," Gabriel said, looking around the room. He found the small pads on the nightstand and grabbed them. "I'm going to roll up your pant legs."

"Whatever for?"

"To help the itching."

"I don't need you to nurse me, boy. I can take care of myself."

"I know you can," Gabriel said, rolling up the left leg to reveal the scarred stump. He put the stimulator on it, and could see the relief in his father's eyes.

"What kind of voodoo is this?" his father said, reaching out to roll up his other pants leg so Gabriel could attach the stimulator.

"Do you know where you are?" Gabriel asked.

"I'm old, Gabe. I'm not senile. Alpha Settlement, Calawan system."

He was better than usual, but not completely straight. He didn't seem to know he had lost his legs. Gabriel put the stimulator on the right stump.

"Don't know why they hurt so much," Theodore said. "Too much running, I suppose."

"General Cave was here to see you," Gabriel said.

"Alan? He left a few minutes ago."

"What did you two talk about?"

"Just shooting the breeze, son. He stops by a few times every week. Talked about all the bullshit he has to deal with. Bullshit I for one am glad to be out from under."

"Did he mention the Magellan?"

Theodore's face changed to hear the name of the ship. "They want to take her," he said, his voice suddenly distant.

"You know?"

"I do now." He lowered his head. "It's wrong, son."

"I know."

"They're pissing on her grave. I told Alan that. He thinks sorry means jack to me. So what we haven't found a weapon to break them yet. So damn what? Nothing is invincible. You know that, boy, don't you?"

"I do, Dad."

"I told him I was going to stop this garbage. That I'm going to go before the Council and tell them what I think of what they want to do. I won't let it happen. They ain't going to do that to me. You hear me, son?"

The words were strong. The man behind them looked weak and frail. Tears were rolling into his eyes.

"I hear you, Dad. I'm with you."

Gabriel knew his father would never make it in front of the Council. He could see him fading away with each passing heartbeat, his eyes losing their sudden burst of soul.

"You're a good boy, Gabe. A good son. I'm proud of you. Your mom would be, too." Theodore shook his head. "So damn tired, son. Think I'm going to rest a while. You're late to school again anyway, ain't you?"

Gabriel reached out, helping his father shift so he could lay back in the bed. He was grateful he had gotten thirty seconds of the real Theodore St. Martin before the meds had hit him again.

"Can you get your mom for me, son?" Theodore asked. "I just want to see her face one more time before I go to sleep. I want her to sing to me like she used to."

"I'll get her, Dad," Gabriel said, fighting to keep himself from tearing up. "Just wait here, okay?"

"I will. You're a good boy, Gabriel."

Gabriel positioned his father's head on the pillow, turning away and heading out of the bedroom, wiping at his eyes as he did. He slipped out of the home, walking right past Sabine and Doctor Hall without saying a word.

Man Of War

In his head, all he could hear was his father's voice.
"They're pissing on her grave."
Not if there was anything he could do about it.

16

They were lucky that when they hit the water, it was deep enough to break their fall and not their limbs.

It didn't mean they hit the surface softly, or that there was no pain involved. Loose cabling in the narrow shaft got caught on Donovan's arm as he fell, wrenching it back and causing an agonizing throb from the shrapnel wound while turning him over and putting him in an awkward position.

Seconds later, he hit the water almost flat on his back, the force pushing his shoulder forward, snapping it back and sending another shiver of pain through his limb. He swallowed water as he sank a few feet below the surface, feeling a panic at the idea of escaping the Dread machine only to drown. He kicked his legs, pushing himself back up, breaking the plane a moment later. He used his good hand to cover his mouth and help silence his coughs.

"Donovan?" he heard Diaz whisper. It was dark down here, and she had the only light.

It appeared next to her face a moment later, providing just enough illumination for him to start swimming slowly toward her.

"I'm here," he whispered in reply. "Coming to you."

He could still hear the Dread above them, the earth shaking and bits of debris being knocked loose with every heavy step. They would have disappeared from its sensors the moment the water doused them. There was nothing it could use to track them where they had gone. The only question was whether or not it would decide to obliterate the area in an effort to kill them.

He reached Diaz a moment later. Her head was poking out of the water; her wrist held up next to it to provide the light. She smiled as he reached out and put his hand on her shoulder.

She opened her mouth to speak, but he put his finger to her lips and shook his head. There was no sense risking being picked up. They had to stay quiet until the enemy left.

They were still for a few moments. The water was too deep to stand in, and now Donovan saw that the top of a subterranean garage was only a few inches over their heads. They tread water as quietly as they could, leaving soft splashes and a faint bubbling in the distance as the only sounds, which echoed in the small space.

They kept their eyes locked on one another, not wanting to be separated down here. The wound on his back stung sharply, and he wondered how clean this water was, and where it had come from. Not to mention, how had Diaz known it was down here? It was a question for later.

Later came soon enough. A few more minutes passed, followed by the sound of the mechanized armor trudging away through the city above.

"You're bleeding," Diaz said before Donovan could say anything.

"I've got some shrapnel in the back of my shoulder," Donovan replied, still whispering.

"Does it hurt?"

"You better believe it. It isn't serious unless it gets infected or I bleed to death. Either way, we need to get out of here and get back to the base. Doc Iwu can patch me up."

Diaz didn't answer right away. She had a concerned expression on her face.

"What is it?" Donovan asked.

"I found this place during one of the scouting missions before we made our run. The shaft, I mean. I saw it had water in it, and I remembered it in the case of an emergency. Better safe than sorry, right?" She smiled, the water dripping from her lips as she did. "I don't know how to get out of here. I don't even know if there is a way out of here."

Donovan pointed up. "There's one way out if we can climb it."

"With one arm?" Diaz asked.

Donovan tried to flex his other shoulder, stopping halfway because of the pain. There was no way he was going to be doing any kind of climbing, and Diaz wasn't strong enough to carry him out. If it had been the other way around, and she was the one with the shrapnel, it might have been different.

"You can climb out," he said. "Go back to base and get me some help. If you can't make it, leave me here. I'll see if there's a way out."

"Are you loco? I'm not leaving you here."

She swam over to the shaft, the doors just visible above the water. She lifted her arm as high as she could to shine the light on it.

"It doesn't matter anyway, Major," she said. "The walls are smooth metal, and the cables are at least twenty feet over our heads. We're both stuck down here."

17

"I hope Sanchez and Cameron made it out. Someone needs to report back that the package was delivered," Donovan said.

"I'm sure they'll be fine. Sanchez isn't a rookie. She knows how to hide, and she'll take care of Cameron."

"And we'll take care of each other. That's how it goes, right?"

"No way, amigo. You're wounded. I'll take care of you. My brother would kill me if I didn't get his best friend home alive."

"Your brother would kill me if I didn't get his sister home alive," Donovan said, smiling. At least he had gotten trapped down here with someone he knew and trusted. "Let's see if we can find a way out."

"Not yet. We need to pull the shrapnel out of your shoulder and get it wrapped. You're turning the water a nice shade of pink."

She lowered the light to the surface so he could see. He hadn't realized how much blood he was losing, and the sight of it made him feel a little queasy.

"Don't pass out on me," Diaz said.

"How are we going to bandage this submerged?"

"We'll have to figure something out, won't we? Give me your shirt."

"What?"

"Your shirt. We need something to wrap it with, and I'm not giving you mine."

Donovan laughed and reached for the buttons of his shirt, undoing them with his good hand. "You'll have to help me pull it off."

Diaz swam behind him, whistling softly when she saw the wound. "Hang on, D. Let me get a closer look."

He could feel her moving behind him, getting her face closer to the injury.

"Okay, it looks like it isn't too deep, but it can't clot with the shrapnel in there."

"It isn't going to clot very well wet either."

"No, but it has to help. I'm going to pull it out on three, okay?"

"Yeah, o-"

Donovan grunted as Diaz pulled the shrapnel from his back. One hand put pressure on the wound while the other worked to get his shirt off.

"That wasn't three," Donovan said.

"It would have hurt more if you were expecting it. Don't be such a baby."

"I'm still your CO," Donovan said.

"Sorry. Don't be such a baby, sir."

He helped her get his shirt off. She used a utility knife tucked under the waist of her pants to cut it into a long strip that she then wrapped around his upper back and shoulder. It took a bit of an effort since they also had to tread water the entire time, but once it was done, he found the pain had subsided substantially.

"There's some good news," Diaz said, circling back in front of him and putting her light against the water.

There was no sign of blood.

"The water's flowing somewhere," he said. "Hopefully, if we follow it, we get the hell out of here."

"Oh, come on, D, it's not so bad. It's like a vacation down here."

"Maybe compared to ten minutes ago. I don't like the whole not knowing how to get out thing."

"We've been through worse."

"We all have, which is why I'm not afraid. I am eager, though."

"Me, too."

"Then there's nothing to do but swim." He reached out. "Take my hand. I don't want to lose you."

She grabbed his hand in hers, using the other to shine the light ahead of them. Donovan flattened out, and they both began kicking.

They reached the edge of the garage a minute later. A solid wall above the water remained solid below it, blocking off their escape from that side.

"There are two more," Diaz said.

Donovan nodded.

They traced the perimeter. They were fortunate the water was temperate, but even so being submerged in it was starting to make Donovan cold. Or maybe it was the loss of blood? Either way, he was shivering by the time they finished moving along the western wall.

"South," Diaz said. "It has to be South." Her eyes fell on his lips. "We need to get you out of here. You're getting a chill."

"Yeah. I'm just about ready to leave. It's a nice place to visit, but I don't want to stay."

They continued swimming, moving around to the southern end of the garage. The entire surface was more solid stone.

"This isn't the outcome I was hoping for," Donovan said.

"I hear bubbling," Diaz replied. "Do you hear it?"

He listened for a minute before nodding. "Yeah."

"Bubbles mean air. Air means an exit, right?"

"I hope so."

They swam across the center of the garage until they found the source of the noise. Large air bubbles were hitting the surface of the water in a steady rhythm.

"I'm going to check it out," Diaz said, letting go of his hand. "Wait here?"

He laughed. "Careful. I might run off with a feisty mamacita while you're gone."

"As if," she said, rolling her eyes. Then she drew in and expelled a few breaths, expanding and gathering air into her lungs. She gave him a thumbs up before vanishing beneath the water.

He could see the light on her wrist fade as she dove, disappearing after a few seconds. He sat in complete darkness, the bubbling the only sound as he counted the time and waited for her to come back up.

He saw the light return as he reached the thirty-second mark. Her head broke the surface a moment later, and she breathed heavily as she spoke.

"I think I found where the air is coming from. The collapse left an exposed pipe. It's six feet wide, at least. A drainage pipe or something. It has a hole in it, and it's venting. It looks big enough for you to squeeze in."

"You want me to squeeze into a submerged pipe? How is that going to help?"

"The pipe is damaged, and if we can cover it and keep some of the air from escaping, we can use it to breathe."

"What happens if the pipe gets smaller further down?"

"We die. Do you have a better option?"

He didn't. "I can't swim down there like this."

"I've got you covered. There's lots of crap on the floor down there. I'll bring something heavy up. Just hold onto me and let yourself sink."

"I never knew you were so resourceful."

"You've barely ever noticed me at all, D. Not as anything more than Matteo's sister."

"That's not true, or you wouldn't be my Lieutenant."

She rolled her eyes again. "You know that isn't how promotions work these days. I just happen to be the second best t-vaulter in Mexico."

"You're number one to me right now," Donovan said.

"Don't get all sappy on me, Major. I'll be right back."

She took in more air and vanished beneath the surface again. Donovan watched the light fade away once more. He'd never realized she had felt excluded from his attention. Maybe because he never wanted Matteo to get the wrong idea about his intentions. He liked Diaz. She was smart, witty, funny, and she had a warm heart. But how do you be friends with your best friend's sister without them thinking you're looking for something else?

Then again, if he had gotten closer to her, could he be certain he wouldn't be?

He couldn't believe he was even thinking about it. It had to be the loss of blood clouding his mind.

The light returned a handful of seconds later, with Diaz swimming hard to reach the surface holding a metal plate that might have come from the bottom of a car. She clutched it tight against her chest, her legs pumping to keep her on the surface.

"Are you ready for this?" she asked, beginning to fill her lungs once more.

He followed her lead, taking quick gulps in and out. Then he reached out and wrapped his arm around her shoulders, putting them so close their foreheads were touching. They kept their eyes on one another as they began to sink.

18

Donovan's lungs were burning by the time the weight of the metal Diaz was holding carried them the seven meters down to the pipe below. From what he could tell in the dim light and murky water, the plasma fire that had caused the garage's collapse had also made a crater on the ground, which had exposed the pipe. He doubted it had always been damaged and leaking. As his feet touched the ground alongside the pipe, he could tell the wound was fairly fresh, and he wondered what could have caused it.

The Dread, of course. The question was, why? And was the damage intentional?

He didn't have time or air to examine it further. Diaz handed him the weight, turning herself over and swimming down into the pipe. She kept her wrist up so he could find her, taking two steps to the lip of the cut and looking in. He wasn't as sure as she had been that he would fit.

He kept his grip on the metal and stepped over the edge, feeling the air bubbles slipping against him as they made their escape. His feet made it in without issue, as did his legs. He clenched his teeth as the jagged edges of the hole approached his upper body and shoulders, closing his eyes and saying a silent prayer.

He felt a scratching along his arm, a piece of the metal digging into his flesh. It was all he could do to stay still instead of panicking and trying to swim, letting the metal slide through and release him. He looked over at his left arm. It was cut and bleeding, but it was nothing compared to his shoulder.

Diaz grabbed at the piece of metal he was holding, pointing at the hole. They lifted it together, laying it across the opening and holding on. The venting air tried to pull it aside, but the added weight helped keep it in place. Donovan was ready to pass out. They had no idea if this plan would work.

It did, well enough. Some of the air escaped, but some of it remained in the pipe, continuing with the flow of water. Diaz nodded, and they both let go of the metal, pushing off the side of the pipe with their feet. He was out of breath, his body begging for him to take in the water. He held his mouth closed, growing desperate for air and imagining Diaz felt the same.

They traveled twenty meters or so, with Diaz holding her hand up to the top of the pipe. She gripped a seam suddenly, tilting her head up and back. Donovan did the same, bringing his face up next to hers in no more than a few centimeters of air.

They both breathed in harshly, taking massive swallows of oxygen. Donovan's stomach muscles were contracting and cramping, sending waves of pain throughout his body. By the look on Diaz's face, she was suffering something similar.

"That sucked," Donovan said, the words coming out in a broken whisper.

"We made it," Diaz replied. "That's all that matters now."

They continued along the pipe with the air bubble, keeping their heads down and coming up every fifteen seconds or so to take a breath, hoping that the pocket was large enough to sustain them. Neither one of them had any idea how long the pipe was, or where it was going.

Or if it went anywhere at all.

An hour passed. Then another. They stopped stroking, letting the flow of the water carry them for a while, floating on their backs with their heads in the air pocket as best they could, holding one another's hands so they wouldn't be separated. Time seemed to fade away with the constant, soft whoosh of the flowing water and the sounds of their light breathing. Each heartbeat began to bleed into the next and Donovan found his thoughts wandering. They settled on the mission, and on the men and women who would never be returning home.

He remembered Diaz's question about Gibbons, and in his mind he saw the man fall dead again, burned by a plasma rifle. She was a good Lieutenant, a skilled t-vaulter. That she had mentioned an interest in anyone meant she was considering giving up the rifle to bear children. She wanted warriors, he realized. Children that would be strong and healthy, like Gibbons had been. Like she was. Offspring were the best way the free females could help the cause. At the same time, no one had ever presumed to stop them from fighting. It was still a choice to be made, not an expectation to be followed.

He turned his head slightly so he could see her, on her back with her head only inches from his. She had her eyes closed, thinking her own thoughts while they floated. Was she thinking about Gibbons, too? About children? He had known her since she had been born. He was seven at the time, and already best friends with Matteo. It seemed strange to him that she would be a mother. He felt too young to be a father, and she was so much younger than him. Was it what she wanted, or what she felt she needed to do? The resistance was slowly dwindling, their numbers dropping every year. If they could clone people like the Dread did, instead of having to reproduce them the old fashioned way, maybe they would stand a chance.

"Do you want to bring a child into this world?" he said out loud without thinking.

Diaz's eyes opened, and she turned her head enough to see him. "What?"

"I was thinking about Gibbons and you. Do you really think it will change anything?"

She positioned her head straight up again. "I want to believe it would," she said. "But I don't know. You're projecting my offhand chatter pretty far."

"I'm tired, and I lost a lot of blood," he said. "I couldn't help but start thinking about everything. I don't know if it's my mind that's tricking me, or if I'm more sane than usual. You've seen what's been happening here in Mexico; I know you have. I've heard it's worse in other places. That the resistance has been wiped out. Japan, Nigeria, Florida. We lose another base every week."

"Those are only rumors."

"Are they? We lost sixteen people today, Renata. How many soldiers does that leave us with?"

She was silent while she listed the names in her head. Just the fact that she could name them all was enough of an answer. "Twenty-six."

"We can't keep going like this. It would take you the rest of your reproductive life to replace what we lost in five minutes."

"So what do you think we should do?" Diaz asked, annoyed. "Give up? Kill ourselves and save the Dread the trouble."

"No. I'm not saying we should ever give up. I think we need to change our tactics or something. Maybe forget about the messengers and focus on fighting our own war. How many people have we lost getting these transmissions out?"

"A lot. We need the space forces. We can't do anything about orbital bombardment without them, and that's exactly what the Dread will do if we start gathering in large numbers again. You remember Charlotte, don't you?"

It was one of the stories that was told around the mess. A free human force of nearly ten-thousand had managed to assemble there. They even swarmed a Dread armor and almost got it to topple. Then the enemy had sent a plasma flume down on them, bathing the armor and the city both. The city was slagged a second time.

The armor wasn't even scratched. In fact, as the legend went, the excited energy had cleaned it up real nice.

"I don't know if we have ten-thousand left in the world," Donovan said.

"Can you try not to sound so dour?" Diaz said. "The last thing we need is to beat ourselves."

Donovan was silent.

"Anyway," Diaz said, "I don't think you're completely wrong. What we've been doing hasn't been working well. I think we've gotten too predictable. The Dread know when we're going to be transmitting. They're waiting for us. We need to take them by surprise."

"How?"

"If I knew that, I'd be the General. Everything we can think of would be easier to say than do."

"How I'd love to get a bullet through that armor of theirs just once," Donovan said. "How I'd love to see the look on one of their faces."

"Fifty years, and nobody even knows what they look like," Diaz said. "To be honest, it is hard to stay upbeat when everything seems so hopeless. But what else can we do? No, I don't think having kids will help the overall fight, but it's still important. We have to keep our hope, or we might as well let ourselves die right here and now."

Donovan locked eyes with Diaz. "Well, I'm not going to let you die, so I guess that means I can't let myself die either."

"I think you've got that reversed, amigo. I'm the one saving you."

"Oh? I'm the man here, Lieutenant. And the CO. I'm saving-"

He didn't get to finish his comment. Without warning, the water, and the pipe they had been traveling in vanished beneath them.

19

They went over the edge together, losing their grip on one another as the pipe opened up and spilled out into a deep well.

Donovan made a better landing this time, keeping his body knife straight and cutting through the pool below, sinking deep enough that his feet scraped the bottom. There hadn't been time to hold his breath, and he kicked furiously to get himself to the surface once more.

His head broke the water, and he took in air while he looked around, suddenly fearful. They appeared to be in a collection area of some kind, with pipes trailing into the large underground space from every direction. He found a small ledge on the south side, where a small control room sat unoccupied, a glowing screen visible through a window; a computer awaiting instructions from handlers that would never return.

Diaz was already at the ledge, pulling herself onto it. He swam more slowly now, letting the apparent safety of the place allow him to relax a little bit.

She was in the control room by the time he dragged himself onto the platform.

"I thought you were taking care of me," he said, struggling to get up with one arm.

"You're the man and the CO. I figured you could handle it."

He regretted starting the macho humor, peering past her at the control screen. "What is this place?"

"Flood control. We were luckier than I realized."

"That pipe only fills when it's been raining a lot?" Donovan said.

"Si. The pipes lead from smaller drainage areas throughout the city, collecting the rainwater and bringing it through here before sending it on to be purified. All that rain the last couple of weeks left the tank nearly full, which is a good thing for us. It would have been a painful landing."

"I can't believe that thing is still working," he said, motioning to the control pad.

"It isn't. The last line says 'critical error.' I think it can cut off the flow to this tank and divert to another one in case it starts to overfill. We're lucky that didn't happen or we would have drowned for sure."

"Lucky us," Donovan deadpanned, shifting his arm. It was starting to throb again, the wound disturbed by the fall.

"We aren't dead yet. That has to be good for something."

"Only if there's a way out."

Diaz pointed behind him. He turned around, smiling when he saw the open doorway and the sign that read "Salida." Exit.

"Perfect," he said. Something had gone right today.

They moved to the door, passing through and following it to the left. There was a second door, there, also open, which lead to a narrow set of iron stairs that smelled of dampness and decay. Donovan grabbed the railing and started to ascend.

"Try to keep quiet," Diaz said. "We don't know where we are, or what might be out here."

"Yes, sir," Donovan replied, saluting her and causing a sharp jolt of pain in his arm.

"Was it worth it?" Diaz asked.

Donovan shrugged and kept climbing, lifting his head so he could see the top of the stairwell. It was a good thirty meters up. The door at the top was closed.

It didn't take long to ascend. They stopped in front of the closed door, and Donovan put his ear to it to listen. He didn't hear anything on the other side, and so he tried the manual handle. It was an old door to an old system. The door clicked as it came free of the latch, and he pulled it open slowly, peering out into the darkness beyond. The area was deserted.

"Come on," he whispered, moving out into the open.

They cleared the doorway, finding themselves inside a small concrete bunker. It was the outer entrance to the system below. A final door rested between them and the outside world.

"When we go through the door, I'll get our bearings, and then we run back to base," he said. "We don't slow down for anything."

"Can you make it?" Diaz asked. "You lost a lot of blood."

"As long as my adrenaline holds out. I'm sure I'll pay for it tomorrow."

"Okay. I'm ready."

Donovan approached the door, listening against it one more time. He could hear a faint noise in the background, a soft hum that could have been anything. It was probably the pump that ran the purification system.

He grabbed the manual handle again and started to turn it. The door was unlocked, and he let it click softly before starting to push it open.

He had only moved it six inches when the sight of what lay beyond made his heart begin to race, and he pulled it quickly and quietly back closed.

"Dios Mio," he said, turning to face Diaz.

"What is it?" Diaz asked.

"I don't believe it," Donovan said, stunned by what he had seen. "We're in. We're inside."

"Inside what?" Diaz's face took on a look of excited curiosity.

"The city. The Dread city."

20

Gabriel couldn't help but smile as Captain Sturges guided the transport into Delta Station's waiting hangar. After everything he had learned during his hours on Alpha Settlement, he was glad to be home.

The BIS touched down on the floor of the hangar, magnetic clamps catching the tiny skids at the bottom of the box and holding it in place while the smaller bay doors were slowly closed. Once they had sealed and locked, the compressed air that was sucked from the chamber was released back in, pressurizing the area. The suppressors were re-activated, returning gravity to the space as well.

The red light in the BIS's cockpit turned green. Sturges turned in his seat to face Gabriel.

"I'm sorry about all of this garbage with the Council," he said, absently tapping the control pad to open the rear cargo door. The transport had been loaded up with foodstuffs and laundered uniforms, among other things. "If there's anything Siddhu or I can do to help, you just let me know."

"Thank you, Paul," Gabriel said. "I don't know if there's anything that anyone can do. It seems the people with the most pull have made up their minds. That doesn't mean I'm not going to try."

"I'm with you, Gabriel. Whatever you need."

Gabriel nodded, squeezing the older man's shoulder on his way to the back. He angled around the cargo and past the crew that was waiting to unload it.

"Captain," the Logistics Officer, Second Lieutenant Daphne O'Dea said, saluting him as he departed.

"Lieutenant," Gabriel said, returning the salute. "Let me know if there are any treats in the resupply, will you?"

"For you or Wallace?" she asked.

Gabriel spread his hands innocently. "Does it matter?"

"Only one of you is cute enough to over-ration. By the way, it's good to have you back."

"Thanks, Daphne. How's Soon?"

She shook her head. "Don't get me started. He's been trying to fix that old inverter again. He nearly blew a hole in our quarters and vented us into space."

Gabriel smiled. Captain Soon Kim considered himself a tinkerer, but he rarely got the things he tinkered with working again. He and Daphne had only been married a few months, and the honeymoon was close to being over. Captain Kim was next up on the mission detail.

"Well, tell him I said hello if I don't see him first," Gabriel said. It had been almost thirty hours since he had slept, and he was planning to head directly to his quarters to drop.

"Will do. See you later, Gabriel."

Gabriel passed across the hangar towards the exit. His eyes wandered to the starfighter bays on his left. They only had five left. Six if he counted the one that had been left on Manhattan. Engineering could probably print more if they were given clearance, but considering current events he doubted that would happen.

He moved from the hangar into the network of corridors that ran across Delta Station. Everything was a mixture of gray metal and small viewports here, a spiderweb of identical hallways that were hard to navigate for cadets fresh out of training. When Gabriel had first arrived, he had made it a point to learn the layout of the station within his first twenty-four hours. Even then, it had taken him forty-eight.

He had no trouble finding his way around now. He had seen every corridor so many times he could point out all of the scratches, dents, and smudges that identified one against another, and he could get anywhere in the base faster than many of the others. Some only bothered to learn their routes and didn't care about the rest. He wasn't like that.

He passed by the gym, waving at the few soldiers inside who were keeping their strength up with basic weights and cardio. It was simple throwback tech that was easy to produce and maintain and just as effective as programmed muscle stimulation and bio-electric conditioning, even if it took more overall effort. From there, he dropped four levels down, further into the spike where berthing was located. As a Captain, he had his own living space on the second level, a fifty square meter apartment complete with a bedroom, bathroom, and den. It was as sparsely produced and decorated as everything else on the station, but it had a full-sized transparency with a nice view of Manhattan, and it was a place to call home.

He finally reached his quarters, having grown more tired with each step he took. It was more than the lack of sleep. He couldn't get his father's words out of his head. Or his tears. Half of the people on the Council wouldn't have been alive if it hadn't been for Juliet St. Martin. He would have hoped they would have more respect for her sacrifice.

He tapped his palm against the door, and it slid aside. Wallace was waiting behind it, as expected. Gabriel could feel his depressed mood turning slightly as the Golden Retriever started whining and wagging his tail, sitting obediently and waiting for him to pour on the attention.

"Hey, Wallace," Gabriel said, stepping over the threshold and reaching down to pet the dog's head. "How are you doing, buddy?"

There weren't a lot of pets in the colony, but there were some, incubated and born in the laboratories in Charlie Settlement from the frozen sperm and eggs that had been loaded onto the Magellan. The colony had access to over ten-thousand species, though only three dog breeds and one cat had been born so far. Wallace had half the genes of

Theodore's pet Golden, Po'boy, who had died during the invasion.

Wallace's tail continued to swish back and forth as Gabriel moved further into his quarters, petting him as he did. Wallace had been a gift from his father after Jessica had died. It was a misguided but otherwise meaningful effort to help him adjust to her loss, and to be honest, to an extent it had.

"Yeah, it's been a rough day at work," Gabriel said. "I missed you, too. Remind me to thank Miranda for taking care of you while I was gone."

Wallace looked up at him, mouth open and tongue hanging out.

"Scientists," Gabriel said, shaking his head. "They don't care about people. They care about proving themselves right. Earth is our planet. Right, buddy?"

Wallace nuzzled Gabriel's hand.

"I saw one of their satellites get blown apart. I know it's possible. Maybe if they put as much energy into figuring that out as they have bent over blurry images of sensor readings."

Gabriel pulled off his jacket and unbuttoned his shirt, taking everything off until he was in a white t-shirt and underwear. He looked out the one-way transparency to Manhattan below, the outline of the Magellan visible beneath a light dust storm. He stared at it for a moment, remembering the look in his father's eyes again before crossing to his bedroom and laying down. Wallace jumped on the bed next to him, immediately curling up on the free side.

They were both asleep within minutes.

21

Gabriel woke six hours later. Wallace was still laying beside him though he had changed position to stretch his body across the bed and lay his head on a pillow.

"Lazy mutt," Gabriel said, reaching over and patting the side of the dog.

Wallace turned his head for a moment and then rolled onto his back so Gabriel could reach his stomach.

"Spoiled, lazy mutt," Gabriel said.

He slid off the bed and onto his feet, crossing to the bathroom. He pulled off the rest of his clothes and stepped into the shower, tapping the regulator that would give him three minutes of hot water every twenty-four hours. No more. No less.

He let the infused water clean off the grime, taking the full minutes before toweling off and throwing on a pair of utilities. He was off-duty for the next three days, and he was hungry.

"Come on, buddy," he said to Wallace, crossing the front of his quarters. "Let's see what's for breakfast."

Wallace's ears perked up at the word, and he rushed ahead to the door. He started whining a moment before a tone signaled someone was at the door.

Gabriel tapped the panel to open it, finding Miranda on the other side.

"Gabriel," she said, surprised. "I didn't know you were back."

"Yup. I hitched a ride with Captain Sturges. I couldn't take being in Alpha any longer than I had to."

Miranda kneeled to pet Wallace, looking up at him while she spoke. "Is it your father?"

"Believe it or not, he was the best part of the trip. It's everything else that's going to hell."

"Oh? What do you mean?"

"You haven't heard the rumors about leaving Calawan?"

"I've heard them. I didn't think they were very serious. You know how we NEA types like to gossip."

"Well, they're serious. Not only that, but General Cave is backing the idea."

Miranda stood, clearly shocked. "General Cave?"

"Even worse, he told my father what they plan to do. I got a few minutes with him before the meds knocked him out again. You should have seen the look in his eyes. I can't forget it."

"They're only trying to do what's best for everyone."

"That's what General Cave and Colonel Graham said. And maybe they are trying to do the best for the people in Calawan. The humans here don't count as everyone."

"You mean Earth? I get where you're coming from, Gabe. I do. I swear. But we've never even been able to hurt the Dread. How are we supposed to help the people on Earth?"

"I've heard that argument before," Gabriel said, suddenly tired of talking about it. "We were headed down to the mess. Do you want to join us?"

"Maybe you've heard the argument, but I don't think you're listening to it. You're as stubborn as your old man." She smiled as though she was giving him a compliment. "Personally, I don't think either choice is that great. Unfortunately, they're the only choices we have."

"So which one do you prefer?"

"Fight or flight? I don't know. My heart says fight. My head says flight."

"You always like to take both sides."

"Because every story has two sides. You should be open to the one you don't agree with some time. You want others to be open to you."

"Only when I'm right."

Miranda laughed. "You're impossible. Come on, I'll grab something with you."

"Let's go, Wally, " Gabriel said. "Time to eat."

Gabriel walked side-by-side with Miranda down the corridor, while Wallace ranged ahead, pausing at the doors to sniff the food behind them. They took the central elevator up to the base of the main saucer, diverting to Delta Park. The park was the station's main recreational area, a one thousand square meter expanse of artificial greenery that did its best to substitute for the real thing.

"Other than the business with the Council, how is your father these days?" Miranda asked as they left the park. "How long had it been since you saw him last?"

"Six months," Gabriel said. "He's, I don't know, well enough? It's hard to say. He spends most of every day medicated and lost in his head. For all intents, he might as well be dead already."

"That's a terrible thing to say."

"The only reason he isn't yet is because he's still waiting for us to win this war. It's all he has to keep him going. My mother believed in God and Heaven, and I know he wants to join her there. The only thing he cares more about is the promise he made to see this through."

Miranda was silent for a few seconds. "It's kind of sad, isn't it? Everything that's happened to him?"

"Yes. You can understand why I'm so against giving up the fight. I also don't believe in giving up on the people that we abandoned."

"Abandoned? That's not fair, is it?"

"My father said he abandoned them. They ran away in the Magellan instead of helping fight back. He's always said it was the one order he regretted following."

"Fight how?"

"Any way they could. Or, in the words of my father, 'wrasslin' with their bare hands until they sank into the bayou.'"

"Your father always had a colorful way with words."

"He still does when he's himself."

They reached the entrance to the mess. Captain Kim was coming out as they were going in, and he paused ahead of Gabriel, smiling and saluting.

"Captain St. Martin. Daphne told me you were back."

"Soon," Gabriel said, dropping the salute and taking his friend's hand. "I heard you almost blew up the station again."

Soon laughed in his deep voice that belied his petite frame. He was just over five feet of fast-twitch muscle, though his spiked hair gave him another few inches. "Lies. Nothing but lies. I almost blew up our quarters. The emergency seals would have closed us off before we could take anyone with us."

"Well, I'm glad I had a station to come back to."

"Yeah, I heard you were on Alpha. I'm sorry, man. At least you made it back here alive. Sturges said you took some nasty damage on that last run."

"It was close. It wasn't the first time. You know how it is."

"I sure do." Soon clapped him on the shoulder. "I've got to run. I'm due for a slipstream drill in thirty. I don't get to skip another rotation to fool around with my wife."

Soon's smile disappeared as he realized the meaning behind what he said. Gabriel felt the twinge of old sadness creeping up, and he forced it back down.

"It's okay," he said instead. "If it were up to me you'd be retiring to keep the population going. We could use some more good pilots."

"Thanks, Gabriel. I only need about sixty more runs to catch up with you."

Gabriel was sure they wouldn't have sixty more runs. If they were going to be leaving Calawan, they would pour every available resource into refitting the Magellan. With the weight of the entire colony behind the effort, he imagined it wouldn't take more than a few months.

"See you soon," Miranda said. Soon rolled his eyes at the old joke and walked away, pausing to pet Wallace's head before continuing.

Wallace wandered over to Gabriel's side, his eyes fixed on the inside of the mess. There were nearly one hundred soldiers inside, seated at the simple tables with a bland stew in front of them. At least they had some real food today.

"That's one of the people we're saving if we leave," Miranda said. "You know if we stay he's more likely than not to die skimming Earth's atmosphere."

"I know," Gabriel replied.

If he could change things, he would. He didn't want anyone else to have to go through what he had, or what his father had.

Some things were bigger than a single person.

Some promises couldn't be broken.

22

"You asked to see me, sir?" Gabriel said, standing in the open doorway of Colonel Graham's office on Delta Station.

Graham looked up from his tablet. His office was an out-of-place aberration compared to the rest of Delta Station. His desk was custom printed and painted, meant to resemble wood as closely as possible. His chair was cushioned. He had three paintings hanging on his walls, carried from Earth in the Magellan. The artist had never been famous before. They were all priceless now.

A second cushioned chair sat opposite him. He waved Gabriel over to it.

"Have a seat, Captain," he said. "I want to talk to you."

Gabriel tried to judge the topic by the Colonel's tone. Graham could be a gruff man, but he could also be very kind. He was somewhere in between.

"Yes, sir," he said, taking the seat, keeping his posture rigid.

"Relax, Gabriel," Graham said, closing the door with a tap on his pad. "This is off the record."

Gabriel let his limbs slouch slightly. "Is my father okay?"

Graham smiled. "He's fine. This is about the other day when you stopped by with Major Choi to see me."

"I apologize if I was out of line, sir," Gabriel said. "You know my emotions get the better of me sometimes."

"First, I said this is off the record. No 'sirs' required. Second, you weren't out of line. You spoke from your heart, and I respect the hell out of that. It's one of the best traits you inherited from your father."

"What's the worst?" Gabriel asked. He already had a feeling he knew the answer.

"Your stubborn determination. Which can be a good quality, too. If I had to pick another one, it would be that you don't shave as often as you should."

Gabriel ran his hand along his chin, feeling the prickliness of it. He had been in the gym when he received the Colonel's summons and rushed to get himself together.

"In any case, after you left my office I had a long conversation with Major Choi. I'm not saying I agree with you. Not yet. I do want to hear more about your experience."

"You have the data recorder," Gabriel said.

"We do, but I haven't heard the contents yet. I wanted to get your perspective first-hand."

Gabriel told Colonel Graham about the mission, starting from the moment he left the slipstream, and ending when he re-entered it. Graham leaned forward when he related the part about the enemy starfighter destroying its own satellites, interested in every detail Gabriel could give him.

"Was there anything about the weapon that seemed strange to you?" Graham asked.

"No. It seemed like a standard plasma cannon to me. Except when the bolts hit the satellites, they blew as if they had no armor at all."

"Incredible. Fifty years, and it's the first time anyone has seen anything like it. Is it coincidence or providence that you witnessed it right before the Council is set to meet about what to do with the colony?"

"I don't believe in fate," Gabriel said.

"Neither do I," Graham replied. "But I do believe in God, and that's the question that's keeping me up at night. I thought I had made up my mind about leaving, but then you dropped that bomb on me, and now I'm not so sure."

"If there is a God, why would He let the Dread kill billions of innocent people?" Gabriel asked. That was the question that had often kept him up at night. It was the reason he asked for luck and kept the crucifix as a charm instead of a religious symbol. His mother had faith, and look where it had gotten her. "And don't say He works in mysterious ways."

"Freedom of all His creations. Including the Dread. That doesn't mean He's happy with what they've done, or that they won't pay for it when they die. I had thought maybe He had other things in mind for us, that this new planet would be an Eden. I'm not the only one. That's what the Council is calling it. Did you know that?"

"No."

"It is. Anyway, my heart says we should stay. My head says we should go."

"Spaceman Locke said the same thing. If you're spiritual, what does your spirit say?"

Graham was silent. He stared at Gabriel as if he could find answers there.

"The Council is convening tomorrow. I'm going to be taking a transport down to Alpha to attend. I want you to come with me."

"Why?"

"Faith. I want you to talk to the Council."

"So I can get myself court-martialed?" Gabriel asked.

"If God wants us to stay and fight, He'll send His message through you."

Gabriel wasn't about to attribute his passion to someone else's will. "Do you really believe that?"

"I do."

"Then I guess I'll see you tomorrow," Gabriel said. "Is there anything else, sir?"

"No, thank you. You're dismissed."

Gabriel got to his feet and saluted before turning on his heel and heading out the door. Colonel Graham could call it providence if he wanted to. He could claim it was the work of an all-powerful being, and who knew? Maybe it was. He'd been having that argument with himself for years, and it always ended with his mother and his home world lost. How did Graham, or his father for that matter, manage to stay with God when God hadn't stayed with them?

He was sure he would never know.

23

"Are you serious?" Diaz asked, pushing past Donovan and opening the door to a hairline crack.

She pulled it closed a few heartbeats later, turning to look at him.

He knew what she had just seen. The small control room for the drainage system was sitting in the corner of an expansive area beneath the Dread's impenetrable cocoon. Looking up, he had seen the dark carapace made visible by an organic light that seemed to run in jagged lines along it, a bluish-white illumination that accented ridges and dips and extrusions on the material that he had never witnessed before.

Ahead of them, he had seen what he assumed was a machine of some kind. It was large and dark and made of a compound he didn't recognize. It was as though they had taken liquid oil and molded it into parts, and then assembled those parts and connected them with more of the dark material in tubes and channels that gave the entire thing a menacing and lifelike appearance.

He had heard it humming while the door was open, and had seen how the ground seemed to vibrate below it. That was all he had taken the time to absorb before his fear had made him close the door again. He had no idea if there were any Dread in the area, and now that they had managed to get into the city, he found himself scared of the idea of seeing one of the aliens. If they did, they would be the first free humans to lay eyes on them.

"I don't know what to say," Diaz whispered. "Or if we should be scared or excited."

"Excited?" Donovan asked.

"This is a pretty incredible opportunity. No one has ever been inside before."

"You don't know that. It could be no one has ever been inside and made it back out."

"Well, we're inside, and whether we choose to be scared or not, there's only going to be one way out." She pointed at the door.

"I'm trying not to be afraid. It isn't working that well."

"I'm with you on that, amigo."

They stared at each other in silence. Donovan tried to get his nerves and his breathing under control. They were going to have to go out there. It wasn't like they had a choice unless they wanted to stay in the control room and starve. Except he doubted that would happen either. The Dread hadn't destroyed the building or the drainage system. In fact, it was possible they were using it for something, which meant they were no safer here than out there.

"You still have your knife?" he asked.

Diaz laughed. "What good is that going to do against them?"

"None if they're armored. We know they use clones for at least part of their army, and the clones are just like us."

"Actually, they're just like each other. Literally. And better armed."

Donovan forced a smile. The trauma they had already been through was making them giddy. He could feel himself shaking, his frayed nerves begging for release. He struggled to get them under control. He was still the CO of this unit, even if it only consisted of one other soldier. It was his duty to lead.

"Then we'll have to be sneaky. We're t-vaulters. We're good at that. How's my shoulder?"

Diaz circled behind him to check it. "It looks like it stopped bleeding. How does it feel?"

"It hurts. I'll live. Come on."

Donovan returned to the door, slowly pushing it open a third time. This time, he opened it enough to stick his head out and take in more of the area.

The machine right in front of him was only one of a dozen identical devices, arranged in a circle around the center of the massive space. What looked like thick cables ran from each of them to the middle, where a large platform rose to the top of the structure in an hourglass shape of bundled cord. As before, he could see the ground vibrating beneath and around each of the machines. The cords leading to the ceiling were shifting as well though the effect wasn't as noticeable in the air.

What he didn't see were any other life forms, alien or otherwise. They were safe for now.

"What do you think it is?" Diaz asked, following him out of the room.

They stayed close to the small, cement building, tracing its walls to the rear. The side of the alien structure was only a dozen meters away at the back and gave off a faint odor that Donovan had never experienced before. It was sweet and rich; a pleasant smell.

"It may be their power source," he said. "Or one of them, anyway."

"What do you think would happen if we destroyed it?"

"Probably nothing good for them, but considering we only have a utility knife? I don't like our odds."

Diaz nodded, and they moved toward the wall. When they got close enough, they both reached out to touch it at almost the same time.

The material was cool to the touch, smooth and solid as steel or iron. Leaning in for a closer inspection, he could see tiny veins of various shades of gray moving through it and along it. He didn't know if they were intentional or simply the coloration of whatever it was made from. The other thing he noticed was that the shape of it was uneven. Not only were there sharp ridges in seemingly random places in the material, but there were also gentle slopes and valleys that he would never have noticed without running his hand along it.

"It's amazing," he said.

"It's also the death of humanity," Diaz replied.

Donovan removed his hand. "Do you see a way out?"

"There," she said, pointing to a break in the material a short distance away. "It looks like a corridor."

"Let's try to stay in the shadows as much as possible, and hope they don't have an alarm."

Diaz smiled. "I bet they don't expect anything to get in here. If we had a little bit of C-4, we could blow this entire area, no problem."

"We'll be sure to come back with some."

They made their way across to the adjoining corridor. It was much smaller in scale, ten meters high and wide. It was also darker and more foreboding, with the bluish light filtering from the ceiling in regular intervals and casting the chitinous material in an eerie light. The hallway ended a few hundred meters back, forking into a pair of adjoining corridors.

There was still no sign of life. The only noise to be heard was the soft humming from the machines behind them.

"I feel like this is a good time to say something witty and inspiring," Donovan said. "Nothing's coming to me."

"Let's try not to die," Diaz said.

"Good enough."

24

Donovan and Diaz navigated through corridor after corridor, taking random turns to the right or left fork based on educated guesses of which direction they were facing and which direction might lead them out of the Dread city, careful not to move in a way that would bring them back to where they had started.

An hour passed with no sign of anything beyond the dim hallways, which all began to look identical after a while. The only sound was the light slapping of their bare feet on the cold floor. The only comfort was the fact that they weren't alone.

They had spent years in the shadow of the massive alien base. They had spent years in hiding, fearful of what lay behind the black walls. Only now they were behind the black walls.

And there was nothing.

For Donovan, it defied expectation or explanation. Where were the Dread? From the outside he had assumed the aliens were thriving beneath their protective cocoon, taking advantage of the humans they had enslaved. It was common knowledge that they had come to harvest humanity's genome, to splice humankind's DNA into their own as centuries of scientific rather than sexual reproduction had destroyed their diversity and left them weak and riddled with illness. It was understood that they had rounded up people by the thousands, testing them for compatibility and quality and using those who matched their criteria for specific applications like the identical bald soldiers.

That information had led him to think the enemy numbered in the millions or at least had millions of slaves. Maybe they had stumbled into a low traffic area, but millions of anything would be sure to make some kind of noise or be some level of obvious.

"Maybe they don't use this area anymore," Diaz whispered, apparently thinking along the same lines.

"Whatever that is back there is up and running," Donovan replied. "Which doesn't suggest it's been abandoned."

"Then where is everybody?"

"Your guess is as good as mine."

They had given up slinking along the sides of the hallways twenty minutes earlier, moving at a faster pace by walking right down the middle. It was so quiet Donovan was sure he'd hear something coming before it was able to sneak up on them.

"We know the perimeter of the city is over one hundred kilometers long," Donovan said. "If the density is low enough it would make sense there would be nobody here."

"Who maintains everything, then? Unless they have a central monitoring system."

Donovan stopped walking, his eyes scanning the walls, ceiling, and floor around them. "Let's say that they do. Do you think they know we're here, and they're just watching us? Waiting to see what we'll do next?"

Diaz bit her bottom lip, considering. "No. Why would they need to monitor inside their walls?"

"We don't know where they came from. Just because human technology is inferior to theirs, how do we know theirs isn't inferior to someone else's? If there are two intelligent life forms in the universe, it stands to reason there are three or more."

"You're reaching, D," Diaz said. "Besides, if they're watching us there isn't anything we can do about it. We have to find a way out."

They started walking again, though Donovan paid more attention to the structure around them now, looking for anything that might resemble a sensor or a camera. Diaz was right. If they were being watched, so be it. The Dread had chosen not to intervene, at least not yet.

Ten more minutes found them at another intersection. Donovan was about to ask Diaz which way she thought they should go when he realized the structure of the corridor had changed. The hallways on both sides of them were no longer completely straight, instead curving gently until they vanished into the distance.

"I bet this corridor makes a ring," Diaz said. "Now we're getting somewhere."

"Stay alert," Donovan said, moving to the inside of the curve. It wouldn't hide them for long, but it was better than nothing.

They turned to the left and began following the curve. As they moved further in, new corridors began to appear on the outer side of the ring, while indents began lining the inner.

"Doorways," Donovan said, feeling a sense of fear rising with his heart rate.

"Somebody has to be here, don't they?" Diaz asked, taking her knife from her waist and holding it up defensively. Any of the doors could open at any time.

They kept going. Eventually, the inner curve revealed a corridor that dove deeper into the center of the circle. Donovan could see what appeared to be a green laser stabbing through the middle of that hallway, signaling the center of the ring. He had no idea what it was, and he wasn't eager to find out.

"Which way is north?" he asked. His sense of direction was fine outside when he could check the sky.

"This way, I think," Diaz said, pointing toward the corridor across from them. It led away from the circle, down another long, straight passage.

"Let's keep going north until we can't anymore. Otherwise, we'll be lost in here forever."

"Agreed."

They started heading for the northern corridor.

A soft swishing noise sounded to their right.

One of the doors was opening.

There was no time to think. No time to consider. It was fight or flight.

Donovan threw himself at the figure coming out of the doorway, hitting it hard with his injured shoulder, acting so quickly he never got a look at what he was attacking. He felt his arm smack against a rough frame, and he bit his tongue to keep from crying out at the pain his assault caused him.

Then he was falling, tangled up with the enemy and landing on top as they both crashed on the floor inside the room.

Donovan squirmed and scrambled, trying to get his feet under him and put a few inches of distance between himself and whatever he had hit. He could smell the same sweet odor again, and see a small patch of stark white flesh and silver hair layered over a bony ridge.

The alien hissed beneath him, trying to shake itself loose. Donovan lifted himself slightly, getting a good look at an orange, humanoid eye. Then Diaz was in the room beside him. She fell to her knees, her knife coming down hard, burying it in that orange eye. Cranberry colored blood began to run out, and the body went limp below him.

"Take that you son of a bitch," Diaz whispered angrily, releasing a sharp breath.

The door slid closed behind them.

25

Donovan rolled off the corpse below him, his shoulder throbbing. He came to his knees on the opposite side, his eyes only the second pair to ever take in the sight of the enemy.

"I never knew what to expect," Diaz said, her body trembling.

The pierced orange eye was matched with a second, anchored to a face that was decidedly humanoid. Between them was a tiny, flat nose, a small arc with a pair of nostrils that led down to very human-looking pink lips and white teeth, the mouth hanging slightly open in a forever silent scream. Tracing the outline, he saw the ears were also small and pressed tight against the head, while some small, bony ridges created an almost reptilian shape to the upper portion of the skull. Short, fine, silver hair grew from the scalp behind the ridges, giving the alien a near-demonic appearance.

Except nothing about it suggested it was demonic. In fact, the white skin made it look more like an angel. Donovan's eyes trailed down a milky neck to narrow shoulders and a small frame, dressed in simple black cloth that appeared to be composed of a similar material to the unbreakable armor. A pair of slippers covered the feet while four-fingered hands lay exposed at the alien's sides.

Diaz reached down, pulling at the cloth and lifting it away from the Dread's waist. The dead alien was clearly a male.

"So much like us," Donovan said, barely able to breathe.

"Maybe now," Diaz said. "We don't know what they looked like before. They've been using human genes to fix themselves."

"I can't believe you killed one." He realized he was shaking, too.

"Me neither." She pulled the knife from its eye. "I can't say I feel sorry for it."

Donovan finally pulled his eyes away from it, quickly scanning the room. It appeared to be living quarters of some kind. A transparent enclosure sat in the center of the space; alien symbols illuminated in a grid against the surface and what appeared to be a mask dangling from the top of it. Behind the enclosure was a more traditional human mattress, complete with white sheets tucked into the frame it sat on, which blended in with, or was protruding from the wall behind it. A seam that suggested a storage area sat on the left of the enclosure, while an archway was on the right.

They got to their feet. Donovan approached the enclosure, making as good of a mental image of it all as he could. He peered through the open archway into what had to be a bathroom. A small tube protruded from the wall at the right height for urinating into, while a second tube extended from the wall in a position that was clearly intended for defecation. It was both familiar and completely alien at the same time, a conjunction of advanced technology and crude adjustments in response to the form the Dread had taken.

He couldn't help but wonder what they had looked like before.

"I wish I could read this," Diaz said, stopped in front of the enclosure and staring at the symbols. They were simple lines in even, measured strokes that bore a very vague resemblance to the Roman alphabet.

"I wish I had a way to record all of this," Donovan said.

He returned to the body on the floor, patting it down. He felt an odd protrusion over the chest, and he pushed aside the alien's clothing until he found a round, flat, black pin the size of a fingernail.

"I wonder what this does," he said, unclipping it and holding it up.

"I wonder what any of this stuff does," Diaz said. She was trying to figure out how to open the seam in the wall. She ran her hands along it until it split in two, sliding apart to reveal its contents.

"Their wardrobe is pretty boring," Donovan said, looking into the storage area. Shelves of black cloth lay inside.

"No hobbies, either," Diaz said. "The room has nothing else in it. What do you think they do for fun?"

"Destroy civilizations," Donovan said. "It's too bad none of its clothes are even close to fitting me. I could use a shirt."

Diaz grabbed a piece of the cloth and unfolded it. It looked way too small for the alien. She pulled at it, finding that it stretched well. "I think it'll work," she said. She tossed it to him, along with a pair of the pants. Then she started unbuttoning her shirt.

"What are you doing?" Donovan asked, catching the cloth. It was incredibly light and soft.

"Changing," she replied, undoing the last button and holding the shirt open just enough that Donovan could see the center of her bare chest between her breasts. "You could try being a gentleman."

Donovan had forgotten his manners, and he felt his face heating up as he turned the other way. "You could have warned me first."

"You saw me unbuttoning. Don't turn around, I'm changing my pants. You should change yours, too. Leave the shirt. I'll tear some new bandages for you with this."

Donovan did as she suggested, slipping out of his torn and filthy pants.

He pulled the pants up, a little uncomfortable over the way it hugged against his groin, and then turned around. The black material had stretched around Diaz's form, pulling tight against her body in a way that likely revealed a little more than she wanted.

"Try not to stare," she said, reaching into the closet and grabbing another shirt. She put the knife to it, intending to cut it into strips for his shoulder.

It bent and shifted beneath the knife, but it didn't break. She tried stabbing it instead. It seemed to solidify against the force, not allowing the point through.

"The compression should keep enough pressure on it," Donovan said. "Help me get the old bandages off."

Diaz nodded and reached for the disgusting shirt. It was torn and soaked with water, sweat, and blood, and smelled awful.

"When did you grow up?" Donovan asked as she dropped the soggy wrap on the floor. He knew Matteo's kid sister had held a crush on him for years, but she had always been Matteo's kid sister. It was the first time he had noticed she wasn't a little girl anymore.

"Puberty was six years ago," Diaz replied. "Like I said, you've never paid me much attention before." She stepped away from him. "Maybe you see me now?"

26

Donovan tugged at the alien material that covered his arms. It stretched so easily, and yet when he tried to jam the knife into it, it became as hard as stone or steel.

"I wonder if this stuff can stop a plasma bolt, too," he said. The material was incredibly comfortable though the nature of it did leave him feeling a little exposed. At least he wasn't alone in that.

"What do we do now?" Diaz asked.

"We can't stay here," he replied. "That thing was going somewhere, which means it's probably going to be missed."

"First things first, then." Diaz pointed to the door. "How do we get out?"

Donovan smiled. "Good question."

He stepped over the dead alien, examining the hatch and the frame around it. Human doors had manual knobs or levers or a touchpad control. He didn't see either of those. He couldn't believe they were going to get stuck here, discovered and killed because they couldn't open it.

"Maybe it's voice activated?" Diaz said.

"I hope not. We don't speak alien."

"Next time you tackle an alien, make sure you stay out in public."

"Yeah, I'll try that."

Diaz laughed softly, coming over to help him, running her hands along the wall near the hatch. "There could be a control hidden in the wall, like the symbols on whatever that enclosure thing is."

"It looks like a breathing apparatus of some kind. Look at its face. That nose seems too small and improperly formed to breathe easily."

Diaz glared down at it for a second. "It's disgusting."

They spent another minute trying to work the door. Donovan slammed his head back against the wall, angry with himself for his ineptitude. "This is ridiculous."

"What about sensors? Maybe it works by detecting that he's leaving?"

"Only him?"

Diaz shrugged. Donovan backed up and then walked toward the door as if assuming it would open ahead of him.

It didn't, leaving him with his nose right against the metal.

"Damn it," he cursed, tempted to slam his fist against it.

"You can say that again," Diaz said. He could tell she was getting uncomfortable with the situation, and the earlier stress relieving lightheartedness was wearing off. "What if it only works when one of them does it?"

"That would be good security, but I wouldn't think they need it."

"You wouldn't want someone just walking into your room on you."

Some of the humor returned to her eyes, and Donovan dropped his eyes to the floor. He had been fourteen when eight-year-old Renata had walked in on him unannounced and caught him masturbating.

"I can't believe you remember that."

"It was another two years before I knew what you were even doing," she said. "It's nothing to be ashamed of. Lots of people do it."

"Do you?" he asked.

"I don't think that matters, does it?"

He wasn't sure if she was being dodgy because she was ashamed, too, or because she didn't want to make him more uncomfortable.

"It might."

She stared at him for a moment.

A tone sounded in the room. It seemed like it came from everywhere.

They both froze, their eyes darting around the space in search of somewhere to hide.

There wasn't anywhere.

"Mierda," Diaz whispered.

Donovan looked at the dead alien, still sprawled on the floor. "There's only one thing to do," he said, moving closer to the door and crouching down, ready to attack.

The tone sounded again. Diaz joined him, handing him her knife. "I'm with you."

A muffled voice followed the second tone, more localized this time. Donovan returned his attention to the Dread until he remembered the pin. He unclipped it from his top. Someone was speaking through it. The voice was female, the words in a language he didn't know.

"I think someone missed him," Diaz whispered.

Donovan passed the knife back to her.

"What are you doing?" she asked.

"Change of plan if the door opens."

"Yes, sir."

They stood and waited. The tone sounded a third time, and the voice through the pin grew more concerned.

A short hiss was the only warning they had before the hatch snapped open. Donovan didn't waste any time, stepping forward and grabbing the newcomer, yanking them inside and wrapping his arms around them from behind, his hand falling over the mouth.

The alien struggled in his grip, making noises beneath his hand and trying to get away. The hatch closed behind them as he held on, her struggle causing his hand to slip.

Teeth came down on his hand, biting through his skin and drawing blood. An elbow hit him hard in the gut, and he lost his grip. The woman pulled herself away, waving her hand toward the hatch. It slid open, but Diaz tackled her again before she could get out. It closed a second time.

Donovan recovered, moving to help Diaz. She had the alien on the floor, her knees digging into its legs and her hands holding its arms down.

"Stop moving," Diaz hissed.

It wasn't a Dread beneath her.

It was a woman. A human woman.

27

She stared back up at them, her large blue eyes wide with fear, her body trembling in kind. She had fair skin and reddish-blonde hair that spilled out around her shoulders. She was wearing the same black outfit as they were though hers was more in the style of a dress and hung more loosely from her frame. She wore the same black pin as the Dread. She also had a second one next to it. It was the same shape and size, but a luminescent blue in color.

"A clone," Diaz said to Donovan.

"I saw how it opened the door," he replied.

"Then we don't need it."

She motioned her head toward her knife, which she had dropped on the floor.

Donovan picked it up and approached them. It was obvious to him that the clone was terrified. It knew what he was going to do.

"Donovan, do it," Diaz said.

Donovan knelt down, putting the knife to the clone's throat. A tear rolled down the side of its face. They were trained from an early age to recognize that enemy humans weren't human. That they were made, not born and raised. There were stories of the early resistance, from before the Dread built their cities and the alien operations were more out in the open. People had seen the factories where the first clones were created, even if they had never seen the Dread outside of their armor before today. It was the scientists who had guessed what they were using them for.

They had been taught that clones were as good as robots. They didn't think. They didn't feel. They followed instructions programmed into them. Organic machines that looked like you and me. To mess with our heads and make them harder to kill? Or because it was simply easier to make a person given the resources available on the planet?

"Major," Diaz said, using his rank to appeal to the soldier in him.

He was hesitating, and he knew it. The clone was crying. He had been raised to be a soldier. To do battle and fight a war. He had no problem killing the enemy when it was trying to kill him.

This was different.

"Give me the knife. I'll do it."

Diaz lifted her right hand to take the knife. Donovan pulled it away. The clone could have used the chance to try to escape, but she didn't. She continued to lay beneath Diaz, sobbing.

"No," Donovan said. "She might be useful. Yeah, great, we can open a door. We might need a little more than that to get out of here."

"D-"

"No. It's my decision. Look at her."

"It."

"Her. Genetically, she's a human just like us."

"No, she isn't. She's a machine. The enemy."

"She isn't trying to get away, and she's terrified."

"Oh, please. They're probably programmed to cry crocodile tears in self-defense. Please give me the knife."

"No. Get off her. That's an order, Lieutenant."

Diaz and Donovan stared at one another. Then Diaz reluctantly rolled off the clone.

Donovan held the knife over her. "If you scream, you die." He pointed

116

it at her and then pantomimed cutting his throat.

"I understand," she said.

Donovan felt a chill at the shock of her words. "You speak English?"

"I speak seven human languages. English, Spanish, German, Japanese, Chinese, and Arabic." She stared up at him. "I've never met a human before. Your interaction with one another is intriguing."

"Who are you?" Diaz said, clearly confused.

The clone sat up, moving slowly and wiping the tears from her eyes. She seemed much less frightened now that she knew they weren't going to kill her.

"My name is Ehri," she said, her voice putting an odd emphasis on the 'eh' that sounded more like a growl. "That was Tuhrik. He was my Dahm."

"Dahm?" Diaz said.

"It is difficult to describe in your tongues. Not a master because that would suggest I am a slave. Not a partner because he did hold dominion over me." Her face wrinkled slightly. "More like a commanding officer." She looked at Diaz. "You called your husband Major. Is he also your commanding officer?"

"Husband?" Diaz said.

"I have read many teachings on the topic of human culture. It was my duty as second-" she paused, trying to think of a suitable word. "Scientist. Tuhrik was a scientist. I was his most senior assistant."

"I'm not her husband," Donovan said. "What kind of science do you do?"

"Alien sociology and genetics."

It took Donovan a second to realize when she said alien, she was talking about them.

"Why does a geneticist need to read about human culture?"

"It is one thing to emulate the biology of a thing. It is something else to understand the individuality. By understanding a culture, we can better assimilate it."

"Individuality?" Diaz said. "You're a clone. One of thousands. All exactly the same."

"You are wrong in that, Lieutenant," Ehri said. "Yes, there are hundreds who share my identical sequence of DNA, sampled many years earlier from a human that the Domo'dahm - that is something akin to a King, or Prime Minister, or President - found very compelling. However, there is only one Ehri who is second to Tuhrik. I have earned that distinction through the value of my work under him. If we were all the same, there would be no distinction made between us."

"What about the soldiers?" Donovan asked. "The clones sent out to hunt us?"

"They are simpler creations, yes. Even they have an individuality. It is only less defined."

"You said assimilate. Is that what the Dread do? Invade planets, kill billions, and steal their culture?"

"You have long called us the Dread. We are known as bek'hai. That was not always our way, but like humans, we have evolved to suit our need for self-preservation. Our home planet became uninhabitable. We were forced into scientific reproduction to cover our losses, which were many. These clones of ourselves were flawed, unable to reproduce naturally, and so we continued to make copies. Our genetic diversity was lost, and we needed to find an intelligent species to help us restore it. We found Earth."

"You could have asked for help," Donovan said. "Instead of destroying our civilization to save your own."

"It was the Domo'dahm's decision to take it. He rationalized that humankind would not allow such use of its own. Despite your petty differences, you are a species that is very loyal to one another."

"We are, aren't we? You say that like it's a bad thing."

"Not at all. Perhaps if we were more alike, our situation would have been avoided."

"So you screwed up, and we have to pay for it?" Diaz asked.

"Yes."

She said it simply and without emotion. Donovan had to move in front of Diaz to keep her back.

"You bitch," Diaz said.

"Lieutenant," Donovan said, grabbing her. "Get a grip on yourself."

It was the perfect opportunity for Ehri to steal his knife and stab him in the back of the neck. She didn't. Instead, she waited while Diaz backed up.

"You aren't afraid of us," Donovan said. "Why?"

"You've already expressed your desire to keep me alive, and I have never met humans before. The original collection was completed before I was made. We know much about humankind before we arrived, but little of how you have adapted to our occupation, other than that you have continued to resist it despite your obvious technological inferiority. The Domo'dahm does not find such intellectual endeavors worthwhile, but Tuhrik believed they were invaluable. He might have even spoken with you, had you not killed him."

"You don't seem too upset that we did," Donovan said.

"Our future depends on replacing the drumhr, the intermediate genetic splicing of bek'hai and human, with a new, more robust iteration. We are closer than ever to achieving natural reproductive capabilities once more. Tuhrik would be satisfied to know that this conversation occurred as a result of the end of his life."

Donovan could barely believe it. There was no human alive that would be so willing, no, almost happy to be captured by the enemy. Yet here was this clone telling him that she thought to be here with them was a good thing, and that her CO would have approved. The concept was more alien to him than the corpse on the floor a meter away.

"You are fortunate that you attacked Tuhrik," Ehri said. "Most of the bek'hai do not share his opinion of humans. They resent that they required you to survive. They resent the physical weaknesses that you have burdened them with, such as the need for oxygen. We had to construct the regeneration chambers to restore them to health on a daily basis."

Donovan looked back at the clear enclosure. He had been right about its purpose. "Burdened them with?' he said. "They could have picked a different planet."

"There was no other planet. Intelligent life is not rife throughout the universe. There is one other that we know of, and they would have defended themselves easily against our assault."

Donovan wasn't that surprised to hear there were other aliens out there.

119

He was surprised to hear that they were even more powerful than these aliens.

"I don't suppose they'll be dropping by Earth anytime soon?" Diaz asked.

"No."

"You aren't worried about telling us all of this?" Donovan asked. "We've been fighting for years to get even the smallest shred of intel, and you've just spilled it all like it's no big deal."

"We have never sought to hide our nature from humankind, or you would know nothing about us at all. We did what we had to do, as you have done what you must. I don't know what brought you here, or how you got through our walls, and I don't care. That is a question for the military to worry about. I am a scientist, Major. I seek knowledge and understanding that will better the goals of my species. That is what I was made to do. That is my motivation for being. Considering that, how might I best understand you if you have no platform from which to understand me?"

"Fair enough, I guess," Donovan said, feeling every bit as inferior as Ehri claimed they were.

Her motives didn't align with the human way of thinking. She was talking to them, the enemy, for no other reason than to use the experience as some kind of scientific study. It was crazy.

"Besides, Major, this may be my one and only chance to further my studies and come to a true understanding of current human culture before you are eliminated. The Domo'dahm has decided that the remnants of humankind are to be exterminated within the year. Even if you manage to escape, you will not survive for long."

28

Gabriel's eyes swept across the chamber, taking a quick inventory of everyone present. It had been two years since he had last been to a Council meeting.

That was the time when his father was awarded the Medal of Honor and honorably discharged from active service.

He could still see the scene in his mind. His father was newly injured, grimacing in pain and cursing up a storm while the Council tried to tell him why it was a good idea for him to retire.

"I have no intention of retiring until the day my chest stops rising and falling for good," Theodore had said. "Pain ain't nothing but a reminder, and I've been reminded of what those alien bastards did every day since we left Earth."

The last time, Gabriel had sided with the Council. His father was seventy-eight years old, and to be honest, the accident had been his fault. He didn't have the vision he once did or the mental acuity. He was a danger to himself and those around him. It was sad but true.

He winced involuntarily as he recalled the way his father had chewed him out for taking the Council's side. Theodore had called him every bit of Cajun slang he had ever heard, and when he was done with that he had switched to English. Gabriel had taken it, sitting and letting his father dump all of his anger and hurt and frustration on his shoulders. He had stayed while the General had bawled into his hands. He had left only once his father was out of energy and asleep.

It had taken four months for him to work up the nerve to go back.

Most of the Council was already assembled. He hadn't been in front of them since the last round of elections, and he only recognized half of the faces. The council was always made up of twelve people. Six men. Six women. Two pairs each from Alpha, Beta, and Gamma settlements. Ten of them were present, along with General Cave, Colonel Graham, Major Choi, Captain Sturges, and three people Gabriel didn't know. Well, two. He recognized the younger man as the one from the pod. The scientist. He guessed the other two were scientists as well. A man and woman, young enough to have been born in the Calawan system and old enough to be one of the first.

"Captain St. Martin," Major Choi said, noticing him at the back of the room. She went back to meet him.

"Major Choi," Gabriel said, saluting.

"We're in the Council Chambers," Choi said. "We're all civilians in here. People of the NEA."

Gabriel smiled. "Right. How have you been, Vivian?"

"Not bad. I'll be better once this business is done. Are you ready to hit them where it hurts?"

Gabriel had spent the last three days trying to work out everything he would say. He had written the beginning of a speech and erased it over one hundred times. In the end, he decided he would wing it and just say whatever came to mind.

"As ready as I'll ever be."

"I went to see your father before I came here," Choi said. "He isn't looking too good these days. Sabine said they had to increase his dosage to keep him calm."

"I saw him a few days ago. It's this bull that's killing him. He and

General Cave used to be best friends. Now he sees him as a traitor."

"It's a shame when people wind up on opposite sides of something like this. I have a lot of respect for General Cave, but he's wrong. Plain and simple."

Gabriel noticed General Cave looking his way at the same time Major Choi said it. He smiled and nodded politely to the General, not making the mistake of saluting him as he had Choi. He would never lose respect for the man, but that didn't mean he was on his side in this particular battle.

He felt a soft breeze behind him, turning to find the two missing Council members at his back. They were easy to identify by the simple medallions they wore around their necks. He knew them both. Charles Ashford and Lucille Guttmann. They had both been part of the Magellan's maiden flight, and advanced age had left Charles overweight and Lucille walking with a cane, which was the reason for their late arrival.

"Gabriel," Lucille said, smiling. "I didn't expect to see you here."

"Hi, Gabe," Charles said.

"I didn't know you two had been voted onto the Council," Gabriel replied. "It's good to see you both. How long has it been?"

Charles laughed. "I think you were still in diapers, the last time I saw you."

"Come on, it can't have been that long."

"No, but you were Second Lieutenant St. Martin at the time."

"I didn't realize it had been so long."

"If you'll excuse us, Gabriel," Lucille said. "We're already running late, thanks to my useless old rear end."

Gabriel smiled and moved out of their way, taking a seat next to Major Choi. Colonel Graham joined them a few seconds later.

"Colonel," Gabriel said, giving him a larger nod than he had General Cave. They had taken the BIS down together earlier in the day.

"Gabriel." Graham's face was grim.

"Is everything okay, Colonel?" Gabriel asked.

"I hope so."

Gabriel didn't like that kind of reaction from someone who was supposed to be his ally in this. "What's going on?"

"God gave me the answer I was looking for," Graham said. "It wasn't the answer that I wanted."

Gabriel was about to ask him what he meant when the echoing bang of one of the medallions on the table at the front of the room called the meeting to order.

29

The Speaker's name was Angela Rouse. She was the youngest person on the Council, the same age as Gabriel and one of the biggest critics of the NEA's military arm. Gabriel knew that no matter what he said, she would never vote in favor of remaining behind. He was okay with that. She wasn't the only person whose vote mattered.

Of course, Colonel Graham's attitude beside him was leaving him lacking in confidence about their chances. Something had changed since Captain Sturges had dropped them off earlier. Some new information had come to light. What?

"I am hereby opening the fifth meeting of the twenty-third New Earth Alliance Council," Angela said. "Are all Council members present and in sound mind and body?"

"We are," they all responded.

Angela reached down and tapped a key to start recording the meeting. "This is an out of cycle meeting to discuss certain information that has come to light in recent days regarding both the activity of the NEA Space Force and the future of the civilian population of the NEA. The goal of this meeting is to hear from relevant parties and arrive at a decision. Either remain in the Calawan system and continue our surveillance of Earth or recondition the starship Magellan once more to carry all surviving members of the NEA to a newly discovered Earth-type planet, which will be referred to as Eden. Are there any questions before we begin the discussion?"

There weren't.

"Okay. I understand we will be hearing from Chief Astronomer Guy Larone, as well as Colonel James Graham to present both sides of the current argument. I'm sure I don't need to remind the Council that your decision should be made from your perspective of what is best for every member of the New Earth Alliance, and not from any past loyalties, friendships, or nostalgia."

"Angela," Captain Sturge's wife, Siddhu, snapped. "We're well aware of our responsibilities."

The two women made sour faces at one another, giving Gabriel a feeling this meeting was going to be more contentious than he had expected. It seemed the Council was already well divided on the issue.

"Colonel Graham, would you like to make your case first?" Angela asked.

Gabriel glanced over at the Colonel, whose eyes shifted to avoid his. He turned his attention back to Angel as Graham stood and straightened his uniform. She had a pleasant look on her face.

Something was definitely wrong.

Major Choi could see it too. She put her hand on his arm, and they looked at one another.

"What's going on?" she mouthed.

He shook his head. He didn't know, and he didn't like it.

Colonel Graham reached the front of the room.

"Thank you, Angela," he said. "Members of the Council, assembled guests." He turned to acknowledge them all, his eyes passing over Gabriel again. "I came here today to present an argument about the importance of the work the Space Force is doing, both in continuing the reconnaissance of Earth and in maintaining the status of the Magellan as a starship preparing for war. I came here to today to present Captain Gabriel St. Martin. He is the son of Retired General Theodore St. Martin, the man who saved the lives of everyone in this system, past, present, and future. He came here to present his compelling and impassioned perspective of our responsibilities to those we were forced to leave behind." He paused, his eyes finally finding Gabriel a dozen meters away. "Unfortunately, I can't do that."

A tense silence followed, with every member of the Council appearing confused except for Angela. Gabriel sought out General Cave. His face was stone. Whatever was happening, he knew about it already. Of course, he did.

"As you know," Colonel Graham continued, "Captain St. Martin returned from a reconnaissance mission three days ago. While our missions as of late have consistently resulted in an empty data recorder, we did finally receive another transmission from our brothers and sisters on the ground. It contained a recorded message from the Mexico based resistance, created by General Rodriguez based on a transcript he received from General Alan Parker in New York. I'd like to play that message for you now."

Colonel Graham reached into his pocket and removed his tablet. He tapped it a few times and then placed it on the desk in front of the Council.

A holographic image rose a foot above the device, spreading into a small but realistic visual of a man in a simple green uniform with a battered, tarnished pin on the chest.

"My comrades beyond Earth," he said, his face tight. "My name is Colonel Christian Rodriguez. You have seen my face before, in transmissions dating back almost a dozen years. Since the Dread arrived over fifty years ago, we have been fighting the good fight, gathering as much information as we can and passing it on to you in hopes of one day finding a way to defeat their technology."

The hologram bowed its head for a moment before continuing.

"The Dread have recently begun to step up their military presence throughout the resistance inhabited regions of the planet. Already, we have confirmed the destruction of bases in Jakarta, Indonesia, Cairo, Egypt,

Osaka, Japan, and Kenya, South Africa. Our base here in Mexico is under constant threat, having lost over a third of our fighting forces in the prior three months. Our analysts are convinced that the Dread have tired of our pecking at them for the last half-century, and of passing intel along to you. It may be that we are drawing nearer to discovering their secrets. Or it may be that they have other plans that require ending the resistance once and for all. I don't know, and I don't think I ever will."

He paused again, looking off to the side. He bit his lower lip, clearly uncomfortable with what came next.

"My comrades beyond Earth. I don't know what your situation is. I know that fifty years have passed, and you have been unable to help us. I know that you have been trying your best. I know that some of your pilots and ships have been lost. I'm sorry, my friends. This is a fight that we cannot win. We have tried, but we have failed. The resistance is on the verge of collapse and will be disbanded soon, our larger groups breaking into smaller ones in an effort to evade detection. All of us here are grateful that you did not abandon us to our fate. Your presence has given us a strength that has allowed us to continue for all of these years.

"Even so, the day has come where I must ask that you move on. I know the ship you escaped on was designed to travel much greater distances than you have. If you have the chance to find a better life somewhere else, I beg you to please take it. Please carry on our civilization and our legacy. Maybe one day you will discover the technology to defeat the Dread armor. Maybe one day, you will avenge us.

"This will be the last transmission sent. Good luck, and Godspeed."

30

The recording ended. The hologram vanished.

The room was still. Silent.

The only sound Gabriel heard was the thumping of his pulse in his ears. The only thing he felt was the heat of his anger and anguish rising into his face, at the same time the skin along his arms prickled from a sudden, intense chill.

What the hell had just happened?

Everyone in the room was in shock, except for Angela, Colonel Graham, and General Cave. They had known. They had heard it earlier.

It was over.

Just like that.

He felt sick. He felt weak. He wanted to cry. To punch something. To close his eyes and not wake up. What was his father going to think when he heard about this? Would he even survive the news?

Colonel Graham picked up the tablet and made the long walk back to his seat. The room remained silent.

Gabriel looked at him as he sat. Graham's eyes were apologetic. He had decided he wanted to keep fighting as much as Gabriel did. It seemed God had other plans.

"Do we even need to hear Guy's report?" Charles asked. "I think the way forward is looking pretty clear."

"Is the Council ready to vote?" Angela asked.

"Aye," they all responded. Even Captain Sturge's wife, Siddhu.

Gabriel had come to argue, but there was no argument left. Even the people on Earth didn't want the New Earth Alliance to help them anymore.

"Okay. All in favor of retrofitting the Magellan and preparing for the trip to Eden, please raise your hand."

Every hand in the Council went up without hesitation like a dozen knives through Gabriel's heart. He felt each one individually, stabbing into his soul and stealing everything he had ever believed in.

Beside him, Major Choi gripped his arm tighter. "It will be okay," she said softly, trying to help him through it.

"Very well," Angel said. "The Council moves to-"

"Um. One minute, Councilwoman Rouse," a voice said from her right.

Gabriel's head felt like it was about to explode, but he still managed to turn it, finding that one of the scientists, the one from the pod, had stepped forward.

"Is there a problem, Reza?" Angela asked.

"Hmm... Well, it's not a problem per se," the scientist replied. "I mean, it is a problem, but it isn't completely- well, it is kind of related to this."

"Reza, we talked about this," the other male scientist said. He had to be Guy. "Your numbers are off."

"Hmm... No. I don't think so. In any case, I think the Council needs to know about this before they make any decisions."

"That's why you wanted to come here? To question our work?"

"I wanted to come to make sure everyone here is informed."

"Informed about what?" Angela said.

Guy moved ahead of Reza. "My apologies, Angela. I-"

"Informed about what?" she repeated.

The man stepped ahead of Guy. "The slipstream calculations to Eden. They're wrong."

"They are not wrong," Guy said.

"They are," Reza insisted.

"Guy, be quiet," Angel said. Guy closed his mouth, his face turning red. "Reza, tell us."

"There was an error made in the slipstream equations. Eden is too far away for the Magellan to reach it. To be precise, Guy's calculations assume a one-year retrofit and project out the slipstream currents to that date, making an estimate of plus or minus three months based on the wave power. I've checked every number three times, and that's just wrong. The travel time is going to be six months at a minimum, and the slipstream variation may be double that based on the planet's location."

"English, please," Lucille said.

"The Magellan was only designed to carry ten-thousand. There are twenty-thousand of us, give or take. If we try to make it to Eden, we'll starve to death," Reza said.

Angela didn't look happy with the news. "Guy?"

Guy made a face at Reza before turning to Angela. "Sarah and I both did the calculations, Angela. We are one hundred percent confident that they're correct. And, unlike Reza here, neither one of us flunked advanced calculus the first time we took it."

"That was a bullshit grade," Reza said, angry at the comment. "Mrs. Ramini hated me."

"Really, Reza?" the female scientist said, finally speaking up.

"Enough," Angela said. "Reza, can you prove the calculations are off?"

"I can show you my work."

"And we can show you ours," Guy said. "Angela, we've known each other for years. You know my work is solid. I'm not the Chief Astronomer because of my good looks."

Reza laughed at the comment, causing Guy to turn on him.

"One more time, Reza, and you'll be staying on Alpha for re-training. Maybe the military wants you."

Reza made a point of clamping his mouth closed before backing up a few steps.

"You can decide who you want to believe," Guy said to the Council.

"Sarah and I have fifty years of experience between us. Reza has only been in Astronomy for three years."

Angela looked over the rest of the Council, checking their expressions.

"I trust you, Guy," she said. "I think the rest of the Council does as well."

Reza didn't say anything at that comment. Instead, he stormed from the meeting room.

"General Cave," Angela said. "I expect a full report on the current configuration of the Magellan on my desk in two days, along with an estimate of how long it will take crews working double shifts to refit her. It's clear the Dread have tired of the humans on Earth. What if they get tired of us being out here, so close to them, as well?"

"Of course, Angela," Cave said. "I would like to point out that we have no reason to believe the Dread know we're out here. There has never been any sign of them anywhere near this system."

"There's a first time for everything, General. I don't want us to be here when that happens."

General Cave spread his hands in submission.

"Thank you all for coming," Angela said, turning to address both the Council and the assembled guests. "I hereby call this meeting adjourned." She tapped her touchpad, stopping the recording. Then she tapped her medallion against the table, ending the meeting.

Gabriel remained motionless in his seat as the Council members got up and began to file from the room. Graham exited without trying to say anything while Major Choi continued to squeeze his arm.

General Cave approached him a moment later, kneeling down to get to eye level. "I'm sorry, Gabriel," he said. "I never intended for things to go like this."

Gabriel stared at him, still unable to find any words. It was over because he had made it out with the message. It was over because he had survived.

"Do you want me to tell your father, or do you want to do it?" Cave asked.

Gabriel was silent. If only he had died, this wouldn't be happening.

There would still be an argument left to be had.

"You should do it, Gabriel," Major Choi said.

Gabriel looked at her. He wasn't going to cry in front of them. He pulled his arm away from her, glaring at General Cave as he got to his feet.

He left the chamber without a word.

31

"So, what do you intend to do?" Donovan asked, staring at Ehri. Her statement had chilled him to the core. Not because she intended it that way. Because it was true.

"I will observe," she replied.

"You won't call the guards or give us away?" Diaz asked.

"No. I wish to study your critical thinking patterns, threat processing capabilities, and problem-solving skills."

"Even if that means we kill some of your kind?"

"Yes."

"I guess that's why you said you would be better off if we were more alike. No human would ever agree to watch their own kind die in the name of science."

"I have studied Earth history. That may be true more recently, but it was not always so. Do you know of Nazi Germany, and what you called World War Two?"

"I've heard of it," Donovan said. "I don't know the details."

"It was not one of humankind's finest moments," Ehri said. "Though I have been able to draw some parallels between the leaders of that time and the Domo'dahm."

"How do you become the Domo'dahm?" Donovan asked. "Inheritance? Election?"

"Neither. Genetic testing. We look for markers that highly correlate with strong leadership. We call them the pur'dahm. These bek'hai are raised to become Domo'dahm. Of course, only one will, and only if the current Domo'dahm dies. It is extremely competitive. Even so, simply being one of the chosen elevates a bek'hai to what you might call a prince."

"Are they all as violent as the current ruler?"

"Just like I am different from my clones, the Domo'dahm are all quite different. Tuhrik was once a pur'dahm. He abandoned the cell to pursue his desire to study humans."

"So you're saying if we can kill this Domo'dahm of yours, we might be able to get a replacement that will stop trying to destroy us?" Diaz asked.

"It is not that simple. No. My suggestion to you is to find your way out of here. To take what you have learned to your people."

"I thought you were just an observer?"

"It is only a suggestion."

"Thanks for the idea," Donovan said, turning to Diaz. "I'm starting to think; this is a one time opportunity. There's no point in going back to base with nothing but a few alien vocabulary words."

"I agree. We should try to find something more substantial. Something that can help us survive, and maybe even fight back."

Donovan turned back to Ehri. "The other bek'hai in here. Are they armed?"

"Do you mean bek'hai, or clones?"

"Both."

"The soldiers are. Most others will raise an alarm if they see you."

"They won't attack us?"

"Only if they are armed."

Donovan stared at the clone. She had a pretty face. A sweet, compassionate face. She was biologically human. He had to remind himself she was still the enemy. All of her talk of observing could be nothing but talk. They had no way to know if she would raise the alarm as soon as they left this room.

"You're wondering if you can trust me," she said.

"Yes."

She stood up. He held the knife, following her across the room to a blank space on the wall.

"Put your knife to my back." She reached back and lowered her dress enough to expose her skin. "Here. A heavy stab will sever my spine."

"What are you doing?" Donovan asked.

"Earning your trust. Duck down. You don't want to be seen."

Donovan did as she said, pressing the knife to her porcelain flesh. She waved her hand, and the wall turned into a video screen.

"Surhm, Aval, Trinia, your attention," she said in English.

Three identical versions of her stopped what they were doing, turned, and stood at attention before her. The hand holding the knife tensed, as Donovan prepared to stop her from giving them away.

"Dahm Tuhrik has chosen to remain in his chamber for today. Please continue your work as assigned."

"Yes, Si-Dahm," they replied together.

"Also, remember to practice your human languages. Understanding is the key to assimilation, and the future of the bek'hai."

"Yes, Si-Dahm."

She waved her hand, and the screen vanished.

"You can remove the knife now," she said.

Donovan pulled the knife away. Ehri turned to face them. "I have now had the opportunity to steal your weapon and use it against you. I have had the opportunity to signal an alert that would guarantee your capture. I have also shown you that I have not lied to you about Tuhrik's studies. Is there something else you would like me to do to prove that I will not betray you to the others?"

Donovan glanced over to Diaz. She was thoughtful for a few moments and then shrugged.

"I can't think of anything," she said. "It's your decision, D. Trust her or kill her?"

Donovan handed the knife back to Diaz. He trusted Ehri with a certainty that surprised him. That fact gave him an idea.

"I'm going to trust you, but I also have a proposal."

"A proposal?"

"If you want to study humankind, you need a bit more exposure than just the two of us trapped in a maze. The sample size is too small, and you won't learn anything about who we are when we aren't under the gun."

She smiled softly. "What do you suggest?"

"Do a little bit more than observe. Help us get out of here, and then come with us." He figured she would say no, but there was no harm in trying.

The offer seemed to catch her off-guard. She took an involuntary step back. "You want me to help you? You want me to come with you? Why would I do that?"

"You're a scientist. You want to study humans. The best way to do that is to spend time with us."

"Donovan, you can't," Diaz said. "We don't know-"

"I can," Donovan interrupted. "It's my decision, remember? Look, you said it yourself. There's no way we can win in the end. So what's the harm in helping us get out of here, and getting to spend some time in our world? You clearly don't care if some of your kind die in the process, and that's the worst that can happen."

She stared at him in silence. He began to wonder if he was wrong about her. Would she change her mind and raise an alarm instead?

"I admit, I am intrigued by the idea," she said at last. "More than intrigued. I am excited by the potential. But also concerned. The Domo'dahm will send an army to destroy your base once it is located. There is a high probability I will die with you, and all of my learnings will be lost. It is one thing to sacrifice a few bek'hai in the name of science. It is another to sacrifice them for nothing."

"There isn't much I can do about that other than to promise to do my best to keep you alive," Donovan said. "It's high risk, high reward all around."

She was silent again, considering. Finally, she held up her right hand with her index and pinkie finger extended, and the rest of her hand closed.

"Put up your hand like this," she said.

Donovan copied the posture.

"This is how the bek'hai make deals with one another. Press your fingertips to mine."

Donovan did. The skin on her fingers was softer than anything he had touched before, and he could swear he felt a cool electricity pass between them as they made contact.

"We have a deal, Major. This touch is my bond."

"This touch is my bond," Donovan repeated.

He wasn't sure if that was part of the routine. It just felt right.

32

"Follow behind me," Ehri said. "Stay close."

She approached the door to Tuhrik's room, waving her hand and opening it. She took a step out into the corridor, checked both directions, and then continued moving. Donovan and Diaz filed out behind her. Donovan spared a glance back into the room, at Tuhrik's dead body, before the door slid closed. Whatever twist of fate had brought them here and guided them to that room, that Dread, and finally to Ehri, he was thankful for it. He had no idea how they would escape without her.

Even with her, it was no guarantee.

Ehri swept down the corridor, moving to the inner portion of the circular hub. The green light was visible ahead of them, growing in intensity as they drew nearer.

"Where are we going?" Donovan asked.

"The light is a transport mechanism," she said. "It will carry us to another part of the ship."

"That's the second time you said ship," Diaz said. "You mean this city is really a starship?"

"Yes. I suppose you are too young to have seen the bek'hai invasion."

"My grandfather always said the alien ships were massive," Donovan said. "I always figured he was exaggerating."

"All of the bek'hai live within a starship, each one connected to the other through constructed tunnels."

"We arrived through a drainage pipe. We came out in a huge room with a bunch of machines arranged around a central spire."

"A power generator. The energy is sent to the ships around it so that they don't need to cycle their reactors. This allows us to reduce maintenance and keep the ships ready for departure."

"Why do you need to be ready to leave?"

"We do not. It is an artifact of our past. When our planet collapsed, we were nearly destroyed for good."

"Collapsed?" Donovan asked.

"Yes. We mined it for every precious metal and resource it could provide. We didn't realize that by removing so much material we were weakening the very soul of the world. Small earthquakes turned into larger and more frequent earthquakes until the planet became unstable. Shortly after, it shook itself to death."

They moved past hatches on either side of the corridor. Ehri didn't seem concerned that they would open, and Donovan guessed she knew for certain that they wouldn't. The green light was right on top of them now, and Donovan could see it wasn't a normal light. There was a near-transparent platform at ground level, and shimmering motes flowed within the luminescence.

"We must step in together, or we will be separated," Ehri said.

"How does it work?" Diaz said, looking uncertain about it.

"Are you familiar with quantum entanglement?" Ehri asked.

"No."

"It is something like that. This one teleports vertically."

"How do you control direction?"

"With your hands. You will see."

They reached the lip of the light. Ehri reached out and took Donovan's right hand with her left, and Diaz's left hand with her right. As before, he marveled at how soft her skin was, and how alive it felt beneath his palm. Judging by Diaz's expression, she was experiencing something similar.

"Here we go."

Ehri stepped onto the platform with them. Donovan felt a moment of panic, afraid they were going to plummet straight down, where only more of the light awaited them. Instead, Ehri lifted his hand, and he could feel he was rising. He could see the floors slipping past his eyes too fast to count.

Seconds later, she lowered her hand, and they came to a stop.

"This level is equal to the ground level outside," she said. "The exit is not far, but there are more bek'hai soldiers up here than there are below. Below is for the passive."

"Exit?" Donovan said. "Wait a minute. I thought you were going to help us?"

"I am helping you to escape."

"We aren't ready to escape," Diaz said. "It doesn't do us any good to get out of here if we have nothing to bring back."

"You have me," Ehri said. "I have a large quantity of information about the bek'hai that I am willing to share."

"Do you know how the armor works?" Donovan asked.

"Armor?"

"The black carapace that covers everything. We've never been able to defeat it, not even with our best weapons."

"Your weapons are inferior."

"I know. Until we can overcome it, we have no chance of winning."

"I told you that you will lose."

"Yeah, well, I'm not ready to lose yet. If you don't know how to defeat it, is there someone here who does?"

"I'm certain there is," Ehri said.

Donovan came to a stop. "Why the sudden freeze?" he said. "Are you having second thoughts?"

"I made a promise, Major. I will not break it. I don't know much about the carapace, as you put it. It is not my area of study. If you want me to bring you to someone who might, we will have to go back down. The longer we linger here, the more likely it is you will be killed, and I am not eager to see that happen. I do not want to lose my opportunity to witness human interaction."

"We can't leave without something," Diaz said.

Ehri was about to answer when her eyes narrowed, and she motioned them off to the side of the hallway. A moment later, what Donovan assumed was a bek'hai soldier walked past.

It was taller than Tuhrik. Taller even than Gibbons. At least seven feet, maybe more, with thick, heavy limbs and a much larger head than the scientist had possessed. The same white skin, silver hair, and ridges were partially obscured by black cloth beneath a chestplate of the dark armor. It glanced their way as it passed, not registering alarm when its eyes fell on Ehri, and she raised her hand, three middle fingers extended out in what looked like a form of salute.

It continued past. Donovan could feel Ehri's tension ease.

"We are fortunate," she said. "Klurik is a pur'dahm. He barely sees other bek'hai; I doubt he noticed you at all. Still, we must be more careful."

"We need to go back down," Donovan said. "We may never get another chance like this, and I'm sorry, but the only way us humans survive is for us to come out of here with useful intel. If that means taking another scientist by force, then that's what we have to do. Ehri, if you don't want to be part of this, we can go on our own."

She shook her head. "I told you, Major. I wish to observe how you think and act. Every decision you make is part of that, regardless of my hopes for what I will learn. If you are going back down, then I am going back down."

They turned back toward the transport, only a few meters away. As they stepped toward it, a figure stepped out. A clone soldier. Its eyes grew large as it took in the sight of them.

Diaz didn't give it time to recover from the surprise. She was on it in an instant, her knife slicing cleanly across its neck while her hand covered a mouth that barely had a chance to scream.

"Druk," Ehri whispered beside Donovan. "We cannot go back. Not now."

"Diaz took it out, it's fine," Donovan said, moving toward the transport.

Ehri grabbed his arm. "No. All soldiers are tracked and monitored. They will know he is dead, and they will send a team to discover how."

Donovan looked back at the green light and Diaz kneeling over the dead clone in front of it. Was Ehri lying to get them to leave?

"Major, please trust me," Ehri said.

Again, Donovan decided he would. "Diaz, let's go."

"What?" Diaz said. "D, we can't."

"No choice. Our cover is blown. Come on."

She hesitated.

"Thats an order, Lieutenant."

Diaz ran back to them. They ran together to the end of the hallway. Ehri brought them to a stop when they arrived, cautiously peering around the corner.

"The barracks are that way," she said, pointing to the right. "There is an exit this way."

They went to the left. They hadn't gone far when somebody shouted something in the alien tongue behind them.

"Run faster," Ehri said.

They did. Donovan felt the heat of plasma bolts on his back a moment later, striking the area around them. There was another corner up ahead. All they had to do was reach it.

They did, moving so fast that it made turning the corner difficult. Donovan slammed his injured shoulder into the wall, absorbing the intense pain, momentarily blinded by a plasma bolt that hit the wall in front of him. The wall sizzled for a moment but remained unharmed by the blast.

"Donovan," Diaz said, urging him forward. He was too slow compared to her and Ehri. He fought off the pain and surged ahead.

"How far?" he heard Diaz ask.

"A few more corridors," Ehri replied.

"We aren't going to make it."

It was his fault. He wasn't a fast runner to begin with, and his injury was only making it worse.

"Go. Leave me here, I'll hold them off."

He shouldn't have said it. Diaz came to an abrupt stop, forcing Ehri to stop a moment later.

"Not going to happen, amigo," Diaz said. "Keep moving or we all die."

"There's no time," Ehri said. "We'll have to try to lose them and come back. This way."

She waved her hand in front of a hatch Donovan hadn't even seen. It slid open to reveal another corridor. It was smaller than the one they were in and barely lit at all.

"Do not slow down," Ehri said, running ahead of them.

She moved through the passage like she had done it a thousand times, navigating from one corridor to another, one door to the next. Diaz and Donovan struggled to stay behind her, following her through the bowels of the alien starship. Donovan wished he had more time to admire the technology and to make sense of what each piece of equipment did. Earth had been in its space-faring infancy when the Dread had arrived, and his only experience with it was climbing through part of the wreckage of the Chinese colony ship Wèilái.

He lost track of how long they were running for. Ten minutes? Twenty? What he did know was that they didn't see another living thing the entire time. For all the systems buried beyond the main livable space of the starship, it seemed that little needed to be done to maintain it.

Finally, Ehri came to a stop in front of a hatch. She waved her hand, and it slid open. "In here."

Donovan's chest was pounding, his breathing heavy from the exertion. Diaz was in better shape, but still breathing hard. He looked at Ehri. She wasn't winded at all. "Where are we?" he asked.

She smiled. "Go inside."

She was silently asking him to trust her again. He didn't hesitate this time, nodding and stepping through the doorway.

"Dios Mio," he heard Diaz whisper behind him.

"Why would you do this?" Donovan asked.

33

"You wanted me to help you," Ehri said. "This was all I could think of."

Donovan's eyes darted around the room. It was a small space, no bigger than a supply closet. It was the contents that made it count.

He reached out, putting his hand to one of a hundred plasma rifles that rested in racks on the floor while his eyes fell on a suit of the black armor near a second hatch in the front of the room. It was way too big, even for him, but just seeing it left him in awe.

"An armory?" Diaz said. "You brought us to an armory?"

"You deserve a chance to fight your way out," Ehri said. "The odds are still against you, but if you escape you will have earned it."

Donovan lifted the rifle from the rack. Of course, he had held the same kind of weapon before. When they were taken from fallen clones, they were always inactive and unable to be used. This one made a soft humming noise as he wrapped his hand around the grip. A small display of alien symbols appeared on the side of it.

"It isn't secured," he said, feeling a sense of awe to be holding an active version of the weapon.

"No. The coding process occurs when it is lifted by a soldier. You do not have the genetic markers for the process to occur."

"You're saying we can walk out of here with this?" Diaz said, lifting a rifle of her own.

"If you survive, yes."

Diaz looked at Ehri as though she wanted to hug the clone. "We'll survive. Won't we, amigo?"

Donovan nodded. "Can we go back the way we came?"

"Yes." She lifted her head slightly. "They are still tracking us. We won't get back out without a fight. Come on." She motioned toward the door.

"Aren't you taking one?" he asked.

"I will not harm my own," Ehri said.

Donovan couldn't argue with that. They followed Ehri back out into the depths of the ship, retracing their steps. They hadn't gone far when Ehri waved them into a small niche in the wall. The soldiers appeared a moment later, moving efficiently through the space while scanning it for signs of their passing.

Donovan lifted the rifle, sighting down the barrel. "Diaz," he whispered, using his other hand to direct her. She raised her rifle, taking aim.

"Make it painless for them if you can," Ehri said.

Donovan pulled the trigger. There was no kick from the weapon, only a gentle wave of heat as the plasma bolt launched across the area and hit its target in the chest. The clone crumpled to the ground.

Diaz fired at almost the same time, catching her target in the chest as well. The other clone soldiers scrambled to find cover and at the same time figure out where the attack was coming from. Donovan hit another as it moved toward a pipe that ran from floor to ceiling.

"We can't afford to get bogged down here," Donovan said. "Ehri, which way?"

He looked back at her. The alien scientist's face was completely pale. She had to be wondering if she had made a mistake.

"Ehri?" he asked again.

"That way," she replied, regaining herself. "Down the corridor to the third crossing, turn right."

"Did you get that, Diaz?"

"Yes, sir."

Donovan took point as the return fire began coming in. He crouched low, checking on Ehri to make sure she was staying down as well. They had the high ground, giving them a strong advantage in the fight. He fired down at targets as they moved away from their cover to shoot back.

"Be careful of your rate of fire," Ehri said. "If the symbols turn yellow, it is a warning that the weapon is overheating. If they turn red, you are running out of power and the weapon will need to be recharged."

"Recharged?" Donovan said, suddenly aware of how many shots he was taking. He was stupid for thinking the alien weapon would have unlimited ammunition.

"It takes approximately one thousand bolts," Ehri said.

He was glad to know he wouldn't be running out of power soon. He fired more slowly, taking better aim as they finished crossing the space and reached the corridor. They started running again as soon as they did, heading back the way they had come.

"Where is everyone?" Donovan asked a short time later. They were nearly back where they had started and had yet to encounter any other soldiers.

"They'll be waiting for you at the exit," Ehri said.

"Wonderful," Donovan replied. "How are we supposed to get past them?"

"I know another way out."

"You seem to know everything."

Ehri smiled at the statement. "I am educated; that is all. I hunger for knowledge of all kinds. It is my reason for being. This way."

She led them off in another direction, bringing them through a second series of twists and turns until they finally reached a narrow passage that ran along the top corner of a massive hallway. Moonlight streamed in from a huge open portal at the end, and Donovan could see the green of the landscape growing around it.

"The launch tunnel," she said. "They won't expect you to go out this way."

"How do we get down there?" Diaz asked.

"There is a transport at the end, near the opening."

Ehri led them to it. Donovan stepped into the green light without hesitation this time, enjoying the feeling of the quick, controlled fall to the lower level. He waved open the hatch ahead of her, eager to get away.

They stepped out onto the floor of the ship, only a few meters away from the outside world and their freedom. Donovan could just barely make out the outline of Mexico City in the distance, a wisp of smoke still rising above it from the earlier battle there. The pipe had carried them a good ten kilometers.

He took a few steps forward.

One of the Dread stepped out in front of them from the side of the opening. Donovan recognized it immediately as the pur'dahm that had crossed their path earlier.

He had been unarmed that time. He wasn't unarmed anymore. A large rifle rested in his hands, and a large, primitive knife hung from a belt at his hips. The soldier was also wearing a mask with tubes coming out the sides, leading to something behind his back.

He barked something at Donovan, pointing the rifle at him. Donovan stood motionless, his weapon aimed back at the bek'hai warrior.

"Klurik," Ehri said, moving between them. "Step aside."

"You don't command me, lor'hai," the bek'hai said in choppy, guttural English. "Are you helping this lor'el?" He sounded amused. "I thought it was you. I knew you would come here."

Donovan glanced over at Ehri. It was obvious these two had some kind of history, and it didn't seem like a positive one.

"They were trapped. It is just to allow them to return to their kind."

"The Domo'dahm has ordered all lor'el dead."

"Then let them die with their own when you discover their hiding place. If you discover it."

The choking noise had to be a laugh.

148

"I will find it myself," Klurik said. His head shifted. Donovan couldn't see the bek'hai's eyes, but he knew the alien was looking at him. "Drop the weapon, and you may go."

Donovan tightened his grip on the rifle. Where was Diaz, anyway?

"I'm going with him," Ehri said.

Another laugh. "You are lor'hai. You do not make decisions on your own. Did Tuhrik put you up to this?"

"He asked me to accompany the human. He wants me to study them. I agreed to help this one escape in exchange for the chance to observe."

"The Domo'dahm-"

"Is above such things," Ehri said. "It was Tuhrik's decision to make."

"Very well. I cannot promise your safety when we locate the lor'el."

"I don't need you to protect me."

"There was a time when you respected me."

"And there was a time when you respected me," Ehri said. "Before you decided the lor'hai were not worthy of respect."

Klurik lowered his rifle. "Drop the weapon, and you may both go."

Donovan looked over at Ehri again. She nodded, and he threw the rifle to the ground. Klurik's head shifted to follow it. A plasma bolt burned past Donovan's ear, catching the bek'hai in the chest and throwing him to the ground.

"Got him," Diaz said. Donovan turned around, finding her at the edge of upper passage, aiming down at them.

Donovan hadn't realized he was holding his breath. He let it out, bending over to retrieve the rifle.

There was movement in front of him.

Donovan grabbed the weapon, dropping to his knees and turning toward the motion. Klurik was on his feet, the knife in hand. A slight burn mark was all that remained of Diaz's attack. The armor had absorbed the blast.

The bek'hai lunged at him, a rough growl pouring from behind the mask. Donovan fired the rifle, watching the plasma bolt hit the armor. It pushed at the alien, but he was ready for it this time, and he took the shot without slowing.

"Major, the switch on the left side," Ehri said.

Donovan knew the alien weapon well enough to know what she was referring to. He found the switch and flipped it down. The rifle began to vibrate, suddenly feeling lighter in his hands. Klurik was almost on him, the bek'hai completely airborne as it sought to run him through.

He pulled the trigger. This time, the plasma bolt struck the chestplate, burning into the alien and through and striking the oxygen tank on its back.

It exploded.

The force of the blast threw Donovan and Ehri backward, covering them in the enemy's blood and gore.

Donovan cursed as his shoulder hit the floor and was wrenched back out of position. It hurt so much; he wanted to stay there and wait for it to stop throbbing. He knew he couldn't. He dragged himself up, getting to his feet at the same time Diaz reached him.

"Donovan," she said, running over and throwing her arms around him.

He threw his good arm around her waist to hug her while he turned to find Ehri. She was standing with her face dripping the bek'hai's blood; her expression horrified.

"We need to go," Donovan said. "Ehri?"

The clone looked back down the launch tunnel as if she were trying to decide what to do. She had come to observe how humans lived, not how her own kind died.

"Ehri?" Diaz said.

The alien scientist looked back at them.

"I'm ready," she said.

34

Gabriel rolled over, trying to ignore Wallace's attention as the dog attempted to get him out of bed. His bathroom was two levels up, and he had to go.

"Leave me alone," Gabriel said, pushing at the dog's side with his hand.

Wallace didn't quit.

"Okay. Okay."

Gabriel pushed himself up, turning to sit on the edge of his bed. He blinked the sleep out of his eyes, running his hand over his face. He hadn't shaved since the Council meeting, and a rough growth of hair was sprouting.

He stood up, ambling unevenly toward the door. Wallace rushed ahead of him, waiting and wagging his tail.

"Don't do that to me," Gabriel said. "There's nothing to be happy about."

Wallace ignored him. Gabriel opened the door, and the dog dashed out into the hallway. That was the problem with dogs. They were always happy. It didn't matter what went wrong. It didn't matter if you felt like your whole world was falling apart around you.

He ran his hand through his short hair, his door closing behind him. The corridor was empty save for the two of them, and he was thankful for that. It had been challenging to avoid everyone else on Delta Station for the last three days. He could imagine what they would say. He could imagine what they were already saying about him, about his father, and about the end of the war.

He was still wearing the same uniform from the Council meeting, wrinkled and messy and certainly smelling awful. He knew anyone who saw him like this would find his reaction pathetic.

Especially his father. He winced as his mind returned to the thought that he had run away instead of dealing with the outcome like a man and being the one to go to Theodore and tell him that his fight was done. He knew what he was doing was wrong. He could hear his father's voice in his head, telling him he was a coward, and that no St. Martin ever shirked their responsibilities because they didn't get what they wanted. He could hear him calling him a baby, a spineless gator, and worse. His father had a colorful vocabulary, and he was never afraid to use it.

So why was he doing it? Why was he wallowing in self-pity, when he should have been attending the meetings Colonel Graham had scheduled to prepare Delta Station for breakdown and abandonment?

Because it was his fault this was happening. It was a thought he couldn't shake. The Dread starfighter had chased him hard, and his ship had taken enough damage that it needed to be grounded and repaired. He had considered himself lucky at the time, but now he realized it was just another cruel joke, courtesy of the God he didn't believe in. How many times in the last few days had he been tempted to take the crucifix his mother had left him and crush it beneath his boot? How many times had he stood in front of his window and stared down at the Magellan as if he could will things to be different?

His mother had believed, so much so that she had stayed behind, sacrificing herself to get others on board in her place. So much that she had chosen the love of an unseen, un-present thing over the love of her husband.

This was how He was repaying her? Making her death for nothing?

He made his way down the corridor, redirecting Wallace to take the stairs up the two levels to the park. There wouldn't be any traffic on the stairs.

He moved like a robot, his emotions careening from angry passion to total despair, and generally settling on a simple numbness that drove his feet forward. Wallace ranged ahead of him until he went too slowly, and then the dog would return and nudge at his legs.

Daphne and Soon were in the park when the hatch slid open and Wallace ran in. Gabriel had a strong desire to turn around, to get out before they saw him. It was early. They should have still been in bed. Most of the station was. They noticed the dog and then turned to him. He could see the pity register on their faces as they took in the sight.

He hated it.

He hated himself more.

He knew he needed to get out of the malaise. He knew he was supposed to be stronger than this. He was General St. Martin's son. The Old Gator's son. Weakness wasn't supposed to be in the vocabulary. He didn't want to feel this way, but he didn't know how to stop it.

"Hey, Gabriel," Daphne said, approaching him with none of the caution her husband was displaying. "How are you?"

Gabriel took a few seconds to answer. "I've been better."

She stepped forward, putting her arms around him. The move took him by surprise, and before he knew it, he had tears in his eyes.

Soon joined them more slowly, standing beside his wife and putting a hand on Gabriel's shoulder. When Wallace trotted back over, he used his free hand to pet him.

"You've always been passionate," Daphne said, looking up at him. "You get that part from your father. You've always run on your emotions. I think you must get that from your mother because from what I've heard your father can run cold as ice in any situation. It makes you strong, Gabe."

"No, it doesn't," Gabriel said, trying to get control over himself. His father would be so disappointed in him. The thought made it worse. "I'm a damn mess, and I can't stop myself."

"It isn't your fault," Soon said.

"Yes, it is. It was my mission, and I survived it."

"Come on, Gabriel. You can't do that to yourself. The 'what if's, the 'if only's. It doesn't work. For anyone. Ever. If it weren't your mission, it would have been someone else's. It might have been mine. Would you prefer if I were dead?"

Gabriel shook his head. "No. I don't mean it that way."

"I know you don't, but you aren't looking at the whole picture. You're seeing it from one perspective. A selfish one that wants to punish you for being alive."

Selfish? How was he selfish to want to have died? To have given his life to keep fighting?

"You're hearing your father's voice in your head, aren't you?" Daphne asked, finally pulling away. "Telling you that you're a failure? Telling you that you aren't enough like him?"

"Sometimes," Gabriel admitted. "And sometimes I hear him calling me every Cajun curse he knows because of the way I've been handling the fallout. I'm a failure on both sides of the ball."

"You aren't a failure for caring," Daphne said. "You've poured all of your energy into this war for the last fifteen years. You've gone on more runs than any other pilot over that time by more than double. You've put your life on the line over sixty times."

"You've also had your share of loss," Soon said. "Nobody expects you to take this like it's nothing or Colonel Graham would be ready to court-martial you for failure to show for duty. You're beating yourself up when nobody else is."

"My father is," Gabriel said.

"You know that for a fact?" Daphne said.

"I know him. I know who he is."

"From what you've told me, he isn't conscious enough of the time to be beating anything up."

"He's been waiting for me to come to him and tell him we've solved the secret of the Dread's armor. Every time I've been to visit him, I could see it in his eyes. Even when he barely knew where he was, or who he was, I could see it. I won't ever get to tell him that. And not only that. I should have been the one to tell him about the message from Earth, and I chickened out of that one, too."

"Gabriel-" Daphne started to say.

"And then there's my mother," Gabriel said, continuing over her. "Failing her memory is the worst of all. She was counting on us to win this war for her. It was her damn dying wish."

He could feel the anger rising again, the tears preceding it. He clenched his jaw and his fists, once more tempted to curse God for whatever part He had in this.

"It was always a long shot, Gabe," Daphne said. "You know that."

"It doesn't matter. I've always believed we would. I still believe we can."

"You heard the message from Earth."

"I don't care. I know our situation is bleak, but I don't know how to give up hope in it. I don't know how to let go of it."

"Maybe that's the real problem," Daphne said.

Gabriel froze, staring at them both. Was that the real problem? His entire life had revolved around the war with the Dread. He had literally been pulled out of cold storage and inserted into a surrogate womb to be born to fight them. Most children of the NEA were assigned to their future roles shortly after birth. They had assigned him before he had existed as anything more than a sperm and egg.

And now it was over, and he didn't know how to live without it.

"Gabe, are you okay?" Soon asked.

Gabriel nodded. "Not yet. I feel a little better. I should have talked to you sooner. Thank you."

Daphne smiled. "Anytime, Captain."

"Come on, Wallace," he said.

35

Gabriel went back to his quarters, finding a small measure of energy returning as he walked. He was still feeling depressed, and he still wanted to fall back on his bed and close his eyes.

He didn't want to do it as much as he had before he had taken Wallace up to the park.

It wasn't much, but it was something.

He fought to cling to that, to use it to push the feelings of hopelessness and loss from his head and his heart. He had handled Eva's death better than this. He had mourned, of course, but he had also volunteered to pilot the next mission. There was no better cure for the loss than getting back out there and doing what they had dedicated their lives to do.

Now that there was no more getting back out there, he realized he had to find something else to do. Some other way to contribute. He had to put his mother's memory aside. He had to put his father's promise aside. He had to drop all that he had ever been and turn into something else.

How?

He slipped into his quarters, feeling the depression returning in a hurry. There was nothing else for him. He was a starfighter pilot. He was a soldier born into a war, and now that the war was over there was no place left for him. He didn't have any other skills. What good would a starfighter pilot be on Eden?

He went over to his small storage cabinet and opened it, finding a nutrient bar inside. He tore open the package and broke it up in his hand before tossing it on the floor. Wallace hurried over to it, gobbling it down before Gabriel could make his way back to his bed.

Wallace jumped on the mattress, blocking his path. Gabriel stared at the dog's face. The big eyes, the lolling tongue, the content smile. His spirit was fighting to bring him back. So was his pet.

"Okay," Gabriel said, fighting against himself. "I'll clean myself up."

He wandered into the bathroom, grabbing his razor and sliding it along his face. It took a lot of effort, and every motion left him feeling exhausted. He was tempted to quit a few times, but each time he began to turn around and let his face stay half-shaven Wallace was standing there, still looking at him.

He finished shaving, peering at himself in the mirror. He looked awful. Pathetic. He closed his eyes, pushing that thought away. If he couldn't accept himself for his loss, he was never going to get back on his feet.

He slowly removed his clothes, his muscles burning from the work though he was hardly out of shape. He stepped into the shower, finding just enough time to get his hair washed before the water ran out. He hoped the flow had gotten enough of the old sweat and dead skin cells from the rest of him that he didn't smell too badly. He dried himself off, wrapping the towel around his waist and moving back out into his bedroom.

He eyed the bed. Wallace was sitting on it, a ball between his front legs.

"I'm not playing with you," he said.

Wallace looked at him with hopeful eyes.

Gabriel noticed that his comm was flashing. It had probably been flashing for days, but he had been too lost to care. He circled around the bed, ignoring Wallace as the dog picked up the ball in his mouth and turned with him, dropping it on the other side.

He tapped the control pad and scanned the list of messages. Colonel Graham. General Cave. Major Choi. Miranda. Daphne. Captain Sturges. Reza Mokri.

He paused at the name, mixed in with the others. Reza? The same Reza who had been at the Council meeting?

He didn't know anyone else with that name.

He tapped the message. The list was replaced with Reza's face, a little too close to the camera.

"Captain St. Martin," Reza said. "Um. I'm sorry to bother you, sir. I. Um. I know you don't really know me, but I saw you at the Council meeting a few hours ago. Um. I saw your face after Colonel Graham played that recording, and I, um, I mean, everyone knows about your father."

Reza was nervous. His olive complexion was more pale, and his eyes kept dropping down from the camera. He glanced back over his shoulder every few seconds.

"I need your help," he said. "What I said at the meeting about the calculations. I. Um. I'm not wrong, Captain. I'm certain I'm not. There's something going on here. Something that smells." He glanced over his shoulder again. "Eden is real. It is. I believe that. We can't reach it. I know that for sure. I've run the numbers. I've run simulations. It won't work with everyone boarding the Magellan. We'll run out of food and water." He looked over his shoulder. "I. Um. I think the others may be planning something. I think they intend to leave some people behind. Maybe the military? I don't have any proof. I wish I did. I can prove the math doesn't work. Come to Gamma to see me, Captain. I'll show you. We need to convince General Cave. He's the only one who can stop it."

Gabriel could see the door open behind Reza. Guy and Sarah entered the room. He must have been sending the message from the lab. Did he not trust his personal comm?

Reza knew they had come in. He leaned in a little closer.

"Come to Gamma, Captain. Help me. Please."

The message ended, switching the screen back to the list.

Gabriel sat in front of it, shaken, but not in a bad way. He could feel

his doldrums lifting like an evaporating cloud.
He had a new mission.

36

Gabriel smiled when Miranda's door slid open. "Hey, 'Randa."

Miranda looked surprised to see him. He had expected that. "Gabriel? Is everything okay?" She looked down at Wallace, standing beside him. "Hey Wallace. Who's my good boy." She kneeled down to pet him.

"Can I come in?" Gabriel asked.

"Of course." Miranda stood and led him into her quarters.

As a Senior Spaceman, she had her own room but it was a quarter of the size of Gabriel's. Soft music was playing in the background, and her comm was active, playing an old movie. He couldn't tell which one it was from a glance.

"What's up?" she asked as her door slid closed. "I heard from Daphne you were in pretty lousy shape this morning. You look okay to me."

"That depends on how you look at it. I've been pretty depressed since the Council meeting. This whole thing with Eden and the war. I'm sure you've heard."

"Everyone knows. I was at Colonel Graham's meeting earlier. They're planning to break down the fighters for their parts."

Gabriel felt a chill. "Already?"

"It's going to take a few weeks, but yes. Graham is under strict orders to get Delta Station out of operation within three months. They need the materials to refit the Magellan."

"Then we don't have a lot of time."

"Time for what?"

He hadn't realized he said it out loud. "Nevermind. I wanted to ask you for a couple of favors."

"Yes, I'll watch Wallace," she replied. "Where are you going?" She paused. "You aren't going to do something stupid, are you?"

Gabriel laughed. It felt good to laugh about something. "If I tell you, will you promise to keep it to yourself?"

"Gabriel, I know you're upset, but-"

"It isn't like that. Do you promise?"

"Fine. What?"

"Can I borrow your shower?"

"What?"

"I ran out of water, and I haven't bathed in three days."

"That's what you wanted me to promise?"

"No, but I'd like to finish cleaning myself up, and then I'll tell you."

She shook her head. "You're impossible. You're lucky I haven't used it yet. Go ahead."

Gabriel leaned down and kissed her on the cheek before heading into the bathroom. The small space didn't have a door, but he didn't mind. Miranda was like a sister to him. He quickly stripped, finished showering, and redressed himself.

"Now, spill it," Miranda said, pausing her movie as he came out of the bathroom.

"While I was out of commission, I got a message from a scientist named Reza Mokri. Do you know him?"

"It doesn't sound familiar."

"He's on Guy Larone's team. He was at the Council meeting the other day. He interrupted the meeting to try to tell the Council about a problem with Astronomy's calculations for the trip to Eden."

"What kind of problem?"

"According to his message, the trip is going to take a bit longer than advertised, and the only way to make it with enough food and water is to cut some of the population out of the exodus."

Miranda's face paled. "What?"

"Exactly. Reza suggested that there may be a plan in place to make sure it's the military personnel who get left behind."

Miranda was silent for a moment as she thought about it. "That doesn't make any sense. We have to be off Delta in three months. That isn't nearly enough time to get the Magellan ready."

"Are you sure? The ship is configured to support five-thousand right now. How long would it take to renovate some of the space into bunks, a hydro-garden, and a few extra recycling units for air and water? A month, at most?"

"Not for twenty-thousand."

"What about for ten-thousand?"

Miranda considered it, and then shook her head. "You can't be suggesting that there are people in the NEA who would leave others behind. They would essentially be murdering them."

"I don't want to believe it, and until I speak to Reza myself, I don't completely. He thinks it's true, and I don't get the feeling he's out of his mind."

"He could be looking for attention, or to get back at Guy for something. I've heard he can be a hard man to work for."

"It's possible, which is why I need to go to Gamma and talk to him. If there is something going on, I need to find out what it is and try to stop it."

"I don't know, Gabriel. You're a pilot, not a policeman. You should go tell Captain Tehrani about the message Reza left, and let him handle it."

"No. I can't. Reza came to me directly. He kept looking around like he was certain he was being watched. I don't know that I can trust Tehrani."

"She's a good person."

"She's also friends with Angela Rouse, who looked a little too happy about the message from Earth."

"What about your duties here?"

"I already put in a request for another week off. Colonel Graham granted it within five minutes. He knows there's nothing for me to do here."

"I'm not going to try to change your mind. God knows that I can't. You've got that St. Martin stubbornness. You're sticking your nose somewhere that you shouldn't. Be careful not to get yourself court-martialed or arrested."

"I'm only going to go talk to him. If anything does happen, you'll take care of Wallace? You're his favorite."

Wallace was laying on the bed, on her pillow.

"Something better not happen."

"If it does?"

"You know I will."

"Thanks, 'Randa. I left you access to my room. Feel free to hang out there if you want some more space."

Gabriel turned to leave. Miranda put her hand on his shoulder, and when he turned around she hugged him.

"Seriously, Gabe. Be careful. I already lost one best friend."

"They're scientists. They can't possibly be scarier than trying to outrun the Dread."

37

It had been seven years since Gabriel had been to Gamma settlement. He and Jessica had left their sperm and egg deposit with the registry on that trip, to secure their place as future parents once they were retired. Located on a small moon orbiting Taphao Thong, it was the most remote of the settlements, designed that way to both keep it obscured should the Dread ever show up in the system, and to protect the other settlements from the experimentation that occurred there. While the scientists took extra caution not to destroy anything, working with new technology meant there were never any guarantees.

Colonel Graham had authorized him to take a starfighter down to the settlement, since they would need to be delivered there for breakdown anyway. Sitting in the cockpit thinking that this might be the last time he was ever behind the sticks was a melancholy experience that might have led Gabriel back into his depression, if it weren't for the fact that his mind was otherwise occupied.

Miranda couldn't believe anyone in the NEA would be willing to let some of its people die to get the rest of them to Eden. While Gabriel didn't want to believe it, he was able to think that it was possible. He had seen Councilwoman Rouse's face when Guy had made his report, and how quickly she had sided with the Chief Astronomer. Was it because they were conspiring together, or was it because he was looking for something to fill the void left by the decision to end the war? Or maybe he was just looking for someone else to blame?

Gabriel adjusted his thrust as he neared the moon, bringing the fighter in more slowly than normal. The equipment in the settlement was sensitive to pretty much everything, which meant all kinds of extra rules around how things operated around it.

He eased the fighter through the open hangar, following a line of lights to the bay where they wanted him to land. He deftly maneuvered the vectoring stick, spinning the fighter in a neat one-eighty as he lowered it to the floor. He felt a wave of sadness as the small skids touched down, running his hand along the perimeter of the cockpit while he waited for pressurization. He lingered for a minute after the safety light had flashed to green before opening the shell and climbing out of his seat. He pulled off his helmet and set it down reverently, grabbing at his crucifix before hopping down and sending a thought to his mother.

The airlock slid open as Gabriel reached it. Lieutenant Curtis was on the other side, standing at attention as he approached.

"Captain St. Martin, sir," Curtis said, saluting.

"At ease, Lieutenant," Gabriel said. "I'm dropping SF-6 off for tear down. Has my return trip been arranged?"

Curtis shifted into parade rest. "Yes, sir. Spaceman Durvy will be ferrying you back to Delta in four hours."

Gabriel had asked Graham to arrange for him to have some time on the moon so he could tour the facilities. He hadn't been specific about the length of the trip to avoid possible suspicion, and he was happy to know he would have more than enough time to meet with Reza. He had sent only a single, obscure message to the scientist hours earlier in case the man's belief that he was being eavesdropped on was valid. Reza hadn't gotten back to him before he had left, so he figured he would find him now.

"Thank you, Lieutenant. Can you point me in the direction of Astronomy?"

"Astronomy, sir?" Curtis said, one of his eyebrows raising in curiosity. "Going to pick a fight?"

"Not quite," Gabriel said, smiling. "Would you want to assist if I were?"

"I'm friends with a lot of the team here, sir. Still, it would be tempting."

"I'll let you know if I change my mind."

"Yes, sir. Take the pod to the north wing, when you get off, go into the main concourse and turn left. Walk about half a kilometer."

"What about residential?"

"All of the scientists are segregated based on discipline. They don't like to be too far from their work. When you get to Astronomy, there will be a door to the lab in front of you. The passage to residential will be on your left."

"How do they manage it when an Astronomer marries a Chemist?"

"Excuse me, sir?"

"Never mind. I've got it. Thanks, Lieutenant."

"Of course, sir."

Gabriel took his leave of the hangar, casting one last longing glance back at the starfighter before he did. He followed the directions to the pod, climbing into the first that arrived and traveling the short distance to the central concourse. Like Alpha, this was where administration for the settlement was handled. Unlike Alpha, the area was nearly deserted in the middle of the day. He had always heard that scientists tended to be less social than other people, and his few trips to Gamma had proven it.

He crossed the concourse, drawing looks from the few people who were present. The soldiers in the space came to attention and saluted him as he passed while the others simply stared. He was sure most of them knew who he was, even if he had never met them. He was a rare enough sight in Alpha Settlement. He was like dark matter here.

A second pod ride brought him to the north wing of the settlement. The concourse was almost as quiet here, though it seemed they had chosen to use the hub as a food court. Three dozen scientists sat in random locations around simple tables, while a single cooking station prepared what smelled like fresh vegetables and synthetic meats. Gabriel had barely eaten in the last few days, and now that he was regaining some of himself the scent was more than tempting.

Like before, the scientists watched him pass. A few of them even waved or nodded their heads to acknowledge him. Others looked away when he made eye contact, embarrassed to be caught staring. He waved back to those who were friendly, and ignored the ones who weren't. He also scanned each face, looking for Reza.

He turned left and headed down the next corridor, stopping when he reached the full-sized hatch labeled 'Astronomy.' As he had guided the fighter in, he had seen the orbital telescope they used to scan the distant universe. Its construction had cost three times the resources as all of Delta Station, but both the science community and the Council had believed it was worth it.

He had been a child at the time, but his father should have seen the writing on the wall back then that the people were losing faith in their ability to overcome the Dread occupation.

He stepped up to the hatch. It slid open at his proximity, revealing another corridor that branched off into the science complex. He had no idea where he was going, so he just started walking.

He hadn't gone far when he nearly bumped into Guy Larone as he was exiting one of the rooms. The Chief Astronomer drew back in surprise at the sight of him, his posture and his expression instantly defensive.

Or was it guilty?

"Captain St. Martin?" Guy said. "I didn't expect to run into you here."

Gabriel struggled with his temper, fighting to keep it at bay. He really was getting back to normal.

"Reza invited me to have lunch with him," Gabriel lied. "Have you seen him?"

Guy's eyes twitched. "Lunch? I didn't realize you and Reza were friends."

"If you had, it would have given you more ammunition, right?"

Gabriel replied, immediately angry at himself for not being more reserved. He smiled. "I'm kidding. We aren't friends, or weren't, I should say. We've been commiserating over the fate of the people of Earth together. There is one scientist in the NEA with a conscience."

He could have kicked himself for going over the line again. Guy stared at him, obviously angry. The scientist shook it off.

"Well, in any case, you won't find Reza here. He's been shipped off to Alpha."

"To Alpha?" Gabriel asked.

"After his performance in front of the Council, Mr. Mokri decided that it would be a good idea to try to hack into off-limits portions of our datacenter to prove his inane theories. Needless to say, built-in safeguards alerted the IT Department to his shenanigans, and he was summarily both fired and arrested. I'm sure he would have told you, had his comm access not been revoked."

It was Gabriel's turn to stew. Maybe if he had checked his messages earlier, the scientist wouldn't have done something so stupid. He had come to Gamma under a false pretense, and now he would need a reason to transfer between settlements.

"You believe him, don't you, Captain?" Guy said while Gabriel was trying to think of a good excuse to use on Colonel Graham for bringing the SF-6 to Alpha.

"I didn't say that."

Guy laughed. "You don't need to say it. I'm not stupid, Captain. I know you despise my team for our discovery, and for ruining your game of make-believe war. It wasn't us that drove the last rivet into the starship. You can thank General Rodriguez on Earth for his surrender. The idea that we would make up numbers that are the basis of transporting every life in the Calawan system to Eden is not only preposterous but personally hurtful. Just because we believe in two different ways forward doesn't mean that we're monsters."

"I never said you were," Gabriel said. "Like I said, we were supposed to have lunch. We set it up before I left Alpha the other day. I had no idea what he was planning. Anyway, to be honest, I did want a little more clarity regarding his statements. Considering that there's a question about the numbers at all, and considering my position and the position of my father, I don't believe that is out of line."

"No, it isn't," Guy agreed. "I would be happy to show you the calculations if you're interested. Just give me some time to prepare, and we can meet to discuss them."

"Why do you need time to prepare? They're only numbers."

Guy laughed. "Only numbers? If that were true, you could do my job. Do I tell you flying a starfighter is only a matter of manipulating a pair of sticks?"

"Maybe another time, then," Gabriel said. "I only reserved enough time to eat and run back to Delta."

"Very well, Captain. Let me know when your schedule allows a longer visit."

"I will," Gabriel said. "If you'll excuse me."

He turned and headed back toward the exit. He could feel Guy's eyes on him, watching him leave. The confrontation left him with a bad feeling that Guy was full of shit.

38

The prison on Alpha Settlement was located in the central hub, through a secured hatch that led down into a subterranean area above where the large dome's anchors had been sunk into the earth. It wasn't a large area. The vast majority of offenses in the NEA were minor things like fistfights or verbal altercations or the occasional theft or vandalism by a minor. These crimes often led to a maximum of a day or two in prison for the citizen in question and meant they only needed a dozen cells for the entire population.

When Gabriel arrived, he learned that only four of them were occupied. He didn't know what the other three offenses were for, but the guard in charge of documenting visitors to the prison was happy to talk to him about Reza. Mr. Mokri was the first hacker to be arraigned in at least twelve years, and between his two-week sentence and Guy's request that he be re-assigned, it turned out he was somewhat of a fifteen-minute celebrity in the settlement.

That fact worked to Gabriel's favor since he needed something to use to convince the Spaceman to let him in to see Reza. He had no official reason to stop by, but he also didn't think that whatever the scientist had to say could wait. The short hop from Gamma to Alpha had given Gabriel time to consider, and the idea that Reza had been framed had wormed its way into his head. It was Guy's attitude that had done it. Gabriel's father was arrogant, but the Lead Astronomer put that arrogance to shame. There was something there. Something Guy wasn't saying.

He was sure of it.

Fortunately, Spaceman Lee was a fan of Gabriel's exploits and an even bigger fan of the Old Gator. He was more than happy to let Gabriel in to meet Reza and to keep quiet about it. After all, what harm could Gabriel do in talking to him?

The cells weren't much different than the standard residential quarters, save for their slightly smaller size and open, barred entry. Each was identical, equipped with a simple bed and mattress, a small room with a toilet, and a comm unit for watching movies or reading.

Reza was laying on his stomach on the bed cradling his handheld, looking as distracted by it as he had at the loop station. He didn't notice when Gabriel approached with Spaceman Lee, continuing to tap on the device with his thumbs.

"You've got a visitor, Reza," Lee said.

"I thought I asked you not to let anyone in to see me," Reza said without looking up. "Are they media?"

"Reza, it's Gabriel St. Martin," Gabriel said.

Reza's head snapped in Gabriel's direction. He looked flabbergasted that the pilot had come to see him. "Captain St. Martin. You were the last person I expected here after I never heard back from you."

"Spaceman Lee, can you give us a few minutes alone?" Gabriel asked.

"Of course, sir," Lee said. "Do you want to go in?"

"Yes, please."

Lee put his thumb against the door. It unlocked, and he held it open for Gabriel, who went inside. Reza shifted to a sitting position so Gabriel could join him.

"I'll be back in twenty minutes," Lee said before leaving.

"Sorry it took me so long to come," Gabriel said. "I took the news about the resistance pretty hard."

"You're here now," Reza said.

"Why are you here?"

Reza shook his head. "Ugh. So stupid. When I didn't hear back from you right away, I thought maybe I could entice you to listen to me by getting at least a little bit of proof about my claims. I had seen Guy and Sarah's original workup on Eden on our servers, the one with the skewed numbers. I wanted to transfer a copy to you. But Guy knew I wasn't going to let things be, so he set a trap for me, and I wound up here. Like I said, it was stupid, but I needed to get your attention. You're the only one who can help me."

"Why am I the only one? If you had irrefutable proof that the math is wrong, then-"

"I tried to tell the Council," Reza said, interrupting. "You saw where that got me. The Larones have all the experience, and I'm just an upstart who switched out of mechanical engineering because I was bored."

"You switched out of ME? Because you were bored?" To Gabriel, there was nothing boring about trying to improve machines. Especially their weapons systems.

"Yes. I thought Astronomy would be fun. I've been trying to put together this theory on slipspace and phasing that I think could change the way we look at the streams, and maybe increase our time and distance estimates to ninety-nine point nine percent accuracy. That's what I'm working on now, and that's why I'm sure the numbers are wrong. The bulk of my astronomical effort has been with slipspace. So, Guy is trying to discredit me."

"Getting arrested doesn't help with that. I came over here with the idea that you might have been set up."

"I know, I know. It was so dumb. No, I didn't get set up. I did it to myself, and I probably lost the only tiny shred of proof I have."

"Only that the math is wrong. What about the other thing you said? What about the idea of leaving people behind?"

"Exactly. I told you; it doesn't work any other way, but I can't even get anyone to consider the possibility if I can't prove the smallest part of it.

Well, except for you. You believe me, don't you?"

Gabriel stared at Reza for a few moments. "I'm not sure what I believe."

Reza leaned back, smacking his head against the wall. "Ugh. If I can't convince you, I can't convince anyone."

"You have to admit, the idea that there are members of the NEA conspiring to leave a good portion of the population behind is hard to swallow, when the worse offense we have around here is a food fight. You're talking about leaving people to die."

"They're willing to leave the people on Earth to die. What's the difference?"

Gabriel didn't have an answer for that.

"Who do you think is involved?" he asked.

"The Larones, of course," Reza replied. "Councilwoman Rouse. Councilman Giorno. Maybe a few others on the Council. Definitely some of the lead scientists beyond Guy. The head nerds are like an exclusive club, and they stick together."

"What about in the Space Force?"

"I'm not sure. I don't think so."

"It would be a major betrayal to go against one of your own," Gabriel said.

"Yes. The question is, how do we prove what they're planning?"

"Why did you say we?"

"The power of suggestion? I don't know how without the original, unaltered slipstream calculations, and I can't get them without you."

"You said they're locked away on a server on Gamma."

"They are."

"So how am I supposed to get them, assuming that I'm willing to help you?"

"You're a Space Force officer. You're legally allowed to request access to any file you want to see."

"I am?" Gabriel asked. He had never heard of that before.

"Yes. Since Space Force is also responsible for policing the settlements, you have rights to view any non-private document within the

NEA. Obviously, most pilots don't know about this, or if they do they don't care. It would be ripe for abuse if it weren't for the fact that, as you said, the worst offenses we have around here are usually food fights."

He shook his head, staring down at the floor.

"Unfortunately, not this time," he said.

39

"We aren't far now," Donovan said, pushing through the heavy brush.

It had taken the three of them nearly ten hours to make their way from the Dread starship to Chicoloapan, a suburb of Mexico City that had been leveled in the initial invasion. Like the capital, it was a ruined mess of destroyed buildings and dead vegetation, littered with debris and corpses picked clean by local wildlife.

"How can you keep your base so close, and remain undiscovered?" Ehri asked.

She had been incredibly inquisitive for the entirety of the journey, constantly asking questions of both Donovan and Diaz. Her energy level remained the same despite the trek while Donovan was just about ready to collapse.

"You'll see when we get there," Donovan said. Most of the answers he had given had been along the same lines. The bek'hai scientist was like a curious, impatient child.

They ambled along an empty street, with Diaz in constant motion, on full alert and scanning the sky for signs of enemy scouts, her captured plasma rifle held in a ready position. They had avoided a number of the machines getting away, with most of them tracking closer to the Dread colony. Ehri said it was because the pur'dahm in charge of the search wouldn't believe that they had managed to slip away. Apparently, arrogance wasn't a uniquely human trait.

There hadn't been any other sign of scouts in the last few hours, though there had been one flyover by a larger Dread ship, a starfighter. They had stopped and hid when they heard the whine of its engines approaching, watching it pass by pressed against the side of a rubble pile.

"How's your shoulder?" Diaz asked, checking in on him.

She had been much more attentive to him than she had ever been in the past, asking him how he was feeling every so often, her face strained with concern. It was a side of her he had never seen before, and while part of him liked it, another part wanted his cool as ice Lieutenant back. The whole episode had left him feeling all kinds of things he hadn't felt before, and he attributed it to loss of blood and lack of food and rest.

He expected that once both of them had slept the episode off they would go back to their professional respect and personal indifference.

"It hurts," he replied. "I need Doc Iwu to clean it out and make sure there isn't any shrapnel stuck in there. I bet there is."

"How do you manage such pain?" Ehri asked.

"The bek'hai don't feel pain?" Diaz said.

"Of course they can feel pain. We have medicines to remove it. Why suffer from something so unnecessary?"

"Pain teaches you to respect the fact that you're alive," Donovan said.

"In what way?"

"Because you never know how long you have. How many days or weeks or years before you get sick, or shot, or something."

"The bek'hai do not consider such things. We are each allotted the equivalent of one hundred of your years."

"Allotted?" Diaz said. "You mean you kill yourselves on purpose?"

"The bek'hai body cannot survive much longer than that because of the weakened genetic chain. Typically by that time we are ready to die. Perhaps once the integration has been perfected this procedure will change."

"I can't imagine surrendering my life," Diaz said.

"I cannot imagine wanting to survive in a body that no longer functions." Ehri said.

Donovan was about to chime in when he noticed a flash of light from a nearby rooftop. He glanced over at Diaz, whose eyes shifted, acknowledging that she had seen it, too.

"Ehri, whatever happens next, stay calm, okay?" he said. "I won't let them kill you."

"What?" Ehri said.

A dozen armed men and women poured out of the debris around them. They were ragged people in the same green cloth Donovan had been wearing earlier, except they had tattered boots covering their feet.

"Don't move," one of them said.

"Captain Reyes," Donovan said. He could imagine what the resistance soldiers were thinking, seeing him dressed in the enemy's cloth. "Major Donovan Peters. Identification code alpha-echo-foxtrot-four-seven-nine."

"Lieutenant Renata Diaz," Diaz said. "Identification code foxtrot-hotel-zulu-six-four-eight."

Captain Reyes froze along with the rest of the soldiers. He stared at Donovan, his eyes squinting despite the darkness.

"Donnie? Is that you?"

"I gave you my codes, Captain."

"The Dread take people. They make copies. How do I know you aren't one of those?"

"A copy wouldn't have the code. That's the whole point of using them. Besides, we've only been gone one day."

Reyes didn't lower his rifle. He pointed it at Ehri instead. "Who is this?" he asked.

"Captain, stand down," Donovan said.

Reyes stepped forward, his hands shaking slightly as he got closer to Ehri. "Who is this, Donnie?"

"We need to meet with General Rodriguez," Diaz said. "It's important."

"Is that a Dread plasma rifle?" one of the other soldiers, Corporal Wade, asked.

"Yes," Donovan replied. "But it's better than that, Miguel. It isn't secured."

A surprised murmur raced across the squad.

"Quiet," Captain Reyes said, still pointing the gun at Ehri.

She continued to follow Donovan's instructions, remaining completely calm, her hands at her sides, palms facing out. She reminded Donovan of a statue of the Madonna he had seen once.

"Who. Is. This?" Reyes asked again, his voice balancing fear and anger.

Donovan stepped toward him. Reyes backed up, pointing the gun at him again. "Don't. Just stay there, Donnie."

"That's Major to you, Captain," Donovan said. "Lower your weapon. That's an order."

"I don't think so. You walk in here dressed in whatever that leotard thing is, carrying an alien weapon with a freaking alien clone in tow, and you think I'm going to listen to you?"

"Julian," Diaz said.

"No. Shut up," Reyes said. "We haven't stayed hidden all these years by being stupid."

"You're being stupid right now. We're carrying active Dread plasma rifles. We could have already blasted you all to mush if that was what we wanted."

"Then you wouldn't know where the base is."

"I already know where the base is, jackass. I'll take you there if you stop pointing your gun at our prisoner."

"Prisoner?"

Ehri looked over at Diaz, unhappy with the title.

"Yes, prisoner," Donovan said. "We captured a Dread scientist. We need to bring her to General Rodriguez."

Reyes looked at Ehri again, his face twisting, losing its fear and turning to pure anger. "Dirty alien piece of-" He swung the gun toward her again.

Donovan stepped toward him, grabbing the rifle and yanking it up as Reyes pulled the trigger. The shot echoed across the landscape. Donovan wrenched the weapon from Reyes' hands, and then hit him in the face with the stock.

"You idiot," Diaz hissed. "They'll hear that for sure."

"You broke my nose," Reyes said, laying on the ground.

Donovan didn't care. His shoulder was throbbing, the wound pulled open by the motion. Reyes had always been too impetuous to be a good soldier, but beggars couldn't be picky. He was young and healthy and wanted to fight. Those were the only requirements, and even the young and healthy part could be overlooked.

"We need to get out of here," Donovan said. "Form up and let's go. That's an order, soldiers. You too, Reyes. Doc Iwu can fix your dumbass nose."

Reyes scowled, rolling over and getting to his feet. The group ran along the street, turning left after half a kilometer. Diaz took the rear, keeping a constant eye on the skies for signs of scouts.

They continued another eight hundred meters, to the edge of a collapsed building. A small space was visible at the bottom, barely large enough for a person to crawl out of.

"Let's go, people," Donovan said, stopping at the opening and waving the soldiers in. One by one they dropped onto their stomachs, rifles on their backs, crawling hand over hand into the small hole.

"No wonder they cannot find it," Ehri said.

"It gets better," Donovan replied. "You understand how much trust I'm putting in you right now?"

"Yes, Major. My touch is my bond."

"Right."

The rest of the soldiers went in ahead of them. Reyes glared at Ehri as he dropped to his knees. "She doesn't look like a prisoner to me," he said. "She isn't even bound."

"You have your own troubles to worry about, Captain," Donovan said. "Don't think I'm not going to report you for discharging your weapon in the open near the base like this."

Reyes was fuming, but he dropped to his stomach and disappeared a moment later.

"Anything?" Donovan asked when Diaz reached the hole.

She nodded. "Not drones. Something huge to the north, near the tree line. It's still a few kilometers away, but it definitely picked up the noise and is coming this way."

"A mechanized tactical armor," Ehri said. "You don't want to be out here when it arrives. I hope your base is well shielded from sensors."

Donovan smiled. "Don't worry. It is."

40

The collapsed space they had to crawl under continued for ten meters at a slightly downward angle. For Donovan, it seemed more like a thousand meters, as every motion of his arm going forward to pull himself along like a snake sent waves of pain up his back, and they didn't have time for him to take it slow and easy.

There was a drop at the end of the tunnel that usually meant reaching out hands-first and rolling to the ground. Fortunately, Diaz waited with Corporal Wade and they helped him down. Ehri stood off to the side, turning in a circle to examine the space.

"What is this?" she asked.

There wasn't much to see just yet. The floor and ceiling were both thick lead with a small crease in the center, and there was a second lead-shielded door to their right. It was open for now.

"You'll see," Diaz said.

They made their way to the door, ducking through and into a narrow, winding stairwell that dropped over one hundred meters. Corporal Wade stopped and pulled the door closed behind them, spinning the central mechanism to lock it. Then they started to descend.

The ground shook above them as the Dread's mechanized armor neared the position.

"Are we out of range?" Ehri asked.

"We should be," Donovan said. "The space we crawled through is a reinforced and lined air vent, and the part of the ceiling that isn't collapsed is the same. The sensors shouldn't be able to penetrate it. That's how we've been able to stay so close without being found."

The vibrations above them stopped.

"We've heard them pass over before," Diaz said. "It won't find us."

They continued the descent, winding a spiral on the stairs. There was another reinforced door at the bottom that was also still open.

"Oh," Ehri said. Donovan looked at her. She was smiling. "I finally figured out what this is. A missile silo, right? For nuclear warheads."

"Yup," Donovan replied. "Sans missile. It was launched at one of the Dread ships during the invasion. I'm sure you know how that turned out."

"Clever. Very clever. It was designed to stay hidden from sensors. The perfect hiding place."

"It is for as long as your kind don't know it's here."

"How did you know it was here?"

"We found a schematic while we were looting a military base a hundred klicks from here, after we had to abandon our last hideout. We weren't sure we could make it without being spotted, but once we did, we've been safe here for quite a while."

They reached the bottom of the steps and approached the door. A figure swung around in front of them, blocking the path. He had a gun in his hand, and like Captain Reyes, he raised it and pointed it at Ehri's head.

"Prisoner, Major?" General Christian Rodriguez said. "Then why are you telling her your whole life story?"

Donovan stepped between Rodriguez and Ehri without thinking. "General Rodriguez, sir. Please. I can explain."

The General smiled. "I'm sure you can, Donnie. We're going to have to lock it in the fridge until you do."

"The fridge?" Ehri said.

"Don't worry. It's an old industrial refrigerator. It was used to store the rations for the crew that worked down here, in case of emergency. The cooling pumps blew out years ago. It's cold, but not that cold."

"Unless you have superhuman strength, you aren't getting out of it," Rodriguez said.

"There's no need to point the weapon at me, General," Ehri said. "I will go willingly."

"Diaz, Wade, bring her down. Donovan, you come with me."

"Yes, sir," Diaz and Wade said. They walked on either side of Ehri, through a small control center and down a long corridor leading to the living area.

"Yes, sir," Donovan said. "I need to see Doctor Iwu at your convenience, sir."

"Are you hurt?"

Donovan nodded, turning to show the General his back. Even though the material couldn't be cut, a large stain of blood covered the area around the injury.

"Ouch. Five minutes, and then you can see Iwu."

"Yes, sir."

Donovan followed Rodriguez through the base along the same path Diaz and Ehri had taken a few seconds earlier. The three of them were already well ahead, walking at a much brisker pace. Ehri glanced back at him once. There was no hint of fear on her face. Only the same look of intense interest and curiosity.

"Did Cameron and Sanchez make it back?" Donovan asked as they walked.

"Si. They told me you were separated when the mech showed up. That you and Diaz drew it away so they could escape."

"Yes, sir."

"It was a brave thing to do."

"I would expect anyone else to have done the same for me in that situation, sir. It was the right thing to do."

"You're braver than most, Donovan. That's probably why you're still alive."

"I wouldn't be if it weren't for Renata. I sent her away as a decoy. She came back for us."

"Disobeying orders?"

"It worked out for the best, sir."

"Yes, I suppose it did."

The connecting tunnel ended at another heavy door, which was hanging open. A guard stood to one side of it, ready to close it in an emergency. On the other side sat an open supply room, a special room the resistance called the Collection. The accumulated non-essential possessions of the resistance were piled inside, loosely separated as though bringing them together in such a way could knit back a history of humankind. It had seemed almost quaint at the time, but the twenty-third-century resurgence of physical nostalgia - photographs, books, handmade arts and crafts and the like - had been a Godsend to the wanderers of the present. It was a solid, tangible connection to the past, to all they had once had, and a memory of what they had lost.

They crossed a series of corridors and doorways from there until they reached General Rodriguez's office. Donovan did his best to ignore the stares he was receiving on the way through the base. He knew how out of place he must look. How alien. He was self-conscious of it, and at the same time proud. They had brought a treasure back with them.

The office was located in the corner of the first floor; a simple, barren, and rarely used space with an older desk sat in the center flanked by a pair of chairs.

"Close the door," Rodriguez said, moving to the other side of the desk. He remained standing.

"Yes, sir. Am I in trouble sir?"

He spoke as soon as it had shut. "In trouble? Are you joking with me, Donnie? Let me see it."

"What?"

"The weapon, Major."

Donovan had forgotten he was still holding the alien plasma rifle. He held it out across the desk. Rodriguez took it, holding the grip and pointing it at the wall while staring at the active display.

"Wow," he said, shaking his head. He looked at Donovan. "Fifty years, Donnie. Fifty freaking years, amigo. How many of these things have we picked up, and they've been completely worthless? How many have we taken apart but couldn't get them to turn on?"

"It's better than that, sir," Donovan said. "We always wondered why they have that toggle on the side. Activating it changes the bolts somehow. They're able to pierce the Dread armor."

Rodriguez's eyes snapped from the gun to him. "You know this for certain?"

"Diaz used the other one to kill an armored Dread warrior."

"Seriously? You killed one of them? Do you have any idea what this means?"

"I have some idea."

"You don't know the half of it." He paused, wiping at the corner of his eyes. "I brought you in here because I didn't want the others to see me cry. I'm supposed to be the tough old General. Where did you get this? And those clothes you're wearing? That isn't cotton. Oh, and that woman you brought with you, the clone?"

"Just to be clear, General, you aren't mad that I brought her?"

"Should I be?" he asked.

"No, sir. She's earned my trust."

"That's good enough for me. You're a hero, Donovan. You and Diaz both. You may have just changed the entire face of this war." He paused again, lowering his voice. "I hope it isn't too late."

"Too late for what, sir?"

"We'll talk about it later. You need to see Iwu. We have a lot of work to do, and this changes everything." He shook the rifle. "Give me the short version."

Donovan spent the next few minutes briefing General Rodriguez on everything that had happened from the moment they had erected the needle. The General remained silent throughout, stroking the top of the weapon like the priceless artifact it was. His eyebrows went up as Donovan recounted in more detail how Diaz had killed the armored Dread, and a smile crept across his face.

"So we came back here. Everything was fine until Captain Reyes turned into an asshole with Ehri, like he's the only one whose family was killed by the Dread."

"I'll deal with Reyes. He won't be leaving the base again anytime soon. I know the Dread are sweeping the area right now because of his stupidity."

"Do you think they'll find us?"

"No. I sent Suarez up to collapse the vent just in case they decide to get too curious. It'll take a few hours to open it up again, but it's worth it."

"Yes, sir."

"Now, have Iwu clean you up and pass those threads over to Carlson so he can peek at it under his microscope. Here." He picked up the rifle. "Get this over to him, too. Tell him not to do anything to make it stop working, but we need to know everything we can about it, especially how it can get through the enemy's armor. Bek'hai, you said?"

"Yes, sir." Donovan took the rifle from Rodriguez. "What about Ehri, sir?"

"You trust her, and she looks like she trusts you. She'll stay under guard until you can escort her. I want to know everything she knows. I've been waiting a lifetime for an opportunity like this."

"Yes, sir."

"Dismissed, Major."

Donovan opened the door and left the room. He didn't see the wave of frightened concern that passed over General Rodriguez's face behind him.

41

Donovan found Chief Science Officer Carlson in his usual location. Face down on his cot in the barracks.

He had decided to drop the rifle and the alien clothing off first, grabbing a new pair of greens from Corporal Gosh in supply and carrying them with him to the bottom floor of the bunker. He didn't disturb Carlson right away, instead taking his time in getting the black cloth off his body. The pants were easy. The top wasn't. He grimaced in pain as his tugged at it.

"Whoever you are, and whatever you're doing, can you please stop?" Carlson said, his voice muffled from being buried in the pillow. "We have a separate room for that."

"Either shut up or help me get this off," Donovan said.

Carlson rolled over. He was an older man, a little pudgy, with thick gray hair and a large nose. He was disheveled in a button down collared shirt and slacks beneath an old and stained white lab coat. "Donnie. You made it back." He shifted back and forth a few times to get enough momentum to pull himself from the cot.

"Diaz and I both made it," he replied.

Carlson made a motion to give him a hug, but Donovan put up his hand.

"You wanted me to stop groaning, remember?" He turned so Carlson could see his back.

"Why aren't you with Iwu right now?"

"The General wanted me to bring you this." He pulled at the clothes. "And that." He pointed to the alien rifle, resting on an adjacent empty mattress.

"Is that-"

"Yes."

He forgot about Donovan, reaching for it. "How? What?"

"I'll tell you all about it later. The General said to examine it, but whatever you do, don't break it."

Carlson picked it up like it was an egg. "I don't believe it." He turned toward Donovan. "You're the damn messiah."

"I wouldn't go that far. Are you going to help me finish getting out of this, or what?"

"Right. Sorry, Donnie." He smiled as he put the weapon back down. "I got a little excited. Geez, I still can't believe it. I've been here since we found the place, and I never thought I would live to see the day."

"Is that why you spend so much time sleeping?" Donovan asked.

"I'm not sleeping. I'm thinking."

"Yeah, right."

Carlson grabbed at the alien cloth, helping Donovan wiggle out of it. The motion opened the wound again, and blood trickled warmly down his back.

"Don't waste your time with me," Carlson said. "Go see Iwu. I'm going to bring this down to the lab and get my people working on it. I'm glad I've been sleeping so much lately. I don't think I'll be resting again for a while. I'm so stoked."

"I thought you were thinking?"

Carlson laughed. "Shut up."

Donovan didn't put his shirt on, leaving his top half bare while he made his way back up one level to the infirmary.

"Where's Doc Iwu?" he asked George. The blonde-haired tween was one of the Doctor's four assistants-in-training.

"Hey Donnie," George said. "You've got a little blood on your side there."

"Thanks. That's why I came to see Iwu."

"She's in the back with Diaz. Let me take a look. Maybe I can help you? Take a seat over there."

He pointed at a small stool in the corner, near the racks of carefully labeled and organized medications that had been grabbed from anywhere they could find them.

Donovan sat down, turning his back to the boy.

"How does it look?"

"Hold on, I need to clean it out." He opened a few nearby drawers, removing some cloth and disinfectant. "This is going to sting."

"I'm used to it."

George worked at cleaning the wound. Donovan winced but didn't make a sound. The stinging was nothing compared to crawling through the tunnel.

"It's deep, but superficial. I imagine it's a bit sore?"

"You could say that."

"I'll stitch it up and get you a sling. Rest the arm for a week and you should be fine."

"George, don't take this personally because you're a good kid, and you're working hard at this, but I'd really like Iwu to take a look at it."

"I understand," George said. "Nailah's been teaching us that confidence is one of the most important traits of a good Doctor. You have to be sure that what you're doing is right. Which I am."

The slight turn on the statement wasn't lost on Donovan. "A little bit of arrogance doesn't hurt either, does it?"

"Nope. Nailah should be out any second. Diaz is in better shape than you."

"Doctors also need to not ogle their patients," Donovan said.

The door to the private examining room started to open. George lowered his voice. "I'm working on it, but between you and me, Diaz is gorgeous."

Donovan got to his feet. "Just wait until you reach puberty."

Diaz came out of the room first, smiling when she saw Donovan. She also had a fresh pair of greens on, though her alien outfit was still in her arms. "I'm glad Rodriguez didn't keep you too long," she said. "What did he say?"

"I'll tell you later," Donovan replied. "Is Ehri okay?"

"Why are you so worried about her? She's fine. It's probably boring for her in the fridge, though. There's nothing to look at, and nobody to interrogate."

Was that a hint of jealousy he was sensing?

Doctor Nailah Iwu was behind Diaz, and she also gave Donovan a wide, bright smile. She was an elegant woman, tall and thin, highly educated and well-spoken. "Major Donovan Peters," she said. "It looks like George has already started my work for me?"

"I'll catch up with you later, amigo," Diaz said, surprising him by leaning up and kissing his cheek. She left the room before he could respond.

"He has a laceration across his right scapula, ma'am," George said. "It's deep, but none of the muscles were cut. I recommended stitches, but Donnie wanted you to look at it first."

"George knows what he's doing, Major," Iwu said.

"I'm sure he does. It's just important to me that I'm ready for duty as soon as possible, and you can't argue that you're a master with stitches."

She laughed. "I've had too much experience. Come on back, I'll take a look. George, you too."

They followed her back into the examination room. It was necessarily low-tech, as it was difficult to keep the more advanced medical machinery operating with the limited resources they possessed.

"Sit facing away from me," Iwu said, patting the padded table.

Donovan did as he was asked. He felt Iwu's cold hands on his skin a moment later.

"George's prognosis is completely accurate."

"I told you so," George said.

"George," Iwu chided.

"Sorry, ma'am."

"Let me stitch this up. Keep the level of your arm below your head for the next week and you should be fine."

"No sling?" Donovan asked, looking over at George.

"I don't think that will be necessary."

George shook his head and looked away.

"Do you want something to bite down on?" Iwu asked. Stitches weren't a good enough reason for them to waste painkillers or numbing agents on.

"No, thank you."

"Suit yourself."

He could hear her moving behind him in quick, precise motions as she prepped the stitches.

"Here we go," she said.

He felt the first stab and closed his eyes, recalling his conversation with Rodriguez as she closed up the wound. The General had called him a hero. That was something to be proud of, and the part of the meeting he wanted most to hold onto.

He couldn't. Instead, his mind kept going back to a single statement the General had made and wondering what he had meant.

"I hope it isn't too late."

42

Gabriel was back on Gamma less than two hours later, after making up an excuse for Colonel Graham about how he wanted one last ride in the fighter before turning it in. Graham was gracious in accepting the reason, even though it was within his rights to dress Gabriel down for his actions. Gabriel wasn't going to risk angering the Colonel, and so he arranged for the transport to return him to Alpha when he was finished on Gamma, ostensibly to visit his father.

Lieutenant Curtis laughed to see him back so soon, and he was even more amused when Gabriel took a few minutes to relate his conversation with Colonel Graham. Once he had Curtis loosened up, he made his next move.

"So, Lieutenant," Gabriel said. "I have it on authority that officers in the Space Force have the right to access any files stored on shared resources?"

Curtis seemed surprised by the question. "I haven't heard of that."

"Look it up if you aren't sure. Article seventy-one, paragraph three." Reza had shown him the law on his handheld. It was a real thing in the

NEA law books.

"I believe you, sir," Curtis said. "I'm not sure why you're bringing it up, though."

"I need to make a copy of a file that I know is here on Gamma."

"I thought you came for a tour?"

"I did, but I also came to get the file."

Curtis seemed unsure. "I'll have to talk to Doctor Shore."

"Shore is a civilian," Gabriel said. "He has no jurisdiction over something like this."

Gabriel watched Curtis' expression. Reza didn't think any of the members of the military were in on the conspiracy. That didn't mean he was right. Curtis was stationed with the science team full-time. If any of the Space Force were going to side with them, it would be him.

"Look, it's not a big deal," Gabriel said. He made a face that he hoped looked somewhat pathetic. "I made a bet with the receptionist on Alpha. Danai. Do you know her?"

"No, sir."

"Well, she agreed to go out with me if I could prove the Eden mission was real, and that we really are going to get out of this system. I talked to Guy before I left, and he told me they had the report on their servers."

"Why didn't you ask Guy for the report?"

"Guy hates me," Gabriel said. "I only asked him to confirm it existed. You've probably heard I've been a little out of sorts the last few days."

"There have been some rumors, yeah. They said you and your father were both devastated over the resistance giving up the war."

"Exactly. I'm just looking for a little distraction; you know what I mean?"

Curtis smiled. "I hear you, Captain." He bit his lip. "It's on the books, right?"

"Yes."

"You promise?"

"Yes."

Curtis nodded. "Okay. I happen to be friends with the head of IT here. Come on, we'll go stop by her office. She can get you what you need."

"I assume you're referring to the file?" Gabriel asked.

The Lieutenant laughed openly. "Yeah. I would prefer if you keep it to business with Felicia. I've been trying to get her to go out with me for the last three months."

"Why won't she?"

"You know those types. They can be hard to get to warm up."

Gabriel didn't know. He smiled and nodded anyway. "Okay. I won't flirt with her. All I want is the file."

"Follow me, sir," Curtis said.

Curtis assigned one of his subordinates to keep an eye on things and then they made their way from the hangar to the loop station, taking a pod to the central hub. Once there, they took the elevator up to the second level. The door to the IT department was secured with a fingerprint scanner. Curtis put his finger to it, and it slid open.

The office was open and basic, rows of desks lined up neatly in the front, with racks of computer equipment behind glass in the back. The servers had originally been on the Magellan, and by the looks of it, there was early activity to disconnect it all and return it to the starship.

"There she is," Curtis said, pointing to a thin woman on the other side of the glass. She was with another tech, pointing at a neatly organized row of cables that dropped from the ceiling.

Curtis went over to the glass and knocked on it. Felicia looked at him, made a less than enthusiastic face, excused herself, and exited the room ahead of a blast of cool air.

"Can I help you, Lieutenant?" she asked.

"Hi, Felicia. How are you today?" Curtis said.

"I'm fine. I'm in the middle of something. Some of us have actual work to do."

Three months, and this was as far as he had gotten? Gabriel had a feeling she wasn't cold. The Lieutenant was just annoying.

"Excuse me, Felicia," he said, approaching them.

"Yes." Her eyes fell to the name badge to his shirt. "Oh, Captain St. Martin." She smiled. There was nothing cold about it. "How is your father?"

194

Gabriel glanced at Curtis, who responded with a shrug.

"He's doing well, thank you for asking. I'm sorry if we're bothering you, and I don't want to take too much of your time. I was hoping you might be able to help me with something."

"Really? I can't imagine how an IT girl would be able to help you with anything."

She was still smiling, her expression soft. He had told Curtis he wouldn't flirt with her as a joke, but it seemed she wanted to flirt with him.

"That's where you're wrong," Gabriel said. "I need to retrieve a file for Colonel Graham's review, but I have no idea how to locate it."

"Oh? I can probably help you there. Which file?"

"Astronomy's report on the Eden migration," Gabriel said. "Guy Larone wrote it."

"Why don't you get it from Guy?"

"You probably know he isn't a big fan of the military."

She laughed. "No, he isn't, is he? If it's his private report, you'll need his permission for me to pull it."

"Actually, he doesn't," Curtis said, trying to get back into the conversation. "Article... Which one was it again, Captain?"

"Article seventy-one," Gabriel replied. "NEA law says I don't need permission, which is good because he would never give it to me."

Felician bit her lip. "I've never heard of that law."

"How often does anyone need it? You must have a copy of the Articles you can pull up if you want to check."

"You don't mind if I take a look?"

"Why would I? I don't want you to get in trouble."

Felicia led them to her desk. It was sparse, save for a photo of a man Gabriel recognized, standing with a younger version of her.

"General Cave is your father?" he asked, suddenly feeling stupid for not putting two and two together. He knew the General had a daughter named Felicia.

"Yes. He used to talk about you and your dad a lot, you know. He has a lot of respect for both of you. There was a time he wanted the two of us to meet, to see if we hit it off. Then he decided he didn't want me to be involved with a pilot." She was speaking as she was navigating through the Articles on a large touchscreen.

"I can understand that," Gabriel said, his mind reaching back and inserting Felicia into a potential alternate timeline. She seemed like a nice enough person, and she wasn't hard to look at. "We don't tend to live very long."

"You have. Ah, here it is." She scanned the lines, reciting some of the words out loud. "It looks legit. I've got you covered, Captain."

She dove into a different part of the system, flipping through all kinds of data until she found what she was looking for. "Do you want me to push it to your account?"

"Actually, can you give me a copy?"

She reached down and opened a drawer, pulling out a small square. She tapped it against the touchscreen and then handed it to him. "Would it be possible for you to bring this back?" she asked. "We don't have an unlimited supply of these."

Gabriel had a feeling from the way she was looking at him that she wanted him to come back more than she wanted the storage square back. "Sure. I'll do my best."

"Great. Maybe we can get something to eat while you're here?"

He looked at Curtis again. The Lieutenant was shaking his head. "I'd like that," he said. "It may be a while though with everything going on."

"You'll have more free time once we're all on the Magellan," she said. "If I don't see you before that, I hope I'll see you then."

"I'll definitely return this to you by then," Gabriel said. "Thank you for your help."

"Anytime, Captain."

"Gabriel."

"Anytime, Gabriel."

Gabriel reached out and took her hand, giving it a light shake. He put the storage device in his pocket and headed for the door with Curtis trailing behind him.

"What was that, sir?" Curtis said once they were back on the elevator.

"I needed the file," Gabriel said. "Besides, I told you I wouldn't come on to her and I didn't."

"You could have been a little less open to her advances."

"Why? I'm not interested in her romantically. That doesn't mean she wouldn't make a good friend. By the way, I appreciate your help with this."

Lieutenant Curtis didn't look happy, but he seemed satisfied with the answer. "You're welcome, sir."

43

"I've got it," Gabriel said, holding the square up so Reza could see it.

The scientist lifted his attention from his handheld, his eyes falling on the square. "I knew I could count on you, Captain." He got to his feet, approaching the bars. Gabriel passed the storage device through.

Reza tapped it against his handheld and then navigated through to it. He scanned it quickly, nodding as he went while Gabriel waited.

"Well?" Gabriel asked a minute later.

Reza tilted his handheld so Gabriel could see the screen. It was filled with mathematical equations he didn't understand. "This is it. The original version. All of this is advanced math that you probably don't care about." He scrolled the data to the bottom. "Here's the important part. Look at that number."

Gabriel tracked Reza's finger to the line that said .001. "What is it?"

"The odds of reaching Eden. One thousandth of a percent."

"Those aren't good odds."

"No."

"I don't see how this proves anything."

"I have a copy of Guy's second report. The doctored one." He manipulated his handheld until he got to the same spot. "Take a look."

99.95.

"I can show you where he changed the calculation if you want. It's buried in the algorithms. Essentially, he reduced the variable until he got the number he wanted."

"Which variable?"

"Souls on board," Reza said.

The idea of it was chilling.

"And you swear that if you show this to the Council, they'll believe you?" Gabriel asked.

"If they don't, you'll know something is really rotten. I can share these two reports with any scientist on Gamma, and unless they're part of the conspiracy they'll jump all over this error."

"That's a problem, isn't it? It's going to be the good guys versus the bad guys. We need more proof than that."

"No, not proof, Captain. Support. If we can get enough people to believe this, we can at least get a stay of execution."

Gabriel considered it. If what Reza was saying was true, whoever didn't agree with his assertions would be outed as a possible traitor, which was good. It might not be enough to change the outcome, which was bad.

"We should bring this to General Cave," he said. "He was open to the Eden trip but he's not going to betray his soldiers to get there, and he has a lot of pull with some of the Council."

Reza nodded. "That sounds like a good start. Can you get me out of here so I can show him?"

"I don't know. I'll be right back."

Gabriel went to the front to find Spaceman Lee. The Spaceman stood and saluted as he entered.

"I'd like you to allow me to take Reza Mokri out of the prison," Gabriel said.

"Sir? What for?"

"He needs to speak with General Cave. He has some information that I believe the General would find valuable."

"I'm not allowed to do that, sir."

"I know you aren't supposed to. Does it explicitly say anywhere that you can't?"

"Not everything has to be spelled out for me to know that it isn't proper, sir."

"And in most cases I would agree with you, Spaceman. This is a bit of an unusual circumstance. You know you can trust me, and it isn't like there's anywhere for me to steal him to. I wouldn't ask if it weren't important."

"Even if I wanted to, I would need to get clearance from my Commanding Officer."

"Who is that?" Gabriel asked.

"Major Choi."

Gabriel smiled. "Can you reach her for me?"

Lee reached to the screen on his desk and tapped into the directory. Major Choi answered the request a moment later.

"Major," Lee said. "I'm sorry to bother you -"

Gabriel moved in front of the guard. "Major."

"Gabriel? What are you doing at the prison?"

"Where are you right now, Major?"

"Above your head in the concourse, getting something to eat. What's going on?"

"Would you mind meeting me down here? It's important."

He could tell she was thinking, trying to determine for herself why he was asking for her.

"This is about Mokri, isn't it? Gabriel, I know you're upset about the Council's decision, but-"

"Please, Vivian," Gabriel said. "For me."

Choi sighed. "Okay. Only because it's you. Give me five minutes."

"Thank you, Major," Gabriel said.

The screen returned to the directory. Gabriel left Lee and returned to Reza.

"Well?" Reza asked.

"I'm still working on it. Major Choi is coming down. I need you to show her what you showed me."

He looked unhappy about the news. "I thought you said General Cave would see me?"

"I have to get you out of this cell first. Major Choi is a friend of mine, and she's on our side. Convince her and she'll get you in front of Cave."

He seemed to relax. "Okay. Okay. I'm running a diff on the two reports that will show exactly what changed between versions. That should help me explain everything more easily."

"Whatever helps."

Reza continued staring down at his handheld while Gabriel waited, leaning against the wall. Major Choi arrived early, entering the cell block with Lee behind her.

"Major," Gabriel said, coming to attention and saluting.

"Relax, Gabriel. I'm here as your friend. Mr. Mokri."

"Major," Reza said, looking nervous.

"Spaceman Lee, you're dismissed," Choi said. The Spaceman saluted and left them. "Gabriel, what is this all about."

Gabriel explained the situation as best he could, with Reza filling in the details. Major Choi seemed unconvinced until he described how he had gotten the original file from the servers on Gamma, and Reza showed her the discrepancies.

"I don't want to believe this could be true," she said, staring at Reza's handheld. His diff program had highlighted the changed number in red. "Never mind what this means for the Eden mission. What does it mean for humanity if we're willing to sacrifice so many?"

"It means people are getting desperate," Gabriel said. "I understand why they would want to get out of Calawan and go somewhere green. I've seen Earth. So have you. Neither one of us is stupid. The allure is there."

"And the temptation may be too strong for some."

"Strong enough they'll let thousands of people die," Reza said. "It isn't right."

"No," Choi agreed. "It isn't. Both of you are coming with me. We're going to find General Cave, and we're going to put a stop to this right now while we figure out what the complete truth is."

"I knew I could count on you," Gabriel said.
Choi smiled, putting her hand on his cheek. "Always, Gabriel."

44

Gabriel was thankful he had enlisted Major Choi's help. All of the activity around planning for the trip to Exodus left General Cave's schedule full, and would have made it nearly impossible to get a minute to speak with him without her influence.

As it was, she had to put in a communication with Colonel Graham to explain that Gabriel was helping her with an important task, and to request he be permitted to spend the night on Alpha. Graham was not only understanding but discreet as well. He didn't ask her why she needed him.

It was evening by the time they arrived at Space Force headquarters on the top floor of the central dome. They were standing in the lobby and waiting for Cave to finish a prior meeting. He had ten minutes between appointments. Ten minutes the General had been planning to spend eating his dinner, which would now have to be skipped until the early morning.

"It better be good," Cave had said to Choi. "If it weren't coming from a St. Martin, I wouldn't bother at all."

Gabriel knew it was good. He wasn't sure if it would be good enough. Reza had been heads down, staring at his handheld since Choi had released him from the jail. The astronomer was doing everything he could to arrange the data in a way that would be digestible to non-scientists.

"You should see your father after this," Choi said.

He didn't like that the Major had to keep telling him how to be a minimally responsible son. At the same time, he was more nervous than ever about seeing his father. It was Choi who had told Theodore about the resistance's message, and the plan to abandon Calawan. She said he had responded very similarly to Gabriel, turning over in his bed in silence and refusing to speak to anyone since. His condition was also getting worse, and the doctor had doubled his dose of medication to keep him nearly unconscious.

"I know. I'm going to. I should have been the one to tell him. I still feel like dirt about that."

"Good," Choi replied. "Let it bother you until we talk to Cave, and then let it go. We have bigger things to worry about now, and you can't change the past."

"Right."

"Major Choi," Spaceman Owens said. "The General will see you now."

"Thank you," Choi said.

They followed Owens through the corridors, past the visitor offices to the rear of the HQ. Owens approached the door first, knocking lightly. It slid open a moment later.

"General Cave, sir," Owens said, saluting and standing at attention. "Major Choi, Captain St. Martin, and Mr. Reza Mokri here to speak with you, sir."

"Send them in, please," Gabriel heard Cave say.

"Yes, sir." Owens shifted his hands to motion them into the room.

"Major Choi reporting, sir," Choi said, saluting and stepping to the side.

"Captain St. Martin reporting, sir," Gabriel said, doing the same.

"General," Reza said. His voice was barely more than a whisper as his nerves started to get the better of him.

"Relax, all of you," Cave said. "Take a seat."

The General's office was the largest in the NEA, as well as one of the fanciest. It not only contained the standard desk and chairs, but also a large conference table with a holographic projector in the center. An oil painting was also mounted on each wall of the room. The three of them each chose a seat on one side of the table.

"We can start in one minute. I'm waiting on, ah, there you are."

Gabriel was confused. He hadn't expected anyone else to be at the meeting. He turned his head toward the door as Guy and Sarah Larone walked in. Angela Rouse trailed behind them.

"I feel like we just walked into an ambush," Choi whispered.

"How the hell did they know about this?" Gabriel replied. He had a feeling he knew. He could picture Lieutenant Curtis running to Guy after Gabriel had left, eager to tell him what had happened to get some kind of childish revenge because Felicia liked Gabriel and didn't like him. Was it any wonder why?

"This isn't good," Reza said. "Not good at all."

Guy met Gabriel's eye as he was greeted by General Cave, letting a small smirk crease the corner of his mouth. Sarah was less subtle, glaring angrily at them while Councilwoman Rouse wore her same general look of amusement.

"Please, sit," Cave said, directing everyone to the table. He moved to the head. "I only have ten minutes, so we'll make this quick. Before anyone says anything, Gabriel, I understand that you went behind Guy's back to get a copy of a specific file from the servers on Gamma and that you got that file from my daughter."

"It was perfectly legal, sir," Gabriel said.

"Yes, it was. That doesn't make it acceptable behavior for an officer."

Gabriel wasn't surprised at the General's reaction. "You are correct, sir. Given any other option, I would have chosen a different course."

"You're undermining everything we're working for, Captain," Guy said.

"Be quiet," Cave said, forcefully enough to cause Guy to sit up a little straighter. "I wasn't done. I've spoken with Councilwoman Rouse about this situation. I understand what the contention is, and what you are trying to prove. Gabriel, Vivian, Reza, the truth is that you are only looking at half the story. As hard as it may be for you to accept, the resistance on Earth has chosen to disband and disappear. Without them, there's no reason for us to continue our military efforts. We don't have the resources to make a true attempt to take back Earth on our own. Is that part understood?"

"Yes, sir," Choi said immediately.

Gabriel was more hesitant, but he reluctantly agreed. "Yes, sir."

"That being the case, the only issue I see here is whether or not Eden is truly a viable planet to send the people of the New Earth Alliance to. My answer is that we have been scanning the stars for the last fifty years, and this is the first real possibility we've had. We can't stay here forever. You all know that."

"You're saying that even if half of us die, it's better than being here?" Reza asked.

"Half of us will not die," Sarah said. "That's a story you keep making up to scare people."

"I do not. General, let me-"

"I said, be quiet," Cave said, his voice low and harsh. It was more frightening at a whisper than it was at a shout. "I'm saying that what you're calling a conspiracy is a possible reality we may just have to deal with. If we can't go to Earth, and we can't stay here, then we have to go somewhere else. If Eden is the only somewhere else even some of us have a chance of reaching, then that is how it has to be. In other words, it doesn't matter which of you are right or wrong. The facts are the facts. There is only one way any of the human race survives, and that way points to Eden."

Reza sighed and slumped back in his seat. Gabriel stared at the General, a painful mixture of emotions stirring in his gut.

"You used to be a man I respected," he said, unable to stay quiet. "A man who would never give up. You promised my father you would be there with him. You swore you would help him avenge my mother's loss, as well as the loss of billions of others. You have given up, though, haven't you? You're too old, you've been away for too long, you miss the air and the grass and the rain. Whatever your reason, you've aged into nothing but a damn coward."

"Gabriel," Choi said beside him.

Cave didn't react to the outburst. He was calm when he spoke. "You need to open your eyes, Captain. We've lost Earth, and the only way we don't lose everything else is to go to Eden. In your head you know it's true. Your heart is loyal, and I admire that in you. Don't let it lead you to foolishness."

Gabriel felt his pulse racing. He was going to be court-martialed if he wasn't careful.

He didn't care.

"It already has, or I wouldn't be sitting here. I was stupid to think you would come through for my father. You admire my loyalty? You've forgotten what that is. I'm sorry, Reza. I tried. This whole colony is being run by a bunch of-" Gabriel stopped himself, shaking his head. "It doesn't matter." He looked over at Angela. "Congratulations. You've managed to convince one of the people I used to respect the most to agree to genocide. I hope you're proud of yourself."

Angela gasped and opened her mouth to reply. Gabriel stood and headed for the door.

"I haven't dismissed you, Captain," General Cave said.

"Go to Hell," Gabriel replied. His training had taught him to respect those above him in rank, but he couldn't pretend he had any respect left for the General.

He was a warrior without a war.

What did it matter anyway?

45

Gabriel's mind was a chaotic mess of anger and disappointment, sadness and rage. He stormed from the Space Force offices, shoving Spaceman Owens aside as he tried to respond to the General's request to stop him. It was too bad very few of the military personnel on Alpha were actually armed.

He made it to the elevator and headed for the ground floor. Cave would be livid with him, he knew. The General would have him arrested and brought to the prison he had just gotten Reza out of. Then he would be left to rot for a while until Cave came to see him, spoke to him calmly, rationally, and logically, and then let him go. The old man didn't have the fire left in his gut to give him a real dress down. He didn't have the energy to chew him out like a soldier.

Gabriel wasn't ready to be brought in. Not yet. He could feel how his emotions were swirling within him. He knew he had only two options left. Fall back into his terrible depression, or stand up and fight like the soldier he was. Like the man his father would be proud of. Even if the only victory he could muster would be to evade the MPs long enough to go and see Theodore.

General Cave was siding with the scientists. The idea of it was so alien to him; he could barely believe it was true. Cave owed Theodore his life. He owed him his daughter. It didn't matter that the resistance on Earth had failed. As Cave himself had said, that wasn't the point anymore. The point was that he was alive because Juliet St. Martin hadn't abandoned him. He was here to make the decision because he was saved by an act of charity that he refused to pay forward. Would he rather let half the colony die than stay here for a while longer? Would he rather turn his back on her sacrifice than make one of his own?

What if the entirety of the NEA voted on the decision with all of the facts in front of them? How many would want to risk being one of the ones left behind? How many would want to determine the fate of their friend or neighbor?

The problem was that neither General Cave or Councilwoman Rouse would let them know the full extent of the truth. He wondered if the rest of the Council even knew what decisions were being made without them.

The thoughts fueled him as he reached the loop station. He was happy to discover there were no guards nearby. Would Cave go through the trouble of calling them in for emergency duty just to grab him? The General may not have liked being told to go to Hell, but he didn't think so.

A pod arrived a minute later. Gabriel climbed in, taking the short ride to Residential. His mind was still a maelstrom of emotion as he hurried through a quiet concourse and up to his father's apartment. He had half-expected to find an MP waiting for him there, but the area was still clear. If Cave wanted him that badly, he would send someone here to look for him, which meant he didn't have a lot of time.

Sabine was asleep on the sofa. She woke with a start when his entry caused the lights to go on.

"Huh? Gabriel? Is that you?"

"Sabine? It's okay. I'm sorry. I need to talk to my father. It's important. What are you doing here?"

Sabine sat up. "Your father's sleeping. The doctor raised the doses on all of his medication. I was ordered to stay and keep an eye on him. He isn't doing well."

"Is he dying?" Gabriel asked.

The fight began draining from him in a hurry. A part of him had always believed that his father was only alive to continue the war, and that learning it was over would kill him. At the same time, the idea of it seemed like uneducated superstition. If only people had such complete control over their mortality.

Either way, he wasn't ready to lose his father. Not yet. He had run away before. Now that he knew the truth of things, he wasn't going to do it again. Not when it meant thousands of people might die.

"He's old, Gabriel. His injuries have taken a toll on him, and his will to live is fading."

"How much longer does he have?"

Sabine shook her head. "I don't know. If it was imminent they would have contacted you. A week or two?"

A chill coursed through him. He had so little time left to spend with Theodore, and he had been wasting it feeling sorry for himself.

"I'm going to talk to him anyway," he said, heading toward the bedroom. "If the Military Police or General Cave show up, can you stall them for me?"

"What? Gabriel, are you in trouble?"

"Nothing I can't handle, but I need to see my father first."

He ducked into the bedroom before Sabine could answer.

Theodore St. Martin was lying in bed, eyes closed, hands out at his sides. An IV hung beside him, the end of it jabbed into his wrist, while a monitor was connected to his finger, taking his vitals and projecting them on the wall behind the bed. A blue line ran in a slow, rhythmic pattern across it, showing a currently steady pulse.

None of the equipment had been there four days earlier, and the sight of it helped return some of his anger. At that moment, he saw his father's condition as a symbol for everything he had ever believed in. Sick. Dying. On life support.

It was no way for anything or anyone to end. Especially someone like Theodore St. Martin.

"Dad," Gabriel said, sitting in the chair next to him. "Dad, wake up."

Theodore's eyes opened. He turned his head to the side, staring at Gabriel with a clarity the younger St. Martin hadn't seen in months.

"Gabriel. About damn time you got here. Thought I'd go near insane waiting for you to show and send your old man off to the bayou in the sky with the respect I deserve."

Gabriel stared at Theodore, trying to figure out what was happening. His father was supposed to be near death. Instead, he seemed full of life. He had heard that people who were sick often regained all of their faculties right before they passed on as if God gave them one last round to say their goodbyes. He felt his eyes begin to tear, realizing that his father had been waiting for him so that he could finish his journey.

"What are you choking up for, son?" Theodore asked.

"I'm sorry," Gabriel said.

"What for? Come on now, Gabe. Don't sit there blubbering like a little school girl. Spit it out."

"I should have been here more often. I should have come sooner. I should have been the one who told you about Eden."

"Yeah. Damn right you should have. You can make it up to me now by helping me get the hell out of here."

"What?" Gabriel said, his emotions swinging again. He was completely confused. "Dad, what do you mean get out of here?"

Theodore reached over with one hand and grabbed the IV, pulling it slowly from his wrist. He held it up to Gabriel. "You know what this is, son?"

"Yes. It's the medicine that's keeping you alive. Dad, I don't want you to die. Not yet."

Theodore's dry lips curled into a smile. Gabriel hadn't seen that expression since before the accident. "Who said a damn thing about dying? There ain't no meds in that there bag. It ain't nothing but saline."

"What?"

"You having trouble with your ears? You keep saying what? What? What? I need your help, son. There's trouble brewing, and we don't have a lot of people we can trust."

Gabriel started to say "what" again. He stopped himself, shaking his head. "I don't believe this is happening."

"Get your head out of your ass, Gabriel. This ain't no dream. Geez, it's a damn nightmare more like. They're spitting on her grave, son. Your mother. My bride. General Cave thinks I'm going just to sit here like a damn fool invalid while he destroys her memory? Son of a bitch tried to poison me, son." He waved the IV needle at him. "Medication? This ain't medication to help. You get me? It's control."

Gabriel couldn't believe what his father was suggesting. "You're saying Cave has been drugging you? Why?"

"To keep me quiet. I've still got a lot of pull in this colony. He doesn't want anyone interfering with his plan to get to greener pastures."

"I'm totally confused. Four days ago you were pathetic and broken."

"You ever call me that again, I'll whoop you so bad you can't sit for a week." He smiled. "I was, son. I was. Just like you, I ain't immune to it. You want to apologize to me for wallowing? No. I've been stuck in the mud for years. Ever since I lost my wheels. It took your mother's intervention for me to open my eyes."

"What do you mean, mom's intervention?"

"When you didn't stop by after the Council meeting the other day, Cave did. He told me about the message. Hell, he showed me the damn thing. I was barely lucid then, but maybe more than he was expecting. I could see the satisfaction in those eyes when he played the message you picked up from Earth."

Theodore removed the finger monitor and pushed himself to a sitting position. He wasn't wearing civilian clothes beneath the covers. He was wearing SBU fatigues.

"Grab my chair," he said.

Gabriel did, rolling it over and positioning it for Theodore. His father swung himself over and into it, looking ten years younger as he did.

"He didn't recognize General Rodriguez," Theodore continued. "I did. He was only seventeen the last time I saw him. Not Space Force. Army. Nothing but a Private back then. He was in the platoon in charge of guarding the Magellan. Stick your hand under the pillow."

Gabriel leaned forward and reached beneath Theodore's pillow. His hand landed on metal, still warm from his father's head. He pulled the gun out, turning it. It was his father's original service piece. A standard projectile pistol. Bullets, not plasma.

"Dad? Why am I holding your gun?"

"I recognized General Rodriguez," Theodore repeated. "That dog is still alive. Which means your mother might be, too."

46

Donovan had one more stop to make before he went back to General Rodriguez, leaving the infirmary and heading across to the nursery.

"Hey, Mom," he said, opening the door and stepping in. He instantly found himself surrounded by toddlers, six in all between one and three years of age. Wanda Peters was sitting in the middle of them with one of the children on her lap, asleep. She looked weary and worried.

At least, she did until she saw him.

"Donovan," she said, a huge smile growing across her face. "You're back."

"Rodriguez didn't tell you?"

"No. When did you get here?"

"About an hour ago."

Wanda lowered the child to the floor. He didn't even seem to notice he was being moved. She got to her feet and wrapped Donovan in a hug.

"I was worried about you."

"You always worry about me. I always come back."

"Thank God. That doesn't mean you always will."

"Then I'll die happy, knowing I was trying to make a difference. Tell me you slept?"

"A little. I'm almost starting to believe you're as invincible as you do."

"You'll probably find out soon enough, but Diaz and I did it, Mom. We got into a Dread city and captured two of their weapons. We killed a Dread."

His mother nodded. "Never be proud of killing anything, Donnie. That's the road to Hell."

Donovan wasn't surprised at her statement. For all the Dread had cost them, she remained adamant that life was precious. All life. Maybe that was why she surrounded herself with it.

"Okay, Mom. I'm not as much proud of that as I am that we got the guns. If Carlson can figure out how they work, it can change the entire face of the war. We might be able to fight back."

"Good. Maybe if they see we aren't so helpless they'll decide to leave."

The door opened behind them. Donovan turned to see Matteo's head poking through it.

"Major Peters," his friend said, entering the room. Matteo Diaz was an olive-skinned, athletic god. At least, that's what most of the women on the base whispered to one another. His dimpled smile cemented the reputation. "I figured if you were done with Iwu I would find you over here."

"Matteo," Donovan said, clasping hands with him. "Your sister told you where I was?"

"Actually, it was General Rodriguez. He wanted you to go see him as soon as you were done with Doc Iwu."

Donovan was eager to find out what Rodriguez was thinking. The General's words still resonated, chilling him to the core.

"Doc Iwu?" Wanda said. "Did you get hurt?"

"No. Standard operating procedure, you know that. I've got to go."

"He leans too hard on you, Donnie," Wanda said. "You just got back, and he won't even give you time to sleep?"

"I can sleep later. Thanks for caring, Mom." He kissed his mother on the cheek.

"I'm glad you're back. I love you."

"I love you too, Mom. I'll stop by again later."

"Get some rest first. That's more important than checking in on your mother and a bunch of rugrats."

"Yes, ma'am," Donovan said, saluting.

"Get out of here," Wanda replied, slapping him on the arm.

He held back from wincing at the twinge of pain. He didn't want her to know he had been injured. She worried enough already.

He left the nursery with Matteo, heading toward the stairs.

"Renata told me you got hit."

"Yeah. Some debris buried itself in my back. We were this close to getting blown to ash." He put his thumb and forefinger together. "Iwu cleaned it out and stitched it up. It wasn't bad enough to waste meds on."

"How does it feel now?"

"As long as nothing hits it and I don't have to raise my hand, I'm fine."

"So, you know it's my birthday this weekend, right?"

Donovan laughed. "Are you serious? I almost died."

"Yeah, but you didn't. Which means you got me something, right?"

"I've got something for you. You aren't going to like it."

"Oh please, amigo. You say that every year, and every year you get me something great. Like that date with Ronnie. Man, I wanted to kiss her forever."

"I didn't have to do much to get her to go out with you. Have you looked in a mirror lately? Besides, that ended in disaster."

"Beautiful disaster."

They ascended the steps to the first floor and headed toward Rodriguez's office.

"Are you in on this?" Donovan asked.

"No. Officers only. I'm just a lowly handyman."

"This base wouldn't run at all without you and your father."

"Thanks for saying so. Which reminds me, I've got a leaky pipe I need to patch. I'll talk to you later, bro."

"Later, Teo."

They split up at the next corridor, with Donovan continuing on to Rodriguez's office.

"General Rodriguez," Donovan said, walking in. "Major Peters, reporting as requested." He saluted sharply.

"At ease, Donovan," Rodriguez said. He was standing behind his desk, a concerned look on his face.

Donovan quickly scanned the room, noting the presence of Colonel Montero, Major Sharma, and Diaz.

"Lieutenant Diaz, can you get the door?" Rodriguez asked.

"Yes, sir," Diaz replied.

"Donovan, I've already briefed Colonel Montero and Major Sharma on what you told me earlier. The reason I called you back so soon is because I have some time-sensitive information that I believe it's important to share."

Donovan glanced at Diaz, who shrugged.

"As you know, we've been in contact with other resistance bases around the globe for some time, including the installation in New York where General Parker is based. Three weeks ago a missive went out from General Parker, outlining the movements of the Dread as they had been reported in. Mexico isn't the only region that is falling under expanded enemy scrutiny, and it was reported that a number of bases around the globe were discovered and destroyed."

Rodriguez paused to let that information sink in.

"The result of this series of defeats led General Parker and his advisors to re-examine the resistance's strategy in dealing with the Dread occupation. The outcome of this is that he passed a message to every known resistance base across the globe that we were to disband at once into smaller groups and make every effort to avoid the Dread."

"What?" Diaz said, beating the rest of them to it. Donovan felt his pulse quicken, and the chill returned. Looking at the other officers, they were feeling the same thing.

"He ordered us to stop fighting and focus on survival," Rodriguez said. "He also made a special request to have me record a message informing the space forces of his decision."

Donovan shook his head. He couldn't believe it. "No. You've got to be kidding me," he said, not meaning to voice his feelings out loud.

"I'm sorry, Donovan. You're a little too good at your job. Your team delivered the message yesterday."

47

"You're saying we told our only allies in this fight not to come back? On the same mission we recovered a weapon that can kill the alien bastards?" Diaz asked, a tremble in her voice.

"General, why didn't you tell us about General Parker's orders?" Colonel Montero asked.

"I was waiting to ensure the message was delivered. Then I was waiting to see if Major Peters and Lieutenant Diaz made it back. How could I know what they would bring back with them?"

"You couldn't, General," Major Sharma said. "None of us could."

"What's done is done," Donovan said. "We have to decide what to do about it. You said before that you hoped it wasn't too late. I think I know what you meant now."

"Thank you, Major," Rodriguez said. "I appreciate your attitude. That's why this couldn't wait."

"What do you mean?" Montero asked.

"You want to make another t-vault, don't you sir?" Donovan asked.

"Yes."

"Sir, you just told us you sent a message to the colony not to come back," Sharma said.

"I did. And it is highly likely that they will follow that directive. It's also entirely possible that they won't."

"They've been returning like clockwork for over twenty years," Donovan said. "We know they've lost ships doing it, and yet they keep coming."

"There is a chance they'll make one more trip to confirm the message. There's a chance they'll keep coming even if no one ever replies. We stopped transmitting for months and they still came."

"We didn't tell them not to," Sharma said.

"It's foolish to assume they'll come back," Montero said. He smiled. "It's also foolish to assume they won't."

"My thought exactly," Rodriguez said. "We have to stay on schedule and make another run, to tell them what we've discovered. We have a couple of weeks. Maybe we can even uncover the secret to overcoming their shields by then."

"That's a big maybe," Diaz said.

"It is, but at the very least we can tell them we have an active weapon, we know it can hurt them, and we're working on it. We can tell them to disregard the previous message."

"What about General Parker in New York?" Donovan asked.

"We need to get a message to him, too. We have to hope just as much that it isn't too late to keep the resistance from falling apart here on Earth as we do out among the stars."

"It should be easy enough to get a message to them," Major Sharma said.

"It still takes time," Rodriguez replied.

Messages flowed from one base to another over an Internet of sorts; a collection of computers connected via a spiderweb route of cables that the Dread had so far ignored. It was all peer-to-peer, incredibly slow, and often subject to blackout. From the way Matteo had explained it, it was a miracle that the system worked at all. Fixing pipes wasn't the only thing he was handy with.

"When is the next expected match in the pattern?" Donovan asked.

The space forces always returned when the slipstream matched a specific set of wave patterns, ostensibly to keep the Dread from guessing when they would arrive. It was more than likely the Dread knew but didn't care.

"Three weeks," Rodriguez said.

"That's plenty of time for my arm to heal," Donovan said.

"We have a bigger problem than that, General," Diaz said. "Most of our team was killed during the last mission, and we lost the transmission equipment."

"Understood," Rodriguez said. "I'm going to put the word out to the base looking for volunteers for this run. As far as our chain-of-command is concerned, we aren't even supposed to be continuing operations right now. I'm not going to order you two back out there, either. There's no guarantee the space forces will return. In fact, it's more likely you'll be killed out there for nothing."

"I wouldn't call it nothing, sir," Donovan said. "I would call it hope."

Rodriguez smiled. "You keep going like you are, Major, and you'll have my job soon."

"If I survive."

"I'm not making you go, Donovan."

"I know, sir. Consider me volunteered."

"Me, too," Diaz said without hesitation.

"Sir, if I might," Colonel Montero said. "I'd like to volunteer as well."

"Are you sure, Jose?"

"Yes, sir. The bigger the team, the better the chance we can pull this off. Besides, I'm getting soft sitting on the sidelines and watching cadets beat each other up."

"Very well. Harpreet, do you want to throw in as well?"

"I would sir, but we all know I would be more hindrance than help with this bum knee of mine." Major Sharma turned to Donovan. "If there's anything else you need, I'll do whatever I can."

"Thank you, Major," Donovan said.

"We've got three weeks, people," Rodriguez said. "Donovan, if you can stay behind for a moment? The rest of you are dismissed."

"Yes, sir," they said, filing out of the room and leaving Donovan alone with Rodriguez again.

"About the prisoner," Rodriguez said.

"Her name is Ehri," Donovan replied.

"I wasn't sure if I should say anything. I'm not even sure if it's important or not."

"What is it, sir?"

"The clone. Ehri. I've seen her before."

Donovan could tell the General was uncomfortable with the subject though he had no idea why. "I'm sorry, sir. I don't know what you're talking about."

"I was there. Did you know that? In New Mexico during the invasion. I was only a Private then, a freshly minted soldier put on guard detail. It was a boring job for the first three months. Every day, I would head in and stand in front of a pair of locked doors leading to the biggest underground hangar you could ever imagine." He smiled.

"I've heard this before, sir. You were stationed in New Mexico, guarding the Magellan."

"I knew the Captain who was in command of her. Not well, but I knew him. Theodore St. Martin. They called him the Gator because he was from an old Louisiana family, and because he was an incredible pilot. They said that once he got something in his teeth, he never let it go. He also liked to curse in cajun."

Rodriguez's eyes were distant as he recounted the memory.

"I knew his wife, Juliet, too. She was the sweetest, most kind-hearted person I've ever met in my life. Compassionate, sensitive, devout. They don't make a lot of people like her.

"Anyway, the invasion had been going on for three days when the order came to round people up to evacuate on the Magellan. She wasn't fully ready for travel, but they didn't have a choice. The top brass chose who would go. Military mostly, with training in every discipline they thought would be useful to a new world, plus their families. I wasn't invited.

"The Dread found out about the Magellan the second they fired up the reactors. They couldn't see her because she was underground, so they didn't get the position precise. That's the only reason she made it off the ground in the first place. Like I said, I wasn't invited, so I was doing my best to help the others on board. The problem was that they weren't ready, and the Dread attack turned the whole thing into chaos. They had to leave in a hurry, and they were going to wind up with only half a boat full of people.

"Then Captain St. Martin's wife, Juliet, appears out of nowhere, running through the base and screaming at the admins and the janitors and everyone she could find to get the hell on board. She yelled the same to me. I had a choice then, Donovan. A choice to leave or to stay. To die right then and there, or maybe live a full life out in the stars. You know which choice I made. I stayed with Juliet, helping her get people onto the ship. I stood next to her on the surface and watched the Magellan get off the ground. I watched how Theodore piloted that behemoth like it was a schooner on a lake of glass. I've never seen anything like it. The plasma flumes were so heavy into the pit, and somehow he got the Magellan around them. It was like he knew where they were going to be before they got there."

His eyes refocused, and he stared at Donovan.

"We escaped from the base in New Mexico, heading south. We got caught in one of the Dread's round ups. I escaped. Juliet was taken."

"Ehri is a clone of Juliet St. Martin?" Donovan said.

Rodriguez nodded. "I don't know how much of her originates with her creation by the Dread, and how much comes from her genetic relationship with Juliet St. Martin. If she's anything like her template, she may be way more important to this war than those rifles could ever be."

48

Gabriel put the gun down on the bed. "You can't be serious. You're seventy-eight years old. She would be eighty. Living on Earth. No medical care. Being hunted by the Dread."

"You didn't know your mother. Pick up the gun."

"Why?"

"Because I need my hands to roll the damn chair. Pick it up, Captain."

"Don't start using my rank on me. You aren't enlisted anymore, remember?"

"I'll tell you where you can put that piece in a second. That wasn't by choice."

"You crashed a fighter into a transport and killed four people because you were so afraid you had lost your touch. You had to get out there and prove you could still do it, and guess what? You couldn't."

This was an old fight. One that had been continuing whenever Theodore was alert enough to have it.

"It was a damn mechanical failure," Theodore said.

"The engineers said-"

"Engineers? They said what they had to say to cover their own asses. Don't you get it, son? This is the way things work. Just like General Cave and that bitch, Rouse."

"The investigation didn't turn up anything."

"Because the investigator had to rely on the engineers. Pick up the damn weapon."

"Why? To do what, Dad? Go and kill General Cave?"

"That traitor should get off so easy. He knew I would fight his decision, so he had the doc jack me up so full of shit that I could barely think. All I could do was sit here and die. He didn't know I recognized Rodriguez. He didn't know what that meant to me. He thought I was inconsolable. He left, and ten minutes later Sabine comes in and says I've been ordered a higher dose of meds. It took every ounce of strength for me to tell her no.

"Vivian, bless the woman, came by an hour later. I was in and out the whole time, but after seeing Rodriguez, I wasn't going to let anything in the world stop me. I told her what I saw. She told me everything that Cave didn't. I ain't a highly educated man like them scientists, but I ain't stupid either. I told her I needed to get clean, and I couldn't do that with Cave trying to keep me quiet. So when they came with the IV, she followed up and swapped it out for a placebo."

"Sabine told me you were in a bad way."

"Withdrawal from the meds. Damn near killed me, for sure, and my stumps hurt like a son of a bitch. I've got a couple of bottles of pills to help keep me going insane from it, but I have to say, drugged ignorance was bliss. Will you pick up the damn gun now?"

"No," Gabriel said, eyeing the weapon. "I still don't know what you want me to do with it."

"Why'd you come here, son?"

"What?"

"Why did you come to see me now, at this particular late hour?"

"I wanted to see you. To apologize-"

"Don't try to bullshit me, boy. I've been able to tell when you're lying since you were in diapers. What's the real reason?"

"I had a meeting with General Cave. Rouse and the Larones were there, along with Vivian and the scientist who said they lied about the math, Reza Mokri. Cave basically said that it doesn't matter if half the colony dies to get to Eden, we're going to Eden."

"Instead of heading back to Earth," Theodore said. "Fifty-percent casualties for a half-promise. Or we could be going home."

"We can't fight the Dread."

"You can't fight slipstream equations either, son. That isn't stopping them from trying. Besides, those are the words of a quitter, and I didn't raise a damn quitter. I know what happened next because as much as you hate it, you're still too much like your old man. You told Cave off and stormed out, didn't you?"

"Yes."

Theodore laughed. Gabriel couldn't remember the last time he had heard his father laugh. "And then you came here. Why?"

"I wanted to talk to you, to ap-"

"Don't bullshit me, boy."

"I wanted your advice. I wanted to know what you would do with everything I've learned."

"Now we're getting somewhere. Pick up the gun, Gabriel. You want to know what I would do? That's step one. I knew you would be by once you couldn't take it anymore. Once you saw Cave for the worm he's become. I was hoping it wouldn't come to this, but we've just about run out of reasonable options."

"Come to what?" Gabriel said, reaching for the gun again.

"I made two promises to your mother. I promised to keep fighting, and I promised to take care of the people who made it out because she didn't. I ain't letting them break those promises. I ain't letting them kill thousands on a wing and a prayer, and I ain't giving up on Earth without a fight."

Gabriel wrapped his hand around the grip and lifted the weapon. His father was putting into words everything he had been feeling. The difference was that his father had the experience to have already guessed it would be up to them to do something about it.

"So what are we going to do?" he asked, putting his other hand over the crucifix around his neck.

"I knew you wouldn't let me down, son. You're everything good about your mother, and everything bad about me." He laughed again. "The Magellan was given over to my care before we ever left Earth. As far as I'm concerned, that means the old girl is mine.

"You and me, we're going to take her."

49

"You want to steal the Magellan?" Gabriel said, his grip on the gun loosening slightly. "We'll be executed for treason."

"Like I said, it ain't stealing. Maggie is mine, placed into my care by General Tomlinson fifty years ago. I'm still on the docket as the registered CO. Idiots never bothered to take my name off because the old girl isn't going anywhere. At least, they don't expect it to be going anywhere."

"That doesn't mean you can lift off without permission. Like it or not, you aren't commissioned."

"Which explains why I was waiting on you. According to Choi, it's a legal gray area."

Gabriel was surprised. "Choi knows about this?"

"Hell, yeah, boy. I told you; she was swapping the spit for me."

"I know. She knows you plan to take the Magellan?"

"She knows. She wasn't too keen on the plan, but I think she'll have a new opinion after your little meeting with Cave. Come on."

Theodore rolled his chair toward the living area. Gabriel grabbed the back of it, holding him.

"Wait a second, Dad. If we do this, we're going to leave everyone here stranded. There aren't enough materials in this system to print another Magellan."

"Then I guess we ought to bring her back in one piece, eh? If we succeed, everyone lives. If we fail, at least everyone gets stuck together. Why the hell do we want to perpetuate a race of backstabbing, immoral, idiot babies? All or nothing. That's the only way to play it."

Gabriel couldn't stop himself from smiling at that statement. It was a classic comment from his father, and he had missed it.

"Now, either let go of my damn chair and be part of the solution, or give me the gun so I can shoot you myself. I'm not going to have my only son be part of the problem."

Gabriel let go of the chair. At the same time, the tone for the front door of the apartment sounded.

Gabriel slipped around the front of Theodore, rushing to grab Sabine's arm before she could respond to the tone. "Wait a second."

Sabine turned around, surprised and angry. Her eyes began to tear when she saw Theodore roll out into the room.

"General St. Martin," she said, hurrying to him and bending over to give him a hug. "You're awake."

"No thanks to the garbage they were poisoning me with," Theodore said, tapping Sabine's back in a more cordial embrace. "You're fired, by the way. I won't be needing a nurse anymore."

"What are you two planning?" Sabine asked, noticing the gun.

The tone sounded again. Gabriel trained the gun on the door. Theodore commanded it to open.

Major Choi stood in front of it, clutching Reza by the arm.

"Gabriel." Her eyes fell on the gun. "I see you talked to your father." She looked past him. "We don't have a lot of time, sir. I talked Cave into letting me deal with Gabriel, but when we don't come back he's going to get suspicious."

"I'm ready to go," Theodore said.

"Where are we going?" Reza asked.

"You wanted to save people?" Choi asked.

"Yes, ma'am."

"Now's your chance."

Gabriel led his father out of the apartment, tucking the gun in the back of his pants and covering it with his jacket. He couldn't believe everything that was happening. First, his father was awake and in relatively good health, and now he was on the verge of stealing the New Earth Alliance's only starship. It was crazy and exhilarating at the same time.

"We can't fly the Magellan with four people," Gabriel said as they hurried across the upper level to the elevator.

"I've got a plan for that," Theodore said.

"Fly the Magellan?" Reza said. "Wait a second. Are you serious?"

"Vivian tells me you're an engineer, and that you have a specialty in slipspace. Is that right?"

"Yes."

"Do I look like some damn teenage girl or your friend from astronomy class or something?" Theodore snapped. "Yes, what?"

"Yes, sir," Reza said, his face turning red.

"Good. You're exactly the kind of person we need."

They reached the elevator and rode it down to the main concourse. Once there, they began moving across it together, drawing stares from the few residents who were still awake. They probably thought they saw a ghost to see General St. Martin crossing the space in his wheelchair.

They were halfway to the loop station when a pair of MPs entered the concourse. They were each holding a plasma rifle, and they took up a guard position on either side of the station entry.

"Damn," Choi said. "I guess he doesn't trust me, either."

"Or Sabine told him what was going down," Gabriel said. "You shouldn't have been so obvious in front of her."

"Me?" Theodore said. "You're the one holding the gun."

"Have you looked in a mirror, Pop? The fatigues don't exactly say 'out for a stroll.'"

"How do you want to handle this, General?" Choi asked.

"My eyes are still a little fuzzy from being half-dead. Do you know the soldiers?"

"Hafizi and Diallo," Choi said.

"I don't know Hafizi. I know Diallo. Gabe and I will handle this."

They approached the loop station entry. As they neared, the two soldiers blocked the way. "Captain St. Martin. We're under orders from General Cave to bring you back to Space Force HQ."

Theodore cut Gabriel off before he could speak. "Lucy. It's been a while."

Diallo shifted her attention to him. "General St. Martin? I thought you were sick."

"I'm feeling much better. I'm afraid Gabriel can't come back to HQ with you. I'm a frail old gator, and I need his help."

Diallo laughed. "You don't look that frail to me, sir."

"You're right. I lied. The truth, Sergeant, is that General Cave is a yellow-bellied couillon, and if he wants Gabriel he'll have to come and get him personally. Now, me and mine are heading over to the Magellan so we can win the war General Cave is afraid to fight. That leaves you with two options, Sergeant. One, shoot us. Two, help us. What's it going to be? And don't take forever to decide. We're on a tight schedule."

Diallo glanced over at Hafizi, who looked uncomfortable with the whole situation.

"I said no lollygagging, Sergeant," Theodore said.

Diallo shifted her rifle, leveling it at Hafizi. "I'm with you, sir. Ali? Come along or hand your rifle over to Captain St. Martin."

Spaceman Hafizi hesitated for a few seconds before shouldering his weapon. "I'm in," he said. "I never served under you, sir, but your reputation precedes you."

"Good man," Theodore said.

"This is outright treason," Reza said nervously.

Theodore spun his chair on one wheel to face the scientist. "Treason, boy? Treason is breaking promises to thousands of people stranded on Earth. Treason is poisoning your best friend to keep him quiet. Treason is making up numbers to support personal goals, and treason sure as shit is giving up ten thousand souls for the sake of a new home world. This ain't treason, son. This is justice."

Reza's face was red again, but he nodded in agreement. "Yes, sir."

The growing group entered the loop station. An empty pod entered less than a minute later, and they filed in, with Hafizi helping Gabriel get his father into the transport.

"You sent a message to Sturges?" Theodore asked.

"Yes, sir," Choi replied. "He's passing the word on to the crew on Delta that he trusts."

"Delta?" Gabriel asked. "What word?"

"Boy, you sound like a parrot," Theodore said. "As you were so kind to point out, you can't fly a damn starship with four, nay, six crew members. And we sure as hell can't run reconnaissance on Earth without any starfighters. We need people that will follow you and me, and that means Delta."

"Me?" Gabriel said. "I'm just a Captain. I'm not anything special."

"That's your mother talking again," Theodore said. "To which I say, bullshit. You're the most decorated pilot in the NEA. You've survived over sixty-eight sorties. You're the only one ever to do that. You could be sitting pretty on Alpha making babies with any lady in the universe, and instead you're still going back out there. Where I'm from, that's called having balls, and people respect men with balls."

Gabriel smiled. His father had that special way with people that few others possessed. He knew exactly what to say to build a person up or tear a person down.

The pod came to a stop, and they climbed out. There was no direct route from the settlement to the Magellan. They would have to take a transport to the starship.

They hurried from the loop station to the hangar. Bay Six was occupied, and Choi steered them toward it.

"How long do you think it will take for you to be missed?" Gabriel asked Diallo.

"We're supposed to report in when we have you." She pulled a handheld from her pocket and checked the time on it. "I suppose we should have you by now." She held down a button on the device. "This is Diallo. We have Captain St. Martin in custody, and are en route to HQ."

"Affirmative, Diallo," Owens replied.

She pocketed the handheld. They reached the airlock for Bay Six, and Choi put her thumb on the scanner to open it. A transport was waiting inside, with Captain Sturges and his wife Siddhu standing on the ramp leading into the BIS.

"General St. Martin," Sturges said, snapping into an attentive salute.

"Captain Sturges," Theodore replied. "Siddhu. It's good to see you both."

"You too, Theodore," Siddhu said, leaning down to kiss his cheek.

"We don't have any time to waste," Sturges said, waving for them to board the transport. Theodore wheeled himself up, looking to Gabriel as if he were getting stronger with each passing minute. "I've got clearance for a supply run to Delta." He pointed to the pallets of food and materials to bring to the station. "I think that stuff will come in handy on the Magellan, don't you?"

"Damn handy," Theodore said.

Sturges hit the control to close the ramp and headed toward the cockpit. Gabriel followed him, taking the co-pilot seat.

"You could have told me about this sooner," Gabriel said.

"And ruin the surprise?" Sturges replied. "Your father said you needed to understand before we could count on you to bring your best game. We have no margin for error here, Gabe."

"I know. Whatever happens, thank you for being part of it."

"I'm loyal to your father and you to the day I die, Gabriel. Thank you for giving this old pilot one more mission that will mean something."

"Are you sure it will?"

"Absolutely. Now, let's steal a starship."

50

"BIS Two, this is Control. You're off course. Is everything okay, sir?"

Sturges looked over at Gabriel. "I guess they noticed that I'm not headed toward Delta Station." He leaned over and tapped the comm. "Control, this is BIS Two. I appear to be having a vectoring thruster malfunction. One of the venting ports may be jammed. I'm investigating."

"Roger, BIS Two. Do you need recovery, Captain?"

"Not yet. I'll let you know if I'm about to float off into space."

"Yes, sir."

"How much time will that buy us?" Gabriel asked.

"Enough."

Gabriel looked through the viewport. The Magellan was already below them, but Sturges was letting the transport drift past it to keep up the ruse.

"The bigger problem is that there's already a transport docked to it," Sturges said, pointing to the rear of the ship, near the port-side slipstream nacelle. It was tiny compared to the starship.

"Who is that?" Gabriel said.

"No idea. I've been keeping an eye on the work orders. There isn't anything scheduled to start until next week."

Gabriel pulled the gun from his waist. "I hope I don't need to use this thing."

"Me, too."

"How long until we dock?"

"Five minutes."

"I'll tell my father about the other transport and get everyone ready."

"Roger."

Gabriel moved to the back of the transport. His father was already holding court, positioned in the center of the group and telling the assembly about Gabriel's mother.

"Dad,' Gabriel said, cutting him short. "Sorry to interrupt, but we're almost at the Magellan. There's a small problem. Another ship is already docked there."

"What?" Siddhu said. "There were no work orders on her this week."

"That's what your husband said," Gabriel replied. "I guess plans changed."

"Or someone else is trying to take her before we do," Theodore said. "I'm glad we picked you up on the way over, Sergeant."

"I don't want to kill any of our own," Diallo said.

"Me neither," Theodore agreed. "Although I have found that an active plasma rifle pointed at your face can be a very effective negotiating tactic." He spun his chair toward Gabriel. "I want you to take point with Diallo and Hafizi."

"I'm a pilot, not a foot soldier."

"I think I've been asleep a little too long, son. You used to recognize when I was asking, and when I was giving you an order. Or has this old gator lost your respect?"

"No, sir," Gabriel said, snapping to attention. "My apologies, sir."

"Good man. Sweep the corridors up to the bridge and clear a path. If whoever is on the ship ain't there and they get stuck riding along, too damn bad. Major, if you would do me the honor of escorting myself and Mr. Mokri here to the bridge, I would be much obliged."

"Of course, General," Choi said.

"Siddhu, wait for your husband and stay with the transport, just in case."

"Yes, sir," Siddhu said.

Gabriel joined Hafizi and Diallo near the docking collar on the side of the BIS, a rounded rectangular hatch with an airlock between them and the vacuum outside. He could see the side of the Magellan growing larger ahead of them, the massive scale of the starship stealing his breath. He had only been on the ship a few times before, and not since before he had gone to officer training. He had forgotten how majestic the Magellan was.

"Wow," Hafizi said beside him.

"First time?" Gabriel asked.

"Yes, sir. I've only seen her from a distance."

"Imagine what she would look like with guns," Diallo said.

"I don't want to imagine it," Gabriel replied. "I want to make it happen."

"Yes, sir."

They stood and watched as the ship drew close enough that the matching docking collar came into view. Captain Sturges guided the transport expertly, getting it aligned right next to the collar before the vectoring thrusters pushed the two together. Gabriel pressed the control pad next to the airlock and felt the slight vibration as the clamping mechanism shifted into place, taking hold of the BIS and pulling it the last few inches to the collar. Once the two ships were joined the outer hatches of each opened, revealing similar airlocks on both sides. Gabriel waited while the two corridors pressurized, and then those doors also slid open.

"Stay close, don't shoot anything unless it shoots at you," Gabriel said. "These are our people, and they probably don't know why we're here."

"Yes, sir," Hafizi and Diallo replied.

The three of them walked through the joined airlocks, passing from the transport into the Magellan. The inside of the starship was dark, with only emergency lighting providing a dim glow.

"They didn't even turn the lights on," Diallo said.

"They probably can't," Gabriel replied. "Only a registered officer has control over Maggie. I don't know which Major is assigned to the retrofit."

They moved out into the corridor. The Magellan would be a maze to anyone who was unfamiliar with her layout, due to hundreds of corridors that all looked nearly identical. While there were plenty of physical signs indicating the current floor and the direction of the passage, even that was of limited help when everything looked the same.

Fortunately, the route to the bridge was one of the easiest, and Gabriel still remembered it from his last time on board. He led the two MPs in that direction ahead of the rest of the group.

"I can't believe this ship was made on Earth," Hafizi said, reaching out and running his hand along the cold metal walls. "So much history."

"What's it like, Captain?" Diallo asked. "Earth, I mean."

"It's beautiful from a distance," Gabriel replied. "White clouds. Blue oceans. When you get closer, you can see how much it's hurting. The Dread haven't been kind to the planet. Their structures litter most of whatever landscapes they didn't burn from orbit. It's home though. Our true home. Not some far away place that half of us might never see. It isn't too late to fix it, if we can get it back from the enemy."

"Yes, sir," Hafizi said.

They reached one of the three dozen or so elevators sprinkled throughout the ship. This one would bring them up into the quarterdeck. The bridge was on QD3. Only the sensor equipment and a maintenance level that had been converted to a damage control buffer sat above the large, open layout of the ship's command center.

Gabriel put his hand to the control pad of the elevator, expecting it to light up with a list of destinations. Instead, a red 'X' flashed on the interface above a message that read, "Access denied. Security lockout."

"What does that mean?" Hafizi asked.

"The elevators were locked out the last time a crew was in here working on things."

"Can we still get to the bridge?"

"Yeah. We have to take the stairs. It's only twenty floors."

"It figures," Diallo said.

"We could wait here for the General," Gabriel said. "His fingerprint should override the lockout. Of course, I don't think he would be too pleased to find us hanging out here."

"I'll take the stairs," Diallo said.

"Sounds good to me," Hafizi agreed.

The emergency stairwell was in an adjacent corridor. They opened the manual hatch and ascended quickly, not wanting to arrive behind the rest of the group. They exited into a second corridor and turned left, taking a short walk to the bridge's entry.

As they neared, Gabriel could hear low voices speaking inside. He raised his hand, ordering the MPs to a stop.

"This is going to be our salvation," one of the voices said. A man, judging by the tone of voice.

"For some of us," a female voice said. "Not all."

"You can't back down now, Sarah. Not when we've made it this far."

Sarah? Gabriel took in a sharp breath. He recognized Guy Larone's voice. Was this a joke? Were they going to be everywhere he went?

"I'm not backing down. It's just. It's troubling. You heard Captain St. Martin. I'm sure he isn't the only one who feels that way. I bet most of the military does, and they're the ones with the weapons. If General Cave can't reign him in, he can make a lot of problems for this trip."

"General Cave will get him under control. Take a look out there, Sarah. What do you see?"

"Gas clouds, stars, the usual."

"But no home."

"No."

"That's why I wanted to bring you here. I wanted you to see. I wanted you to be able to picture it more clearly. In six months, we could be staring out this same viewport at a pristine oasis of life. A perfect blue and green marble. A new home for humankind."

"I hope so. I want to see it. But the sacrifice-"

"There are no easy decisions left, love," Guy said. "The Dread took them all away. My father used to tell me about the invasion. About the pillars of fire, and how every military in the world was powerless against them. He was so grateful to have escaped, and yet so pained by what we had all lost. In two or three generations, no one will remember the ones who were left here or on Earth. No one will remember ever living in Calawan at all. Even Earth can be erased from people's memories. Destroy the videos and images, and in time it becomes nothing more than a myth. A bad dream. That is the beauty of time. A beauty matched only by your own."

Gabriel glanced over at Diallo and Hafizi. Diallo made a face like she was about the vomit, while Hafizi rolled his eyes. Was Guy trying to solidify his wife's resolve, or was this foreplay? And where was the pilot who must have brought them here?

"I love you, Guy," Sarah said.

"I love you, too."

Gabriel stepped quietly forward, pausing as he reached the open archway onto the bridge and looking up at the engraved plaque hanging above it. "IN GOD WE TRUST. U.S.S.S. Magellan. 2264." He could hear the couple kissing just out of his view.

He was going to enjoy this part.

He held up Diallo and Hafizi, stepping around the corner on his own, raising the gun and pointing it at Guy and Sarah's interlocked faces. They didn't notice him until he let out a soft cough.

"Hello, Guy. Sarah."

The scientists broke their embrace, their faces turning pale with sudden fear.

"Captain St. Martin? What are you doing here?"

"Apparently, we're stopping you from erasing as much of human history as you can. You had good reason to be worried about me before. You have even more reason to be worried now. We're taking the Magellan before you can fulfill your dream of leaving innocent people to die so that you can reach your Utopia."

"On what authority?" Guy asked. "You don't have access to this ship's control systems."

"He doesn't," Theodore said, rolling around the corner, flanked by Choi, Reza, Diallo, and Hafizi. "But I do. Good evening, Maggie."

51

The bridge jumped to attention in front of them. First, the lights that ringed the large space faded on to a comfortable brightness. Then the screens in front of each of the stations flashed to life like a row of dominoes, starting with the smallest screen on the right side of the raised Command chair and dropping down into the pit in front of it, running right to left across half a dozen pods organized around a large starmap station that dominated the forward position ahead of Command.

"Good evening, Colonel St. Martin," the ship's computer replied in a neutral female voice.

"It's General now, Maggie," Theodore said. "I know it's been a long time."

"Twenty two years, six months, eighteen days, twelve hours, forty-seven minutes, sir," Maggie replied. "Congratulations on your promotion."

Theodore chuckled. "You're a little late, but thank you. Gabriel, you'll take the helm. Reza, that pod over there is navigations. Go sit there and don't touch anything. Vivian, I expect you'll be my XO."

"Yes, sir," Gabriel said.

"I'm honored, sir," Vivian said. "What about Colonel Graham?"

"If the Colonel joins up, he'll be in charge of operations, same as he is on Delta."

"You can't do this," Guy said, remaining stationary with the gun aimed at him. "I'll have you arrested."

"Are you some kind of dumbass, boy?" Theodore said. "You're alone on a starship that I control, with no way out except past the gun pointed at your head. How exactly are you going to have me arrested? By the way, Gabriel, you can lower the weapon and get us underway."

"Yes, sir," Gabriel replied, lowering the gun. "Sir, you need to clear the security locks."

"I do, don't I? Maggie, can you clear all security protocols?"

"Protocols cleared, sir," Maggie replied.

"Thank you."

Gabriel stuck the gun back in the waist of his pants, grinning at the Larones as he descended the raised platform into the pit and took a seat in the front pod. The seat was very similar to that of a starfighter, as were the flight controls. The Command chair had a similar setup, as it was typically the ship's Commander who did the most intense piloting. The helmsman generally served as a backup when the Commander was attending to other duties, and to keep the ship on course during more mundane travel.

He dropped his right hand to the control pad there, navigating through it without looking until he brought the systems status up. The software on the Magellan was identical to the operating system on the starfighters, except a little more complex.

"Vivian," he heard his father say. "You've read the technical manual, correct?"

"Yes, sir. It was at least fifteen years ago."

"I'm sure it'll come back to you. I'm an old gator, and I still remember how it all works. Can you take the engineering pod for now? We need to heat the reactor up, and she can be a little temperamental. I need you to monitor the subsystems to make sure we don't go killing ourselves."

"Of course, General."

Gabriel looked back and up to where the Larones were standing near the edge of the pit.

"As for you two," he heard his father say. "We don't have a brig, or I'd lock you up there. We also aren't about to go shooting people because that would make us killers like you. I can't let you leave, since you've already threatened to have me arrested, and I didn't like that. Let me see, what's left?" There was a pause while Theodore considered. "I'll tell you what. You promise to follow my orders, and I won't ask Sergeant Diallo here to rough you up a bit."

"You just said you wouldn't hurt us," Guy said, sounding frightened and angry.

"I did not, boy. I said I wouldn't kill you. Hurting is another matter entirely, and if you keep testing my patience I will proceed with putting it on. Are we clear?"

"You won't get away with this," Guy said, remaining defiant.

"Guy," Sarah said before Theodore could respond. "I'm sorry, General. We'll follow your orders."

"Your wife is a smart woman. Pretty, too. It's a shame you two are so cold. You could be such a boon to the colony. I'm taking her word as yours. I hope it's good."

"It is, General," Sarah said. Guy remained silent.

"Go on down and join Reza at the nav station. If he tells you to jump, you damned well better jump. Understood?"

"Yes, sir," Sarah said. She and Guy appeared on the steps a moment later. She was pulling him by the arm, with Hafizi staying close behind.

"Maggie," Theodore said, his voice shifting as he moved to the Command Station. "Initiate startup series."

"Yes, sir," the computer replied. Immediately, the ship began to hum and shake.

"I don't remember that from last time," Theodore said. "Vivian, do we have an issue?"

"We blew a power converter on the secondary reactor," Major Choi said. "Diverting power through the alternates. I hope."

The ship stopped shaking, the hum vanishing as well. From the bridge, there was little indication that the starship was waking up.

"Main positron reactor stable," Choi said. "Secondary and tertiary stable. Quantum phase generator online."

"Navigation looks like it's online," Reza said.

The screen in front of Gabriel changed, revealing a three-sixty view of the Magellan, positioned in the center as a skeletal frame of the starship.

"Helm is online," Gabriel said.

"All systems are nominal," Choi said.

"After all of these years," Theodore said. "You still purr like a kitten, Maggie."

A tone sounded from the empty pod next to navigation.

"I can only think of one person that might be calling me already," Theodore said, receiving the same communication alert at the Command station.

Gabriel tapped his control pad a few times. The controls unlocked as the starship finished its initiation sequence. "We're ready to go, General."

"Do me a favor, Captain, get us on course for Delta Station while I take care of this couillon," Theodore said. There was an audible click as he sent the communication to the entire bridge.

"Teddy, what the hell do you think you're doing?" General Cave said, his voice sharp with anger.

"Why, hello there Alan," Theodore said. "I was hoping maybe you would give me a shout. In case you failed to notice, I'm taking my ship, and I'm moving it away from assholes like you."

Gabriel adjusted the suppressor energy levels, trimming the gravitational pull and using a small amount of hull thrust to begin lifting the Magellan from the surface of the planet. As he did, a cloud of dust began to rise around the fringes, rising into the atmosphere and swirling around the ship like a cape.

"You have no authority to do any such thing, Theodore," Cave said. "You were honorably discharged. Don't make me change that to dishonorably."

Theodore laughed. "Honor? You want to lecture me on honor? Take a look in the mirror, Alan, and hope it doesn't crack at the sight of your lying mug. You're slipperier than a gator in a swamp, and I ain't about to let you poison the few good and brave men and women of the Alliance who still believe in it."

"We've been friends for a long time, Theodore. Don't make me-"

"Make you what?" Theodore said. "You ain't got a damn thing that can hurt the Magellan, and so you ain't got a damn thing that can hurt me. Hearing you were going to abandon Juliet's memory and the people we left behind, that was the worst you could do. You know what happens when you disturb a viper's nest, Alan? It bites."

The communication cut off abruptly. Gabriel turned his head to look back at his father. Theodore was looking at him, and they shared a moment of satisfaction.

"Let's hurry things up a bit, son. I don't want to give Cave time to do something stupid."

"Yes, sir," Gabriel said, increasing the thrust.

The Magellan was already ten kilometers from the surface of the planet. Gabriel increased the power to the main thrusters, arranged in an 'X' pattern along the back of the starship. At the same time, he decreased the power to the outer suppressors. They were high enough that the weak gravity would no longer tether them to the ground.

"Reza," Theodore said. "Can you start plotting a slipstream path? Not too close to Earth, we don't want to get blown up before we can plan our next move."

"I've already started, sir," Reza said, flipping through the interface with the ease of someone who spent most of their life staring at a screen. "When we have some time, I can also make corrections to the operational algorithms to improve path efficiency."

Theodore raised his eyebrow. Gabriel smiled at the sight of it.

"Good man," Theodore said. "Captain Sturges, do you read me?"

The comm station clicked again. "Roger, General."

"Is everything on schedule?"

"Yes, sir. Captain Kim reports we have over sixty percent of Delta Station on our side."

"Sixty? That's low. Damn low."

"You've been out of action for quite a while, Dad," Gabriel said.

"There's a lot of young blood on Delta that doesn't even believe you're real."

"Bah. It's enough to handle Maggie. It'll have to do."

Gabriel smiled, turning back to the helm. Delta was approaching in a hurry.

A green triangle appeared on the HUD in front of him, a fighter launching from Gamma. The same one he had delivered earlier.

The triangle flashed, turning from green to red as the Magellan's new combat systems picked up an active weapon signature locked onto the starship.

"Uh, Dad," Gabriel said. "We have a small problem."

52

"You've got to be kidding me," Theodore said, getting his own view of the incoming fighter. "Who the hell did Cave find to send out here?"

Gabriel had a feeling he knew. There was one soldier on Gamma who might want to get in the General's good graces, and would certainly enjoy a chance to be a thorn in his side.

"Lewis," he said. "He's an asshole Lieutenant in charge of security on Gamma. He doesn't like me because Cave's daughter came onto me. I didn't know he was trained to fly a fighter."

"Felicia?" Theodore said. "Heh. Alan kept trying to keep her away from you. I'm happy to hear all of his efforts were for nothing."

"I'm not interested, Dad."

"Why not? She's a good looking girl. She's got good hips."

"Hips?" Gabriel said. "Who says that?"

"Do you think you could try paying attention to that fighter out there?" Guy said. "It's shooting at us."

"What does Maggie look like to you?" Theodore snapped. "This is a starship, not a damn speedboat. There's a reason combat starships carry fighters."

Gabriel looked up, watching the fighter zip past the bridge, firing its ion cannon at the surface of the Magellan. The heavy armor absorbed the attack without flinching, but that was the idea. Cave wanted to show Theodore he was serious, not inflict costly damage to the ship.

He watched the triangle circle around the skeleton of the Magellan, returning for a second run. The comm station toned.

"I knew you'd be calling me back," Theodore said.

"I don't want to make this hard," General Cave said. "Gabriel, put the Magellan back where you got her, and I promise we won't imprison you or your father."

Gabriel looked back at Theodore, shaking his head. The starfighter came back around, strafing the heavy armor with its ion cannon again.

"General, do you remember when I told you to go to Hell? Why are you still here?"

Cave didn't respond to the statement. "Theodore, if you want to be a hero, this isn't the way to do it. I can have Lewis target your thrusters and cause damage to the Magellan that can't be repaired. And then what, Teddy? The people of the NEA will hate you for breaking the most important asset we have, and neither one of us will get what we want."

"You wouldn't," Theodore said.

"Oh, no? Do you want to try me?"

Theodore was silent while he considered. Gabriel watched as four green triangles appeared on the HUD, all of the starfighters on Delta Station launching at high velocity and making a hard turn to head their way.

"You know what, Alan? I think I do," Theodore said, having seen the fighters as well. "You're a snake in the grass, and I just found myself a few mongoose."

He was the one to close the connection this time, cutting Cave off before he could respond.

The fighters were closing on the Magellan. Lewis must have noticed them, because he altered his vector, gaining some distance between them.

"General St. Martin," a new voice said over the comm. "This is

Captain Soon Kim, Alpha Squadron Leader. It looks like you could use an escort."

"Damn right we can, Captain. It's good to have you with us. My boy tells me you're a stellar pilot."

"He does? He's never told me that."

"I didn't want it to go to your head," Gabriel said.

"Too late," Soon said, laughing. His fighter buzzed past the bridge before spinning around and taking position above and to the front.

Delta Station was getting close, and Gabriel began slowing the ship for docking. Lewis' red triangle was growing ever more distant on the display.

"I'm going to ease her in," Gabriel said, switching his attention between the view from the bridge and the representation of the Magellan's position on the screen.

"No need, son," Theodore said. "Maggie can take it from here. Maggie, initiate docking procedure Delta."

"Yes, sir," the computer replied.

"Come on, Gabe. We've got some new guests to meet and greet."

Gabriel rose from his seat, joining his father. Theodore had already managed to swing himself from the Command Station to his wheelchair.

"Impressive," Gabriel said.

"Hurts like a son of a bitch," Theodore said, pulling one of the pill bottles from his pocket. He popped the top and dumped two of the red capsules into his mouth, swallowing them dry. "Hafizi, you're with us. Vivian, you have the bridge. Maggie, add security protocol beta for Choi, Vivian. Rank of Colonel."

"Yes, sir," Maggie replied.

"Colonel?" Major Choi said. She abandoned the engineering station, ascending the steps and taking over the Command chair.

"We can't have Graham getting too pissy about his assignment."

"You aren't authorized to raise my rank."

"Hah. I'm not authorized to do a damn thing, according to all of you people. And yet, when I look around, it seems that I'm still the one in charge."

Choi smiled. "Yes, sir."

"Keep her warm for me," Theodore said, rolling off the bridge ahead of Gabriel and Hafizi. They had to move quickly to keep up.

"Your father is something else," Hafizi said.

"You have no idea," Gabriel replied.

It had been so long since he had seen his father. He had gone to visit his physical husk a few times, sure, but the mind had been missing for years. To watch him up and at it gave him a pleasure he hadn't even known he was lacking.

Whatever happened from here on out, there was nothing that could take that away.

53

The airlocks between Delta Station and the Magellan slid open. Gabriel stood beside his father, eager to see who had decided to join them.

He smiled when Wallace was the first one through, running ahead and jumping up at him excitedly.

"Hey, buddy," Gabriel said, patting the dog's side.

Wallace shifted his attention to Theodore, sticking his nose in the General's face and trying to lick him.

"Okay, okay," Theodore said, trying to gently shove Wallace's face away. "I know, it's been a long time. Yeah, yeah. You can be my XD. Okay."

"General St. Martin," Colonel Graham said, having crossed the space between them while they were being assaulted. He came to attention and saluted sharply.

Gabriel looked up. The crew of Delta Station was waiting behind their Commanding Officer, at strict attention with spacebags on the ground beside them.

"Colonel Graham," Theodore said, returning the salute. "At ease,

James."

The Colonel shifted to a parade rest. "I can't believe you did this, sir," Graham said.

"I've been acting a fool for a long time, I admit. I wised up. So did you."

"Yes, sir." Graham's eyes shifted to Gabriel. "I was looking for a sign. I wasn't expecting it to park right outside my station." He looked back at Theodore. "I'd like to present most of the crew of Delta. They're all loyal to you and the mission, sir."

"Are they good men and women?" Theodore asked.

"The best," Graham replied.

"Let me see."

"Yes, sir." Graham turned around. "Company. Present."

The members of the crew marched forward in a perfect line, doing a good job remembering their days as cadets. They stopped when they reached the edge of Delta's airlock, a line of people that vanished back into the station. Gabriel could see Miranda a few rows back, and if Soon was out there running escort he was sure Daphne was in the mix somewhere as well.

Over one hundred hands snapped up in a sharp salute. Theodore and Gabriel both returned it.

"My fellow members of the New Earth Alliance Space Force," Theodore said, raising his voice loud enough that even the crew in the back were sure to hear. "I wish I could say this is going to be easy, but it ain't. Most likely, we're all going to die. As I like to say, it's better to die for something than to die doing nothing. If you don't agree, now is your chance to walk away."

They waited in silence. None of the assembled soldiers moved.

Theodore smiled. "In that case, welcome aboard." He lowered his voice, looking at Graham. "Colonel, I want you to be my Operations Officer."

"Not XO?" Graham asked. He was clearly disappointed.

"Please don't hurt an old gator's feelings, Jimmy. You know I respect the hell out of you. Right now, I need everyone to do what they do best and for you that's getting these people and this ship organized. What do you say?"

Graham nodded. He was a loyal soldier. "Of course, sir. Who do you need on the bridge?"

"A couple of engineers, someone to handle the comm, and a pair of systems techs. That should be enough to start."

"Consider it done. I'll send them up once I find them in the line."

"Uh, sirs?"

The new voice came from behind them. Gabriel spun, surprised that he hadn't heard anyone coming. Graham glanced up, and they all stared at the newcomer. She was young, maybe nineteen or twenty, with short brown hair and a pretty face. She couldn't have been more than three months out of training.

"My apologies. I'm Second Lieutenant Sandra Bale, sir."

"You're the pilot who brought the Larones over?" Gabriel guessed.

"Yes, sir," she replied. "I was waiting in the transport for them to come back. When the Magellan took off, I left my ship and found Captain Sturges. We talked about what you were doing, and he told me to find you." Wallace stepped over to her, sniffing her hand. She looked down at him and smiled, running her hand along his fur. "I've never seen a dog before. He's so soft."

"Lieutenant Bale, don't take this the wrong way," Gabriel said. "But where did you come from? If you're a recent graduate, you should have been assigned to Delta Station."

"And I don't know you," Graham said.

Bale's face turned red. "This is awkward," she said. "I haven't actually graduated yet."

"What?" Theodore said.

"General Cave needed someone to bring the Larones over to the Magellan, sir. He asked me to do it."

"How do you know him?" Gabriel asked.

She looked even more embarrassed. "We met last year, sir. At one of the restaurants on Alpha."

"Hoo-boy," Theodore said. "You're doing the dirty with him?"

"Dad," Gabriel said.

"It ain't none of my business, I know, but last I knew Alan was a married man. You're telling me you're his mistress?"

"I prefer not to think of it that way, sir," she replied. "Yes, we were in a relationship."

"And now you want to get off my boat. Is that it?" He pointed to the airlock, where Delta's soldiers were still standing at attention. "There's the exit. I'm keeping the transport."

"Actually, sir, I want to stay."

Theodore's eyes narrowed. Gabriel could tell his father didn't trust her. "Really? Why?"

"I didn't know what he was doing. What they were planning. I don't agree with it."

Theodore rubbed his chin. "Bale. Bale. Where do I know that name from? It sounds so familiar, but I just can't get it solid in my noggin."

"My father was David Bale, sir. He was a scientist. His father was Roland Bale. He was an administrator who happened to work on the base where the Magellan was docked. Your wife saved him. I mean, I know everyone is here because of you, but it's more than that."

"Is it?" Theodore said. "I don't remember every civilian that made it onto the Magellan. I suppose it doesn't matter. Even if Alan wants you to spy on me, there ain't much you can do from out here."

"I'm not a spy, General," Bale said. "I care about the people of the NEA. All of them."

"Then welcome aboard, Lieutenant. Colonel Graham here will get you settled with everyone else."

"Thank you, sir," she said.

"Go and join the others," Graham said.

"Yes, sir."

Bale went over to stand at attention at the front of the line.

"Do you really think she's a spy?" Gabriel asked.

"Her? I doubt it, but you never really know a person, do you? I thought I knew Alan Cave and I hate being wrong."

"Amen to that, sir," Graham said.

"Get your people loaded and ready, Colonel," Theodore said. "I want to be underway within the next half-hour."

"Yes, sir."

"Let's go, Gabriel. And bring Wallace with you. He is the XD, after all."

"Executive Dog?" Gabriel asked.

"Damn right."

"Yes, sir."

Gabriel walked beside Theodore as they made their way back to the elevator while Wallace ranged ahead and sniffed at different spots along the wall.

"Was there anyone you didn't see in the crowd that you were hoping to?" Theodore asked.

"It was hard to see to the back. We have enough pilots for the Magellan and the starfighters, and then some. Assuming you let Second Lieutenant Bales fly, that is."

"Why wouldn't I let her fly? She may be a cute little dollie type, and she may have messed around with Alan, but I don't think she's dumb enough to try anything that stupid."

"Let's hope not. So, we have a ship. We have a crew. We're going to Earth. Then what?"

"What do you think? We need to make contact with the resistance."

"We don't contact them. They contact us."

"Well that's the problem right there, ain't it?"

"A problem we haven't been able to solve in twenty-seven years."

"Not true, son. We know how to solve the problem. We just ain't ever had a good enough reason to order someone to do it."

Gabriel stopped in the corridor. He knew exactly what his father was suggesting. And who he was suggesting.

Theodore turned his head to lock eyes. "You know I wouldn't ask you to do it if I didn't think you could."

"I barely made it out last time at full tilt," Gabriel said. "What makes you think I can enter the atmosphere and survive at air speeds long enough to broadcast."

"Because you're my boy, and you're the best."

"That isn't a great reason. You're biased."

"I ain't biased that you're the best. You've proven that you are."

"I've never flown outside of a vacuum."

"Same thing. Mostly."

"You know it isn't. You can't flip a fighter over in place when you've got friction and gravity."

"Nope. Neither can they."

"So what if I pull it off? What if I can contact them? Then what?"

"We'll tell them what you told Graham and Choi. That the enemy's weapons can damage the armor, and that they need to get their hands on some."

"You don't think they already know that?"

"Nope. They never reported that they did, only that the weapons have some kind of security on them that they can't crack. Hell, if we can get one of those maybe we can crack it ourselves. We've got Mr. Mokri on board, and from what I've heard, he's a regular Einstein."

"Someone would have to land on the planet's surface to pick it up."

"Yup."

Theodore was still looking at him.

"Right," Gabriel said. "Survive the frying pan, jump into the fire. I get it."

"This is about the entire human race."

"I know. It's bigger than both of us. That doesn't make it any less frightening."

"Fear is a gift, Gabe. Fear gives you the edge you need to stay alive."

"Then I must have the sharpest edge around."

"You damn well better. I lost your mother. I don't want to lose you, too."

54

"We're away, General," Gabriel said, increasing thrust to put some distance between the Magellan and Delta Station.

He watched out the viewport as it vanished off the port side and they made their way toward empty space. His conversation with his father had left him equal parts frightened and excited. He had been born to be a warrior. He had been born to fight back against the Dread. When he had been at his lowest, all he had asked for was the chance to do something. Now that he had that chance, he didn't want to waste it.

"Mr. Mokri," Theodore said from his position at the Command Station.

"Yes, sir," Reza said.

"How are those calculations coming along?"

"They were done ten minutes ago, sir. I'm sending the sequence over to the helm now."

"I've got them," Gabriel said. "Setting slipstream sequence."

"Maggie can handle this for you, if you want, Captain," Theodore said.

"No thank you, sir. I prefer to handle it myself."

"As you will."

Gabriel tapped out the commands that would finalize the coordinates. Then he adjusted the throttle, opening up the thrusters. From inside the ship, there was little indication of the change in power or speed. Instead, Gabriel relied on the display to alert him to their current velocity. They had a nice long runway to get the Magellan into the slipstream.

"Sir, I'm getting a ping from Alpha," Spaceman Locke said from her position at the comm station. Gabriel had been pleased when she had entered the bridge with the rest of Graham's picks for duty. "It's General Cave."

Theodore laughed openly. "Put him on the general broadcast."

"Yes, sir."

"Alan. Here to wish us luck?"

"Believe it or not, Teddy, I am," Cave replied. "Whatever you think of me, I'm not your enemy. The Dread are. I want you to succeed, and I want you to bring the Magellan back in one piece. It's the only way any of us survives."

"That's awful gracious of you, Alan. I have every intention of bringing her back. Thank you for your support."

"I'm sorry it had to come to this."

"I'll take it any way it comes," Theodore said. "In your own convoluted way, you saved me from myself. I'll remember that." He used his controls to close the channel.

Gabriel watched the counter continue to climb, the Magellan nearing slip velocity. He tapped his control pad, preparing to activate the quantum phase generator. A silent reverence settled over the bridge as the rest of the assembled crew seemed to realize all at once what it was they were actually about to do.

He looked around the room. Miranda caught his eyes with hers, responding with a smile. Reza nodded to him. Guy and Sarah glowered, but Sarah nodded as well, showing him a hint of respect. The three engineers Graham had chosen huddled over their monitors, keeping a close eye on the systems as they prepared to slip.

Up on the dais, Theodore was leaning forward in his seat, watching space outside with an expression of eager determination. He had waited fifty years to return to Earth. Fifty years to attempt to avenge what the Dread had done.

That wait was nearly over.

Gabriel returned his attention to the display, holding his finger over the control pad. As the indicator hit slip speed, he dropped his finger and set the QPG to work. A sudden deep rumbling rippled through the Magellan before fading away.

"All systems nominal," the Chief Engineer, Technical Sergeant Abdullah said. "Everything looks good."

"Entering slipspace," Gabriel said. He couldn't see the nacelles, but he didn't need to. They bore the same distinctive construction as the wings of each starfighter, and would carry the remainder of the Magellan out of phase and into the slipstream with them. He knew it was happening when the stars began to fade away, and the ship started to shake slightly as it surfed along the edge of the wave.

"What's the ETA, Mr. Mokri?" Theodore asked.

"Seven hours, sir," Reza replied.

"Not bad," Theodore said. "Not bad at all."

Gabriel clutched at his crucifix, closing his eyes. He had never been sure about God, but he figured it couldn't hurt. The ship stopped shaking, and everything went silent and still. He opened his eyes and stared out at the empty black expanse ahead of them.

"Slipstream joined," he said.

They were on their way.

55

"I'm here to retrieve our guest," Donovan said, approaching the woman standing guard in front of the fridge.

Sergeant Wilcox saluted. "Yes, sir," she said, shouldering her rifle and moving to the handle of the large, stainless steel box.

"Thanks, Amanda," Donovan said. He had known Sergeant Wilcox for almost his entire life. Their parents had met up during the escape from Los Angeles and traveled to Mexico together. They had dated for a little while in the past, and she was still the only girl he had ever been with.

"I can't believe you caught an alien," she said, putting her hand on the cool metal. "What are you going to do with it?"

"Number one, I didn't catch her. She came voluntarily. Number two, she's a she, like you are. Not an it."

"She wasn't born. She came out of a tube or whatever as an adult. As far as I'm concerned, that makes it an it."

Donovan was tempted to chide her for being out of line with a superior officer. How dumb would that look? He was the one who had made the conversation casual. "She has breasts and a vagina, and her DNA is one-hundred percent human."

"Are you sure? Have you seen her naked already?"

Donovan shook his head. He wasn't even sure about the DNA part. The military clones were genetically altered. It was more than likely Ehri was, too. As for seeing her naked, he liked to think of himself as a gentleman. That didn't mean he didn't think she was attractive.

She was also the enemy. Whether he trusted her or not, that didn't change. She was confident the bek'hai were going to stomp them to dust, which was why she had helped them in the first place.

"Just open the door, Sergeant," he said, smiling. They had only dated for a little while because she had been too argumentative. It was as if having sex had given her leave to question or counter everything he said from then on, for no other reason than she seemed to enjoy it.

"Yes, sir," Wilcox replied, a hint of amused smugness in her voice. She wanted to get to him, and she had. She pulled the door open.

Ehri was sitting in the back of the fridge on a few sacks of grain they had managed to harvest from a field further up the mountain, and surrounded by a multitude of long-preserved edibles that had been foraged from anywhere their scouts could find them. She had a pleasant, slightly bored look on her face, which brightened instantly when she saw him.

Donovan stared at her for a moment before speaking. He still wasn't quite sure what to make of the story General Rodriguez had told him. Apparently, Ehri was a clone of a woman the General had known. A woman who had not only saved the lives of thousands, but who had also worked incredibly hard to help organize the early resistance. Obviously the Dread had also found value in her genes if they were using her as a template for their scientists.

"Are you okay?" Donovan asked.

"Yes, I'm fine," Ehri said, getting to her feet.

She looked different. Less alien. Donovan realized it was because they had taken her dress and replaced it with whatever surplus they had found to fit her. A simple pink t-shirt that Donovan knew belonged to Diaz, and an old pair of jeans. They had also been kind enough to give her sneakers. He doubted her feet were as used to being bare as his own.

"They are interesting," she said, tugging at the sleeve of the shirt. "Not as soft or as warm as I am accustomed, but I do feel a sense of-" She paused, trying to decide on the word. "Freedom, maybe? I have always appeared the same as the others, and now I don't."

"You look like you were born here," Donovan said.

"I am happy to try to fit in. Subjects do not act the same when they know they are under observation. It takes time for them to forget you are there."

"I thought you haven't studied humans directly before?"

"I haven't. We also do research on the drumhr to measure the integration and ascertain fit."

"What does that mean?"

"Splicing bek'hai genetic code with human genetic code tends to introduce new traits. Those traits are human in some cases, and entirely new in others. We have to monitor these traits to ensure we don't create something we do not want."

"Such as?"

"Earlier alterations produced drumhr who were extremely violent."

"You killed billions of humans. Isn't that violent?"

"No. That is war. By violent, I mean they would attack others with no provocation. They would eviscerate them, decapitate them. There was one case of what you would call rape."

"Are you sure that wasn't too much of the human traits?" Donovan asked. The end of human civilization hadn't only produced rebels. It could be a very dangerous world out there.

"I did not say it wasn't. Either way, it was an unacceptable alteration. This was all before I was made. I know these things from research notes."

"I see. Well, General Rodriguez put me in charge of keeping an eye on you. He's also given me permission to allow you access to most of the base as long as I'm with you."

"What about when you aren't with me?"

"You'll either be in here, or in the nursery."

"The nursery?" She made a face that was both nervous and touched. "You would trust me with your children?"

"They aren't mine. And yes, I do trust you, though not everyone here will or does. I expect you'll get a lot of looks, and you'll probably hear whispers."

"I have studied humans. I expect as much."

"Right. As for the nursery, I'll leave you there when I can't be with you because my mother runs it. She'll keep the others off your back."

Ehri smiled. "Your mother? I should very much like to learn of this kind of familial interaction. The bek'hai no longer have a concept of parenthood, or of children."

Donovan had already guessed that. So had General Rodriguez. They had decided to leave Ehri with Wanda at times for that very reason. The human she was created from, Juliet, had been extremely compassionate and loved children though she had none of her own. And of course, they wanted to win Ehri over to their side. It could lead to her revealing more valuable information than she otherwise would. They hoped that connecting her to the inherent qualities of Juliet St. Martin would be the path of least resistance.

"Good," Donovan said. "I was hoping to give you something you would find of value to your study. In payment for what you gave us."

"You would have figured out the plasma weapon eventually. The bek'hai will never understand the value of natural offspring. It has been lost to them for too many centuries. This learning will be of great benefit."

"I get the feeling you want me to go away and leave you with my mom right now."

Ehri laughed. "I am excited about the prospect, yes. I also enjoy your company, Major."

Donovan felt a twinge in his chest. He pushed it aside. "Right now, I'm to bring you to Doctor Montoya. He's the administrator for our base, and as a former psychologist, he's also a bit of a sociologist himself. He wants to ask you some questions about the bek'hai."

"Yes. Of course. As I said, I will share whatever information I can. I do have two questions."

"What is it?"

"One, are we going to eat soon? I have not had a meal since we met."

Donovan smiled. "Yes. Right after we speak with Doctor Montoya. I haven't eaten in almost two days myself. I'm so used to it; I hadn't even noticed."

"Do you have a shortage of food?"

"No. We have this storage, plus a larger one downstairs where we keep the game we catch. It's cooler down there. We're lucky the ovens still work here. It's because I spend a lot of time out of the base. On missions to transmit our signals mostly, but I've also gone with the scouts on occasion to search for things we can use. What was your other question?"

"Do you have a place to void?"

"Void?"

"A toilet?"

"Oh." Donovan could feel his face turning red. How had he forgotten she would need to relieve herself? Her body was still human. "Of course. I'm sorry."

"I know you are unaccustomed to me, as I am unaccustomed to you. We will each learn from the other, and regardless of when or how the bek'hai destroy your people, we will perhaps change the course of the universe through this understanding."

"I'd rather do it without being destroyed," Donovan said.

"I know, and I am sorry for that. The will of the Domo'dahm cannot be altered by any of us."

Donovan's mind wandered back to the sight of the plasma bolt cutting through the Dread warrior's breastplate. Maybe Ehri's statement wasn't as true as she thought it was?

He was going to do anything he could to make it false.

56

Walking Ehri through the halls was as surreal an experience as Donovan had ever experienced. He had expected that she would receive angry stares, comments whispered just loud enough for her to hear, and maybe even an attempt at violence from someone as stupid as Captain Reyes.

He was wrong.

Of course, the people watched her. They stared as he escorted her out of the fridge and through the hallways, first to the bathroom and then to Montoya's office. They kept their eyes glued to her in a curiosity mixed with wonder and some small bit of resentment. The outright hatred wasn't manifest, though. Was it because they had heard about the weapons they had brought back? Had word already spread that she was responsible for helping them escape? Or had General Rodriguez sent his own whispers throughout the base, asking the people to be calm and kind and welcoming because this clone could hold more keys to defeating the Dread than they even understood right now?

Whatever the reason, Donovan was thankful for it. He could tell Ehri was as well. She smiled at the people who looked on her with wonder. Her expression was priceless as she took it all in. And when she saw a young girl run across a hallway in front of her, she nearly had tears in her eyes for the experience.

"What do you think?" Donovan asked as they reached Montoya's office.

"This is everything I ever dreamed of. The videos and photos do not compare. I will be a hero to my peers for the information I am gathering."

"What about the child?"

"Amazing. Beautiful."

Donovan opened the door to Montoya's office. The doctor was sitting behind the desk, leaning back in his chair with an ancient book cradled in his hands. He set it down carefully before standing at attention.

"Major," Montoya said. He was middle-aged, with a bald head and a pair of old, round glasses resting on a small nose. He was dressed in a worn pair of slacks and collared shirt. "And Ehri, is it?" He circled the desk as they entered, reaching out to shake Ehri's hand and smiling broadly. "I can't tell you what a pleasure it is to meet you. I've studied everything I can about the Dread, but there's so little that we know. Every word you speak will be new information for us."

"Surely not every word, Doctor," Ehri said.

"You speak English so well."

"I speak seven human languages."

"Incredible. Please, both of you, have a seat."

There were two chairs against the wall. Montoya grabbed them and dragged them over.

"You have an hour, Doc," Donovan said. "Ehri hasn't eaten, and neither have I."

"Oh. I can't possibly get through all of my questions in an hour."

"She'll come back."

"Okay. Let me do my best then." He returned to the desk, reaching down and taking a legal pad from a drawer, along with a pencil.

It was low-tech, the best they could manage. There were only three functional computers, and they were needed to maintain the link to the other resistance bases. Anything he wrote now would be transcribed and distributed later.

"Please state your name, age, and place of birth for the records."

"My name is Ehri dur Tuhrik. My physical body is equivalent to that of a twenty-four-year-old human. I was released from the generation chamber seven years ago. My place of birth is the bek'hai mothership."

Doctor Montoya was writing everything down as quickly as he could.

"You say you were released from the generation chamber. Can you describe what a generation chamber is, and how it functions?"

"Of course. The generation chamber is how the bek'hai reproduce. It is what you would call a cloning device. It is essentially a vat of nutrients in which base genetic material is submerged and excited in order to make it grow. A generation chamber produces a fully formed and adult bek'hai in approximately eight weeks."

"Eight weeks?" Donovan said. "You went from a single cell to a seventeen-year-old human in two months? And you've been alive for seven years since then? How do you have such an extensive education?"

"If you don't mind, Major," Montoya said. "I'll ask the questions. Ehri, go ahead. I'm also interested to know."

"First, during the generation process, targeted electrical currents are used to implant a standard set of directives and information into the developing brain. We leave the generation chamber already able to speak the bek'hai language, dress ourselves, and perform other functions an adult bek'hai is expected to perform. Second, each lor'hai, or clone, regardless of type, has a purpose. A specific job that they are intended to do. As a scientist, I dedicated all of my time to study beneath Dahm Tuhrik, eventually becoming his Si'dahm. His second."

"So you're saying you have no children at all?" Montoya asked.

"No. The bek'hai culture had children once, many hundreds of years ago. That has not been our way for quite some time."

"Then do you have relations?"

"Relations?" Ehri asked, confused.

"Sexual relations. Intercourse."

"No. It is a process that my team would like to re-introduce. As it is, the bek'hai can generally be divided into three classes. If you are not a warrior or a scientist, you are a servant of warriors or scientists."

"You said you want to re-introduce sexual intercourse? Why?"

"Our survival depends on it. Only certain kinds of genomes are acceptable for us in the generation chamber, despite many years of efforts to perfect the technology. Over time, this greatly retards genetic diversity. With our integration of humankind, we have a much larger pool of potential genetic code, but without natural reproduction, this pool will shrink and dry up once more."

"What kind of challenges have you faced?"

"Neither warriors nor scientists see the value in what you call relations. To them, it is primitive and animalistic. We have had some success with the servants, but their value is limited and we don't desire to over-diversify them."

"So you're saying that because servants are inferior, you don't want too many of them?"

"Yes."

"Like humankind?"

"There are parallels that may be interpolated, yes."

"You sound like a lawyer I used to know."

"Lawyer?"

"Never mind. You aren't an alien, in a sense, correct?" Montoya said. "You're a clone of a human woman."

"That is correct."

"What about the aliens? The real Dread? What do they look like?"

"I do not know."

The answer surprised both Doctor Montoya and Donovan.

"You don't know?" Donovan said, forgetting himself.

Ehri smiled at his speaking out of turn. She looked at him. "I have never seen a pure bek'hai. There are very few remaining. Even the Domo'dahm is a drumhr."

"Drumhr?" Montoya said.

"Half-human, half bek'hai," Donovan said. "I've seen them. You said you live around one hundred Earth years. Your kind has only been here for fifty. Why aren't there more of the original?"

"Major," Montoya said, trying to take charge of the interview again.

"Do you want to know?" Donovan asked.

"Yes."

"Then stop correcting me and get your pencil ready."

Montoya made a rejected face and readied his pencil. Ehri almost laughed at the reaction, her mouth parting in a small smile.

"The bek'hai were very sick. Only a small percentage have survived to the date of their surrender. The years since we arrived on this planet have produced healthier bek'hai in the form of the drumhr, but even they have their limitations. We are improving with each generation."

"I think I understand," Montoya said. "I want to come back to speak more on Dread, er, bek'hai culture, but for now let's talk about something else. Can you tell me more about your technology. Things like communications, transportation, computation."

"Shields," Ehri said. "Or the plasma weapons? I know you very much want to know how the bek'hai are able to both protect themselves and harm themselves the way they do. Even if I could answer that question for you, I wouldn't. That is something you will have to work out for yourselves, if you can."

Montoya stared at her, a sour expression crossing his face. "I have one more question, and then we can break for the day so you can get more settled. What do the bek'hai think about your treachery? How does such an action make them feel, in context with your culture?"

Donovan could tell by Montoya's face that he had been hoping the question would shake her, maybe as a test of her loyalty to both the Dread and the promise she had made to him.

She reacted with the same calm confidence as she had handled everything else.

"Some would label me a traitor, and wish me dead. Others will call me a hero for what I have sacrificed to be here, and for the knowledge I will gain if I survive."

"What do you mean, if you survive?" Montoya asked.

"This base is well protected, and well hidden. I believe you will survive here for some time. You will not survive here forever."

"Is that a threat?"

"No, Doctor Montoya. That is the simple truth of your situation. It requires no intervention from me, and I plan to provide none. As I have told Donovan, the Domo'dahm wishes all resisting humans dead within the year. The pur'dahm will do all in their power to make it so."

Montoya's face was pale, his hand shaking with a combination of fear and anger as he finished writing his notes. "Major, will you bring Ehri back tomorrow at the same time? I'll prepare follow-up questions based on what I've learned today."

"Sure," Donovan said. "Do you want to head to the cafeteria with us, Doctor?"

Montoya looked at Donovan as if he were insane. "No, thank you. I don't have much of an appetite right now."

57

"That went well," Donovan said, leading Ehri downstairs to the cafeteria. "Did you have to mention the part about your kind killing all of us again?"

"My apologies, Major. It is only-" she trailed off.

"Only what?" he asked.

She pursed her lips. She seemed conflicted to him. "I have seen little of this base or its people so far, I admit. Even so, I get this sense of an attitude that is permeating through both. It seems that while your kind believes things are bad, it is simply the new normal. That you have grown accustomed to it, and have become complacent and satisfied as a result."

Donovan glanced over at her. "You picked all that up just from talking to Montoya?"

"It isn't only Montoya. I saw it in you when we met as well. Even trapped in the bek'hai mothership, you seemed almost arrogant, despite your situation."

"Arrogance is a very human trait," Donovan said. "As is selfishness and jackassery."

"Jackassery?"

"Acting stupid. Like Reyes did. It's true that some of the people here have gotten too comfortable with how things are. Most of those people are refugees and civilians. They have important roles here on the base, but they never go out there. They don't see how the world has been burned. The arrogance you sense is a defense. A way of controlling fear. When you've been living afraid for so long, it just becomes a way of life. Montoya was not as much afraid of you as he was of what you represent."

"What I represent?"

"Yeah. Superiority. The future. I think everyone here knows the score. Humankind is dying, and unless we get lucky or do something smart we won't be here a year from now. We've been fighting an uphill battle for fifty years. A war where we were the only casualties until today."

"I understand. How do you manage it so well, Major?"

"Fear?"

"Yes."

"I invite it. It shows me how much I care. The alternative is to drown in it, and I can't stand the thought of that. You don't seem to be afraid of being here. You didn't hesitate to come back with us, and you seem more excited than frightened."

"I'm not afraid. Not of this. Perhaps because the bek'hai do not value life the way humans do. We are made to adults in a number of weeks while you take years to mature. It is even worse for clones. Even clone scientists are servants of a kind."

"That's what I don't understand," Donovan said. "Don't take this the wrong way, but what are the bek'hai's overall purpose? Do you love one another? Do you experience things outside of your assigned roles? Do you even have free time to do anything you want to do? It seems that as a whole, you're missing a lot of what makes life worth it. Maybe that's the real reason you don't value it very highly."

"I loved my Dahm. I love learning."

"What about music? Dancing? Jokes? Laughter? Celebrations?"

"Perhaps there is some of that among the pur'dahm," Ehri said. "I was made for a different purpose."

"And you don't desire anything else?"

"No."

She said it softly. Donovan wasn't convinced. "So being here to learn is the only reason to enjoy being here? What about the experience of what you learn? What about the meal you are about to eat? Or the emotions and the personalities of the people you will talk to?"

"I came to observe you, and I will return my observations to whoever is named the new Dahm."

"You were the Si'dahm. Shouldn't you become Dahm?"

"I cannot. I am not drumhr."

"And that's okay?"

"Yes. That is our way."

Donovan looked over at her again. They were almost to the cafeteria, and her face was flushed, her eyes cast down to the floor. He would ask her again once she had experienced a little more of a life of freedom.

Maybe she would be honest with him then.

58

"Colonel Choi, Captain St. Martin, Mr. Mokri, Mr. Larone, Mrs. Larone, come on up and join me, will you?" Theodore said in a booming voice.

Ten quiet, tense minutes had passed since the Magellan had entered slipspace, riding a wave of distortion across the vastness of the universe toward Earth. Most of the crew knew one another, or at least knew of one another, but it didn't diminish the level of eager discomfort they were feeling. They had disobeyed their superior officer. They were traitors and deserters, all of them.

At the same time, they respected Theodore and his point of view, one that fell much closer in line to their upbringing and training. To a man, with the exception of the Larones, they didn't want to run off to another planet. They wanted to stay and fight, even if the odds were impossibly stacked against them.

Gabriel rose from his pod, smiling at Miranda as he headed toward the back of the bridge with the scientists. Now that they were in the slipstream, he didn't need to do anything. Nobody did. Once the wave was joined, they would only need to worry about disengaging at the right place and time.

"Yes, sir?" Colonel Choi said, saluting Theodore when she reached him.

"Let's take a walk, shall we?" Theodore said. "There's a conference room across the corridor. I already called for Colonel Graham. I want to talk to the five of you."

"What do you want from us?" Guy said, looking at his wife. "Do you think we're going to help you?"

Theodore laughed. "I know you're going to help me, son. Because if you don't, this ship is going to get blown to flotsam, and you're going to be on it when it does."

"You're a damned psycho," Guy said, getting angry. "Keeping us here against our will, forcing us to take this trip with you. You don't get it, do you old man? Nobody in the NEA wants to fight this war anymore. They want a real home. A place where food grows in the ground, not on a wall."

Theodore leaned on his arms as if he was going to try to stand. He paused when he realized he couldn't, keeping himself in the position.

"Nobody?" he shouted, causing Guy to flinch and step back. "Who in the damned hells are you calling nobody? There ain't a soul in this universe who calls my son a nobody, you son of a bitch. There ain't a person on Earth or on Calawan that questions the value of the men and women who gave up everything to be on this ship, to fight for what they believe in, and to have the guts that you so sorely lack. Now, you will get in line, you will help us do what needs to be done, and you will do it with quiet respect, or I will throw you off of my starship. Do you hear me, boy?"

Guy clenched his jaw, somewhere in between anger and fear. Sarah stepped in front of him. "I'm sorry, sir," she said. "Guy doesn't handle change well."

"Well ain't that sweet," Theodore said. "Welcome to the present, Mr. Larone. Change is inevitable. I'm an old man, and I ain't afraid of a little change. I invite it. Now, let's take that walk."

Gabriel helped his father into his chair this time. Theodore's arms were shaking and tired from holding himself erect to yell at Guy. They followed as he wheeled himself off the bridge and a few meters down the hall. The opposite door was open. Colonel Graham was already present, and he saluted sharply as Theodore entered.

"At ease, Jimmy," Theodore said. "Everybody grab a seat."

The chairs on the Magellan were plush cloth, much finer than anything they had in the settlements. Gabriel was surprised at their comfort as he took his seat next to his father. Not surprisingly, Guy took a position at the opposite end, keeping himself separate from the others while Sarah sat halfway between.

"You always been a peacemaker, Mrs. Larone?" Theodore asked.

"I don't see the point in conflict. Not now. If the only way we survive is to help as best we can, then that is what both of us will do." She glared at Guy. "Or you can find a new wife."

Guy looked like he wanted to say something. He remained quiet.

"The reason I asked you here is so that we can plan our first mission," Theodore said.

"Which is?" Colonel Graham asked.

"I'm going into the atmosphere," Gabriel said.

"What?" Colonel Choi said. "General-"

"I'm doing it," Gabriel said. "Thank you for your concern, Colonel. I can take care of myself."

She didn't look happy, but she nodded.

"Gabriel is going to take one of the fighters in and fly it low to try to get in contact with the resistance," Theodore said.

"The resistance is disbanding," Guy said. "You heard the message."

"I heard it," Theodore said. "But I know how people like me think. Just because one man wants to stop doesn't mean they all do. Besides that, we have information for them that they might find valuable. Hell, it might change the whole face of this war."

"How are you going to transmit to them?" Reza asked. "You have no idea what band they'll be listening on, if they're listening at all."

"That's why I need scientists, Mr. Mokri. Scientists like you and the Larones. You have a background in engineering, and they have both broad-based theoretical training and a specialty in waveform patterns. I ain't the smartest berry on the tree, but I think that ain't too different from slipstream patterns, is it?"

"No, sir," Sarah said. "I have some experience with communications systems. I spent a year over there during my training."

"That was fifteen years ago," Guy said.

"I remember most of it. Seriously, Guy. Either help or shut up."

"Fine. I've done some work on the fighters in the past. The phase generators, mostly, but I have a general understanding of the equipment on board."

"Good man," Theodore said, warming immediately with Guy's compliance. "I knew we could count on you. Now, what do we need to do to get the message to the resistance?"

"Besides a low altitude sweep?" Reza said.

"Yes."

"Well, what can you tell me about Earth communications before the invasion, sir?"

"There was nothing but dirt and smut on the Internet. I can tell you that much."

"The Internet, right. A hardened communication system, designed to withstand disruption by any number of natural disasters, or in this case an alien invasion. That's our best bet for an attack vector."

"I like how you speak, Mr. Mokri."

"Thank you, sir," Reza said, blushing. "So, without satellites or wireless links, they'll have to be using wired connections. It's unlikely the Dread attack damaged underwater or underground cabling, so we should be in luck there."

"You can't transmit a wireless signal into a wire," Sarah said. "It needs to be received wirelessly."

"There has to be a receiver still active somewhere. It's a network, so all we need to do is hit one access point. I assume the data transfer protocols are the same as what is on the Magellan, sir?"

"There ain't been anyone to update them."

"Okay, so if we can get the gain high enough we can pump the signal out, and hopefully it will hit a functional device that can transfer it to whatever resistance computers may be up and running. If we assume that technology has been dormant on Earth, we can base our design on the equipment here on the Magellan."

"We'll need a lot of power to put out that kind of signal," Guy said. "Add to the friction of the atmosphere, and we will need to boost the starfighter's energy stores significantly."

"I have techs that can help with that," Colonel Graham said.

"I knew you would," Theodore said. "Now, you see what we can accomplish when our backs are against the wall?"

Colonel Choi was shaking her head. "So, Gabriel flies his starfighter into the atmosphere and makes a sweep of the surface, transmitting a signal to the resistance. I'm going to assume he makes it because he always has. I'll assume the resistance gets the message, too. Then what?"

"We'll wait near Mars, using the planet to stay hidden. Gabriel comes back, and then we wait. Mr. Mokri, how long until the next regular reconnaissance slip?"

"Sixteen days, sir."

"We'll wait sixteen days. Then Gabriel will go back to pick up whatever message they left for us. We'll decide what to do after that once we can reestablish communications."

"What if the Dread come looking for us?" Sarah asked.

"Then we'll play 'spot the gator' until we either launch the mission or die," Theodore said.

"You've got it all figured out, don't you?" Colonel Graham said.

"You're damned right I do," Theodore replied. "Everybody does their part, and maybe we can start turning the tide of this war. Now, let's get to it. Dismissed."

59

On a ship as large as the Magellan, slipspace was a chance to finally get a little downtime. It hadn't occurred to Gabriel that he had been running for nearly twenty-four hours without sleep until Colonel Graham had been summoned to the bridge along with a small replacement crew, and they had all been sent to their quarters to get some sleep.

"I didn't even know I had quarters," Gabriel said.

"We did yours and your father's first," Daphne replied.

They were walking down to his room. Theodore had requested Gabriel be put a little closer to the launch tubes, so that he could be ready if he was needed. Ready for what? He had no idea.

It didn't matter. He felt alive on the Magellan, as if all of his years of training and all of the missions he survived had all been leading up to this moment. Unlike some of the other crew, he didn't share the mixed emotions over disobeying Cave's orders.

"How do you like her?" Gabriel asked.

"The Magellan? The corridors are a little claustrophobic, and the bunks are tiny. Otherwise, I have no complaints."

"I'm glad you decided to come."

She laughed. "It wasn't much of a choice. I'm not going to leave Soon to fend for himself, and he wasn't about to let you go off and steal all the glory."

"He said that?"

"Word for word."

"I think there will be plenty of glory to go around."

"Me too. Even for logistics officers like me."

They reached the door to Gabriel's quarters. Daphne pulled the handle, giving it a shove with her shoulder to convince it that it wanted to open.

"The hinges need a little attention," she said. "Well, what do you think?"

Gabriel stared in at the room. He had been expecting something simple, like on Delta Station. Instead, the quarters were expansive, with carpeting and couches, and a raised bed, a real bed, on a platform near the back. To the left of it was a large viewport, and to the right an archway leading into a large bathroom.

"You're lucky, you get your own shower. No three minute rule here," Daphne said. "Every drop of liquid on this boat gets processed and recycled, and the tanks are large enough for a crew of thousands, not hundreds. This is the Orbital Group Commander's quarters."

"The COG's quarters? My father didn't say anything about that to me."

"I guess he figured it was obvious."

"I don't know. Soon is just as qualified for the job."

"You're humility would be annoying if you weren't so sincere. Nobody is as qualified as you. Do you like it?"

"It's amazing. I didn't know the Magellan was so opulent."

"Most of it isn't, but it's still a step up from Delta, at least for as long as we have such a small crew. If you think this is fancy, you should see the General's quarters."

"I'm sure I will at some point. Hey, where's Wallace?"

"Soon is keeping an eye on him. I'll send him over."

"Thanks, Daphne."

"You're welcome. Try to get some rest, will you. You can't be a hero with your eyes closed."

Gabriel gave Daphne a quick hug. "You, too. You can't organize a starship with your eyes closed either. You'll keep running into walls."

Daphne turned to leave at the same time Wallace appeared in the doorway. He hurried over to Gabriel, putting his head down to be pet.

"I found this mangy thing hanging out next door," Soon said.

"Are you talking about yourself, dear?" Daphne asked.

"Of course."

"Thanks for running interference out there," Gabriel said. "It's good to have you with us."

"Us pilots have to stick together. I've always got your wing, Captain."

"And I have yours, Captain."

"Come on, Soon. Let's leave the man and his dog to relax for a while."

"Whatever you say, boss." Soon replied. "See you later, Gabe." He put his arm around her waist, and they headed off together.

Gabriel pushed the door closed, and then scanned the room again. In eight hours he would be suiting up to make a run on Earth. A run unlike any other he had made before. He had confidence in his abilities, but he had never flown outside of a vacuum before. None of them had except for his father. He had used the simulator, of course, but that wasn't the same thing.

Nothing was chasing you in the simulator.

He looked over at the bed, and then to the bathroom. He began stripping off his clothes.

If he was going to die soon, he would die clean and relaxed and having enjoyed the longest shower of his life.

60

"Can you hear me okay?" Miranda asked.

Gabriel adjusted his helmet, tapping on the side. "Try again."

"Testing. One. Two."

"It has to be on your side."

"I'll get one of the engineers to look at it while you're gone. It should be fixed by the time you get back."

"It better be."

Gabriel leaned back in the seat of the starfighter, holding his mother's crucifix. He closed his eyes, concentrating on his breathing. This mission wasn't like all of the others. Not just because of the atmosphere. There would be no slipstream ride to Earth. The Magellan would fire him at max power from its launch tubes, bringing him up to speed in a matter of seconds. After that, he would do a light, continual burn that would get him to Earth within ten hours.

He was nervous, and that was okay. It was normal. The fear was normal. If he didn't feel it, he knew he would get sloppy and die. He felt ready. He had showered, slept for a few hours, and woken to a hot bowl of oatmeal waiting at the end of his bed. It was the best food he had tasted for some time, so much better than the nutrient bars.

Gabriel tapped his control pad, and then eyed his power levels. Guy and Colonel Graham's crew had been hard at work during the entire slip, using a spare cell that had been loaded into storage and somehow finding a way to shoehorn it into place beside the primary. It had meant removing the ion cannon's targeting computer, but what good would that do him anyway?

Reza and Sarah had also done their part, running tests against the Magellan's onboard network to determine when they had solved the transmission problem. From there, Reza had gotten the circuit boards in the fighter pulled so he could do some additional soldering on them to expand the capabilities of the equipment. They had done a simple test only minutes earlier, ensuring that the whole package functioned as expected.

As far as Gabriel was concerned, if anyone was going to be called a hero for this, it should be the scientists who had even made his run possible. He hated to admit it, but that included Guy as well. For all of his complaints, the man had come through when it mattered the most.

"We're going to be getting a clear shot in one minute," Miranda said. "Try not to hit anything on your way in."

The Magellan was sitting about three quarters of the distance between Earth and Mars, as close as Theodore dared to take it without risking discovery.

Gabriel laughed. "I'll do my best."

"Gabriel, this is your father," Theodore said, his voice cutting into the comm. "I don't need to tell you what to do, or how to do it. I know we've had our differences over the years, but then, who hasn't? You're a St. Martin, and that makes you a stubborn gator by default. But you're a damn fine pilot and a damn fine son. I want you to know your old man is proud of you, and I know your mom would be proud of you too."

Gabriel felt a chill wash over him. Who didn't want to make their parents proud?

"Thanks, Dad."

"Captain, prepare to launch on my mark," Miranda said, switching the tone of the conversation to a purely professional one.

"Roger. Wish me luck."

"Good luck, Captain," Theodore said. "May God be with you."

Gabriel squeezed the crucifix one last time before letting it drop and taking hold of the control sticks. He took one more long breath and held it for a few seconds before releasing.

"Launching in three. Two. One."

Gabriel was pushed back in his seat as the magnetic launcher pulled him forward through the tube. The lights were a growing blur while he streaked through the tunnel, his pulse quickening in an instant.

Then he was out, rocketing forward through space. Mars was at his back, small and red. Earth was a distant speck ahead of him. It wouldn't be for long.

He turned his head, looking back over his shoulder at the Magellan. It was shrinking fast, growing more distant with each passing second. He could picture his father up on the bridge, watching the starfighter vanish within moments. He wondered what he was thinking, smiling as he did. He imagined his father was telling him to hurry the hell up.

He put his eyes forward again, keeping his attention on the HUD and ready to fire the vectoring thrusters should any solid masses pop up in front of his course.

Ten hours quickly became nine, and then eight, and then seven. The Earth began to come into view as he reached the one hour mark, continually to growing larger ahead of him, slowly morphing from a bright point of white light to a more bluish tinged point, to a small blue sphere.

His thoughts redirected to Jessica. He knew how much she would have wanted to be a part of this. She had always been so passionate about her beliefs, and the war was something she had believed in. It was that passion that had led them to fall in love. It was the same passion that had sent her to her death. He used it now to steel himself against the coming storm. To find strength and focus.

He was a warrior, a soldier on a mission.

He wouldn't be denied.

M.R. Forbes

61

"General Rodriguez," Donovan said, standing at attention and saluting.

"At ease, Major," Rodriguez said.

Donovan adjusted his stance before making eye contact with the rest of the assembly. He had come running when one of Carlson's assistants had found him and asked him to head down to the lab right away, but it seemed even his best time was slower than the General, Diaz, Montero, and Sharma.

Maybe if he hadn't dropped Ehri with his mother first.

It had been three days since Donovan had brought the alien clone back to the resistance base. They had been the three busiest and most fulfilling days of his life. When he wasn't escorting Ehri around, teaching her about human life, or in many cases just allowing her to observe his routine, he was working to organize and prepare for his next mission to make one last ditch effort to contact the space forces. It was more work than usual, mainly due to his need to find at least six more volunteers for the mission, though he preferred to take as many as he could find. The resistance base had a limited pool of potentials to begin with, and many of the fighters weren't in good enough physical condition to make a good runner.

As for Ehri, she was absorbing what it was like for them with alarming aptitude, quickly adjusting her speech patterns to better match theirs, as well as learning everything she could. She spent time with Doctor Montoya, answering his questions. She spent time in the kitchens learning to cook. She spent time with the seamstresses learning to sew. She even spent time with Matteo, watching him repair this and that around the base, and quickly making everyone on the base forget she wasn't human or truly one of them.

Of course, it was the nursery where she was the happiest. Every moment with a child was a learning experience for her, and she delighted in their generally unpredictable nature, finding a great challenge in trying to understand how they thought and functioned, and somehow maintaining her patience when she couldn't. She also enjoyed his mother's stories about him, and about how he had been as a child. Rambunctious and independent. He hadn't changed since then.

"Carlson, we have everyone here," General Rodriguez said, giving the CSO the floor.

"Thank you, General," Carlson said. He had a smile on his face, though his hair was dirty and messy and he looked as if he hadn't slept since Donovan had returned.

Donovan realized he probably hadn't. Carlson had joked about it, but it was no joke at all.

"I've been working on the alien tech that Major Peters and Lieutenant Diaz returned after their last mission. I wanted to give you all a quick update on what I've discovered."

"Do you know how to defeat their armor?" Rodriguez asked bluntly.

Carlson shook his head. "Well. No. Not yet. But we're working on it. The rifle is incredibly complex, and of course, we need to make sure that our work on it doesn't damage it in any way. It's made reverse engineering it a bit of a challenge. We have made progress on the power supply; however, and I think we may be able to design something similar based on it. I know the reactor keeps this place going, but it isn't exactly portable. That's not why I asked you to come down."

"It isn't?" Montero said.

"No. I wanted to talk to you about the cloth."

He had a pair of the pants hanging against a heavily shielded wall beside them, and it was clear he had tried to puncture them with gunfire.

"This material is unlike anything I've seen before. Completely bulletproof, it actually hardens in direct opposition to the amount of force placed against it. Meaning, the harder you hit it, the harder it gets. We've been examining it, and it appears as though it is constructed of nanometer-sized particles that act kind of like springs, loose in general, but coiling up as pressure is applied."

"That's interesting, Carlson, but not that useful," Rodriguez said.

"You're so impatient, Christian," Carlson said. "Okay. This is the super cool part that's got me all excited. So, we left one of the shirts sitting under the microscope while we switched gears to look at the rifles. When we came back, the springs molecules had reorganized."

He opened his mouth, mimicking his total amazement and expecting the gathered officers to respond in kind.

"I don't know what that means," Diaz said.

"Ah. Uh." Carlson shook his head. "I should have known better. It means the cloth is alive."

"What do you mean, alive?" Donovan said.

"I mean, the thing that makes it so impervious is a nano-organism. There are billions of them living on the base fibers of the cloth, which is made of some kind of silk. They seem to be feeding on the cloth, so I imagine that over time it wears down to point of uselessness. This is nothing that you can find here on Earth."

"Okay," Rodriguez said. "I understand why you're excited, I think, but was this really something worth calling us all down here for?"

"Yes, sir," Carlson said. "Don't you see? This cloth is an example of using a biological ingredient in making super strong cloth. What if this is a primitive version of the Dread armor? If we can find a way to kill these creatures, maybe we can do the same to destroy their shells?"

"We have a way to destroy the shells, Carlson," Major Sharma said. "The rifles Donovan brought you can do it. What you need to do is figure out how."

"I said, I'm working on that."

"You were wasting time on a shirt when you could have been learning about the weapons technology. You do understand we're at war, and on the verge of losing it?"

Carlson's face turned beet red. "I understand completely. If you would open your mind the teeniest bit, you would be able to conceptualize the parallels between the cloth and the carapace. The goal here is to defeat the enemy shields, and understanding how they work is the best key to doing so."

"Assuming they are even remotely the same."

"Yes. I do believe the armor is biological in nature, at least in part."

"But you don't know for sure."

"No. What I do know is that I don't have the equipment here to do a more thorough analysis on this. I've seen these rifles before. I've broken them down and scanned them under a microscope. The problem is that even with it turned on, there's nothing new for me to discover here. At least, nothing new that I'm capable of discovering. Considering the nano-tech in the cloth, it is reasonable to assume there is other nano-tech within the weapon."

"The rifle has a switch on it," Donovan said. "A clear indication that it has two different modes. You can't figure out which is which?"

"I can't figure out which does what. Something is happening when I flip the toggle. I can hear it; I can sense it. I can't see it. Not with the equipment we have here. I could try taking the weapon apart and hope that I can put it back together, but that is precisely what you ordered me not to do."

"Damn," General Rodriguez said. "So close, and still so far."

"I can try taking it apart,'" Carlson said.

"No. Not yet. Let me think about it."

"We don't have a lot of time, sir," Montero said.

"I know. We only have two. We can't risk losing either one without being certain we can get what we need from it. Carlson, how confident do you feel that you can take the weapon apart and put it back together in working order?"

"We have some older disabled weapons in storage, maybe if I practice on those a few more times, I can be more sure."

"Okay. Do it. But don't start breaking down either of the active weapons until you come and see me."

"Yes, General."

"And keep your people on the cloth. See if you can find something that will kill the organisms. It was good thinking, bad timing."

"Yes, General."

"Donovan, walk back to my office with me. The rest of you are dismissed."

"Yes, sir," Diaz, Montero, and Sharma said.

Rodriguez exited behind them, with Donovan at his side. "How are the preparations for the run going?"

"As well as can be expected, sir. I only have six in my squad. That's a bare minimum for any run, and considering how heavily the Dread have been coming after us any time we expose ourselves, it doesn't leave me feeling that positive."

"Understood," the General said, rubbing at his mustache. "I can't order people to do this. Not in good conscience."

"I'm not asking you to, sir. If we have to use six, we'll use six. Even if we don't make it back, we'll get the message sent."

"I know you will. I've been reading Doctor Montoya's reports on Ehri. The bek'hai culture is interesting, wouldn't you say?"

"It's different, that's for sure. I can't imagine a world without children, without intimacy, where intelligent beings are so easy to make that most of them are expendable."

"Agreed. Have you been able to get her to tell you anything she hasn't told Montoya?"

"Not yet. I'm still trying to win her over. She loves spending time in the nursery, so I think that's helping. She needs to give us the information willingly, without feeling like I'm attempting to trick her. Anyway, I don't know if she knows any more than what she's said. Her role with the bek'hai was to study us."

"She may not, but like I told you earlier, if genetics play any role in who a person is then getting her on our side can be one of the most important things we do."

"I'm still not sure how," Donovan said.

"Neither am I. Maybe it's because I held Juliet St. Martin in such high esteem. I don't know. It's a gut call."

"One that I don't disagree with, sir."

"Are you still planning to take your team off-base tomorrow?"

"Yes, sir. We all need to stay sharp somewhere that isn't as safe as down here."

"What about your shoulder?"

Donovan lifted it over his head, ignoring the twinge of pain as he did. He couldn't afford to let Rodriguez know it wasn't healed yet. "Almost as good as new, sir."

The General smiled. "Good. Dismissed, Major."

"Yes, sir."

62

"Captain Gabriel St. Martin mission recording sixty-nine," Gabriel said, starting the in-flight recorder. "Time to Earth, nine hours and thirty-four minutes. Engines online. Weapons systems deactivated. All other systems nominal."

He had been firing reverse thrusters for the last ten minutes, slowing the starfighter down to a more acceptable speed. He was close enough now that he could see the orbital defense ring up ahead as a solid line of black that seemed to split the planet in half.

He tapped the control pad until he found the new menu item that had been tacked on. It was nothing but a simple toggle to activate and deliver the transmission his father had recorded earlier. It was also the most important button on the pad.

His pulse had calmed during the journey from the Magellan, and it remained calm as he grew ever closer to the Earth. He was in his element now. He had done this so many times before. True, entering atmosphere would be a new experience, but it didn't change who he was or what he knew, or how much he had experienced. His fears and doubts vanished as he traveled further and further from the starship and his father. Sometimes he wanted so much to make Theodore proud that his reputation became more hindrance than help.

"I'm beginning my run," he said, using the second stick to fire the planar vectoring thrusters and put the ship into a wobbly spin. He needed more than ever to conserve his energy, and making an effort to confuse the defense system before he reached it was one way to do it.

The spheres began to activate as he approached, short bursts of thrust turning them as they extended their weaponry. Gabriel kept his eyes focused on them, ignoring the way the universe was spinning around him.

They started to fire, their blasts of plasma arcing out toward the fighter. Gabriel kept his rotation, turning the stick in tight, precise motions to bring himself out of harm's way. He found an opening in the pattern and swung toward it, bright flashes of energy all around him.

The ring seemed tighter to him than the last time, and it began to close as he maneuvered towards the space. He couldn't spare the energy to go back and make another approach, and if he tried to run horizontal he would be blown to pieces. There was no other choice than to try to go through.

He gritted his teeth, the satellites so close to his ship that he could see the way the plasma formed at the tip of the cannon before firing, so close that each shot nearly blinded him. Somehow he got the starfighter through it, angling the wings and changing his direction just enough to keep himself alive. There was no thought behind it. No planning. It was all instinct and muscle memory.

It was what separated the good pilots from the rest.

Then he was in, past the orbital defense and racing toward the atmosphere. He tapped his control pad, adding a new layer to his HUD to help guide him to the correct angle to spear his way through. A line appeared on either side, moving toward the center as he adjusted. He checked his power supply. Getting in wouldn't use nearly as much as going back out.

The front of the fighter lit up as he sank deeper toward the surface, the heat pouring from the surface. Within seconds he was through, dipping toward the ground. The fighter shook and jostled as it cut through the air. It was similar to joining the slipstream, but felt less controlled, and Gabriel fought to maintain his focus and his nerve. He released the vector control stick, it wouldn't do him much good here, and put both hands on the main.

The alien structure looked so different closer in, and he felt his breath catch at the sight of it. It may have looked large from space. From within the atmosphere it was massive, stretching for miles and seeming to overtake the entire planet. The spires cut high into the air below him, and he could see motion along the black, armored surface.

He jumped in his seat when the first plasma bolt passed next to the fighter He cut the stick hard, feeling the fighter shake more, the airframe working to meet his command. Inertial dampeners kept him from being rocked unconscious by the move, and he cursed himself for being stupid. He flicked the stick in more controlled motions, sweeping side to side as he continued the descent. He could see the world beyond the Dread approaching, brown and green in the distance.

"I'm inside the atmosphere, heading toward North America."

They knew the transmissions generated from somewhere around Mexico, though not exactly where. He tapped the controls to return to the toggle. He was almost in position.

A warning tone sounded in the cockpit as a pair of Dread fighters rose from behind him. He dropped the fighter, sending it straight down toward the enemy city, going into a slight spin as the plasma cut the sky around him. He needed cover, and it was the only cover he was going to get.

A massive machine appeared ahead and to his right, a squat torso on huge legs, with some kind of weapons hanging on either side. It rotated to face him, raising the guns and firing. Red blobs rocketed up at him, and he rolled and dove a little more, getting under them before coming up straight and breaking the descent. He angled to the left, barely skirting around a tall spire before moving back to the right. The Bats were still behind him, struggling to maneuver as well as he could. He recognized he had the advantage, locating a narrow channel in the structure and diving down toward it. A second mechanized ground unit appeared near the top of the channel, unable to angle its weapons in time to fire on him.

Gabriel raced through the channel, his heart beating calmly, nothing but ice in his veins. Fear was foreplay. Now there was only determination.

The channel ended at another spire, and Gabriel pulled back hard on his stick while increasing thrust, launching vertically out of the channel and climbing the side of the structure. The fights had held back to wait for him, and they didn't dare fire without the risk of hitting their own structure. Now that Gabriel knew the weapons would damage it, he felt safe to use it as a shield.

He rolled his starfighter again, finding his direction and adding more thrust. He wouldn't get as wide of a spread coming in low, but he didn't have a choice. He cleared the edge of the Dread city, shooting over a former human city that had been reduced to brown earth and a mixture of partially standing buildings, rusted steel, and rubble. He hit the toggle on the control pad, transmitting the message downward. The enemy fighters had lost some ground, but they were still behind him.

"Transmitting," he said. "I pray to God that someone hears it."

M.R. Forbes

63

Donovan's eyes passed over the five men and women who had volunteered to join him on the t-vault. Diaz, Montero, Cameron, Sanchez, and Wade. They were standing at attention beneath the cover of a hollowed-out building, dressed in greens and barefoot. Two buckets of water and a third of orange clay sat on the ground beside them.

"First, I want to thank you all for volunteering for this mission. Your support of what we're trying to do is a testament to your courage and your faith."

"Thank you, sir," all five replied. They kept their voices low, not wanting to be discovered by a passing enemy drone.

The area around the base had been warmer since Reyes had fired his rifle. The mechanized armor on the scene had been replaced by clone patrols, and then with drones. Only the scouts had gone in or out for the last four days, and even then it was to quickly monitor the situation and get back inside.

Donovan was thankful for the opportunity to bring his team outside. Scanning the soldiers, he could tell that only Diaz wasn't nervous to be too far from home to escape should they be sighted.

Getting used to that fear was one of the most valuable experiences he could give them.

"Lieutenant Diaz, prepare the squad."

"Yes, sir," Diaz said, breaking rank and going over to the water.

She lifted the bucket with one hand, grabbing an attached spray nozzle in the other. She proceeded to douse each of the soldiers with it, soaking their shirts and pants. Once that was one, she retrieved the bucket of clay. "Cover yourself as much as possible. Clothes, too. The clay will dampen your heat signature. Help each other in the places you can't reach."

"Yes, ma'am," they said, approaching the bucket.

Donovan watched and waited while they coated themselves and one another. Diaz brought him the bucket once they were done.

"Would you like some help with that, sir?" she asked playfully.

"I've got it," he replied, smiling. "Thanks."

"Yes, sir."

Donovan grabbed the clay, quickly spreading it over his body. Then he headed for the open air.

The others followed him, quickly moving into a standard wedge formation. Only Wade lagged behind, his slowness immediately drawing Diaz's attention.

"Wade," she hissed. "This isn't a walk in the park. If you dawdle, you die."

"Yes, ma'am."

Donovan scanned the street. They were a good kilometer away from the base, closer to the edge of the city so that if they were caught the Dread might think they were hiding in the mountains. He watched the sky for signs of scouts. He didn't see any.

"Okay, people," he said. "We're going to cross to that rubble over there, as fast as we can. Stay in formation, eyes up and alert. Diaz, you're on point as the spotter. If she sees anything, her hand will go up like this. You see the hand, you find cover, and you stay there until she opens her fist to signal the all clear. Understood?"

"Yes, sir," they replied.

"What if they see us?" Wade asked.

"Rendezvous point is two klicks north. We split up, try to lose them, and meet back there when it's clear. We wait two hours for survivors. If you aren't there in that time, you're probably dead."

"But not always, sir," Montero said. "You weren't."

"We were lucky once. I doubt that will happen again."

"Yes, sir."

"Diaz, on your mark."

Diaz moved up ahead of him, and he replaced her position in the wedge. As the fastest runner, she could afford to watch the sky while she sprinted.

"Okay, let's-"

They all froze, as a heavy clap echoed across the sky, followed quickly by a second.

"What the hell was that?" Diaz said.

"I don't know," Donovan replied. "Can you see anything."

Diaz lifted her head, looking up, turning in a circle as she did. "I don't. Wait. Major, you have to see this."

Donovan joined Diaz, following her finger as she pointed.

"What is that?" she asked.

A dark speck was falling from the sky in a hurry, trailing vapor. It looked like it was out over the Dread city.

"Maybe one of their satellites malfunctioned and lost orbit," he said.

"And is coincidentally falling right on top of their heads?"

"You never know." He watched the speck continue to tumble, and then straighten out and move horizontally. "Okay, not a satellite."

"It's a ship. It has to be."

"A Dread fighter? Why would it be out there? They don't launch them unless they pick up one of ours."

The speck was getting slightly larger, moving in their general direction. Two more joined it a moment later, rocketing upward from the Dread city.

"I don't think that's a Dread ship," Diaz said.

"The run isn't for another twelve days," Donovan replied, his pulse quickening nervously. "If it's the space force, they're way too early."

"Why would they be coming in this low?"

Thin bolts of plasma began to pierce the sky around the black spot, which turned and jiggled to avoid them.

"Definitely not theirs," Donovan said. He noticed the others had moved into position to watch as well.

"If he's one of ours, he's damn good at avoiding them," Montero said.

The three dots continued to descend until they vanished behind their line of sight.

"I wonder what he's doing here?" Diaz said. "There has to be a reason for it."

"I don't know," Donovan said. "We need to get back to base and inform General Rodriguez. Come on."

Donovan sprinted away from the building, heading back the way they had come. He had only reached the end of the first street when he felt the first vibration. He recognized it immediately and threw up his fist before pressing himself against the closest standing wall.

The vibrations intensified in a hurry, coming one after another in rapid succession. Donovan slid along the wall, reaching the end, and then peered around it. He could see down the long main thoroughfare, and while it was littered with debris, the mech was easily large enough for him to spot.

His pulse moved to triple-time, and he made sure to keep his arm up, fist closed. They were still encased in clay. They were still damp. They would be safe as long as they were quiet and remained hidden.

He watched it approach with a measure of awe. He had never had a chance to observe one before. He was impressed with the size and how easily it seemed to move with its near-humanoid shape. It pushed some of the rubble and old cars out of the way as it moved ever closer to him.

Had it seen him? He didn't think so. It would have blown him to ash already if it had. What was it doing?

It stopped halfway to him, the upper half turning, the arms lifting toward the sky and began firing projectiles. Donovan heard the soft whine a moment later, his mouth falling open in wonder as the starfighter rocketed past, barely a hundred meters overhead and angled on its side. He saw the pilot for the briefest of instants before he was past, somehow avoiding the enemy fire and continuing beyond the city.

The mech turned to follow the fighter, and so did Donovan, losing it behind the building before finding it again, headed along the slope and up the mountain. Two heartbeats later a pair of Dread fighters screamed overhead in pursuit.

"Come on, buddy," he said, shaking from the excitement. "You can do it."

The fighter shrank into the distance. The mech started to move, heading back the way it had come and giving up its part in the battle. The two Dread fighters took over for it, resuming their plasma attack.

Once more, the pilot managed to avoid the fire. Then it dipped suddenly, heading for the trees, so low he was amazed it hadn't crashed into them already. The Dread angled down, so intent on hitting him they weren't paying attention to the altitude.

The fighter shifted vectors and streaked up, barely whipping around the side of the mountain and disappearing beyond. The enemy ships weren't as fortunate, and he could hear the echo as they crashed into the woods.

"Yes," he whispered, holding himself back from screaming and remembering to keep his fist up.

He stayed that way for thirty seconds, waiting for things to calm down. There was no smoke coming from the area where the Dread had crashed, just a swath of downed trees. The armor would have protected them from damage, but could they get airborne again from that position? He didn't know.

He looked around, finding Diaz to his left next to a car, with Wade right beside her. He opened his hand. Montero, Cameron, and Sanchez appeared from their cover, and they ran to form up on him again.

"Dios Mio, did you see that, amigo?" Diaz asked excitedly.

"Shh," Donovan replied. "Take us back to base. Silent until then."

She nodded, moving to point and bringing them home.

64

"Major. You're back," Sergeant Wilcox said. "We could feel the rumbling over the base and thought you might have been spotted. General Rodriguez was worried about you."

"We're fine," Donovan said. They were standing at the entrance to the corridor between the silo and the control center. Wilcox had been posted there to guard the door and open it upon their arrival. "Where is the General?"

"He was meeting with Carlson again. What happened out there?"

"I'm sure you'll hear about it. I need to speak to Rodriguez."

Wilcox nodded and moved aside, allowing them to file in. Donovan and the rest of the t-vault team ran through the connecting corridor while the Sergeant closed the door behind them.

They reached the base, and Donovan headed for the stairs down to the lab. He was standing in the doorway leading to them when he heard a shout behind him.

"Donovan, wait," Matteo said. The entire squad turned as one, watching Matteo pull to a stop in front of them, his breathing heavy.

M.R. Forbes

"What's going on"? Diaz asked.

"Do you know where General Rodriguez is?"

"Science lab," Donovan said. "I was headed down there now."

"Tell him to come up to the comm room right away."

"Why?"

"Just tell him, amigo. It's important."

"I will. The rest of you wait here," Donovan said. "Don't say anything to anyone about this until the General says it's okay."

"Yes, sir."

Donovan continued down the steps, hurrying to the lab. He found General Rodriguez on his way out.

"Major," Rodriguez said, his eyes checking Donovan for injury. "There was some action outside. I was afraid your team was in trouble. Is everything okay?"

"We're fine, sir," Donovan said. "I'm not sure if everything is okay. There's something happening out there. Matteo said to ask you to come to the comm room immediately. He said it was important."

"Let's go, then. Tell me what happened to you."

They started walking together, taking a brisk pace back.

"A ship dropped from orbit. At first, we thought it was a Dread ship, but then it leveled out, and the Dread came up and started shooting at it. There must have been a mech nearby because it moved closer to our position and also started shooting. General, it was unreal. The ship was one of ours, and it flew right over our heads, so close I could see the pilot inside."

"Did he engage the enemy?" Rodriguez asked.

"No, sir. It didn't look like he had any weapons."

"Then why would he come in so low? What would he be doing here, anyway? They're early."

"Very early."

They reached the steps, climbing them two at a time. Donovan's team was still waiting at the stairwell for him, and they came to attention and saluted when the General appeared.

"At ease,' Rodriguez said. "I'm glad you're all safe. Donovan told me

300

you had a bit of excitement."

"Yes, sir," Diaz said.

"Follow me. Whatever is happening, you're all an important part of it now."

The soldiers trailed behind Donovan and Rodriguez. They entered the communications room, where three small computers rested on an old metal desk, and wires snaked across the floor to the wall. Matteo was behind the desk, leaning over an old touchpad and staring into the monitor. He looked up.

"General," he said, saluting even though he wasn't part of the military.

"Matteo. What do you have?"

"I still can't quite believe it, sir. I mean, after all of this time, and-"

"What do you have?" Rodriguez repeated.

"Sorry, sir. Our monitoring software picked up an incoming message about ten seconds after the first round of vibrations stopped. It kind of caught me off guard with how fast it transferred because that meant it had to be a local send. But what really blew my mind were the headers."

"Headers?" Diaz asked.

"Information on where and how to send," Matteo said. "General, the message was directed to you, using an old identification tag you provided when we setup the system. According to the headers, it came from a General Theodore St. Martin?"

Donovan felt a chill run through his body. He glanced over at Rodriguez, who had frozen in disbelief.

"Did you say Theodore St. Martin?" he said, his voice barely more than a whisper.

"Yes, sir," Matteo said.

"What did it say?"

"It was sent to you. I haven't looked at it. I came to you right away."

General Rodriguez smiled. There was a tear in the corner of his eye. "That son of a gun. I knew if he were still out there he wouldn't let me down. Let me see it."

Matteo turned the monitor so they could all see. He tapped the pad, and an older man appeared. Donovan assumed it was General St. Martin.

The look of recognition on General Rodriguez's face confirmed it.

"Christian," Theodore said. "You may not remember me, son, but I remember you. I can't say I'm surprised to know that you're still alive down there. You always had this look about you that told me you were a survivor. We got a message from you not too long ago, saying that the resistance was giving up the fight and going into hiding." Theodore leaned forward on his arms, getting closer to the recorder. "Christian, don't you dare do something as foolish as that. This fight ain't over yet. Hell, son, it's just getting interesting."

"He has no idea," Diaz said.

"Shhh," Rodriguez replied.

"If you're watching this recording, it means my son, Gabriel, managed to break through the Dread's defenses and transmit it down to you. Hopefully, it means he also managed to get himself back out. The point is, I risked my own boy to get in touch with you, and I did it for a damn good reason. Gabriel witnessed a Dread fighter firing on the defense satellites in orbit around the planet. He says the Dread's plasma cannon was able to destroy them, meaning their weapons can defeat their armor."

"We already knew that," Diaz said.

"Shhh," Rodriguez repeated.

"What I want you to do is try to capture one of their weapons. I've got a scientist up here who's a real genius, and I think if we can get our hands on one, he can figure out what makes it tick and find a way to use it against the enemy. Now, I know it may not be easy to get one of these weapons, but son, this is it. The last hurrah, if you will. The New Earth Alliance was considering abandoning Earth before we received your message, and I had to take the Magellan despite their protests to keep them from turning tail and leaving you stranded. If you have to give up every last man and woman you've got to make this happen, you need to do it. It's more than just their lives at stake. It's the lives of everyone left on Earth, and at least half the population of the NEA as well. Me and mine are waiting out near Mars for the next standard recon cycle. My son, Gabriel, will be back then. Send a transmission, tell us if you've got it or what the next move is. We'll be waiting."

Theodore leaned back. It seemed as if the recording would end, but then he leaned forward again.

"Oh, and Christian, if you know the whereabouts of my Juliet, I would be much obliged for that information as well. I know it seems a long shot, but there's a part of me that can't let go and is very much praying that she's still alive."

The screen went dark.

65

"Sir?" Donovan said.

Thirty seconds had passed since the recording ended. General Rodriguez hadn't moved a muscle. His eyes were glued to the dark screen; his hands clenched into fists.

The rest of the squad waited silently.

The seconds continued to tick by.

"Matteo," General Rodriguez said at last. "Get a message out to General Parker in New York. Tell him that Mexico base will not stand down, and my recommendation is for him to rescind his order, at least temporarily."

"Yes, sir," Matteo said, immediately shifting the screen back around and sitting at the desk to prepare the message.

"Donovan," Rodriguez said, turning to him. "I don't want to put undue pressure on you, but I can't even begin to express how important your next mission is going to be. I-"

"General Rodriguez, General Rodriguez, sir!"

Sergeant Wilcox barreled into the room, barely stopping before knocking Corporal Wade over.

"General Rodriguez."

"What is it, Wilcox?" he asked.

"Sir." She swallowed, trying to catch her breath. "If you remember, sir, Sergeant Yung and his team left yesterday on a supply run. They just returned a minute ago. They were out of breath from running to get the message back to you, so I ran here for them. Yung said the Dread were headed this way in force."

Rodriguez's eyes bore into her so fiercely she looked away.

"Damn it," he said. "They got us the message, but they attracted too much attention doing it."

"The fighter flew right over the base, sir," Donovan said.

"Between that and Captain Reyes firing his weapon the other day, they have to suspect we're here somewhere," Diaz said.

"Did he say how many?" Rodriguez asked.

"No, sir. He said it was more than he had ever seen in one group before. Both regular clones and others in armor."

"Should we evacuate, sir?" Montero said.

Rodriguez didn't answer. They all knew it was a difficult decision to make. How could everything be falling apart at the same time it was beginning to come together?

"Sir?" Donovan said.

"Yes, Major?"

"General St. Martin said they have a scientist with them who he thinks can figure out how the alien weapons work. He wanted us to get a gun, but we already have one. What we need to do is to get it to them."

"In twelve days," Rodriguez said. "Maybe we can stay hidden down here for that long, but then Gabriel is going to come back, and there will be nothing for him to pick up. They'll assume we've either given up or died, or maybe that their transmission never made it through, and they'll leave again. That's assuming we can stay hidden. If the Dread are sending a large force, I don't think they'll give up until they've found something."

"Or we can evacuate and make a run for it," Montero said.

"Where are we going to go?" Donovan asked. "We've already been on the run. How many will people die if we do? Besides, we know from Ehri that the Dread leader wants us all dead. Who's to say we'll make it out this time?"

"So you want to hide down here and wait for them to storm in and kill us all?"

"Of course not. I think we need to focus on our priorities. I hate to say this, but this base and everyone in it is secondary to getting the weapon out of the area and up to General St. Martin. If all of us have to die to do it, then that's our fate. We're part of the resistance. We have a duty to the mission. We have to fight to the last man, to the last breath to get the Dread off our planet."

"Tell that to my daughter," Montero said. "She's only four years old."

"I'm sorry, Colonel," Donovan said. "I know it sounds cold, but this is the world we're living in. If we don't get that gun off the planet, we're all as good as dead. Not just you and me. Every last human on Earth."

Montero turned to Rodriguez. "I'm not going to sit here and wait for her to die, sir."

"No one wants their child to die," Rodriguez said.

"General," Donovan started. Rodriguez put up his hand to silence him.

"Give me a minute, Major. I didn't survive this long by rushing into things."

"We don't have a lot of time, sir," Diaz said.

"I'm aware, Lieutenant. Matteo."

"Yes, sir."

"You said the transmission was received locally. Do you know where?"

"Give me a minute, sir." Matteo's eyes locked onto the monitor, his hands gliding across the control pad.

"What are you thinking, General?" Montero asked.

"I have an idea. It may get us all killed, but it may also be the best chance we have."

"I ran a packet trace, sir," Matteo said. "The transmission was picked up by an antenna thirty kilometers east of here."

"East?" Montero said. "That would be near the top of Mount Tlaloc.

There's nothing out there, never mind anything with a power supply. That can't be right."

"The antenna id was MTTC-DSN-110. I've got the IP address." Matteo did something with the control pad. "I just pinged it. Whatever it is, it's active."

"Another group?" Donovan asked.

"If it is, they may not be friendly," Diaz said.

"I'm telling you, there's nothing out there," Montero said. "I'm from this area. I would know."

"Matteo, how sure are you about the location?" General Rodriguez asked.

"It isn't a perfect system. Seventy percent?"

"It will have to be good enough. Major Peters, I need you and your team to head out to the transmission site. Matteo, I want you to go with them."

"Me?" Matteo said. "Why?"

"Whatever that place is, it has power and an antenna. We can't wait twelve days for the recon flight to return. We know General St. Martin is waiting near Mars. We need to get a signal out that way, to tell them we have the weapon and that we're waiting for them."

"Waiting where, sir?" Donovan asked.

"On the mountain. You'll bring the guns with you."

"Guns? Both of them?"

"Yes. We can't afford to lose them. Not now. I'd send Carlson with you, too, but he's too damn slow. I do want you to bring Ehri."

"I don't understand?"

"It's like you said, Major. Our top priority is to get the weapon to General St. Martin so his genius can try to do something with it. Unfortunately, right now I think that's also the safest place for anyone to be. Our second priority is to protect the people here who can't protect themselves. I have an idea on that, too. Montero, go ask Major Sharma to help you get our people together in the cafeteria so that I can go over the details."

"Yes, sir," Montero said, leaving the room.

"Sir," Matteo said. "I don't know if this will work. I've read everything we have here about communication systems. It takes a pretty big antenna to reach out into space with any kind of authority. What if we get there and it's somebody's homebrew needle or something?"

"Then you stay alive for twelve days and wait for Gabriel St. Martin to return. You can use the needle to transmit to them. Either way, we'll get a message off."

"Are you sure you want us to bring Ehri, sir?" Donovan asked. He didn't mind keeping her out of harms way, but he wasn't sure what value she would add to the mission.

"Yes. She knows how her people operate, and she seems to have a soft spot for you. She may be able to help you evade the Dread long enough to deliver the message."

Donovan was surprised by the comment. "A soft spot?" he asked.

"That's what your mother told me."

"You've been talking to my mother?"

"I get reports from everyone who is in charge of anything around here, Major. That includes the nursery."

Donovan felt a mixture of excitement and guilt. It had never occurred to him that Ehri might become fond of him. The children, maybe. Not him.

"She's also highly educated and intelligent. She may be able to help with the transmission."

"Yes, sir," Donovan said.

"Take Diaz down to the lab to get the weapons from Carlson. Take the Dread cloth, too. All of it. Use it to stay alive. Come to the cafeteria after."

"Yes, sir. One more question, sir."

"Yes, Major?"

"Thirty kilometers to the top of the mountain? It's going to take us at least a day to get there. If the Dread see us, there's no way we can outrun them."

Rodriguez smiled. "I'm a survivor, remember? I've got a plan for that, too."

66

Donovan and Diaz left the science lab, each wearing the alien clothing beneath their green uniforms and carrying a Dread plasma rifle. Donovan also had Ehri's black dress in a bundle beneath his arm.

They were on their way to the cafeteria, following a short distance behind Carlson and his team as they answered the General's call for all hands. They were close enough to the open space that they could hear the general hum of the assembled as each of the gathered members of their community worked to guess why they had been summoned or calm their suddenly fraying nerves.

"This is it, isn't it?" Diaz said, her voice low. "What did General St. Martin call it? The last hurrah."

"This may be our most important mission, but this isn't it," Donovan said. "If we make this happen, we'll be on the road to fighting back for the first time in half a century."

"Can we make this happen?"

Donovan nodded. A strange calm had come over him since they had left the communications room. After barely surviving so many t-vaults, the idea of having something tangible come from it meant that all of the friends and comrades he had lost over the years had died for something. He would do his best to make sure of that.

"Yes. No one would ever have guessed we would wind up in a Dread starship and make it out alive. Last week, it seemed impossible that we would be able to get our hands on one of these." He shook the rifle. "We can do this, Renata. You and me and our team."

She smiled. "You seem convinced."

"I am."

She stopped walking and turned to face him. "Can I ask you something? Something personal?"

He paused. "Of course. We've known each other for a long time."

"Do you ever think of me? As anything other than a friend or Matteo's sister, I mean?"

Donovan stared at her. He knew there was something passing between them. Two weeks ago he had only ever thought of her as his best friend's sister, and now he saw her as a friend and equal. He appreciated the way they interacted, and the trust he had in her ability to help keep him and the team alive. Maybe there was something more to it? He really didn't know. He had bigger concerns right now.

"Renata," he said. "This isn't the best time."

"There is no best time, D. You know that. Is it a hard question to answer?"

"I can only tell you what I know, which is that I'm glad we're here together, and that we're fighting this war together. I trust you and have faith in you, and I genuinely enjoy your company. I don't know exactly where that fits in the hierarchy of male and female relationships."

He could tell that wasn't exactly what she wanted to hear. A flash of disappointment crossed her face.

"Is it because of Ehri?"

When she said it, she didn't sound like the confident woman she had grown into. She seemed more like a little girl about to have her heart crushed.

"No. It isn't that. My job is to complete the mission and keep as many of you alive as I can. That's all that matters to me right now."

The confidence return in an instant. "I know. I'm being ridiculous, and I'm sorry. It's just that I've had this crush on you since I was twelve years old, and you never noticed me. You did a little bit when we were trapped on the Dread ship. Maybe it was just because you had lost so much blood. Maybe it was something else. Whatever. I didn't want to die without having said anything. I didn't want to die without letting you know how I feel."

"You aren't going to die. Is that understood, Lieutenant?"

"Yes, sir," Diaz said. Then she surprised him, stepping forward and leaning up on her toes to put her lips on his.

He didn't respond to the kiss, caught off guard and unwilling to complicate things. It passed quickly. She pulled away, looking up at him. "I'm sorry, Donnie. I always dreamed of kissing you, and I didn't want to die without doing that once either."

She turned on her heel and continued toward the cafeteria. Donovan watched her for a moment before trailing behind.

The cafeteria was already full when they entered, with all three hundred plus members of the community crowded around the tables and benches, and standing along the walls. They drew some stares when they walked in armed, and some of the people quieted. Donovan scanned them, finding Ehri and his mother standing with the parents of the children in the nursery. Ehri smiled and waved when she saw him.

He made his way over to her, Diaz hanging close at his side.

"What's going on?" his mother asked. "Why did General Rodriguez bring us all together?" She glanced at the gun. "I can guess it isn't anything good."

"Things are going to get rough, Mom," Donovan said.

"We've done rough before. We'll do it again."

"Yeah, we will." He turned his shoulder with the bundle under it to Ehri. "Your bek'hai clothing. Rodriguez wants you to wear it for whatever protection it can offer."

"Why?"

He looked at his mother again. "Some of us are leaving. We have a chance to deliver one of these guns to the space forces. To someone who may be able to decipher the technology."

"Ehri's coming with you?"

"Yes. General Rodriguez wants you with us."

"He believes I can be of use?"

"Maybe. Would you help us if you could?"

Ehri looked at Wanda, and then back at the children. Donovan could see the conflict on her face. She had come to observe, not to help. Except she had started this in the first place by leading them to the weapons. Confident in her kind's success or not, she had to know she was at least partially responsible for what was happening.

"Attention!"

Colonel Montero's voice echoed across the room, bringing the assembled soldiers to attention and silencing the non-combatants. He also spared Ehri from having to answer the question.

General Rodriguez entered the cafeteria a moment later. Donovan couldn't help but notice how old he suddenly looked.

"I'm sorry to bring you all here under these circumstances," Rodriguez said, not wasting any time. "We have a report from Sergeant Yung that the Dread forces are heading this way in a number that suggests they intend to do whatever they must to find this base."

He waited a moment while the crowd reacted.

"I have a plan. Two plans, actually. First, Major Peters and the t-vault squad are going to be heading out following this meeting. Their mission is to deliver one of the captured alien weapons to a member of the space forces that we have been communicating with for all of these years. Both their General and I are of a belief that together we can find a way to defeat the alien armor and start fighting back against the Dread for real."

"Why don't we just offer them their clone back in exchange for our safety?" someone said from the back of the room.

Donovan glanced at Ehri. She didn't seem phased by the comment. In fact, she looked intrigued.

"Yeah. If we had never brought her here in the first place, this wouldn't be happening," someone else said.

"Yeah," one of the women right behind them said. "Why did you have to come here, anyway? Go home you alien bitch. You don't belong with us."

Ehri's face froze at that comment.

"Be quiet," Rodriguez shouted, quieting the crowd. "Are you all loco? This has nothing to do with her, and if you think the Dread give a crap about one wayward clone when they have hundreds more just like her, you're really out of your mind. In case you've forgotten, this is a rebel installation. A military base, dedicated to continuing the war with the Dread. Have you all gotten so comfortable here, you've gone soft? Do you think you have a right to question any of the decisions I make? You know how to get out if you do."

The people were silent.

"Now, here's the second part of my plan, and I need your help to make it work. We're going to leave a small number of soldiers here along with the mothers of the children, or fathers if the mother isn't with us. Everyone else is going to pack up everything they have and we're going to make a run for it. With any luck, the evacuation will lead them away from the base and keep its location secret. Except we won't be evacuating. We can double back once we've split up and lost them."

The crowd was silent this time, but a thick tension was heavy in the air. The plan wasn't that much of a plan at all, and everyone in the cafeteria knew that it meant many of them were going to die. At the same time, they also knew there was nowhere else for them to run to. There was nowhere to go that was as safe as it was down here. In a sense, the idea was brilliant in its simplicity. Some of them would escape and make it back.

Some was better than none.

"Major Sharma and Sergeant Wilcox are going to organize you into groups. Everyone needs to head in a separate direction for this to be believable. I'll be bringing the bulk of the soldiers with me, and we'll do everything we can to draw them away. Understood?"

The room remained silent. Even the soldiers were too shocked to reply. Everything had happened so suddenly; it was hard to digest.

"I said, understood," Rodriguez repeated in a drill sergeant tone.

"Yes, sir," came the reply, loud and strong.

"I'm proud of all of you. Major Peters, gather your team and meet me on the first level immediately."

"Yes, sir," Donovan said.

Rodriguez strode confidently from the room, while Sharma and Wilcox began moving through the gathered crowd.

"Mom," Donovan said, turning to his mother. "I-"

"Shh," Wanda said. "You be careful. Stay alive, and finish this mission. This is bigger than the people here. It's bigger than me. I love you, and I'm proud of you."

Donovan hugged her. "Thanks. I love you, too."

"I know."

He let go and looked at Ehri. She was standing stiff and distant. He knew the Dread didn't value one another as a whole the way humans did. He wondered if they could ever be as downright mean to one another.

"Goodbye, Ehri," Wanda said, approaching her. She wrapped her arms around the clone, hugging her. "I know you want to learn," Donovan heard her say. "Sometimes fear makes humans say and do terrible things, but that's all it is. The fear coming out in words. They don't really mean it. None of this is your fault."

Ehri's face softened, and she raised her arms and hugged Wanda back.

"Now, don't keep the General waiting," Wanda said.

67

"Diaz, go round up the others," Donovan said. "I need a minute with Ehri."

Diaz almost covered up her displeasure before he noticed. "Yes, sir."

"We can talk in here," Donovan said, leading Ehri to one of the offices.

"Your General won't be happy when you're late."

"I know. Are you okay?"

"Yes. Why do you ask?"

"The things the people were saying. I know they must have hurt."

"No. Not at first. Only when Carol turned on me. I thought that we were friends. I watched her son every day."

"My mother was right. It was only fear."

"I know that now."

"I need to know if you're with us, against us, or neutral."

"Major, I don't know."

"You have to know, Ehri. I have to know. Rodriguez wants you with us because he thinks you can help us. You helped Diaz and me back at the bek'hai mothership because you knew this day would come, though I don't think you imagined it would come this soon. You knew the Dread would find us and crush us sooner or later, and then you could go back to your life as a slave."

Donovan bit his lip. He hadn't meant to say slave. After all he had heard of her life as a member of the lor'hai, it had spilled out.

"I'm not a slave," Ehri said. "No one owns me."

"Do you have freedom?"

"I'm here, aren't I?"

"Yes. Here you're free. What about back there? What will happen to you then?"

"I will be Si'dahm to the new Dahm in charge of my team. I will continue to study human culture, and I will write my own discourse on what I have learned of humans in these last few days."

"And then what?"

"What do you mean? That's all."

"Do you think you'll enjoy watching fifty year old videos of humanity, after you've experienced the real thing? Will your work even matter when the Domo'dahm gets his wish and all of us are gone? Will they even need you anymore?"

"Of course. There are always things to study and to learn."

"Really? And the pur'dahm will have a use for an aging clone whose field of science is obsolete? I've been to all of your interviews with Doctor Montoya. You're lying to yourself if you think that will happen."

"I'm not a traitor, Donovan."

Donovan couldn't help but laugh at that. "You gave us the guns. The key to this entire war. You handed them over without a second thought."

"You know why."

"You helped Diaz kill Klurik."

"I did not."

"Come on, Ehri. You distracted him while she aimed her shot. You could have told him she was there."

"It had to be done in order for me to continue my work. That is an acceptable reason in bek'hai culture, and I will face no punishment for it."

"It was more than that, wasn't it? You didn't like Klurik. That much was obvious."

"You're saying I wanted to kill him?"

"Maybe. You didn't like the way he treated you. It made you feel like you were nothing. That's what you want to go back to?"

"There is more to it than that. I miss my sisters."

"You're lying."

"I am not. How do you know when I'm lying, anyway?"

"Your nose wrinkles. It's kind of cute, to be honest with you."

Ehri paused, staring at him. "Donovan, I'm scared."

He hadn't expected his simple, silly compliment to be the thing that drove down her defenses. "Why?"

"I." She shook her head. "I don't know who I am, anymore. I don't know what I am. I followed what Tuhrik taught me. I did what I believed he would have wanted. Only it didn't give me answers, only more questions to go with experiences I never believed I would have. Children." She smiled sadly. "The bek'hai are not evil, Donovan. They seek to survive, like all living things do. Like your people are trying to do now."

"I know they aren't. But they messed up their world. They don't have the right to ours. Don't you understand that?"

"Yes. I do. That is why I'm scared. I understand that they're wrong. I understand that they use me, as they use all lor'hai. We aren't slaves, but we aren't free, either. I feel guilty for hating them for that, the way I hated Klurik for how he treated me. Like a thing instead of an intelligent being. I am alone here, Donovan. The only one of my kind. My DNA may be fully human, but as much as you might accept me, I'll always be set apart. I'll always be different."

"You aren't alone," Donovan said. "I'm here."

"For now. Until they kill you."

"Then help me stay alive. If you know the bek'hai are wrong, maybe together we can do something about it. Maybe we can fix things for everyone, including the lor'hai."

"I'm only a scientist."

Donovan remembered what Rodriguez had said about Juliet St. Martin. "No. You're more than that. You proved that when you helped us escape. You're proving that right now."

"I. I don't know. I-"

Donovan didn't think about what he was doing until he was doing it. He wrapped his free arm around her, pulling her to him, leaning his head down and finding her lips. He kissed her, trying to pour every ounce of his desire for her to stay and help them into it.

She didn't resist him. She melted in his arms, her lips responding awkwardly. She had never kissed anyone before.

"Please," Donovan said. "Help us. Whatever happens, we can do it together, as free people."

She pulled her head back to look into his eyes.

"Please," he said again.

She nodded. Her entire body was trembling.

Donovan wondered if he had just done the right thing. He had no idea how this mess was going to turn out. He could barely believe how quickly they had ended up in it to begin with. He wanted Ehri on their side. So did General Rodriguez. But had he kissed her to win her over, or simply because he wanted to?

He wasn't even sure of that one himself. One mess at a time. It wouldn't matter if he were dead twenty-four hours from now.

"Come on," he said. "We have a delivery to make."

68

Gabriel felt a massive sense of relief as first the planet Mars came into clearer view, and then the starship Magellan appeared ahead of it. It was a black speck at first, a mote of dust against the red planet.

He had never been more grateful to make it back.

It hadn't been easy. The Dread ground defenses had been tight, and only some fancy flying that he couldn't even believe he'd managed had gotten him out of harm's way and back into space. He had seen the two Bats slam into the trees and vanish from his HUD. It had been his last ditch effort to lose them by taking advantage of his fighter's more Earth-friendly design and agility. Fortunately, it had worked.

He didn't know if the resistance forces had received the message. He wouldn't know until he was back on board the Magellan and Guy could check the logs of the equipment. He was almost sure he had caught a flash of movement from the ground and seen someone there in a green uniform, but everything had happened so fast it was just as likely a figment of his imagination.

He hoped not.

He tapped his control pad, activating his comm. "Magellan, this is Captain Gabriel St. Martin. Do you copy?"

"Captain St. Martin," his father's voice replied a few seconds later. "This is Magellan. We hear you, son. Welcome home." He paused again as if trying to decide whether or not to break protocol. "I knew you could do it, Gabe," he continued, throwing protocol aside. "I'm just about pissing myself that you made it back to us."

Gabriel smiled. "Thank you, General," he replied. "I don't know if the mission was a success or not. The enemy position is pretty strong down there."

"Understood. Bring her in and we'll see what we've got."

"Roger. Captain St. Martin, out."

Gabriel navigated the fighter to the waiting hangar, bringing it into the first bay and waiting while the system re-pressurized it. As soon as the light turned green, he popped out of the cockpit, climbed down, and headed to the airlock. A crowd was waiting to greet him as he opened it and stepped through.

"Welcome back, Gabriel," Miranda said, hugging him.

"Nice work, Captain," Soon said, also giving him a hug.

"Gabe," Colonel Choi said, squeezing his shoulder.

Gabriel suddenly found himself face to face with Guy. The scientist looked different, and Gabriel was taken off guard because he was smiling.

"Welcome home, Captain," Guy said, extending his hand.

They locked eyes for a moment. It was obvious to Gabriel that Guy still didn't like him, but he had made the decision to be a team player.

"Thank you," Gabriel said, taking the hand.

"We're glad you made it," Sarah said, hugging him.

"Your father said to go clean yourself up and then to stop by his quarters for a debriefing," Choi said.

"Yes, ma'am," Gabriel replied.

"We should have the logs analyzed by then," Guy said. "Colonel, I'll send the report up to the General as soon as I have it."

"Thank you, Guy."

The crowd dispersed, each member of the crew returning to their duties. Gabriel made his way back up to his quarters with Colonel Choi at his side.

"How is it down there?" she asked.

"Not good," Gabriel replied. "It looks worse from close up."

"This whole thing is such a long shot."

"It's worth it."

"Don't get me wrong, Gabriel. I agree completely. The fact that you're here proves that we can still fight back. We don't have to be victims."

"No, we don't. How is the General holding up?" He couldn't ignore the fact that his father had been bedridden up until two days ago.

"I convinced him to sleep a few hours. He seems twenty years younger to me since we boarded this ship. He's acting it, too."

"He's in his element out here. A man on a mission."

"A man of war."

"Because he has to be. We all have to be. You saw what the alternative is. The kind of people we become."

"It helps that you're with him."

"You, too. You've always been there for both of us."

"How could I not, Gabriel? I can still remember how hard you used to kick me." She put her hand on her stomach. "I've never been more proud than to help give Theodore and Juliet their son, after what they did for me."

They reached Gabriel's quarters. Gabriel was going to salute Colonel Choi. He decided to embrace her instead. "Thank you," he said.

"You're welcome."

69

"Captain St. Martin reporting, sir," Gabriel said as the door to his father's quarters opened. He was greeted there by Sergeant Diallo.

"The General will be with you in a moment," she said. "Welcome back, Gabe."

"Thank you."

His father's quarters were twice the size of his own, leaving room for both a sitting area and a conference table, in addition to the bed. Gabriel started moving toward the sofa until he heard Theodore coughing from the bathroom and the soft splash of water. Was his father vomiting?

"Is he okay?" Gabriel said, taking a step in that direction.

Diallo moved in front of him. "He's fine. He said it was the pain medication. It makes him nauseous sometimes."

Gabriel wanted to go and check on him but resisted. If Theodore had asked Diallo to keep him away, he would respect that. He went to the sofa and sat.

His father emerged from the bathroom a minute later. Gabriel stood as he rolled over, noting how pale his face was. Colonel Choi had mentioned how much better he looked not twenty minutes earlier. Did she know the pills were making him sick?

"Gabriel. Damn glad to see you again, son. Damn glad."

Gabriel saluted him. His father returned the salute.

"Now, don't ever do that in here again," Theodore said. "In here, we're father and son, you hear me?"

"Yes, sir," Gabriel said. His father glared at him. "Okay, Dad," he said in correction.

"Good man. Go ahead and sit, son. I got word from Guy and Reza. They'll be bringing the report up any minute now."

"Dad, are you feeling okay?" Gabriel asked. He cared more about that than the report.

"I'm fine. Just a little nauseous from the meds is all. They were giving me anti-emetics back on Alpha. I don't have any here." He shrugged. "Tell me, what's it like on Earth? It's been so long since I've seen it, and back then most of it was on fire."

"It isn't on fire anymore, at least. There are still things growing there. I saw trees up close for the first time in my life." Gabriel couldn't help but smile at that. Even while trying to escape the Dread, a portion of his brain had been able to marvel. "I might have seen a person, too, but I'm not sure."

"They're down there. With any luck, they saw you. Even if the transmission didn't make it, having you pass so close to the surface has to send a message of its own."

"If they were there, I'm sure I was hard to ignore."

A tone sounded from the door. Diallo was standing next to it, and she stood in front of the hatch and opened it.

"Uh, is General St. Martin here?" Reza said.

"Lucy, I know you want to help me, and I appreciate it from the bottom of my ancient ticker, but I don't need a keeper," Theodore said.

"I'm sorry sir," Diallo replied, stepping aside. "It's the training."

Reza, Guy, and Sarah entered the room with Colonels Choi and Graham.

"Sir," the soldier said, saluting.

"Relax," Theodore said. "We're all friends and family in here."

"We have the results of the logging, Theodore," Guy said.

"Well, don't keep us all squirming. Spill it."

"The transmission was a success," Reza said, his voice giddy. "It was sent, anyway. Obviously, we have no way to know if General Rodriguez, or anyone for that matter, heard it."

"It worked," Theodore said. "Y'all are geniuses. All of y'all. If I had any cigars, I'd give you one."

"Cigar?" Reza asked.

"They're made from a plant that grew on Earth. Tobacco. You cultivate it, dry it out, roll it up, and smoke it."

"Oh. Why?"

"What do you mean, why?" Theodore asked.

"I'm sorry, sir. I mean, what is the purpose of it?"

Theodore stared at him for a moment before laughing. "Heh. You know, I never really thought about it. I ain't sure I know anymore. The point is, the mission was a success. A real team effort, too. Y'all make me proud. Now, we need to start planning ahead."

"We'll assume that they received the message," Choi said. "That means that you'll be making another run in twelve days, Gabriel."

"Standard operation this time," Theodore asked. "Easy-peasy for you." He looked over at the scientists. "You three have some tougher work ahead of you."

"What do you need?" Reza asked.

"We have to assume the ground forces will do their damnedest to get us one of the enemy weapons. Once they do, we'll need to get on the ground to retrieve it."

"I barely made it skimming the surface," Gabriel said. "Dad, there's no way we're landing without getting killed."

"Now Gabriel, don't make me embarrass you in front of the others. No soldier of mine is going to use words like 'no way' without getting under this old gator's skin. Nobody's saying it'll be easy, but we have to believe it can be done."

Gabriel felt his face flush, even though Theodore had gone easy on him that time. "You're right. I'm sorry."

"Reza," Theodore said. "You've been doing a lot of work on slipstream algorithms. What is your opinion on the possibility of exiting a slipstream inside of Earth's atmosphere? And remember what I just said to Gabriel."

Reza looked uncomfortable under Theodore's gaze. "Uh. Hmm. It's a good question, sir. I gather you want Gabriel to be able to leave the slipstream already past the Dread defenses?"

"That's right. I want to take them by surprise. That way we get in and out before they can organize a defense."

"Well. You know. I mean." He paused.

Gabriel could tell he wanted to inform the General that it couldn't be done. That it was impossible. After all, it wasn't a new idea.

"I've done a lot of reading on this subject. There are three main problems with the concept. The largest is that while slipstream velocities are somewhat predictable, they aren't consistent. Right now we can estimate time to arrival with a certain margin of error, but to phase out in atmosphere doesn't have any margin. The disembarkation would have to be millisecond precise, as would the velocity calculations. One tick in the wrong direction, and you could come out in the center of the Earth, or shoot past it by a million kilometers."

"But the shorter the distance, the less error there is," Guy said.

"Right," Reza agreed. "Which is a second problem. There is a minimum distance to phase. Otherwise, you would never be able to turn the system on and off fast enough to arrive at your destination instead of shooting past it. Not to mention, you need to get up to slipstream join velocity in the first place."

"Even at a minimum distance there is still some error," Sarah said. "One thousandth of a millisecond could be the difference between life and death."

"Another problem is exit velocity," Guy said. "You'll be coming out of the slipstream at over twenty thousand KPH. A fighter will be torn to pieces by the sudden air resistance and pressure. Even if it could survive the exit, it would be a challenge to slow enough to keep from crashing into the surface."

"Reza, you told me back on Alpha that you were working on improved slipstream algorithms to better calculate velocities," Gabriel said. "Can you eliminate the margin of error?"

Reza started to shake his head before thinking better of it. "There is still some error. It's much, much less, but it isn't zero."

The assembly fell silent. Gabriel turned his attention to his father, who was sitting stiff and stoic, a thoughtful expression on his face.

"Well," he said at last. "It looks like y'all have your work cut out for you. I want to know what the margin of error is. I want calculations on the effects of air pressure and resistance at speed, and I want proposals on how to mitigate both as much as possible. We don't have the luxury of 'can't' right now. Is that understood?"

"Yes, sir," Reza said. Guy and Sarah nodded.

"You have twelve days. I know you won't let me down. Dismissed."

Gabriel stood with the others. He started to salute Theodore before remembering what he had said. "I'll see you on the bridge, Dad," he said instead.

Theodore nodded. "Take a day off, son. You've earned it."

Gabriel wasn't going to lay around and relax when he knew Reza and the Larones would be working nonstop. "I'll see you on the bridge," he repeated.

His father smiled. "Have it your way."

70

General Rodriguez, Diaz, and the rest of Donovan's t-vault team were already assembled by the time Donovan and Ehri joined them, with Ehri now wearing her original Dread clothing.

"Time is not on our side, Major," Rodriguez said.

"Yes, sir. I'm sorry, sir."

"It was my fault, General," Ehri said. "I-"

"It doesn't matter," the General replied. "All of you, follow me."

The group trailed behind Rodriguez as he moved away from the silo. Donovan hung back to walk next to Matteo, who looked lost and alone amidst the armed soldiers.

"Are you okay, amigo?" he asked.

"Sure. Why wouldn't I be?" Matteo said. "No sweat."

"I've got your back. Don't worry."

"I don't know if I can update the system to transmit. Hell, I don't even know what the system is."

"You'll figure it out. You've read every technical manual we have."

"That isn't saying much."

"I have faith in you," Donovan said, clapping Matteo on the shoulder.

"General, where are we going?" Diaz asked. "The exit is that way."

Rodriguez turned his head back. "There is an exit that way, yes. It's a little too open."

"Too open for what, sir?" Wade asked.

"You'll see, Corporal." He smiled. "I've been saving this surprise for a special occasion. I hoped I would never need to share it with anyone."

They reached the General's office. He circled his desk and stood next to the wall.

"I always figured there had to be another way out," he said. "Even though it wasn't in the schematics we found. I mean, you never know if you might need to evacuate, and exiting near a nuclear warhead seemed a bit stupid. I found this by accident a couple of weeks after we arrived here."

He ran his hand along the wall, feeling for something. When he found it, he pushed.

The solid cement wall suddenly gained a seam, and then it clicked and swung inward.

"Oh, man," Sanchez said. "A secret passage? Too cool."

"If there's another way out, why haven't the Dread found it?" Wade asked.

"And why didn't you tell the others about it?" Donovan asked. "They can use it if the Dread find their way in."

"Your mother knows about it, Major. She'll lead the others here and try to keep them hidden if things get bad. If the Dread are already coming into the base, it's likely they'll be killed if they attempt to leave whichever way they go. That's why we're trying to draw them away."

He brought them into the passage. It was dimly lit by emergency strips along the cement walkway, guiding them a hundred meters forward until dipping down.

"Where does it come out?" Donovan asked.

"You'll see."

Rodriguez started jogging, and the others picked up the pace with him. They followed the corridor nearly half a kilometer. Finally, they reached a heavy lead hatch that was hanging open. An earthy, damp smell permeated the tunnel, making Donovan nauseous.

Rodriguez slipped through the hatch, which led to a ladder.

"The ladder goes down into the sewers," Rodriguez said. "What you're smelling is fifty-year-old shit, garbage, and corpses. I think the stench is too much for the Dread, and that's why they never came this way."

"The bek'hai consider delving beneath the ground to be a sign of weakness," Ehri said. "They think it is degrading, even for a lor'hai. That is why they never search the sewers." She paused. "With the Domo'dahm's new orders, I don't know how much longer that will hold true."

"You learn something new every day," Rodriguez said. "But I guess when your enemy can't hurt you, you don't need to go soil yourself to hunt them down. In this case, it works out in our favor."

Rodriguez descended. The others followed. When he reached the bottom he pulled a wrist light from his pocket and slapped it on.

"The Dread have the right idea," Diaz said, holding her nose with her free hand.

Donovan looked around, feeling even more sick at the sight of the bloated, rotted, bodies that mingled with the rest of the debris in an inch deep layer of brown muck.

"We should have gone out the other way," he said.

"Come on."

Rodriguez led them another kilometer through the sewer to another ladder.

"I'll go up first and make sure it's clear. Wait here."

He climbed the ladder, reaching the top and then using his back to lift the heavy cover enough to see out. Once he was convinced it was safe, he slowly moved the cover off to the side and finished his ascent.

They joined him a minute later, standing in the back of a dark, enclosed space.

General Rodriguez made his way to the wall and pressed a switch. A single light faded on above them, revealing his secret.

"Is that a car?" Matteo asked.

They were in an old garage somewhere within the city. A bench of tools sat along the north wall. A hatch leading out was to the south. The west wall was intact, while the east had collapsed, destroying the rest of the building but managing to keep the single bay hidden.

Rodriguez smiled. "An old car. I think it was parked in here when the Dread came. Maybe they were working on restoring it? You can imagine my surprise when I happened across it."

"It has wheels," Diaz said.

"And an electric motor," Rodriguez said. "Fortunately, it was still holding a charge."

"What year do you think it's from?" Sanchez asked. "Twenty-two hundred?"

"Earlier than that. This thing was probably already a hundred years old when the Dread showed up. I've been coming here every week since I discovered the secret passage, trying to fix her up. It took me three years, but I got her running again."

The group circled the car. It had large, rugged tires and a boxy shape, and was covered in a layer of thick armor-plating.

"I can't believe you were coming here to work on this, sir," Donovan said. "Nobody else knows?"

"Major Sharma knows," Rodriguez said. "He made excuses for me now and then so I could come here. I had a feeling we would need it one day."

"How does it work?" Montero asked.

"I know how it works," Ehri said. "I have studied human transportation extensively."

"Ehri is driving," Donovan said.

"Major, I said I know how it works. I have never driven before."

"None of us have, except for the General."

"It's been a long time," Rodriguez said. "I always hoped I would be able to take her for a spin." He smiled sadly. "It's electric, so it won't give off too much heat for the first five minutes or so. After that, if there are any scouts around, they will spot you. Try to get as far as you can up the mountain before you have to abandon it." He reached into his pocket, withdrawing a small, gray block and a remote. "Explosives. After you ditch the car, blow it up. The heat will help hide you, and if you're really lucky they'll think you crashed and burned, or that they killed you themselves."

Donovan was reluctant to take the explosives. The General had spent so much time to restore the car, only to have to destroy it. It didn't seem fair.

"It's okay, Donnie," Rodriguez said. "It's a tool. A means to an end. Nothing more."

"Yes, sir."

"Now, get in. I'll get the door for you. Don't look back, don't slow down. Three blocks straight out, turn left, head up two klicks. You'll see the old highway there. Head over to it and follow it until you reach the tree line. Head into the trees and go as far as you can as fast as you can. Their mechanized armor will have trouble through the brush. The canopy should help absorb some of the plasma if they send fighters after you."

General Rodriguez took a step toward the hatch. There was no power to open it, so it would have to be pushed up manually.

"General, wait," Donovan said, approaching him.

"What is it, Major?"

"I hope I'll get to see you again, sir. If I don't, it's been an honor."

"The honor is mine, son. That goes for all of you. The bravest of the brave. You know what you have to do."

"Yes, sir," they replied, sharp and low, saluting at the same time.

Donovan retreated to the car, opening the passenger side door. Ehri climbed in behind the wheel to his left. She stared at the controls for a moment while the others piled into the back.

"You're sure you know how to work this thing?" Donovan asked.

She reached up and pressed the ignition. It didn't make any sound, but the dashboard lit up. She put her foot on the small, thin pedal on the right at the floorboard and depressed it slightly. The car inched forward. She moved her foot to the larger pedal and it stopped.

"Yes," she said.

General Rodriguez gave them the thumbs up, and then bent down and grabbed the small handle at the bottom of the hatch. He pulled hard, lifting it up and over his head, getting it just high enough for the car to fit below. He stood there, holding it while Ehri accelerated out into the fading light.

The General had said not to look back, but Donovan did anyway. He saw Rodriguez vanish behind the door.

"We're on our way," Matteo said, his voice shaking.

"Don't worry, bro," Diaz said. "We'll be there in no time."

A figure moved out into the street ahead of them.

A Dread clone, its plasma rifle already raised and ready to fire.

71

The car bucked forward as Ehri slammed on the brakes.

"What are you doing?" Donovan started to say, a sudden feeling of betrayal worming its way into his head.

The Dread soldier's shot was short, judged on where they would have been if she hadn't slowed. She immediately accelerated again, swerving to the left as the soldier adjusted his aim. The next shot grazed the side of the vehicle, leaving a scorch mark on the armor.

Corporal Wade aimed his rifle out the window, returning fire. The clone ducked back and away as they sped past.

"We made it, what, twenty meters?" Matteo asked.

"Relax, bro," Diaz said. "Ehri clearly knows how to handle this thing."

They crossed the three blocks in less than a minute, with Ehri making a hard left turn that threatened to tip the car. More Dread clones were appearing in the streets, answering the call of the first and trying to keep up with them.

"How the hell is the General going to get through this mess?" Montero said. "They're already crawling all over the city."

"We're still a klick out from home base," Donovan said. "It could be less crowded back that way."

The car was whipping past the ruined streets, with Ehri deftly steering it around the rubble. The large tires allowed them to clear large pieces of debris, bouncing the team around inside.

"Drive faster, drive faster," Sanchez said.

Donovan turned his head back to see her staring out the rear. He cursed under his breath as the mechanized armor turned the corner and took aim.

"Ehri, we've got a mech on our tail," he said.

Fire spewed from its arms, and the ground behind them began to explode, creating a cloud of fragmented pavement behind them while the machine adjusted its aim.

Ehri reached a street corner and turned left, escaping the strafing fire as it tore up their expected position.

"We're going the wrong way," Matteo said.

"Would you rather be dead?" Diaz asked.

Ehri turned right at the end of the block and immediately brought the car to a stop.

The road was blocked by a twenty-foot high pile of rubble.

"Back up," Donovan said, keeping his eyes to the rear.

"I don't know how," Ehri replied, looking at the dashboard.

"We can't just sit here," Wade said.

"You'll figure it out," Donovan said, opening the door and climbing out.

"What are you doing, Major?" Montero asked.

Donovan returned to the corner and peered around it. A squad of Dread soldiers had already covered the position, and the mech was still incoming. He aimed the plasma rifle and fired, the first few shots going wide before he adjusted for the lack of recoil. He let the base of the building absorb the return volley, and then fired back again, hitting each of the clones in turn.

They weren't even trying to hide. Not with the mech at their backs.

The car began to go backward, stopping next to him. He jumped in

334

and they continued onward. They were turning right when he saw the mech reach the corner. It was too slow.

The vehicle jumped forward, accelerating quickly through the mess. Ehri steered like a pro, getting them toward the city center where a park had once rested. Now it was a wide-open space, one that they would have to cross to get to the highway beyond.

"Go as fast as you can," Donovan said, scanning the area. A line of soldiers was entering from the west. He could feel the ominous presence of the mech approaching from the south.

Ehri went even faster, letting the car hit the edge of a burned out vehicle and throw it violently to the side. Then they were up and over what had once been a grassy area, now turned to brown wasteland. The Dread mech appeared to their right. The first shots hit dangerously close, sending up a spray of dirt through the open sides before the remainder struck the tail end, the force of the projectiles it was firing hitting the armor rocking the car.

Then they were across, breaking the mech's line of fire and racing toward the highway. The lane ahead of them was clear.

"I can't believe we made it," Matteo said.

Donovan caught motion to his right. A dark blur launched toward them, hitting the side of the car and sending it sideways. Ehri's hands gripped the controls, fighting to keep it stable as it began spinning from the force. Donovan got a glimpse of a pur'dahm soldier rising to its feet and bringing its rifle to bear.

The car hit the side of a wall and came to a stop. A bright flash nearly blinded them as a plasma bolt struck the armor, sinking in but not through. A second passed through the opening and into the wall on the other side, so close that Donovan could feel the heat of it.

A return volley caught the Dread in the shoulder, burning through the armor and damaging its arm, which fell limp to the side and dropped the gun. The pur'dahm vanished a moment later, springing away as Ehri got them moving again.

"Wow," Montero said. "Nice shot, Lieutenant."

The car began picking up speed again, breaking free from the edge of the city and bounding up and across a swath of long-dead grass and trees. Donovan could see the highway up ahead, a long strip of decaying pavement that continued on toward the tree line leading up the mountain. Donovan watched their rear as they crossed the area.

"It stopped following," he said. The echo of rifle fire created a sudden burst of sound.

"The General," Diaz said.

"Godspeed to him," Montero replied. "And to all of them."

"Do you think we're safe now?" Matteo asked. "Maybe they think we're just part of the evacuation and not worth the effort."

"I doubt that," Donovan said. The pur'dahm must have seen that Ehri was driving the car.

Two black dots appeared in the distant sky behind them.

He knew the Dread fighters were headed their way.

72

"We'll make the trees," Ehri said, keeping the car moving faster and faster.

"I don't think so," Donovan replied.

The fighters were closing so quickly there was no way to outrun them.

"Diaz, we have to keep them off-guard."

He cradled the plasma rifle, leaning out through the side of the vehicle, facing the rear. The odds of hitting the fighters were ridiculously low, but if he could at least make them wary, it might be enough.

Diaz joined him on the opposite side, holding tight with her legs and aiming the weapon. They both began to fire into the distance, the plasma bolts piercing the sky, covering a thousand meters before fading.

Ehri swung the car left, nearly peeling Donovan from his perch. The fighters fired back at the same time, swooping down to send plasma bolts at them. They burned the ground next to the car, over and over as Ehri zigged and zagged before momentum carried them past and forced them to turn around and reset.

Donovan looked in at the Dread scientist, her eyes fixed on the road and her tongue sticking slightly out of her mouth in concentration. She had steered them away from the Dread's attack as if she knew when and where it was coming. Was that even possible?

The fighters were coming back. The trees were growing closer. The off-road path had to be close.

"Diaz," Donovan shouted, resuming his cover fire. Diaz did the same, their aim improving enough to force the fighters to wobble slightly. The next volley missed wide; the pilots' aim disrupted.

"Over there," Montero shouted. "The break in the trees."

Ehri turned her head, and then the wheel. They bounced off the pavement and onto the grass, the car jostling over the terrain toward the slope. The fighters were coming back for a third approach.

Then they were below the canopy, smashing through the lighter brush. Ehri had to slow to maneuver around the trees, and Donovan and Diaz ducked back inside before they were decapitated by wayward branches. They had covered a lot of distance in a short time.

Maybe they would make it after all.

They continued up the slope. Donovan tried to watch the sky, but the growth above them made it difficult to see. He was sure the fighters were up there, and he knew they would fire on them sooner or later.

The attack came. Plasma bolts rained through the branches, burning holes in trees and igniting the brush around them. They were tracking the heat signature; their aim pushed off by the interference. Each volley began to come closer and closer.

"I can't shake them in here," Ehri said. "The trees force me into an almost straight line."

A plasma bolt hit the front of the car, digging deep into the armor, which managed to withstand the attack.

"It's time to ditch," Donovan said. "Everybody else out."

"We're still moving," Matteo said.

"If we stop, we die for sure."

Diaz kicked open her door and grabbed Matteo's arm. "Come on," she said, throwing herself out and dragging him along.

The other soldiers opened their doors and jumped out, rolling along the ground. More plasma bolts came down, two of them hitting the rear of the car where the passengers had been moments earlier.

"Ehri, we need to jump," Donovan said. He shoved the explosive against the dashboard and took hold of the detonator.

Ehri pushed open her door and vanished, leaving him alone in the car. He waited for the next plasma bolt to hit before throwing himself from the car and hitting the trigger on the remote at the same time.

The car exploded calmly, the armor keeping it from sending shrapnel everywhere. It was enough to set the interior on fire, and blow through to the engine compartment. Thick smoke rose from the front, and two more plasma bolts immediately dug into it, damaging it further.

Donovan waited thirty seconds before getting to his feet and scanning behind him. The others were still on the ground, likely watching him. He looked up through the brush and didn't see the Dread fighters.

Hopefully, the enemy thought they were all dead.

He waved back and signaled ahead. The rest of the squad began to rise, heading in the direction he had motioned while merging into one unit. They started picking their way through the woods in tense silence, listening for any sign of pursuit.

There was none.

73

The echo of gunfire had faded to nothing by the time Donovan and his squad neared the position where Matteo claimed General St. Martin's transmission had originated. They had climbed ten kilometers up the mountain in less than two hours, a pace that left them all tired and breathless.

"Do you think anyone is still alive down there?" Corporal Wade asked.

"They have to be," Sanchez replied. "No way General Rodriguez goes down like that."

No one else spoke. The words only made them more tense.

They traveled another half-kilometer before they reached their target.

A large building, half-buried beneath trees and moss and vines, the side of it appearing as if out of nowhere directly in front of them.

"I think this is it," Matteo said.

"What is it?" Diaz asked.

"I don't know."

Donovan approached the wall, pushing some of the leaves in front of it aside. He followed the parts he could see upward. It appeared there was a dome on top, though time had merged it with the vegetation.

"I think this is the side," he said. "We need to find the front."

They continued, staying close to the side and moving clockwise around it. It took another few minutes before they discovered the entrance in the form of a dark shadow beneath a line of vines and spider webs.

"Anyone have a light?" Donovan asked.

"I do," Matteo said producing a wrist light. He slapped it on and stayed close behind as Donovan pushed the vines and webs aside.

There was a soft light coming from somewhere inside, allowing them to see the long corridor the entrance became. The illumination was sourced through a window in a simple red door.

"There," Donovan said. He led them to it, running his fingers over the lettering etched into the glass when they reached it.

"Control," Ehri said, reading it.

Donovan looked through the glass. The light was brighter now, and was joined by others. Control was a small room with a monitor and touchpad, along with some other equipment he was sure Matteo would recognize.

He tried the door, finding it unlocked. He pushed it open.

"It's all yours, amigo," he said to Matteo.

"Thanks," Matteo replied. He entered and sat on the stool in front of the monitor, running his hand along the control pad. "This thing is old."

"What is it?" Donovan asked.

"It looks like a mainframe for something. I bet it was on low-power standby for all of these years, waiting for instructions that no one was around to give."

"Until now."

"Yeah." He explored the different screens while the others waited in anxious silence. "If I'm not mistaken, it looks like this building is connected to an antenna outside."

"I didn't see an antenna," Donovan said.

"I think it was on the opposite side."

"Does it transmit, or only receive?"

"I don't know yet. I'm picking through the pieces here." He moved through a few more screens. "Give me time."

"We don't have a lot of time."

"I know."

"Major," Ehri said. Donovan turned and found her standing outside of the control room. "You should come and see this."

Donovan left the others, following Ehri through a second hallway. Each door had a small window in it, and looking through he saw a series of rooms, dimly lit by backup lighting: a small room with a pair of bunk beds, a kitchen, a gym, and finally three adjacent offices.

There was a single book resting on the desk of the first. He pushed open the door and approached it. A layer of dust coated the cover, and he picked it up and wiped it off. Ehri stood behind him, looking over his shoulder.

The book was a plain navy blue with white writing. "Mount Tlaloc Deep Space Network Station 110," Donovan said, showing it to Ehri.

"Deep Space Network?" she said, reaching out and taking the book. She flipped through a few pages. "This is an operations manual for the base."

"Whatever the Deep Space Network is, it sounds promising."

"I know what it is, Major. The DSN antennas were originally installed to communicate with satellites and probes your people launched in the twenty-first century. As your technology improved and interstellar travel became possible, they were updated and increased in number to communicate with and track outbound ships. The bek'hai destroyed all of them during the initial invasion. Or at least, they believe they did."

"This one looks like it was out of use before the invasion," Donovan said. "The entire forest has grown around it."

"Which is likely why the bek'hai didn't know it was here."

"If what you're saying is right, then this base should be able to get a message out to Mars."

"Yes, Major."

Donovan couldn't believe it. Just when everything had started to look hopeless. Just when the head of the resistance had decided it was better to run and hide than to continue the fight. The one thing they needed most had been sitting right in their backyard, waiting for them.

"We need to tell Matteo."

They rushed back to the control room. Matteo was tapping on the control pad.

"I think I have this mostly figured out," he said.

Ehri placed the book on the desk next to him. "This might help."

"Deep Space Network?" Matteo said. "Does that mean what I think it means, amigo?"

"Let's hope so," Donovan said. He turned to Diaz. "We need to secure the area. Take Wade, Cameron and Sanchez and form a perimeter. Do not engage. If you see any Dread coming, send a warning."

"Yes, sir," Diaz said. "You heard the Major."

The other soldiers followed Diaz from the room.

"What should I do?" Colonel Montero asked. It was still strange to Donovan to give orders to someone who outranked him.

"Cover the door, sir. Help pass any messages in from outside."

"Of course, Major."

"This screen has a list of numbers on it," Matteo said. "I wasn't sure what they were, but knowing what this place is helps. I think they're coordinates."

"May I see?" Ehri asked.

Matteo rolled the stool to the side so Ehri could lean over and see the screen. "Yes, you're right. They're updating in realtime."

"Is one of them Mars?" Donovan asked.

Matteo scrolled the list. He went halfway before pausing.

"Si, amigo. One of them is Mars."

74

Gabriel was already on the bridge when Theodore arrived. Only fifteen minutes had passed since their meeting with the scientists, and he was pleased when he noticed that the color and health had returned to the General's face.

There wasn't that much for him to do on the bridge while the Magellan was in a static position near Mars. In fact, there wasn't much for anyone on the bridge to do except sit and wait. Even so, he felt an obligation to be there. He didn't want anyone to think he was getting off easy because he was the General's son. Maybe it forced him to push himself harder than he would otherwise, but he was okay with that. If his efforts motivated the people around him, all the better.

"General on the bridge," Colonel Choi said as the elder St. Martin rolled in. The rest of the crew stood and saluted him.

"At ease," Theodore said.

He got himself to the Command Station and transferred himself from the chair. Then he leaned back in it, taking a breath, before fixing his gaze out of the front viewport. They had shifted their position, moving closer to

Mars and leaving the red planet visible on the port side, large and beautiful. There was nothing but empty space dead ahead.

"Systems report," the General said.

"All systems operating smoothly, sir," Sergeant Abdullah said. "She's as content as a kid in a candy store."

"Heh. Where did you hear that simile, Sergeant?" Theodore asked. "You ain't old enough to have ever seen a candy store."

"My father used to like to say it, sir," Abdullah replied, turning back to face him. "He told me it reminded him of Earth. He was only seven when the Dread came. Was my usage incorrect?"

"No, Sergeant. It was spot on. I was just curious. Carry on."

"Yes, sir."

The bridge fell into a comfortable silence. Gabriel sat back in his pod, mimicking his father by staring out the viewport. Was this the calm before the storm?

"Sir," Miranda said, spinning around from the comm station. "I'm picking up an unidentified signal on the X-band."

"X-band?" Theodore said, sitting forward on his arms. "That's a military frequency. Are you receiving?"

"Let me check, sir," Miranda said, operating her station. "I'm sharing with your station." Her voice was quivering. She glanced over at Gabriel, her surprise obvious. "It's coming from Earth, sir."

"I see that, Spaceman Locke," Theodore said. "Well I'll be. That sly son of a bitch, he's way ahead of me." He paused as the message continued to receive. "Damn it. Those alien couillons. It ain't going to end like this."

Gabriel looked back at his father, his pulse quickening. A message from Earth? How could that be? And what was his father muttering about?

The message must have finished. Theodore's expression gained an even higher level of intensity and focus.

"Colonel Choi," Theodore said. "Get me Reza and the Larones and bring them to the conference room."

"Yes, sir."

Colonel Choi left the bridge to find them.

"Captain St. Martin."

Gabriel stood and faced his father. "Yes, sir?"

"Contact Captain Kim and tell him to get the other pilots organized."

"Sir?"

"Don't question, son, just do."

"Yes, sir."

Gabriel returned to his station, using his control pad to contact Soon.

"Gabriel?" he said, answering the call. He sounded as if he had been sleeping. "What's up?"

"I'm not sure yet. I have orders from the General to prep the flight crew."

"Are you serious?"

"Very."

"Yes, sir."

"Captain Kim is prepping the flight crew, sir," Gabriel reported.

"Follow me, Captain," Theodore said. "Sergeant Abdullah, you have the bridge."

"Yes, sir," Abdullah said.

Theodore was in his chair by the time Gabriel reached him. He had to jog to keep up with his father as he sped down the hall.

"What's happening?" Gabriel asked.

"The resistance got our message. They already have a couple of alien rifles, if you believe that. Not only that, they've used them to kill a couple of the aliens."

"That's great news," Gabriel said. It was about time they had managed to do a little bit of damage against their enemy. "How did they manage to send a signal out here?"

"That's the bad news. The Dread are swarming their position, which may or may not already be overrun or lost. A small team led by Major Donovan Peters traced the source of our message back to an old Deep Space Network station of all things. Hah. They used it to transmit out here. They want to organize a pickup."

"It's ten hours back to Earth," Gabriel said, his earlier misgivings about landing on the surface lost in the moment. "Can they last that long?"

"No. Not now. They had to burn the station's backup power supply to adjust the antenna position and get the message out. Not to mention, the motion is bound to attract the Dread."

"Which means they may be dead already."

"We ain't going there, son," Theodore said.

They reached the conference room. Colonel Choi and the scientists joined them less than a minute later.

"I don't understand," Guy said. "We just spoke to you."

"You remember all that stuff I asked you for twenty minutes ago?" Theodore said. "I need it now."

"What?" Guy said. "General, we can't possibly produce any kind of accurate information in less than twenty minutes. We need time to-"

Sarah put her hand up, cutting her husband off. "I thought we had twelve days?"

"Things change fast in war," Theodore said. "We've got one shot to get our hands on an alien weapon, but the only way we make it is if you get us to Earth in the next thirty minutes."

"Thirty minutes?" Reza said. "General, it can't-" Theodore flashed him an angry look. "Okay. I mean, my algorithm hasn't been tested, but we're far enough out we should be able to get it to work. I assume you want to bring the Magellan close to Earth, but far enough out that the orbital defenses won't start shooting at you?"

"No, Mr. Mokri. I want you to bring the Magellan in past the orbital defense ring."

"What?" Reza and Gabriel both said at the same time.

"General, that's suicide," Guy said. "You'll kill every one of us."

"Maybe I will. Mr. Mokri, what's your margin of error?"

"I'd have to check, sir."

"Guess."

"Plus or minus one hundredth of a second?"

"A slipstream ride from here to Earth will take less than two seconds," Guy said. "That's more than enough to throw the position completely."

"I can get it to one ten-thousandth if I can run the calculations," Reza said.

"You can not," Guy replied.

"Yes, I can. General, I'm sure I can. I have an idea."

"That's the spirit," Theodore said. "Go do what you need to do."

"Yes, sir." Reza turned and ran down the hallway toward his quarters.

"General, this isn't going work," Guy said.

Theodore glared at Guy, opening his mouth, ready to explode.

"Guy, we're doing this one way or another," Gabriel said, interrupting. "Two seconds is too fast for a human to start and stop the QPG. We'll need to automate the shutdown."

"Me? I'm not a software engineer."

"Then go back to your room and get out of my face," Theodore said. "I thought you were coming around to our way of thinking, but I guess you're just a yellow-bellied couillon after all."

"I can do it," Sarah said. "But I need full access to the ship's computer."

"You can use the Command Station. Access code is 7-2-4-8-9-1-5-6. Can you remember that?"

"7-2-4-8-9-1-4-6," Sarah repeated. "I've got it."

"You're a smart cookie. Be careful with Maggie, Mrs. Larone. She's a delicate flower."

"Yes, General." She eyed Guy angrily before rushing from the room.

"Captain, head on down to the hangar and prep your squad. If we survive the slip, you'll be launching directly into the thermosphere."

"And then what, General?" Gabriel asked.

"One of your team needs to touch down on top of Mount Tlaloc in what used to be Mexico. You probably flew over it on your pass. Collect the alien rifle from the ground team and get the hell out of there. The rest of the squad runs interference."

"Interference? We don't have any firepower."

"I don't care how you do it, Captain. Ram them with your fighters if you have to. We need to get that weapon back to the Magellan."

"And then we need to get the Magellan away from Earth."

Theodore smiled. "You let me handle that, son. I beat those bastards once, and I'm damn well going to do it again."

75

"Did it work?" Donovan asked.

"I think so," Matteo said, turning away from the now dead computer.

It had taken nearly twelve hours for Matteo and Ehri to get the transmission sent. The complexity and age of the system had been a challenging barrier to overcome, even with the help of the operations manual. On top of that, their first attempt to reposition the antenna to Mars' azimuth had been met with total failure, as a frayed wire connecting the station to the parabolic transmitter caused the commands to die silently.

The two of them had eventually figured it out, and the message had been sent.

He could only pray that it would be received and acted on.

"Let's round up the rest of the squad," he said. "We need to be out of here and up the mountain to the rendezvous point."

"Do you think the Dread noticed?" Matteo asked. "The antenna wasn't exactly quiet."

They were lucky it had moved at all with nearly one hundred years of vegetation attached to it.

Donovan glanced at Ehri, who shrugged. "I don't know. Anything is possible, which is all the more reason not to linger."

They abandoned the control room, heading for the exit. Colonel Montero was standing against the wall there, staring out into the night.

"Major," he said when he saw Donovan. "Success?"

"Yes."

"Excellent."

Donovan put his fingers to his mouth and blew softly. A reply came a moment later. Then another. Then another.

"Only three," Montero said.

Donovan made the signal again. Again, three whistles in reply.

"Why aren't there four?" Matteo asked.

A plasma bolt lit the night, a red flash that struck Colonel Montero in the chest, sending him flopping backward and to the ground.

"Mierda," Matteo said, ducking back into the building.

Donovan shoved Ehri against the wall, scanning for the source of the shot. No others followed.

"They're on to us," Donovan said. "Damn it." He put his fingers to his mouth and blew a new signal, warning the others. He saw a flash in the trees to the north. Who had gone that way? The echo of rifle fire confirmed the position was under attack.

"We can't stay here, Major," Ehri said.

"I know. We have to get up the mountain."

"What about the others?" Matteo asked.

"They'll follow if they can."

He stuck his head out from the entrance, trying to scan the trees in the darkness. "Their soldiers can see in the dark. Can you?"

"Better than you, but not like them," Ehri replied.

"Do you see anything?"

"No."

"Come on."

He stared out of the building, keeping the Dread plasma rifle raised and ready. He only made it a single step when he heard a branch snap to his left. He backpedaled just in time to regain the cover as a plasma bolt seared into the wall.

"We're pinned down," he said. The soldier had vanished into the woods again, taking advantage of its superiority in the dark.

"We can't stay here," Ehri repeated. "They'll send a fighter to blast this building to dust if the lor'hai can't root you out."

"I don't suppose we can reason with them?"

"No. They haven't been exposed to freedom the way I have. They won't understand it. Not yet."

"So, what do you suggest?"

"We have to make a run for it."

Donovan looked back at Matteo. He was pressed against the wall, his face pale.

"Matteo, are you with me, amigo?"

Matteo didn't answer.

"Matteo? Come on, bro. You need to snap out of it."

More gunfire sounded from the east, and the sky flashed again. The shooting stopped. They were being picked off one at a time.

"Matteo?" Donovan said, grabbing his arm. "I don't want to have to leave you here."

Matteo's eyes shifted. "Donovan?"

"Come on, amigo. It's time to run."

"I don't want to die."

"Stick with me, you won't die. I promise. Okay?"

"Okay."

Donovan inched to the edge of the doorway again, looking out into the darkness once more. He jutted his neck out once more, peering through the opening.

A bright flash ahead of him caused him to duck back, but nothing hit the wall.

He looked out again. Diaz ran to the doorway.

"You're clear, Major," she said.

"The others?"

She shook her head. "I don't think so. I saw Wade get hit. I nailed the bastard who killed him."

He would have time to mourn his people if he survived.

"Fast feet, eyes open," he said.

"Yes, sir."

They sprinted from the doorway, into the trees and away. Branches slapped Donovan's body as he barreled in front of the remainder of his squad, absorbing the blows with the alien cloth. The drop point was five kilometers up the mountain. General Rodriguez had chosen the spot because they could reach it on foot and because there was a small plateau where a starfighter could likely land. It was fairly close. Right now, it seemed impossibly far.

Not that it mattered. It would be nearly ten hours before General St. Martin would be able to reach them from Mars. They had to stay in the area, which meant there was no way to lose the Dread soldiers.

They had to fight, but how? The enemy could see them, but they couldn't see the enemy.

He tried to ignore the cold truth of their situation, but it began creeping through him, a chill that started at his chest and started working its way outward.

They were going to die.

Worse, they were going to fail.

76

"This is Leader One. Fighter Squadron Alpha, sound off," Gabriel said.

"Alpha Two, standing by," Captain Kim said.

"Alpha Three, standing by," Lieutenant Ribisi said.

"Alpha Four, standing by," Second Lieutenant Bale said.

"Alpha Five, standing by," Second Lieutenant Polski said.

Gabriel tapped his control pad. "Fighter Squadron Alpha is standing by, General."

"Roger," Theodore replied. "Hold position and prepare for launch."

"Roger."

Gabriel looked out at the bare metal walls of the launch tube he and his fighter had been placed in. The rest of the squad was arranged in the other four tubes on either side of his, part of the half dozen that lay on each side of the Magellan. He wished he could see into space from where he was. He wasn't claustrophobic, but riding blind when he was used to being in control was making him a little tense.

It had taken Reza almost an hour to return to Theodore with his calculations and an updated slip algorithm that he swore was almost error free, with the important word being almost. Reza had started to try to tell the General that perfection was impossible, but had stopped himself before he got in trouble. Instead, he had turned the algorithm over to Sarah Larone, who used the Command Station to make the changes to Maggie's software. Between that untested math and the better half of the Larones' untested hack into the QPG controls, Gabriel figured there was a one percent chance or so that they would even survive the entry and exit from the slipstream.

And that was being generous.

Even so, he was able to hold on to a certain calm. Either it was all going to end, or perhaps something new would begin. A chance to fight back against the aliens who had taken their world. A chance for humankind to rise up and prosper once more.

To him, it was a chance worth dying for.

"Stand by, Alpha Leader," Miranda said through his comm.

"Beginning acceleration to slip velocity," Theodore said. He had left the comm open so that the squadron could hear.

A soft hum rose in the launch tube as the main thrusters on the rear of the Magellan began to fire.

Gabriel reached down and clutched his mother's crucifix, bringing it to his lips and kissing it. He closed his eyes, thinking of the picture of her that he had grown up with. "We're keeping our promise, Mom," he whispered. Then he smiled. "I bet you always knew we would."

"Ten-thousand," Theodore said. "Maggie, prepare the QPG."

"Yes, General," the computer said.

"Fifteen-thousand," Theodore said. "Get ready."

Gabriel lowered the crucifix, moving his hands to the fighter's control sticks. The slip was going to be short. Shorter than should even be possible. Shorter than might be possible. They were fortunate there was even a current to carry them.

"Eighteen-thousand," Theodore said. "Maggie, darlin', you know what to do."

The ship shuddered slightly as the QPG was engaged, beginning the process of phasing the starship into slipspace. Gabriel breathed in, finding that breath caught in his throat.

"One one-thousand, two one-thousand," he counted in his head.

"Launch Alpha Squadron," Theodore barked crisply.

"Launching," Miranda replied.

Gabriel was shoved back in his seat as the fighter was rocketed forward through the tube. They were still alive, which meant the slip had been successful. He wouldn't know if they had come out as intended until he reached open space.

He remembered to breathe out.

The fighter burst from the side of the starship in unison with the rest of the squadron. Earth was directly ahead of them. The Magellan was already yawing to allow them an easy departure into the atmosphere.

"I can't believe he did it," Soon said over the comm.

"Stay focused," Gabriel replied. "Bring weapons online."

"They won't do anything," Ribisi said.

"Bring them online," Gabriel barked.

"Yes, sir."

They hit the atmosphere, blinding heat pushing off the front of the fighters as they descended. The Magellan lumbered behind them, crossing the planet just out of reach of the gravitational pull, safely behind the net of deadly satellites.

"Follow my lead," Gabriel said. "If anything happens to me, you have to get down and retrieve the weapon."

"Yes, sir," the pilots said.

They continued to descend, coming in hard and fast. The sun was on the other side of the planet, leaving it draped in darkness as they burst into the sky. The Dread had no time to prepare for them. There was no advance warning from the outer defenses. The squadron raced across the landscape, headed for the mountain.

Ten seconds passed. Twenty. The mountain came into view ahead of them, lit only by the multitude of stars and outlined on Gabriel's HUD.

"Cut throttle. Form up, pattern bravo. Eyes open."

He slowed his fighter. The mountain was approaching in a hurry. Even in the dim light of the stars he could see the line of downed trees where the two Dread fighters had crashed. It looked like they had managed to get airborne again.

"Alpha Leader, are you seeing what I'm seeing?" Bale asked.

He wasn't. "What do you have, Alpha Four?"

"The mountain, sir. The western side. It doesn't look like it's very far from the drop point."

Gabriel turned his attention to the area. He didn't see anything at first. Only the shape of the canopy in silhouette against the dark.

A sudden flash below the trees sent light rippling out and around. Three more followed.

"That looks like plasma," Kim said.

"It has to be the resistance," Gabriel replied.

"Alpha Leader, we've got company," Polksi said. "Two bogeys, headed our way from the direction of the Dread city."

"Probably the same two I sent into the trees once already. Alpha Four, Alpha Five, peel off and see if you can keep them distracted. Remember, they can't maneuver as well as you can."

"Yes, sir," Bale and Polski said, breaking from the formation and turning to engage.

"What about us?" Ribisi asked.

"Low and slow, Alpha Three. It doesn't matter if we make it to the drop zone if the rebels don't."

77

Donovan grabbed Matteo's shoulder, pulling him to the side and behind a tree as a bolt of plasma pierced the spot where he had been standing.

"You can't come out from cover like that, amigo. You're going to get yourself killed."

Matteo looked up at him, his eyes glazed over with fear.

They had been making a slow but steady retreat from the Deep Space Network Station to the pickup site, backing toward it while trading fire with the Dread clone soldiers. The battle had started fairly intense, but at this point it was becoming tedious. Donovan had been hoping Matteo would get used to it after he didn't get hit with the first three hundred or so rounds. He couldn't believe his friend was so skittish.

"We can't keep this up," Diaz said, leaning against the trunk of the tree next to Ehri. "We're going to kill our guns before we can hand one over."

"I think we're almost there," Donovan said. "It can't be more than another half-kilometer."

Diaz leaned out, searching the night for the soldiers. "I think we have a break. Let's move."

Donovan grabbed Matteo's shirt and pulled him up. They raced as one unit toward the next line of trees a dozen meters ahead. Plasma bolts flew by, one of them passing so close to Donovan's foot that he felt the tingle as it burned.

They slipped behind the tree, with Diaz firing back as they did. Two shots to conserve power.

"We only need to do that about fifty more times," she said.

"We've already done it at least a hundred," Donovan replied.

"I want to go home," Matteo said.

"You need to man up, bro," Diaz said. "I can't believe my big brother is such a baby."

"Screw you, Ren."

"Shhh," Ehri said, silencing them. "Do you hear that?"

Donovan listened. He could hear the soldiers in the woods. That was nothing new. "I don't hear anything different."

"We need to move faster," Ehri said. "They're losing patience."

"How do you know?"

"Listen."

Donovan did. "I can't hear it, whatever it is."

"The trees are too thick for mechanized armor. They aren't too thick for pur'dahm Hunters."

"Hunters?" Matteo asked.

"Elite warriors. They organize in teams, and fight to the death for sport."

"So much for civilized," Diaz said.

Ehri didn't reply to that. "We need to move faster," she repeated.

"Okay," Donovan said. "Let's go."

"We aren't clear," Diaz said.

"It doesn't matter. If we don't make it-"

"Then what, D? What if we don't make it? General St. Martin isn't coming for at least another nine hours. Nine. We're going to be out of bolts way before then, and if we aren't it will only be because we're dead. I know you're being the strong commander, but you have to know that's true."

"We aren't dead until we're dead," Donovan said. "Now move it, Lieutenant. That's an order."

Diaz clenched her jaw, nodded, and got to her feet. "Fine."

They started to run. A hail of bolts pounded the area around them, forcing them back into safety.

"They're laying down suppressing fire to keep us pinned," Diaz said.

"We have to try again. We don't have a choice."

"I knew you were going to say that."

They prepared themselves a second time. They were just about to break cover when a series of rumbling pops echoed across the mountainside. He looked over at Diaz, who was looking back at him.

"It couldn't be," he said.

"Those were sonic booms," Ehri said. "At least six of them."

"Is he here already?" Diaz asked.

"We have to get to the drop point. Now."

The assumed arrival of the space forces gave them new energy. Donovan pulled Matteo up again, holding on as they made a run for it. He ignored the enemy fire at his back, focusing only on making it through the brush without tripping on a branch or a root. He had no idea how General St. Martin could have gotten here so fast, but they had to make it to the plateau. It was the only thing that mattered.

They kept going, slipping through the foliage and somehow managing to make it through without being hit. They covered fifty meters, then one hundred. Donovan's legs were burning, but he didn't dare stop. The fact that he was still alive was a miracle in itself.

They pushed through the trees and into a small clearing. It took Donovan a few seconds to realize he was standing on the plateau.

The pur'dahm Hunters were already waiting there for them.

"That's why they kept missing us," Diaz said, pulling up short, her breathing hard. "They were herding us here."

Tense seconds passed as the two sides stood and stared at one another. Donovan glanced over his shoulder at the movement in the trees. A dozen clones spilled out behind them.

"I'll go talk to them," Ehri said.

"Why?" Donovan asked.

It was too late. She was already ranging ahead.

"Who speaks for you?" Ehri shouted to the pur'dahm.

They looked different than the other bek'hai soldiers he had seen. Their black armor covered every inch of them, encasing them in an impenetrable carapace. Donovan shifted the plasma rifle in his arms. It wasn't impenetrable right now.

"Buhr gruhmn. Orik dur Lorik."

"Speak English, Orik dur Lorik," Ehri said.

"I do not take commands from the lor'hai," Orik said. He reached up and tapped the side of his armor. It slid away, revealing his face. Tubes ran from his nose to the oxygen tank Donovan knew would be on his back.

"And yet you did as I asked," Ehri replied.

Orik's face twisted in anger. "I chose for myself. This is not your affair, Ehri dur Tuhrik. You have had your time to study the humans, as your Dahm wished, even though it cost his life."

"Four days? What was I to learn of them in four days?"

"You shouldn't have armed them with our weapons if you wanted more time. You shouldn't have let them kill Klurik."

"He wasn't one of yours."

"It matters not."

"The Domo'dahm promised me time."

"And you promised not to interfere."

Donovan stared at Ehri. She was speaking as if she had been planning on joining them. How could that be if their entry into the Dread ship had been an accident?

Unless it hadn't been an accident.

Had she manipulated the entire thing? It seemed impossible, but if they had been spotted scouting out the transmission site, it could be that she had arranged for the clone soldiers to attack in a way that would steer them toward the elevator shaft. It could be that she had seen them enter the ship, and had arranged for Tuhrik to leave his quarters at the same time they arrived.

"I needed a proper catalyst," Ehri said.

"The Domo'dahm did not approve it."

"He gave me approval when he allowed the study. Do what you must to learn what you must. Those were his exact words."

"The Domo'dahm has always been illogical to that face," Orik said. "I don't know what he ever saw in that human, to give her such favor. Her genetics weren't even compatible."

"I need more time," Ehri said.

"It is over, Ehri. The human base is destroyed. The ones who were trying to escape are all dead."

Ehri looked back at them, her eyes apologetic. Donovan shook his head, silently pleading with her not to turn them over to the Dread.

Diaz reacted differently, whipping the plasma rifle up. "You alien bitch," she said. "We trusted you."

The pur'dahm raised their weapons on the other side of the plateau, five rifles all pointed at Diaz.

The entire clearing erupted.

78

Gabriel squeezed the trigger, loosing pulse after pulse of ions at the line of Dread soldiers standing near the far side of the plateau, while a similar assault tore at the clone soldiers standing behind the rebel fighters. Captain Kim and Lieutenant Ribisi's attacks were more effective than his, the ions shredding both the stone around the clones and the clones themselves, sending them sprawling in sprays of blood and gore.

The armored Dread weren't completely immune, the ions still powerful enough to push at them, knocking them off-balance and causing them to fall.

Then he was past, shooting by the drop point and making a tight vector to come back around again. He didn't know if their intervention would be enough to give the resistance the upper hand. If he was quick enough, he could knock the Dread soldiers back a second time.

"Alpha Leader, this is Alpha Four. We just lost Alpha Five."

Gabriel felt the wrench in his heart at the sudden news.

"I could really use some help back here."

"Alpha Two, pick up the slack for Alpha Four," Gabriel said.

"Yes, sir," Soon replied, breaking away.

"The enemy assholes are up again, sir," Ribisi said.

"Then we knock them down."

He dropped back toward the clearing, getting visual on the alien fighters. They had reassembled, spreading apart to minimize the chance of being hit. Half of them were turning their weapons to the sky while the other half were aiming for the resistance soldiers. The one who had moved ahead of the rest was on her stomach between the two sides. He didn't know if she were dead. Had they hit her by mistake?

He fired the ion cannon again, the pulses cutting into the line of Dread soldiers a second time. Once more, they fell away under the weight of the assault, losing their aim. He saw a plasma bolt launch from the resistance side and hit one of the Dread in the chest.

"Alpha Leader, this is Alpha Two. We can't shake them."

Gabriel watched his HUD. All of the airborne targets were visible in it as red or green triangles. The greens were moving every which way, and the reds were managing to keep up despite their lesser maneuverability.

"Alpha Three, see if you can sneak up on them. The cannons may at least disrupt their aim."

"Yes, sir."

The final fighter moved away, leaving him alone to finish trying to clean off the mountain. He was running out of time.

He adjusted his flight pattern, setting up to make a third and hopefully final run.

79

Donovan pushed himself to his feet, quickly scanning the line of Hunters ahead of him. They were recovering from the starfighter's second approach, preparing to attack once more.

He ran toward Ehri. She was lying face down and motionless in the center of the clearing. Was she dead? Why was he running toward her, anyway? She had betrayed them. She had lied to them. She had used them like some kind of laboratory experiment.

Was he going to help her or make sure she really was gone?

Motion from the other side alerted him to the Dread soldier who had gotten back up and was now running toward Ehri as well. The one she had called Orik. Donovan fired his plasma rifle, the poorly aimed shots going wide. Orik did the same, his targeting equally poor.

It was a race to reach her. He didn't know what the Dread was planning to do with her. What he did know was that he wanted to be the one to decide her fate. He pushed himself to run faster.

Orik's shots were getting closer. His return fire was still no good, and he was just too damn slow. He wasn't going to make it.

The pur'dahm reached Ehri as Donovan came to a stop, intending to retreat. He had forgotten about the rest of the Dread soldiers in his desperate run, and now he looked further ahead. Only three were still moving, keeping a low profile and shooting back at Diaz, who was covering him. He started adjusting his aim again, a sudden sense of hopelessness overwhelming him. He had been reckless. Careless. Orik stood over Ehri, the bek'hai's rifle already trained on him.

A hand reached up from the ground. Ehri rolled over, grabbing the pur'dahm's wrist and pulling it down, bringing it into her other hand and continuing to yank on it as she shifted. The Hunter was brought off balance, and she used his momentum to get to her feet, spinning like a top and kicking him hard in the side of his bare head. The blow knocked him back a step and pulled the oxygen tube from his nostril, and she used the chance to grab his rifle, turning it in her grip and firing at point blank range before he could react.

She shifted to face Donovan, pointing the rifle in his direction. How was she even able to use it?

A starfighter streaked past. It didn't attack.

"Ehri?" Donovan said. He dropped his gun, holding his arms out in submission.

The battle seemed to pause, as both sides stopped their assault while they waited for Ehri to resolve it.

"I'm sorry, Major," she said.

"Me, too," he replied. He didn't know why. It seemed appropriate.

An explosion echoed from the sky behind him. One of the starfighters, no doubt.

"I didn't mean for this to happen," Ehri said. "I only wanted to learn about humankind. To understand in a way that none of the others do."

"I know," Donovan said. "You started this. It's only right that you finish it."

He spread his arms wide. He wouldn't close his eyes. He wouldn't make it that easy for her.

"Thank you, Major," Ehri said.

"For what?"

"For showing me the truth."

He didn't know what that meant.

Not until she turned, spinning on her heel like a dancer, dropping into a crouch and firing one, two, three plasma bolts. Each one of them struck one of the pur'dahm Hunters directly in the center of the head. They dropped in a neat line.

"I know I tricked you into coming for me," she said, looking back at him. "I wanted to learn about humanity, and in doing so, I realized it was the element of your kind that the bek'hai most sorely lack, and most desperately need. I said I would help you, Donovan. My touch is my bond."

Donovan smiled, remembering the tingling feel of her fingers against his.

"I shouldn't have doubted you," he said.

"Yes, you should have."

A soft whine rose to their left. They both turned in the direction of it, watching as the starfighter approached them.

80

Gabriel gritted his teeth as the sky lit up in the distance and Lieutenant Ribisi's starfighter vanished in a storm of flame and fragments. His pilots were dying, and dying fast. They had to finish this, now.

He was coming in fast toward the plateau, ready for one more assault. There were still a few of the Dread fighters trading shots with the resistance on the ground, and while he couldn't hurt them, he could stop their fire, maybe long enough that the soldiers could finally take them out.

He rocketed toward them, suddenly noticing that one of the Dread warriors and one of the resistance soldiers were both up and running, converging on the body in the center of the action. Who was she, that they both thought she was so important?

He angled the fighter, prepared to strafe the area again.

"Alpha Leader, if you're going to land, you need to do it now," Soon said, his voice desperate. "We've got more fighters incoming."

More? They couldn't handle two. Gabriel quit the attack, launching past the field and beginning a tight turn to get him to the plateau. He was going in, whether the fighting was over or not.

The fighter complained at the force of his reverse, the frame shuddering against the motion, the dampeners working to keep him from passing out. He felt it all the same, ignoring it as best he could. He pointed the fighter back to the plateau and leveled out, checking the HUD. Three more Dread fighters had appeared; they were at most thirty seconds out.

He began his descent, dropping hard and fast. He hadn't seen the action, but somehow the resistance force had won. The Dread were all motionless, and the male soldier was standing with the woman near the center of the area. He adjusted slightly to bring the fighter down right in front of them.

Their heads turned to look at him as he approached. He nearly crashed when he saw the woman's face.

Gabriel's heart began to pound, his mind trying to make sense of what his eyes were telling him. He finished his descent, tapping his control pad to open the cockpit before he had even touched down. The fighter bounced slightly before settling, and he unbuckled himself and jumped from the cockpit.

The two people rushed over to meet him. Two more were running their direction from the other side.

"Mom?" Gabriel said softly as they all coalesced. His hand had absently fallen to the crucifix, clutching it tightly.

The woman's expression changed, softening slightly. She was the spitting image of his mother. There was no doubt about that. He felt a tear on the corner of his eye. Damn it, that wasn't Juliet St. Martin. He knew the Dread used people to make clones. He could barely stand the thought of what that meant for his mother's fate. How would he ever tell his father about this?

"Captain Gabriel St. Martin?" the man asked.

Gabriel nodded.

"My name is Major Donovan Peters." He held out the alien rifle. "I brought you this."

Gabriel was numb as he reached out and took it, his eyes having trouble escaping the clone. He had never met his mother. He had never had the chance to see her in flesh and bone. Maybe she was a copy, but at least he could take this memory and juxtapose it with the others.

"Thank you," Gabriel said, forcing himself to keep it together. "We'll get this back to our ship and handed off to our scientist. How can we contact you, once we reverse the engineering?"

"The resistance headquarters are in New York. If you can, fly over there and send a message, just like you did before. Someone there should hear it."

Gabriel was about to say something to the clone. What was she doing, helping the rebels, anyway? How had they managed to get one of them on their side? There was no time to speak or wonder. The Dread fighters were closing in.

"I have to go," he said. "It was an honor to meet you, Major." He passed his eyes over the others. "It was an honor to meet all of you. You need to clear the area; there are more Dread fighters on their way."

"Yes, sir," Major Peters said. Gabriel didn't understand why. He was the ranking officer.

"Good luck, Captain," the clone said. "Be safe."

Gabriel felt his heart about to burst anew to hear her voice. He clenched his teeth and nodded, and then grabbed the wing of the fighter and pulled himself up. He sat down, placing the rifle between his legs, getting the starfighter back into the sky before the cockpit had sealed.

"Alpha Two, report," Gabriel said, firing his thrusters and launching away from the site.

There was no reply.

"Alpha Four, report. Bale, are you there?"

Again, no reply.

It didn't mean they were dead. He hadn't heard any explosions.

They had the alien weapon.

Now they had to escape.

81

Captain Kim and Lieutenant Bale weren't dead after all. He spotted them as they streaked upward, climbing vertically from a nearby river valley. The topography had interfered with both the HUD and the comm system.

A single Bat was rising behind them, taking a less steep vector as it tried to line up a shot.

The other Dread fighters were almost on them, their thrusters visible in the distance against the night sky.

"Alpha Squadron, this is Alpha Leader. We have the package. It's time to evac."

"Roger, Alpha Leader," they replied.

"Did you see? We managed to dunk one," Soon said.

"Good work," Gabriel replied. "Let's break away from our new friends and get ourselves home."

"Yes, sir."

Gabriel changed direction, ascending in a vector that would put him into formation with the others as they climbed away from the planet. He checked his power supply, noting that he had burned more than half of his reserves. It was enough to get him back to the Magellan as long as he didn't waste any more energy on the ion cannon.

The Bats started shooting, sending streams of plasma bolts toward them. Gabriel shifted the control stick, winding his way through the sudden rain. Bolts flashed in front of the cockpit, his onboard computer sounding off in both warning and complaint. He glanced to the left, to Captain Kim, who was managing to wiggle enough to keep the enemy off the mark. He couldn't see Bale, but her green arrow was still on his HUD. He hoped it would stay there.

They continued to climb, pushing higher and higher. The Dread couldn't ascend as quickly and began to fall behind. The growing distance caused them to intensify their fire, filling the air with so much plasma that Gabriel had no idea how they were avoiding it. Was it divine intervention, or just unbelievable luck?

Whatever it was, it ran out a heartbeat later.

His computer beeped in rapid pulses as he became blinded by the light of a plasma bolt and the starfighter started to wobble. He cursed, checking the HUD for a damage report.

Everything was still operational. The shot had grazed him.

"Alpha Leader," Soon said. "Gabriel. I'm hit. One of the cells is offline. I don't have the power to make it into orbit."

Gabriel looked over at the other starfighter again. It was trailing smoke, and there was a gaping hole in the fuselage.

"Yes you do, Alpha Two," Gabriel said. "Get in behind me and I'll cut the air for you."

Soon's fighter spun sharply, avoiding more enemy fire as he worked his way over. Lieutenant Bale tightened her position up as well, aligning next to Gabriel's wing. They were way up above the Earth now, and he could make out the shape of the Magellan silhouetted against the stars.

They were almost there.

"Alpha Two, what are your power readings?" Gabriel asked.

"Not good, Alpha Leader," Soon replied. "I'm reaching critical."

Gabriel checked his own levels again to compare. He had nearly drained the primary cell, but the secondary was still at half. "You can make it, Soon. Hang in there."

A plasma bolt flashed by, crossing within a meter of the cockpit. The Bats had fallen back. Not far enough.

"Alpha Leader, I'm turning around," Soon said.

"You'll make it," Gabriel repeated.

"No. I won't, and when I run out of power I'm going to fall back to Earth. I'd rather land than crash, and maybe I can draw your tail away. At the very least I can disrupt them and help you escape. Anyway, I'll hook up with the resistance if I can. At least I'll get to spend some time planetside. It looks incredible, even if the Dread are ruining the view."

Gabriel was going to try to argue. He decided against it. Soon had made up his mind, and was already decelerating and rolling the fighter over.

"Damn it, Soon," Gabriel said. "Be safe down there. We'll be back for you. I promise."

"I know you will, Captain. I'll be waiting for you. Tell Daphne I'll be waiting, too, and that I love her."

Gabriel tightened his jaw. "I will."

He watched the fighter in the HUD, accelerating back down toward the Bats. It didn't matter if they collided with him or angled out of the way, as soon as they broke off the chase he and Bale would escape.

The Dread ships parted to allow Soon through, realizing that it was more efficient than being knocked off course in a collision. Even so, they lost nearly a kilometer of ground in the few seconds the evasive maneuvers took.

Gabriel looked forward again. The Magellan was looming large ahead of them as they plowed into the thermosphere, climbing higher and faster. The enemy fire had finally started to ease, and they would be home safe with the Dread weapon in less than a minute.

Without Captain Kim.

Without Lieutenant Ribisi.

Without Second Lieutenant Polski.

Gabriel was used to losing his friends and comrades. So many had died skirting the atmosphere to communicate with the resistance. Seeing it happen felt so much worse. It made it more personal. More painful. He could only imagine what the people on the ground were experiencing.

He glanced down at the Dread plasma rifle.

Not for much longer.

The two remaining fighters cleared the remainder of the atmosphere. General St. Martin's voice carried crisply through their comm systems as soon as they did, breaking protocol by not waiting to be hailed.

"Welcome back, son. What's the verdict?"

"We have the alien weapon, sir," Gabriel said. For all his upset over the deaths of his wing mates, he couldn't help but feel proud of what they had accomplished. All of them.

"I knew you would," Theodore said. "What about Kim, Ribisi, and Polski?"

"Ribisi and Polski are dead, sir. Captain Kim's fighter was damaged, and he was forced to land."

"I'll say a prayer for their souls. Soon is still alive?"

"I hope so."

"He's a good man. He'll survive. Hangar B is open. Bays One and Two."

"Yes, sir."

Gabriel leaned his head back in his seat, closing his eyes for a moment and sending a quick prayer into the universe, that Ribisi, Polski, and all the others would have a peaceful and happy eternity. Then he vectored his fighter to the waiting hangar, guiding it smoothly into the open bay.

He had done his part.

The rest of it was up to his father.

82

Donovan stood at the edge of the plateau and watched the sky as Captain Gabriel St. Martin's fighter rose into it and raced away. His eyes did their best to follow the small glow of the ship's thrusters through the night, finding it difficult with the twinkle of the stars behind it.

Ehri stood next to him in silence, while Diaz and Matteo sat on the ground where the starfighter had been a moment earlier. Matteo had his head in his hands. He was ill from all of the violence. Diaz was trying to comfort him.

"Why did you do it?" Donovan asked without looking.

"I told you why when we met," Ehri said. "All of those words were true."

"What wasn't true?"

"The decision wasn't spontaneous. I spent weeks devising a plan to lead one of you to our ship. The water was the most challenging part. The bek'hai cannot control the weather."

"You set me up to kill your Dahm."

"Yes."

"Why?"

"He was old by drumhr standards. He was one of the first successful splices. The Domo'dahm, the previous one, gave him fifty years, and he had seen forty-eight."

"He was going to die soon anyway, so he sacrificed himself for your plan?"

"Yes."

"You spoke about the Domo'dahm as if you know him personally. How?"

"I am a clone of his heil'bek." She paused. "It is a difficult word to turn into English. It is similar to a significant other, but that meaning is imprecise because the bek'hai do not take mates. Perhaps best friend is more appropriate? I am unsure. As I told you, we all have our own personalities. He always said that mine was most similar to hers. It allowed me to persuade him to approve my study."

Donovan knew she had to be talking about Juliet St. Martin. The question was, did she know? "Did you know the human woman you're a clone of?"

"No. I never met her."

He wondered if he should tell her. Was there any value in it?

"I've always found your kind fascinating," she said. "I wanted to walk among you from the day I emerged. I wanted to understand how any intelligent life could continue with such tenacity and persistence in the face of elimination. I told Orik that four days were not enough, but in truth it took only hours for me to discover those answers. Once I had, I found that I did not want to leave. As I told you, for all of the freedom the Domo'dahm allowed me because I reminded him of his heil'bek; before I came with you I had never been free."

Donovan was silent as he scanned the sky. He could see the flashes of light high above them, the Dread giving chase to Captain St. Martin and his team. He wished there was some way, any way that he could help.

He finally turned to face Ehri, looking her in the eye.

"Is there anything else you weren't completely honest about?" he asked. "Maybe like how you're able to use that weapon."

Ehri was still holding Orik's plasma rifle. She shifted it in her hand. "The Hunter's rifles are not biologically secured. It is a point of pride for them to risk being killed by their own weapon."

Donovan glanced over at the dead Hunters further back on the plateau. Each of them had been carrying one of the guns. "Even if it means us humans have a better chance of fighting back?"

"Especially because of that. They believe that if you can defeat them in battle, then you deserve what you have earned."

"Did you hear that, Diaz?" Donovan asked, looking back at her.

She glanced up at him, but didn't speak. He could tell by her face she was both worried about Matteo, and still angry at Ehri, even though she had saved their lives in the end.

"There is one other thing," Ehri said.

"What is it?" he asked.

"I know how to fight."

"I noticed."

She smiled. "I studied under Klurik for many years. That is how we knew one another. At one time I thought he might ask me to be his heil'bek. Instead, he turned his back on me because I am lor'hai. I told Diaz to wait in the back and take him by surprise. You would not have defeated him any other way."

Donovan was about to respond when a soft rumble rippled across the landscape. The ground started to shake a moment later. He returned his attention up and out. The flashes of light were gone. He scanned the forest, looking for incoming mechs.

He didn't see any.

Ehri didn't react. Instead, she pointed out toward the Dread city. "The Domo'dahm is worried about what we have done, Major."

Donovan followed her finger. He could see the lights rising in the distance. A portion of the alien structure had broken away and was slowly ascending.

"They can't fight that thing," Donovan said.

"No. If it catches up to them, they'll die."

They stood and watched it. Even Matteo lifted his head to see. It continued to rise, gaining speed as it gained altitude, a series of thrusters in the back leaving long trails of heat that brightened the entire sky.

"Donovan, look," Matteo said. He pointed to another point in the sky, to a small dark spot illuminated by the Dread starship's thrusters.

"It's one of the human ships," Ehri said.

Donovan watched the dot cut across the sky. It was growing larger, flattening out a bit and heading in their general direction. Smoke poured from its side.

"It looks like it's damaged," Matteo said.

"But not out of control," Donovan said, trying to guess where it would come down. "I think it's going to land."

"They won't survive ten minutes out here," Diaz said.

"Not on their own," Donovan replied. "We're done here, anyway. Let's grab the Hunters' weapons and go help him out."

There was no questioning. No hesitation. They sprang into action, grabbing the unsecured Dread plasma rifles and vanishing into the woods.

This battle was over. Despite everything, they had won.

Now the real fight would begin.

83

"Sir, sensors are detecting an enemy ship incoming from the surface," Spaceman Locke said.

General Theodore St. Martin moved his hand across the Command Station's control pad, switching his main view to see below the Magellan's belly. The shape of the rising alien starship was obvious when contrasted against the blue marble below it.

"I knew it wouldn't be that easy," he mumbled. Gabriel had made it back safe with one of the Dread's weapons. It was only fair that he would have to find a creative way to get them all away from the planet in one piece.

"Maggie, sound the red alert," Theodore said.

"Yes, General," the computer replied.

The shrill tone of the alarm echoed in the hallway beyond the bridge. Theodore adjusted his position in his seat, using his elbows to sit up a little bit straighter so he could see his crew. He wanted a reminder of the consequences of failure.

He was responsible for every soul on this ship, and he had no intention of letting them die.

He took hold of the Magellan's controls, shifting again in an effort to get comfortable. He had taken a pill not too long ago, but he wanted another one or two to take more of the edge off the pain that was flaring out from the stumps of his legs. There was no way he was going to. They cut back on the agony, but they also made him sick and tired and unable to think.

Right now, what he needed most was to think.

"General, Lieutenant O'Dea reports that Captain St. Martin and Second Lieutenant Bale are safely aboard and Hangar B is sealed," Miranda said.

"Thank you," Theodore replied, immediately pushing the throttle forward. A soft groaning noise could be heard from somewhere in the ship, and the Magellan started to move out of its synchronous orbit. "Time to intercept?" he asked.

"Forty three seconds and closing, sir," Colonel Choi said. "General, how are you planning on getting us through the orbital defense satellites?"

"I'm working on that," Theodore replied.

He had been in this situation before. He could still remember it like it was yesterday, even though it had happened over fifty years earlier. The Dread had been coming down to the surface then, while he had been trying to escape it with nearly ten thousand souls on board. He had zigged and zagged and vectored the massive starship using every trick he knew and a few he had improvised, somehow charting a course through the rain of heavy plasma that was decimating cities around the globe. His ship had been the only one to escape, and yet he had never questioned the how or why of it. As far as he was concerned, it was the Will of God plain and simple, in restitution for stealing his bride from him and in a great desire not to see his creations completely wiped out.

He had always known that God would call him back here. He had always known a showdown would come. That knowledge was the only thing that kept him alive in the years that had followed the escape. It was the only reason he hadn't taken a knife or a belt to his throat after the accident that had taken his legs.

That, and Gabriel.

He had taught his boy to be strong, and he wasn't going to ruin that by taking the coward's way out. His life would end the way it was intended.

Going down fighting.

"But not today," he said to himself.

The ship was too large to steer through the viewport, so he focused his attention on the HUD instead, watching the position of the Dread starship as it grew ever closer, and taking note of the orbital defense ring above. The slip calculations Reza had done had been impressive in their perfection, getting them to the safe side of the satellites. He had told the crew he had an idea on how to get back out, but the truth of it was that he didn't. In part it was because there was a piece of him that hadn't believed they would succeed. In part it was because he had assumed he would think of something before the situation went critical. He had always been better under pressure. He was a sly old gator, and he had a knack for getting himself out of tight spots.

Except the situation had gone critical, and he was still struggling for an idea. He couldn't try to fight back against the Dread starship. Not without any weapons. He also couldn't outrun it. He clenched his teeth.

He had to think of something or they were all going to die.

The Dread's first shot across the Magellan's bow solidified that fact. It was made as a singular gesture of warning, a prelude to the real attack, set to begin at any moment. An attack that would tear the ship to pieces. It would happen more slowly with the extra armor that had been added to the old girl, but slow or fast, dead was dead, and he couldn't let it happen.

The starship shuddered, and something at one of the pods began beeping in a shrill tone.

"We're under fire, sir," Colonel Choi said from her station.

"She can take it," Theodore replied. "Can't you Maggie?" Even so, he adjusted his flight path, rotating the Magellan to give their attacker a smaller target.

The ship shuddered again from another hit.

"We have damage to a power conduit," Sergeant Abdullah said. "Deck 17. Seal door is closed."

Theodore shook his head. They were taking damage already? It shouldn't have been that easy.

Gabriel ran onto the bridge, pausing at the Command Station.

"Captain St. Martin reporting for duty, sir," his son said, standing at attention, holding to protocol in front of the others, even in the middle of an attack.

"Head on down to your pod, son," Theodore said, using his hand to wave him closer. Gabriel stopped next to him. "By the by, if you've got any ideas on getting past the orbital defense, I'm all ears."

Gabriel leaned over to see the HUD. He turned his head, putting his face level with Theodore's.

"I thought we were going to go out the way we came in?"

"What do you mean?" Theodore said. He shouldn't have taken that other pill. It hadn't helped the pain much and it was hurting his ability to think more than he realized.

"Reza," Gabriel shouted up to the scientist, who was sitting at one of the pods with a terrified look on his face.

Reza turned his head at the sound of his name. "Yes, Captain?"

"We need a slipstream. What do you have?"

The ship shuddered again. Another tone sounded from the engineering station, and Sergeant Abdullah shook his head as he tapped furiously on his control pad.

"I don't keep them in my pocket, Gabriel."

"Not the time for jokes," Gabriel replied. "Is there a stream running through the Earth or not?"

"Through the Earth?" Theodore said.

Gabriel looked at him. Theodore recognized that face. He understood the spark of anger in his son's eyes. He had been that way once, a long time ago when he hadn't been a crusty old coonass. When he had been able to think straight. He was losing it, he knew. His reflexes. Maybe his mind. Nothing was right anymore. Nothing was the way it used to be. He knew it by the fact that the answer was so obvious, and yet he had been unable to see it.

He wanted to both laugh at Gabriel's genius and cry at the loss of his own. Instead, he pushed Gabriel gently aside.

"Good man," he said. "I'm smelling what you're cooking."

The ship shuddered.

Theodore worked the controls to the starship, changing their course.

"You had better find me a stream, and you had better do it now, Mr. Mokri," he said.

Reza looked out the forward viewport, and then back at Theodore. "General?" he said softly.

The Earth had rolled into view ahead of them. Theodore continued to angle the starship toward it, pushing the throttle the rest of the way open.

"I said find me a stream, son," Theodore repeated. "Or we're going to make an awful mess on the surface of the planet."

Reza's face paled, and he turned to his station's controls.

"Maggie, prepare the QPG," Theodore said.

"No sequence has been input, General," Maggie replied.

"Nope, and it ain't going to be. Command override three nine seven."

"Command override accepted. Deploying QPG nacelles."

"You can't do this, General," Reza shouted, even as he continued his work. "You can't enter a slipstream inside a planet's atmosphere."

"Why the hell not?"

"You need to get up to join velocity for one," Reza said. "For another, the planet's gravity will make a mess of the stream path and pattern. We have no way to know where we're going to wind up."

"Space is a big place, Mr. Mokri," Theodore said. "As long as it ain't smashed into the ground, I'll take it."

"You don't understand, sir. The gravitational fields accelerate the stream. We could wind up too far from anything to ever get back."

The edges of the Earth vanished to the sides of the viewport. The long bow of the Magellan was pointed straight toward the planet while the Dread ship was on her port side, slowly rolling over to get its weapons aimed and fired once more.

"Stop complaining and start producing," Theodore said.

"Sir-" Reza said again.

"Get me a stream, damn it," Theodore roared.

The Magellan passed into the atmosphere. Theodore checked their velocity. Fifteen thousand kilometers per hour. They were almost there, but the planet's surface was rising in an awful hurry. They had seconds to escape.

"Got it," Reza said, sounding pleased with himself.

"Put them in," Theodore said.

"Yes, sir." Reza tapped his control pad. "Sequence entered and accepted."

They were falling ever faster, passing from the darkness into the great blue below. Seventeen thousand, eighteen thousand. The world was rising to meet them, opening her arms and preparing to take them in.

The ship began shaking violently, the air shoving against the irregular shape of the craft. It was intended that the suppressors would be used in gravity, not the main thrusters. Theodore had no idea if she was sturdy enough to hold together. He thought she was. He prayed she was. He pushed a little harder on the throttle, trying to eke out just a little bit more.

Nineteen thousand. Collision warnings began to sound, and Gabriel had to grab onto the back of the seat to keep from falling over.

"Son, if we don't make it," Theodore said. "I want you to know-"

"We're going to make it," Gabriel replied.

They were out over the ocean, getting so close that Theodore could almost see the outline of the waves below, the Magellan a meteor about to strike.

In that moment, his mind settled on a single instant from the past. The one where he and Juliet stood on a beach in Hawaii, the water up to their ankles as they gave their vows. It wasn't the church wedding she had always wanted, but they had decided they couldn't wait that long.

He closed his eyes, remembering the feel of her hands on his, her lips on his. Whether they lived or died was out of his control now.

He counted his heartbeats.

Thump thump.

Thump thump.

Thump thump.

Thump thump.

The Magellan became translucent, phasing into slipspace, her bow slicing into the water without breaking the surface, sinking like a ghost ship until she vanished entirely.

Theodore opened his eyes.

He was still alive.

All of them were.

About the Author

M.R. Forbes is the creator of a growing catalog of speculative fiction titles, including the science-fiction Rebellion and War Eternal novels, the epic fantasy Tears of Blood series, the contemporary fantasy Divine series, and the world of Ghosts & Magic. He lives in the pacific northwest with his family, including a cat who thinks she's a dog, and a dog who thinks she's a cat. He eats too many donuts, and he's always happy to hear from readers.

Mailing List: http://www.mrforbes.com/mailinglist

Website: http://www.mrforbes.com/

Goodreads: http://www.goodreads.com/author/show/6912725.M_R_Forbes

Facebook: http://www.facebook.com/mrforbes.author

Twitter: http://www.twitter.com/mrforbes

51383256R00218

Made in the USA
San Bernardino, CA
20 July 2017